TASK FORCE: **GAEA**

MEMORY'S CURSE

DAVID BERGER

Email: tchrofengl@gmail.com

First Edition

Task Force: Gaea — Memory's Curse / Written by David Berger, Land O Lakes, FL 34638

Summary: An elder goddess seeks to destroy the Olympeian gods and four heroes must stop her.
ISBN-13: 978-0615871240 (Custom Universal)
ISBN-10: 0615871240
Printed in the United States of America. Layout by David Berger. Illustrations by Michael Hamlett.

ACKNOWLEDGMENTS

To my family, friends, and my partner Gavi: your continuous love and support mean so much.

My unending gratitude goes to friends who have provided me with steadfast support, love and friendship, and consistent objectivity. I truly could not have finished this sequel without you: Michael D'Alessio, Peter Saenz, James Matlack Raney, Topher Cassidy, and Jarrid.

From the beginning, my muse has been Diana, princess of the Amazons: Wonder Woman. With her as my example, I provided the best examples I could of heroes.

Michael Hamlett, your art fans the flames of inspiration.

CONTENTS

THE COSMOS

Before all came the *Protogenoi* — the elder gods — starting with *Khaos*, the primordial mother, who kindled the *First Fires*, the source of all creation.

From her womb came *Gaea*, the earth, *Tartaros*, the pit of torment, *Ananke*, necessity, and *Olympeia*, the first mountain spirit who would become holy Olympos.

Then, *Khaos* birthed *Nyx,* night, and *Erebos*, the darkness; they, in turn, gave the world *Æther*, light, and *Hemera*, day.

Alone, *Gaea* bore *Ouranos*, the heavens; *Pontos*, the sea; the *Nesoi*, the islands; the *Ourea*, the mountains.

With *Ouranos, Gaea* bore *Cyclopes*, one-eyed blacksmiths; and, *Hekatoncheires*, hundred-handed stormbringers —

> *Ouranos* sent these misshapen offspring to *Tartaros*.

Then came the *Titans* — first Olympeians — rulers of Earth; favored by *Ouranos*, they were the sovereign race.

Kronos, the youngest Titan, gelded his father and genitals crashing into the sea begat *Aphrodite*, while *Ouranos'* blood itself spawned goddesses of vengeance, the *Erinyes*.

From *Kronos* and sister *Rhea* came six gods: *Hesteia*, of the hearth; *Demeter*, of the earth; *Hera*, of marriage; *Hades*, of the underworld; *Poseidon*, of the sea; and, *Zeus*, of the sky, slayer of *Kronos* —

Zeus fathered *Athene*, by *Metis*; *Hermes*, by *Maia*; *Hephaestos* and *Ares*, by *Hera*; *Dionysos*, by Semele, a mortal; *Artemis and Apollo*, by *Leto*.

Gods built the pantheon and, ultimately, the mortal world.

PRONUNCIATION KEY

Adyton	AH-doo-tone
Aegis	EE-jis
Aer	Air
Aether/Æther	EE-ther
Akheron	ah-KER-on
Alekto	ah-LEK-toe
Alkinoë	al-kee-NO-ee
Arkadeia	ar-KAY-dee-ah
Cetoi	SEE-toy
Cocytos	ko-key-TOS
Drakones	drah-KOH-nays
Ekhidna	eh-KID-nah
Erebos	EH-re-bus
Erinyes	eh-RIN-yeez
Euenor	AY-nor
Eurynomoi	EH-ree-no-moy
Gaea	GUY-uh
Ge Thêon	Yeh THEE-on
Horkos	OR-kose
Hydor	ih-THOR
Khaos	KAH-ose
Kidemonas	key-day-MOH-nas
Kleisthenes	klee-us-THAY-nees
Leimakides	lay-ma-KEE-days
Leukippe	lef-KEY-pay
Litokhoro	lee-TOH-ko-ro
Megaera	meh-GAY-ra
Mnemosyne	neh-MOH-sin-nee
Moirae	MOY-reh
Naiad	NYE-add
Nephelae	neh-FEH-lie
Nephoskizetes	neh-foh-skee-ZEE-teez
Nyx	Nix
Oikoumene Broteios	oy-KOO-mee-nay bro-TAY-os
Olympeia	oh-LIM-pee-uh
Orthros	OR-thrus
Ouranos	oo-RAN-us
Phlegethon	fle-YEH-thon
Protogenos	pro-to-YEN-os
Ptinotrofeio	tee-no-tro-FEE-oh

Pyr	Peer
Syra	SEE-ra
Tegea	Ti-YEH-ah
Tetrastoikheia	teh-trah-STOY-key-uh
Thalassa	THAH-la-sa
Themis	THEH-mis
Thyroros	Thee-RO-ros
Tisiphone	ti-SI-fo-nee

UNITED NATIONS TASK FORCE DIVISION

TEAM: GAEA

LIAISON: QUINN REYNOLDS

MEMBERS/ABILITIES:

DANELOS FAIRMONT / AEGIS

> HIGHLY TRAINED HAND TO HAND COMBATANT; HEALING ABILITY
> ANCESTRY: APOLLO (OLYMPEIAN) AND ALKINOE (ARKADEIAN)
> WEAPON 1: THYROROS (PORTALBEARER); SWORD OPENS
  DIMENSIONAL PORTALS TO ANYWHERE AEGIS HAS SEEN
> WEAPON 2: IMPACT SHIELD; MANACLE ON LEFT WRIST
  GENERATES INVISIBLE SHIELD

SARAH JACOBS / AETHER

> HIGHLY TRAINED HAND TO HAND COMBATANT; HEALING ABILITY
> ANCESTRY: ATLANTEAN / WICCAN
> WEAPON: RING OF ELEMENTS; ALLOWS HER TO COMMAND THE
  FOUR ELEMENTS: EARTH, FIRE, AIR, AND WATER

BRANDON JEFFRIES / ZODIAK

> HIGHLY TRAINED HAND TO HAND COMBATANT
> ANCESTRY: UNDETERMINED / ADOPTED
> WEAPON: EYE OF OURANOS; ALLOWS ZODIAK TO CHANNEL
  POWERS FROM ZODIAC CONSTELLATIONS

DR. ALETA HALSTON / TALON

> HIGHLY TRAINED HAND TO HAND COMBATANT
> ANCESTRY: AMAZONIAN
> WEAPON: NEPHOSKIZETES (CLOUDSPLITTER); SILVER JAVELIN
  THAT ALLOWS TALON TO CONTROL LIGHTNING

PART ONE:

OBLIVION

I—AGE OF TORMENT

2012, the Modern Era: inside Gaea's vault, the *adyton*.

"A daughter... Zeus and Nyx?" asked Themis, the blindfolded goddess of Justice, the only Titan not entombed in stone in Tartaros with her brethren. "How... inconvenient."

Gaea, Earth Mother, had given her grandson Apollo and her daughter Themis special dispensation to enter her *adyton*, her most sacred repository deep inside the earth where the Scales existed, and he had just told Themis a most intriguing tale about how four mortals restored balance, and only he remembered what happened.

The sun god, who strangely took great solace in the darkest parts of the underworld, stared at the scales that kept the shaky balance of order and chaos.

"Yes, inconvenient to say the least. The sky god and Night incarnate." He paused, lost. "Can you feel it? History has realigned — the time line has shifted." He refocused on Themis. "Three thousand years ago, I had come to this place, if you can even call it *that* since it has no tangible mortal dimension, to find solitude and reflection after the gods imprisoned your brethren Titans after the *Titanoma-*

1

chia, that Great War. In that heavy blackness, I was here, with Gaea's consent. She is my guide, my anchor—I had been given permission to enter this place as I needed to, and she has now allowed you, too. On that day, I spied my father and Nyx in an impossible embrace. They shared no words, and after he seduced her, had been with her as he had been with so many others, he spurned her—as he had so many others. Alone, her rage festered, and I didn't have to be the god of prophecy to know that that wouldn't bode well."

Themis' expression remained unchanged; however, Apollo sensed she wished to know more.

"I have mixed memories of that day, however. As this timeline adjusts, I remember—yes—I remember this event unfolding, that Zeus saw me, and then used that as a reason to banish me to Gaea, so that I wouldn't say anything to Hera. It was during that memory that Nyx destroyed the Sacred Scales after being scorned, or from being ignored after Zeus, Hades, and Poseidon established Olympos for the gods. But, another memory, if that's what it is, tells me that I saw my father and Nyx, but then he returned to Olympos, reluctant to linger too long in her murkiness, regretting his choice. Not long after, bored with immortality, I chose to live a mortal life for a year, but then I dreamed a prophecy about the birth of a great evil, that would destroy the gods, but it was so unclear. I wanted more time for it to unfold to me, so I let it lapse. But, something about it prompted me to uproot my wife and child and move to a different realm… the world of mortals far in the future. I know not when the prophecy shall come to pass."

"I have heard whispers of such a creature, but nothing of her birth. How do you know about this daughter of Nyx? Would not others know, too?" Themis hovered closer to him. "Did you not tell Zeus of this? Should he not know of any threat to Olympos?"

"Within Gaea's embrace, the story remains hidden; such is her shame. The Earth goddess herself told me the horrific story of the birth, and even *she* shuddered as she told me. And, no, I didn't tell Zeus. The images were so murky that he could have done nothing. This is what I know..."

1019 B.C.E. or *Ilikía Olympios (Olympeian Age)*

A churning blackness, Nyx shaped herself in ways that would stagger the mortal mind, collapsing into maelstroms of dark, living clouds, ready to bear her offspring implanted in her by Olympos' adulterous king. With the catacombs of the dead for her nursery, Nyx wanted to bring forth her daughter in the company of the agonized, pitiable souls of those who had never made it beyond the gates of the underworld; they had a great deal to offer her child, and their rejection and pain mirrored her own.

Sidetracked by her thoughts, she almost forgot her role in the cosmos and raced toward the exit of Tartaros, a cave entrance kissed by the air that mortals breathe. As she neared the opening, bright Hemera, her daughter — the Day itself — descended into the Hadean depths, and both *Protogenoi*, elder gods, touched ever so briefly before Nyx bubbled forth into the air, becoming the blanket of obscurity shrouding part of the earth until Day would rise again — mother and daughter in a forever dance.

Taking her place in the sky, Nyx decided it was time: her newest daughter would enter the world in a way no other elder god had.

Two days later, in Megara, Greece, screams of torment and searing pain cut at the air like talons, ripping apart the peace of the healer's tent in the cultist's sanctuary, a humble place in the mortal world where those afflicted by madness came to embrace the darkness of Nyx. A woman, crazed with murderous thoughts and tortured dreams, lay on a woven grass mat, her wrists and ankles bound with worn leather straps anchored to the ground to prevent her from hurting herself or others. Her eyes as black as Erebos, the darkness itself, she became the ideal choice for this birth, a living receptacle for Nyx. Her madness would mix well with the darkness. Ancient primordial entered her human host and the body took on the pregnant form, bloating the abdomen with life.

Soon, echoing cries interlaced with unintelligible mutterings escaped the woman's lips while the healer, his white chiton stained from years of patient's blood, knelt ready to extract the newborn, eager to come forth; he was certainly ignorant of what would come. He preferred the bloody patches on his garment to help him remember each forced amputation or sutured wound, usually brought about by a stony fragment or stick used during an arcane ritual to Nyx. Anarchy bound the cult, it would seem, and spontaneous fights were commonplace. Night incarnate had selected well, largely to reflect the chaos within, but also to see what it would feel like to push her progeny forth as a mortal would. That connection to humanity would prove so very useful.

Following a pain-induced shriek, a volcanic spray of blood and placenta erupted forth as the part human, part primordial being pushed her way into the world of Humankind without the benefit of the healer's aid. Wiping the sanguine discharge from his face, the healer caught a glimpse of this child, and as he felt his psyche melt, he gouged out his own eyes with his fingers, mumbling as his intellect fragmented, foaming at the mouth like a rabid beast. A mortal mind could not comprehend such a primordial in her true form. Soon, he lay still, and the entity moved over to the lifeless body, draining it of its soul as a child takes sustenance from its mother. Not even Hades would want the sack of skin and bones, as it had no spirit to wander the underworld.

Nyx exited the woman's spent body—now a lifeless, vacant, fleshy shell—and coalesced around her daughter, ready to take her back to Tartaros where the newborn would mature among the imprisoned Titans, Gaea's children buried beneath stone and Zeus' curse, and there she would feed off ancient energy originating from Khaos, the mother of the cosmos herself. In such a place of despair, this child would find solace near yet another tomb, a place no mortal could ever see, and no god would ever go. She would grow accustomed to the dead chill of one whose presence no one spoke, for fear even saying his name would rouse him — Kronos, the Titan king.

As the *Moirae* wove the fate of Humanity and the immortal gods, so too had they spun the threads of those who came before them. Part of this tapestry would form a path for the daughter of Nyx, who would be known by all as *The Nebulous One*, for uttering or even knowing her true name would bring on madness. Childlike fingers of Clotho, the youngest of the *Moirae*, on the loom, bound by duty and a yearning, trembled with each pass, and the fabric it brought forth for Zeus' daughter bore the color of blood.

"That was all," Apollo uttered. "Gaea would tell me no more, but I could tell she knew more. It was not like her to be fickle. With what I do know, and what every prophetic bone in my immortal body tells me, I feel my ichor run cold, colder than the tomb of Kronos."

"Where is she now?" Themis asked.

"I don't know. But, I need to see Zeus and pray that he believes me."

Gaea indeed knew more about this child's early days.

Nyx waited in Tartaros for the return of Day so she might become the night sky once more, an eternal cycle she had entered long ago. While *The Nebulous One* drifted around the Titans' rocky tombs, she absorbed even the faintest traces of energy from within the encasements, energy tainted by hatred of the other Olympeian gods — especially Zeus, her father. She felt their rage, their unremitting, seething rage against the youngest son of Kronos. Like mother's milk, this life force leached through the stone into her, and her form churned like a storm-battered sea with every acerbic drop. Each of the Titans remembered the day Zeus' scythe took their lord's life, returning his energy back to all-encompassing Khaos. Each remembered the sacrosanct pact of Zeus, Poseidon, and Hades, the one that turned their own mother, Gaea, against them. Mother Earth was nothing if she not loyal to prophecy, the one that foretold of Kronos' demise by his son's hand. The mantle of power had to pass from father to son.

The Nebulous One glided further away from her mother, tumbling over the rock-strewn floor until even she felt the gelid tomb, the one place in all of creation not even the gods visit. Surrounding the earth sarcophagus, she waited to feel that familiar electric sensation of life, but... nothing. Her frustration subsided, as she slowly comprehended what she had learned from the Titans: Kronos, the son of Gaea and Ouranos, the king of the Titans, truly was no more. His hatred would have been a deep well on which to draw.

After her feeding, she wanted to explore her new home, like any curious child, and found the path through Hades to the place where she knew she could find the one she needed to meet, the one she needed to scorn, the one she needed to kill – Zeus – for he not only had abandoned her and her mother, as he had so many others, but he also was despised by the Titans, and it was their hatred that fueled her. The journey to Olympos from Tartaros, even for Nyx's daughter, would take time. Immune to mortal constraints, she could not be bound by chain or rope, by solid or ether, but time had neither shape nor form, neither matter nor mind, and it could affect her. She would eventually reach the sacred mountaintop, though and would ensure that Zeus understood what it meant to abandon her. Making her way through Hades, though, would teach her much, if nothing else, how nourishing souls could be.

Through the fields of gray asphodel, she wended her

way, rolling like a black tide. Spirits of the dead — pale mist swirling with no human resemblance — paid her no mind, neither knowing nor caring who she was, and they wandered through the fields as the billowing daughter of Nyx wafted around them. Those souls in her path, she devoured. Near Hades' palace of inky marble columns, striated with wispy bits of white, she stopped, looking like a storm cloud that had lost its buoyancy. This was Hades, she thought, the underworld where the dead found their solace or their suffering. She had already felt the deep, aching torment from the Titans, raw emotions able to carve into the densest stone, and now she felt even more at home. Onward she moved, undulating, rolling across the realm, and finding her bearings, until she saw her kin. Hovering on scaly black wings behind the Hall of Judgment, their arms and legs entwined with sleek serpents, three sisters tormented a soul not yet ethereal, but no longer corporeal. Having drowned his newborn child, this once-mortal man would spend eternity in Tartaros, enduring punishments not fit for humans to comprehend. Such was the will of Rhadamanthys, Aeacos, and Minos, the three judges of the underworld. Each had been mortal, and a son of Zeus, rewarded for his good deeds with this post, and so they spoke in one voice, *"Tartaros shall lay claim to you, and none shall discern your screams amid those whose voices you join."*

Despite lacking a body, this former human felt every talon strike ripping through what was left, every snakebite and the soul-melting venom it released, every contemptuous gesture, and he would never again know peace. One of the three winged goddesses, Tisiphone, took perverse pleasure in bringing anguish to him, the murderer of the innocent; the other Erinyes, Alekto and Megaera, assisted in his torment. Daughters of Nyx by Ouranos and sisters to *The Nebulous One*, they only relented when their cloud-like sibling moved closer. Through thought, she conveyed her contempt for Zeus and all of Olympos, relaying how the god of the sky had abandoned their mother. She was going to Olympos seeking vengeance, to tear down the oligarchy of the gods one by one, starting with her father who had wronged the *Protogenoi*. *The Nebulous One* had few emotions known to her for one so young, but the Erinyes saw her deep pain, felt her yearning. To demonstrate what she would do, she swirled around the tortured soul before them, exacting her own revenge on him for his heinous crime. None who knew him would ever remember he existed — such was her power — but his spirit would remember the egregious harm he had done to his infant girl. How appropriate, *The Nebulous One* thought, that he had tripped on a stone after committing the deed, cracking open his skull. As his blood leached into the earth, Hermes dragged his soul to the underworld to face judgment. And now what was left of him would go to Tartaros, to endure whatever agony he deserved, knowing no one would ever mourn him or feel the finest shred of pity.

The Nebulous One left her sisters and headed directly for the meandering caverns that stretched out beneath Olympos. Magaera and her sisters eagerly followed. Others found their path with the Erinyes, too, and those who inhabited the darkest realms of the underworld saw opportunities to glorious and plentiful torment with the daughter of Night.

It would take time to find the right path to Olympos, the new home for the gods; spirits sometimes wandered from their eternal existence, and it would be easy for some to find their way beyond the underworld. Blind caverns and labyrinthine paths meander through the caves, some harboring creatures that dine on lost souls. It could take eons or seconds to find the Olympeian gods. Nevertheless, she would find her prey.

2—THE MERGING

I n another timeline that existed for only one god, the Muses had sung a tale woven by the *Moirae* where *'four not born of godly word'* took up the care of Gaea, protecting the mortal world from the children of Ekhidna, mother of all monsters, whose only purpose was to spread chaos. These mortals, entwined into history to fix the broken Sacred Scales and bring back cosmic equilibrium—the Merging—had one braided strand where their purpose was inextricable. With the prophecy fulfilled, and the pans of Order and Chaos rising and falling once more, what was fabric became lone threads, what was a tapestry of bonds, became nothing, since the loom of the *Moirae* and the loom of Ananke, the goddess of inevitability, became one, and all of history from creation's birth followed different paths, those intended to exist.

True destinies emerged, and certain events would be remembered while others would never have happened, and no one, except Apollo, would ever know that one petty goddess had untangled Fate all by herself.

Before the Merging, as Apollo referred to it, the planet Earth lay shackled with paranoia and fear. Nations of the world with financial means mounted surveillance cameras to buildings, to parking garages, to neighborhood streets, all for the sake of maintaining control—for the betterment of the people, they said. Trust languished while retinal scans and DNA samples confirmed identities where one's word could not; men, women, and children alike felt the yoke of suppression upon them, learning to live like rats in a laboratory, walking with their heads just a little lower. Humanity itself had applied the pressure, preventing society from cleansing itself from its infections: prejudice, trepidation, and despair. Governments created a veneer of peace, with only a shade of surveillance showing through. Prying eyes hid in silhouette. But, everyone knew they were there. Citizens lived with their pulse near the edge of panic. Armed police stood on every street corner, but they remained in the shadows, dressed like civilians. But, everyone knew they were there. Militia from the local government looked like the homeless or taxi drivers or housewives or college students. But, everyone knew they were there. Chaos indeed ruled.

Now, after the Merging, the world's inhabitants, mortal and otherwise, followed a different path, and the three *Moirae* wove the fabric of Fate with darker, deeper colors than before. Helpless citizens sat under a heavier yoke of a planet whose rulers deconstructed the human spirit by controlling every aspect of their lives; in essence, they lived under martial law. A military presence was the norm, and any semblance of ease or harmony was but a fume. Countries not only fortified their borders with troop regiments, arming their soldiers with AK-47s, M16s, SA80s as well as Sarin and Tabun paralytic nerve gasses, but they also built electrified fences topped with razorwire. Border crossings required paperwork, retinal scans, and even DNA crosschecking, depending on the government. The one hope for change, the formation of the United Nations, a desperate attempt to impose some sort of order on a hornet's nest of bedlam, prompted session after session over the years to undo some of the fear mongering. Suc-

cess, although limited, came from the Concordance Pact, where the organized nations in the world agreed to support one another and allow for intercontinental and inter-country travel with a universal passport, but not all nations or police actions recognized such an attempt at peace.

The European Commonwealth, comprised of all countries on that continent except for Italy and Greece, became the greatest ally to the American Conglomerate that included the United States, Mexico, South America, Central America, and Canada. The Greco-Italian Alliance, not part of the Concordance Pact because both Greece and Italy would not allow trade from other outside countries, did send a representative to the United Nations, however, to keep an ear on what was happening in other parts of the world. If anyone were to ask when this descent into chaos began, no one could say; even the elderly remembered their youth when politics, suspicion, and fear simply made up everyday life. Spiritualists and polytheists had always believed this all emerged millennia ago, closer to the dawn of a more civilized world. The monotheists proffered the idea that their divine was angry at humanity and sought to punish all. The pervasive, suffocating malaise kept the world from unifying and rising above and offering much hope.

In a history rewoven, this fabric was no better, providing no shelter from the destiny to come.

3—THE AVIARY OF THE GODS

Apollo left Themis and returned to Olympos, the mountain that sat between moments in time, and sought his father and the other immortals. Before they assembled, he visited his scrying pool in the Hall of Prophecy, his refuge. Looking down into the world, he found his family in Boston, Massachusetts, and sliding his fingers along the surface of the water as one does the pages of a book, he learned that certain things had changed, but much remained the same. Acclimating to the Merging for him would take some time since he had to align memories from the moment the Scales became whole. He and his wife, Alkinoë, the former queen of Arkadeia, lived in the same brownstone; he would delve deeper later to see all that had realigned in this time. From what he could tell, his son, Danelos, his friend and teammate, Brandon, and their other teammates, Aleta Halston and Sarah Bish...no, Jacobs...lived in Boston. Their connection to Task Force: Gaea remained intact: Aegis, Aether, Zodiak, and Aetos... no, she was called Talon now. People he knew in the United Nations or the Task Force Division were different, too: names, gender, and even smaller, less noticeable differences. Apparently, the world still needed this agency, though—a good sign. Some changes, though, stood out: the power of the gods remained in this realm somehow, a weaker version of what had once been. This would test everything Apollo had within him, but he knew he would contend with whatever changed without question. But, now he needed to speak with the other gods.

Time on Olympos didn't pass as it did for mortals, but Apollo certainly felt as if he had spoken for hours about his experiences. Once he had finished, he slumped in his throne, partly enervated by all the talking he had done, but also dismayed, since only he remembered the other time line. Threads in the *Moirae's* loom would certainly be tangled, but the Fates would sort it out one strand at a time; they always did. Even though no chronicle, oral or written, existed of the sun god's penance or what followed, he alone knew, and he brought out so much detail that no one believed he could have fabricated the story. Thirteen immortals stunned into silence was more than he had hoped for, but he didn't think there could be any other reaction. Athene, wisdom's champion, released her owl as she stood, putting her hand on Apollo's shoulder.

"I feel what can best be explained as pangs of remorse for what my brother has experienced and lost. Such perspective on humanity bears a dear price, Zeus. I envy Apollo."

No Olympeian had ever borne witness to such a tale, and the silence that muted them all rang like a death knell to all they had held dear. When gods walked among mortals, they did so as gods in human form, but to be flesh and blood and bone… that humbled even Zeus. Knowing he had done so to his first-born son, whether or not he remembered it, made the son of Kronos impotent for the first time.

"So shall it be!" Thunder rumbled with Zeus' words.

"We of Olympos shall seek to understand that with which Apollo has become intimate: we shall go to Gaea, for one mortal year, when Nyx rises in the heavens. Prepare."

No dissent. No refusal. The Olympeians would honor the sun god the only way that seemed fitting.

Although not what he intended, Apollo saw the logic, however, and he agreed that even the gods needed perspective. Finding two identical snowflakes seemed more likely than getting all Olympeians to agree on anything, but Apollo had done just that, despite that none remembered he had ever lived in the human world.

Zeus needed to know more.

Apollo found his father and Pallas Athene in the Hall of Tribunals, a marble room whose scale and grandeur dwarfed any mortal monarch's palace. Seeing his son enter, Zeus signaled to his daughter, the Aegisbearer, who left in a cloud of butterflies.

"I have thought much about what you have told me," began Zeus. "Were you not the guardian of Truth, I would dismiss this entire story as inventive folly. Why does none of great Olympos recall that creation succumbed to the actions of Nyx? Destroying the Scales would have had lasting effect on every last part of the cosmos."

"It did. As I have told you, you banished me to Gaea, stripped me of my godhood, and forced me to fend for myself as a mortal man. I endured physical and emotional pain, embarrassment, hunger and thirst... all things that we immortals have never known. And, most importantly, I experienced humility. Something, Zeus, that we could all benefit from occasionally," Apollo bowed. "Thank you."

Zeus tried to understand the sincerity in those last two words, but Apollo continued before he could linger on them.

"What I don't thoroughly understand, however, is that some experiences I've had have not changed, but their surrounding events differ. I am loath to speak all of what I know, but I fear you of all the gods should know some of it."

"You have never restrained your words from me, my son. Do not start now. Shrouded in truth, these words will help me to understand your ordeal."

As a younger, less mature god, Apollo never censored himself to his father. Whatever thought appeared in the sun god's mind came from his mouth, like an irrepressible sunbeam, many times to the chagrin of Zeus who would shake his head in disbelief but take those words as those from a child who didn't know any better. To speak of what he knew to the king of Olympos actually made Apollo hesitant, a sign of either maturity or fear — perhaps both. He recalled Zeus' deepening ire and the subsequent humiliation before all the gods as he was stripped of his birthright and dignity, dignity he reclaimed, ironically, as a mortal. But, Zeus was right. Revealing what he knew might be the only way to chase away the darkness that hung over Apollo's heart.

"As I had told you earlier, in that timeframe, you had shunned Nyx after Kronos' defeat, an insult she could not overlook, so she shattered the Scales, causing cataclysm after cataclysm, even the loss of Atlantis. What I didn't tell you was that I was there, in Gaea's *adyton*, sitting in the darkness of Tartaros to find solace and saw you with Nyx embracing beneath the Scales beforehand. Even now, I still do not know if Nyx acted out of being left out of your plans or because you abandoned her, although it really doesn't matter."

Zeus appreciated the euphemism 'embracing' but didn't remember seeing Apollo there when he did indeed seduce Night. But, after that encounter, Olympos' king had returned to his throne, Hera not being the wiser. Or at least he believed. A pale flickering in the sky god's eyes informed Apollo that even Zeus had limits to patience.

While Apollo revealed how events had changed, he came to a realization that stopped him. Those moments that remained the same centered on strong emotions in the historical continuum. The fact that Danelos remained

Apollo's son reinforced how crucial that relationship was to the cosmos, but a detail about this current timeline gave even the sun god a chill.

"I traveled to the *Oikoumene Broteios*, the land of only mortals, from this godly realm, the *Ge Thêon*, because of the dual souls inhabiting each body, a consequence of the Scales' destruction. When my wife Alkinoë arrived, she had to relinquish her immortality, and when my son came over, he was no longer human, and his soul had to be reborn through Alkinoë, this time as mortal. Our son in the Olympeian realm, Demetrios, remained immortal and fully-grown, but his mortal counterpart, Danelos, grew up with no knowledge of his Olympeian heritage. Only later, when Danelos' role in the prophecy became clear did he return to his ancestral home, take Demetrios' soul, and return to the mortal realm, and..."

He stopped, and cold despair, the kind only a parent would know, washed over him. Apollo crumpled to his knees, his empty eyes shimmering. As he closed them, tears traced the lines of his face.

Zeus' argent eyes had never seen his son so absorbed in thought or pain, and even he felt the radiant anguish.

"Dear Gaea," he exhaled, "Danelos, my son now, never lived in Arkadeia. He was born in the mortal realm. All Demetrios experienced, everything I experienced of my son: his journey to Tartaros to rescue Ares, his experiences in the Blue Guard, his relationships, his childhood... never happened."

Omniscient though he was, Zeus had no way to comprehend the agony coursing through his son. He could, however, see that exact emotion painted on Apollo's face, a lack of divine ichor or blood of the gods having left him pallid.

"At the same time, I have memories of Danelos in Boston..." Apollo didn't even finish his thought before he transported himself to the other side of Olympos at the scrying pool in the Hall of Prophecy, a space reserved for private communion between him and his priests. With a gesture, the waters darkened for a moment, but then he channeled his own memories into the pool revealing two distinct panels from the past, one showing Danelos' childhood while the Scales were broken, and one showing his childhood after they were fixed. Calling up the same calendar date for both showed different events, some varying a little, others varying so much it was hard to believe both events had even happened.

Just like when two souls inhabited one person in the other timeline, he retained two distinct sets of experiences, but he could now feel only one soul within himself. Waving random dates and times into the pool, he clearly saw either parallel or diverse moments in time. If he focused on one particular event, though, he could momentarily block the other one, distinguishing one history from the other. At least he wouldn't confuse the two.

Having traveled through the immortal realm of Hades for centuries, looking for a way to Mount Olympos, The Nebulous One finally discovered a portal that led out from the underworld. Emerging in the modern era, she left the valley and ascended the earthly mountain. If one were to have seen her, he would have seen an avalanche, but in reverse; instead of white, powdery snow, this would be living, undulating darkness. Her single-minded mission built up her momentum, and in her wake, the earth seemed scarred. Or, perhaps Gaea recoiled to the touch of one so heinous.

Apollo sat on the edge of the pool, trying to balance all he had learned, but both Gaea and Olympeia, his spiritual mothers, interrupted his meditation with news that sent him right back to his father.

"I have been thinking about your dilemma, my son—" Zeus began.

"Hold, Father! Gaea and Olympeia charge us to leave Olympos and hide, if we can. *'She who feeds on darkness comes to destroy all the gods.'* That very prophecy that sent me to the mortal realm a second time is now finally coming true. *The Nebulous One*, as I have learned she is called, has found her way from Hades."

Zeus and Nyx's daughter was rising from Hades, Apollo told him, and approached Olympos. Even though Gaea and Olympeia, ancient *Protogenoi* that they were, feared nothing in creation, *The Nebulous One* was a force beyond reckoning, one with unknown power and intent. Zeus took commands from none except the *Moirae* and the sisters Gaea and Olympeia. Thunder rang throughout the heavens, summoning every Olympeian to the Hall of Tribunals. If Mother Earth and the spirit of Olympos felt the need to warn them, they should be heeded, Zeus thought.

The sky god's face bore an expression Apollo wasn't used to seeing—apprehension.

At the point where the Nephelae—the cloud nymphs—girded the mountain first, an obstacle that would normally dissuade mortals from continuing on, The Nebulous One pressed on, her touch dissolving the nymphs as well as the mists they embodied. Further up the face of Greece's highest peak, more boundaries fell. If the gods knew of the nymphs' demise, surely they would mourn, but they had their own concerns.

Seated in the Piereia province in northern Thessaly, the tallest mountain in the land—Mount Olympos—rose over the Pindus range with majesty and presence. Just beneath the cloud line, mortal mountain climbers knew to turn back when they encountered markings etched forever into the stone, symbols older than the gods themselves that marked a boundary. Where the Nephelae encircled the mountain was sacred ground, and only those who had been sanctified by the gods or their emissaries could traverse there. Goddesses with no corporeal form, the nymphs became a dense, misty sponge through which any would struggle to penetrate. Should a mortal be bold enough to pass through, sights few humans had ever seen would overwhelm him. Olympos appeared different to each visitor based on godly whim: some would see pillars of marble, a forest of firs, or, perhaps, orbs of light. Here was where the pronouncements of the gods hailed from as well as curses or praises upon mortals and immortals alike. Classical artists imagined it would be beyond gravity, beyond logic, with structures defying every natural law jutting from the mountain itself. In truth, the Olympos Theôn, or Olympos of the gods, had no physical connection to the actual mountain, but rather was an ethereal extension of the rock. The petulant daughter of Nyx and Zeus bridged the gap between the stony crags of the mortal mountain and the mist-shrouded structures of the immortal gods, unaffected by the drastic changes from mortal gravity to immortal atmosphere. The Hall of Tribunals reeked of Zeus, and that would be her first target.

"Where shall we go?" Zeus asked his son. "If Olympos is not safe, and Olympeia herself cannot protect us as she has always done, we are indeed doomed."

For Zeus to express such concern over their safety, he had to be unsure of the outcome of such a confrontation. He knew Nyx, and the power she wielded, so he knew their offspring would have immeasurable possibilities for destruction.

"Not exactly. In communing with Gaea, I have learned secrets, most of which I cannot share, but one that I think she wouldn't mind if I did." Apollo lowered his voice. "Just as Gaea has a sacred *adyton*, her impenetrable inner sanctum, so too did Ouranos."

"If Nyx was able to enter Gaea's *adyton* in that other time, as was I, what makes you think *The Nebulous One* could not enter that of Ouranos?"

"Father, Nyx had gained entry to Gaea's vault through ancient spells that allowed you to go with her, if memory serves. Plus, she knew exactly where to find the magic, and that power does not exist in this time. *The Nebulous One* is but a toddler compared to her mother, and her motives seem much more based on raw emotion than intelligence. Besides, only I will know exactly where this place exists, and it will serve the purpose well. And I alone know how to gain access or can."

His eyes flashing, Zeus transported himself and his son to the great hall where all the immortals gathered.

Apollo muttered a few words in an ancient tongue, and Earthsteel blade materialized. The sword belonged to him before it belonged to Danelos, so the sun god didn't think his son would mind.

"Father, this is a sword of Gaea, called *Thyroros*, the PortalBearer. With this, I can open the place you need to go."

"How is that possible? I am not even sure where this place is," Zeus inspected the blade.

"Trust me. Above our celestial realm lies a place no god has ever seen. Rising beyond the highest point here, above a thicker layer of Nephelae, exists this sacred place."

Zeus nodded. "Very well. We will go now. Let the rite begin!" He thrust his hands skyward, raising his eyes.

Thunderclouds packed the heavens, bringing with them torrents of living rain. Each of the gods raised his or her arms, beginning a chant in that same Olympeian language—a transformation enchantment. Pelted with rain electrified by Zeus' lightning, the gods relinquished their human guises, revealing their true forms, that of Avians. The human forms, reduced to light and shadow, shot forth from the hall, vanishing onto Gaea, only to coalesce in new forms they had never been in random earthbound locations. Gods as mortals they would be, for one year.

Left behind were birds containing the power of the gods: true archetypes. Fair Aphrodite emerged into a diminutive sparrow while her husband, Ares, donned the dark plumage of the vulture, he who scavenged the battlefield for fleshy remains. With ruddy, intoxicated cheeks,

Dionysos took to the air bearing a robin's red feathers, with Demeter going aloft on those of a striped turtledove. As Hermes flitted about, so did his avian shape: a quick hummingbird; Hephaestus climbed higher and higher with a crane's prodigious form. With the bearing of the huntress, Artemis stretched out her hawk's wings, and the queen of the gods, Hera, ascended as a white peacock, its majesty declared by the glow of Apollo's sun-chariot. Wisdom's avatar, a grey owl, replaced Athene's human shape, and she soared higher into the heavens until she surpassed the cloudy barrier above.

The last to depart, the brotherhood of three, shared a look. Hades wrapped himself in his cloak and a blackbird replaced his scowling presence; Poseidon, through an aquamarine mist, became an osprey, and Zeus outstretched his arms, morphing into an eagle, talons grasping chains of Hephaestian gold that supported a shallow tray bearing the fiery form of his sister, Hesteia — she preferred the shifting shape of fire to anything avian, and her flames would be the portal for their vision into the mortal world.

Using his access to the First Fires through Gaea, Phoebos Apollo irradiated the Eye of Gaea in the sword's pommel, igniting its power. He rose toward the cloudy barrier, the blade's presence coaxing the Nephelae to retreat, revealing a barrier of pure energy. As the Earthsteel blade cut into the realm higher than Olympos, each of the birds entered, the last being Zeus' eagle, squawking his gratitude. The portal of clouds enveloped them, welcomed them into the *Ptinotrofeio*, the Aviary of the gods, until such time as their essence would join once more with their mortal forms on Gaea.

With the gods safe for the moment, Apollo rejoined his own family in Boston, realizing he wouldn't see his father, siblings, and the other gods for a long time.

The Hall of Tribunals was empty. Swishing around the marble

corridors and chambers of Olympos, she could smell the stench of her father, but she found no one there. Her body filled entire chambers, and the gelatinous cloud oozed into crevices and secret rooms with ease. No sound came from her. Sliding over objects, silence followed, even more than what was already there. She thirsted for him, his power, and his essence. Maybe, she would take from him something she could survive on for eons. After all, the Titans provided a limited amount of sustenance. Wait... another trail lead to a place above the great hall, above the palatial marble, almost into the ether. But... wait...

Nothing.

More white clouds drifted, hiding the aviary from The Nebulous One. She could almost taste the ichor in the air with the electric energy Zeus generated. Olympos held nothing else for her, so she turned her attention to Gaea's mortals. Surely those who lived below could lead her to what she sought.

To the east, she found another scent. Faint, but it would do.

4—FIRST KILL

Litokhoro, Greece. Six miles east from Mt. Olympos.

"See you tomorrow, Yaya!" Theo Ranopoulos removed his apron. He worked at Dioscuri, a small restaurant on Pidnas Street owned by his elderly grandmother, Eugenia. Working with his family in this place ever since he was able to walk, he had the reputation of being the cornerstone to the business after his father died a few months earlier.

He delivered a quick kiss to the top of her silvery head just before he stepped into the alley behind the restaurant, ready to catch up with some friends at the café about a mile away. Adjusting a leather cap atop his brown curls, he shoved his hands in his pockets and blended into the dozens of passersby, most making their way home for dinner.

"*Kalispera*, Theo!" the shopkeeper chuckled while sweeping the sidewalk, "Off to cause trouble?"

"Of course, Panagioti! And good evening to you, too," Theo said, smiling, waving as he crossed the street.

For the past five years, he and his friends had met around 7 p.m. in the back room of Poseidonis, a dive bar/café on Koutroumpa Street near the edge of town, mostly to assuage themselves from a hard day's work with some ouzo and *saganaki*, punctuated by much laughter and camaraderie until the deep hours of the morning. With the sun having just passed the horizon, the streaky sky left just enough warm orange to pass for skybound streetlights. On the opposite side of town, the lacy moon began to show its delicate silver, and further to the west, the peak of Olympos seemed to exude a dark smoke, but not the wispy feathers of mist or the light puffs of a campfire: this charcoal cloud followed the side of the mountain with purpose and direction, swaying with both serpentine grace and malevolence.

Theo found himself distracted on his street journey, always chatting with either random shop owners or friends he would run into at sidewalk cafés or bistros, or family members who worked all over town and wanted to catch up. Salty breezes off the Thermaic Gulf brought with them pungent aromas of the sea, blanketing the streets with a magical familiarity. Mingling with the social surroundings, local guitarists played, their sprightly strumming injecting a baseline of rhythm into an already melodic atmosphere. Litokhoro's familial backdrop was one of the main reasons why Theo had never left, even though he knew larger cities had much more to offer him.

Between the majesty of Olympos and the simplicity of Litokhoro stood pine, cedar, and fir forests expanding like a fleecy, aromatic green blanket over the landscape. Hikers and nature lovers alike relished the view of the sacred mountain they could camp beneath, perhaps wishing the ancient ones looked upon them with some favor because they showed respect to Gaea and all she represented. Through this sanctuary zigzagged the black cloud form of *The Nebulous One*. Just as a shark can detect the slightest drop of blood in the vastness of the ocean, she knew exactly what she wanted—down to the square foot. Offspring of a primordial being, she moved with great speed, unnatural by mortal standards.

Caught up chatting with his ex-girlfriend, Ianthe, who worked as a barista at the only Starbucks in Litokhoro, Theo used his wry smile, blue eyes, and even his knowledge of what she liked to convince her to join him over at Poseidonis after she finished her shift, offering such enticements as a fun crowd, great music, and even his company, although he knew she wouldn't take that last one as seriously. Having mastered managing Theo's methods, she playfully rebuffed him, even though she still found him charming, and returned to work.

As he walked closer to his destination, he noticed how the sky had darkened a bit, the sun having set completely, pinpoints of street lamps glowing above him like will o' the wisps in a fairy land. The air temperature dropped a few degrees, something atypical this time of year, but Theo simply chalked it up to a possible oncoming rain shower and picked up his pace. Whether it was the cooler air or perhaps the sudden feeling he was being watched, the hair on his arms bristled.

Fog had been known to creep through the town during certain times of year, sticking to the streets like honey, but this darkness rolled into Litokhoro and down Vasilios Konstantinou, a main street emptying as night descended, like quicksilver. Nyx's daughter, harder to discern when her mother obscured the mortal world, closed in on her prey with a stealth unknown to man or beast. With her victim in her view, she moved over houses and around cars like a tidal wave, pushing the air before her into swirls.

Tearing through the center of town, *The Nebulous One* had no designs on just anyone, but those who saw her felt their fear spontaneously shoot from their body in screams. The shrill sounds of panic made Theo turn, and seeing the monstrous horror that is night's child, his heart took on a percussion that made his head throb, and he tore off down side streets, glancing over his shoulder occasionally. As he moved closer to the Gulf, he figured he could eventually evade whatever it was that was following him. He had never seen something so frightening, and all he could see was thick blackness, but an impenetrable blackness. Theo's swerving moved him into parts of town he wouldn't normally visit during broad daylight, but a soul-shredding fear prodded him. He had only come close to that feeling once when he almost fell off a cliff as a boy, having immobilized him back then, but a strong survival instinct kept him going now. Even with that, deep inside, he knew she would catch up.

She was toying with him.

By the time he reached the street Iona Dragoumi, he couldn't run anymore. Theo stumbled into an alley, hoping to hide long enough for this thing to lose him. Somewhere, he'd lost his hat—his favorite hat—and his brown curls dripped with sweat. Hunched over, his hands on his knees, his deep breathing played counter to his heartbeat. Behind some wooden boxes he hunched, praying that he would just survive. What could this thing possibly want from him? What was it anyway?

The streetlights went out. The temperature fell below freezing. A flood of ink filled the alley, tendrils creeping up the brick walls on both sides. His scent was strong, that of the first born. He couldn't have hid anywhere where she couldn't have found him. A child of Zeus herself, *The Nebulous One* could smell that familiar stench, no matter how many generations back, no matter how many thousands of years since Zeus first imposed his will on the woman or goddess whose descendants would eventually give birth to this... man. She felt his mortality outweighing any trace of godhood; he had no idea about his ancestry.

Theo's frosty breath quickened in her presence, and as she flowed closer, he released the contents of both his bladder and his bowels. She had him.

A protrusion of her black self moved toward him, like a faceless neck, and where a face would be, two red eyes glowed, capturing him in her gaze. While not a Gorgon who could turn him to stone, his fear betrayed him enough to do that. Other parts of her coiled around his legs, his arms, his neck, and his torso, leaving only his eyes free. She wanted to peer into his soul while she took what she wanted from him against his will. In her embrace, his body stopped shivering and crumpled to the alley floor, strewn in his own waste.

Streetlights returned moments later. The night air warmed once more. *The Nebulous One* receded from the alley like low tide to find her next victim, the one bearing that familiar scent.

Regaining consciousness, Theo left the alley, his terror lessening into simple fear, gradually evaporating, but he still had no idea what that was and why it wanted him. When he realized he wasn't injured, he saw the state of his clothes, reeking with excrement, and made his way to the beach where he cleansed himself in the frothy waves. Using the darkness as a shield, he found his way home, his parents out for the evening, and a change of clothes, ready to find his companions. Strangely enough, after what happened, he felt at peace.

Around 8:30, he arrived at the café, pushing his way through the throngs to the back room, the place he and his friends used for their evening festivities. Theo hoped to wash away the evening with a few glasses of ouzo. Seated on a worn couch were some of his closest comrades, and just being with them warmed his soul.

"Yammas!" His cheer caused all eyes to fall on him. "Sorry I'm late. Who's buying the first round?"

A man around Theo's age, his arm around a young blonde, squinted through the cigarette smoke. "What? Who the hell are you?"

"Stavros, it's me, Theo," he laughed. "Seriously, is it my turn to buy already?" He sat in an empty overstuffed chair across from the couch.

"Hey, I don't know who you think you are, but this is a closed party." Stavros sat up. "Find your way out."

From behind, Theo heard, "Hey, you're in my chair. Mind finding another one?"

"Sofia! It's me, Theo. Hey, there's plenty of room for

two." He patted the arm. "Stavros is playing with me to-night."

More people walked over, hearing the conversation, each one looking at Theo with that same expression. Every time he greeted someone by name, he or she responded as if Theo were someone unknown, an interloper.

"Guys, okay, the joke was funny for a minute, but seriously — what's going on?"

Stavros, annoyed at having to leave the couch, leaned into Theo's face. "Not sure who you are, buddy, but we're not your friends. Now, get out before I throw you out."

"Andrew," Theo addressed someone else he knew leaning against the pool table. "What's happening here? Did I do something? You're not still mad at what I did in third grade, are you? What the hell is happening?"

The man he called Andrew walked over smiling, and for a moment, Theo thought he would finally get some answers, but then both Andrew and Stavros lifted him up by his arms and shoved him toward the door back into the café. People he thought he knew turned around to rejoin their original crowd, laughing and commenting about how they might need to lock the door if freaks just walked in off the street.

Heading back home, confused and angry, Theo decided to stop by the Starbucks to see Ianthe. Maybe she knew what was going on. Taking a seat on the patio, he saw her waiting on someone.

"Hey, *glikia mou*, any chance I could get a latte?" Theo asked just as she turned to place the other order. He enjoyed teasing her every so often.

Met with a glare, he tried calling her by name.

"Have we met? And, who do you think you're calling *sweetheart*, anyway?"

More attempts to communicate went ignored, and she uttered an obscenity as she pointed him out to her manager. Threatened with bodily harm if he didn't leave, Theo reluctantly headed back to Dioscuri, figuring he would at least get something to eat before he went home. As he always did, he went into the restaurant through the kitchen door in the alley, and when he saw his grandmother chopping onions, he stood behind her and gave her his usual peck on her head. Shrieking, Eugenia turned around, waving her knife.

"Yaya, what are you doing?" He dodged the blade. "It's me, Yaya... Theo!"

"*Vyes exo! Vyes exo!*" Her voice was as shrill as a harpy's.

"Get out? I work here, Yaya. Did I do something?" He blocked the knife with a cutting board. "Yaya, stop!"

It was no use. She wouldn't stop thrashing the knife, and he didn't want her to hurt herself, so he ran back into the alley. He didn't know what else to do. Everywhere he had been, all the familiar places, people just didn't know him. Going home would be too painful, the thought of his own parents not knowing who he was, so he would just wait until his mother went to work in the morning to get some things. The later it became, the more frustrated he grew, unsure what to do or where to go. By 2 a.m., he was sitting on the shore of the gulf, staring out at the shadowy horizon, throwing sticks into the surf. The more he thought about what had happened earlier in the evening, the more he couldn't be certain it actually happened. Maybe he imagined the whole thing? Perhaps he had gotten so drunk at Poseidonis that he blacked out and dreamt that no one knew him. It could happen.

A few hours later, as if the truth of it all forced itself free, his face contorted and his eyes flowed with grief and anger. So much rejection, for no obvious reason. How did his best friends he had spent every evening with for years suddenly not know him? His ex-girlfriend? His own grandmother? Maybe he was actually still unconscious somewhere, perhaps the alley. He just didn't know. He lay back on the damp sand, tears sliding down the side of his head into the grains. While he stared into the sky, speckled with stars, the whisper of wavelets creeping up the sand lulled him to sleep.

Sunrise provided promise, the yellows of sunbeams nudging him awake gently, but when he realized where he was, the bright day felt even more painful—he couldn't hide his fears in shadow anymore. That twinge in the pit of his stomach returned, too.

Walking through town, a jovial place where he had always felt so welcomed, so embraced, Theo now felt abandoned. Faces that normally brought strong memories to the surface stabbed him fiercely, and making eye contact conveyed no connection whatsoever. Behind every pair of eyes was someone he knew, some from years of friendship, yet he couldn't possibly comprehend why he or she didn't know him. It was as if he just didn't exist anymore. Maybe he would have to make a new life elsewhere, but how? Where would he go? He would have to start all over, making friends. His family, however, would be lost to him, forever. Just that thought alone brought back the despair, deep and empty at the same time. Theo hadn't seen them since the day before; they might remember him, he thought, but it was easier for him to separate himself from them before he would see the look in his mother's eyes of a woman who didn't remember giving birth to him, or the eyes of his father who would never recall the fishing trips they had taken in the Aegean Sea.

Sometimes, one reaches that jagged threshold of pain, grief, and despair, a place where logic and lucidity can't take hold. That emotional boundary, once passed, can lead to a path of new beginnings. In Theo's case, his mind had reached a place where he felt solace plunging Yaya's kitchen knife through the heart of his parents, asleep in their bed, since he couldn't bear for them to live without his memory. Sitting cross-legged in his living room, eyes glazed, his mind splintered, Theo traced, with a bloody finger, the outline of his parents in a photograph.

Attracted by his odious crime were the Erinyes, three goddesses whose sole purpose was to bring madness to those who killed their family. Caressing his cheek was the taloned hand, black as oil, of Tisiphone, glossy-scaled serpents on her arm slithering across his face. She and her two sisters, Alekto and Megaera, had followed *The Nebulous One* from Hades, and they would bring justice to those who had sinned, a justice that Themis would never sanction.

When the time arrived, with the madness at its peak, the Furies, as Mankind sometimes called them, would eventually devour him, leaving behind only his entrails, his mortal soul cursed to inhabit Tartaros.

5—TRUTH

With the pans of the Sacred Scales repaired and moving as was intended, random threads of events realigned and attached themselves to one another, so that which might not have existed prior, existed in this correct time. While *The Nebulous One* pursued her quarry, having left Litokhoro behind, in Boston, Massachusetts, Alkinoë went to her son's apartment, although she hadn't gone to see Danelos; rather she sought his roommate. She needed to share something with him, a revelation that had not been true before the Merging.

"My birth mother?" Brandon sat up.

Alkinoë was wringing her hands, her breathing a little shallow, but her eyes never left him. Her long, black hair had been pulled back with a tortoise shell clip, but a few wisps of hair had come loose.

She pulled some strands behind her ear. "I think it be better if we talk about this when Paul, er, Apollo arrives."

In the mortal world, Apollo went by Paul Fairmont; Alkinoë kept her first name.

"Why... why would you tell me this?"

Brandon couldn't look her in the face, but he couldn't

just walk away, so he remained on the couch, leaning on his knees, his fingers laced beneath his chin. After everything he had experienced as part of the Task Force, fighting side by side with Dan, Aleta, and Sarah, he had seen and heard things that would make his blood run cold, but, nothing like this.

A deep sigh. "I had to. I just did. Let's wait—"

She just looked around the apartment, not knowing what to say. In her heart, she knew this was the right thing to do. It just was. Alkinoë had been the queen of Arkadeia, had commanded the Royal Army, and had led countless diplomatic excursions where she had been challenged beyond her comfort zone, but this heartache was like nothing she had ever known; and, it had been plaguing her for months. Brandon paced around the apartment, hoping that Danelos wouldn't come back too soon. He wasn't sure he could handle that: his best friend was now his brother. Everything he had told Dan in confidence seemed almost trivial now after this. Being on missions in parts of the world he never knew existed, he and the others felt like their lives were forfeit on so many occasions. Faced with what you believe to be your imminent death, you share things, delicate things, with those you care about like family. But, what if that same person you felt was like family was now indeed your family? How did that change things, or did it?

Only about twenty minutes passed, but it felt more like an hour, and Alkinoë was startled back into the moment by the knocking at the door. Brandon was closer, so he opened it, and felt a churning in the pit of his stomach when he saw Apollo. Without speaking, Brandon returned to the living room and stared out the sliding glass doors overlooking Boston.

"Brandon? Is everything all right?"

Alkinoë reached out to her husband, and he took her hand. "I have something to tell you. Brandon, you don't have to sit, but just listen. Apollo, I love you so much. I wish I had told you this sooner." She used his true name when things were serious.

Brandon turned around to look at both of them. Apollo, unsure of what was happening, sat next to his wife, her hand tightly gripping his. All he could do was look from one to the other.

"As I'm sure you remember," Alkinoë began, "I used to be the queen of Arkadeia. Well, technically, I still am, but that isn't the point. I had a son, Kidemonas, who was our pride and joy. Being the leader of a powerful society meant I had responsibilities, so my time was limited. We put our son in the care of a nurse, Penthe, who also watched the children of other dignitaries who stayed in the palace. What a gentle, loving woman she was. Remember, Apollo? Anyway, when he was just able to walk, he came in holding her hand one day, tottering into the throne chamber, singing a tune he had learned. Well, I don't know if you would call it singing. It was more like gibberish with music, but it was so adorable. He was trying to sing whatever the song was to me. For weeks, whenever Kidemonas was with us, he would do his best to sing this song. Penthe called it a Macedonian lullaby."

"Yes, I remember." Apollo caressed her cheek. "Why did you think of this?"

"I'm getting to that. When Kidemonas was about two years old, Apollo and I had made the decision to come to this world, the mortal realm, because he had already spent a year here when he chose to see what it was like to be human, and prophetic vision worried him. Arkadeia, like many other god-formed societies, existed outside the realm of normal time and space. We could interact with the local tribes or other major nation-states, but we could also choose to conceal ourselves from the world and exist in secret. Themyskira, Sparta, Athens... all of them could make that decision. When Apollo and I came here, time passed differently, so we arrived in 1978. We bought the apartment on Commonwealth Avenue and settled into a mortal life, all three of us.

"One afternoon, while I was at the supermarket, I had

Kidemonas in the cart. I turned toward the cereal shelf, my right hand still on the cart's handle, and when I turned back, he had vanished." She squeezed Apollo's hand.

"You didn't hear anything? See anything at all?" Brandon said, momentarily distracted from his own quandary.

"I never heard a thing. Well, I called the police and then Apollo, who was the liaison between the Greco-Italian Alliance and the United Nations. Law enforcement searched the vicinity as well as the local train stations and the airport, but they found absolutely nothing. If I didn't know better, I would say that a god or daemon had taken him, but there were reasons why that couldn't have been true. Even Apollo, with his Olympeian gifts, couldn't find Kidemonas, and that surprised me. To be able to hide from a god, the kidnapper would have to have been a god, or a daemon. After two months, the police gave up their search. They had no clues of any kind to follow.

"Life went on. I then discovered that I was pregnant. I must have become pregnant before I left Arkadeia, because almost six and a half months later, I gave birth to Danelos. I never forgot Kidemonas, however, and having another son made the loss even harder to bear."

At this point, Brandon sat on the chair across from them, intrigued more by what had happened, but still confused as to his connection.

"A few months ago," Alkinoë continued, "you and the others had come to our apartment, Brandon. It was the day after Task Force: Gaea had defeated that group of hydras that had been brought to life by that cult claiming to be Olympeian Resurrectionists. We told Danelos to bring you, Sarah, and Aleta over for dinner so we could celebrate with you, since we hadn't seen you in a few weeks. Remember? I digress. I was in the kitchen preparing dinner when you came into the dining room to get on your computer. I distinctly remember seeing you in the dining room, collecting some papers, and humming. It took me a moment, but as soon as I remembered that song, I dropped a glass. You came into the kitchen to see if I was all right."

"I do remember that, actually. You'd lost all color in your face," Brandon said. "But, are you saying I'm your son? I just don't see how that's possible. I mean, I know the Jeffries adopted me. They were pretty up front about it when I was old enough to understand. I just don't remember learning a song like that or living in a Greek city. If I was two years old when that happened, surely I'd have some memories, right?"

Apollo walked over to Brandon, putting his hand on the young man's shoulder. "You were awfully young, though, Brandon. Alkinoë and I came to the conclusion that someone who needed money abducted you. We don't believe the Jeffries were involved, but when we questioned the agency, all they knew was someone claiming to be your father paid someone at the agency to take you. And, it's not uncommon for you to forget your past, since you were so young when you were with your new family."

Brandon nodded along with Apollo's words, almost convinced. "But, why did you choose today to tell me?"

"Think about it, Brandon," Alkinoë's voice softened.

"My birthday. Today is my birthday. Of course." He glanced at a few envelopes on the table. "Alkinoë. Apollo. Look, I'm sorry. This is a bit much for me to take in. I have to get to the university. Do me a favor, please. Don't tell Dan. Not yet. I want to be there when he finds out."

Everything would just be all right if she could hold him, she thought, but she couldn't do anything except let him walk out the door. Apollo and his wife stared out the sliding glass doors at the city, reflecting on that day almost thirty years ago. Alkinoë, Her Royal Majesty, Queen of Arkadeia, Commander-in-Chief of the Royal Army, who had fought innumerable battles against creatures of the underworld as well as adversarial nations—and won— collapsed into her husband's arms and wept.

6—MARK OF THE ERINYES

Task Force Ops. Boston Division. 0630 hours.

At 6:30 a.m. every morning, Quinn walked through the door of the command chamber in the basement, put her eyes up to the retinal scanner, and laughed to herself whenever the computer said, "Insufficient data entered. Fingerprint analysis required to verify identity." With all of the advancements in technology, she mused, why the United Nations couldn't figure out a way to register blindness as one of her identifying qualities was incomprehensible. Every day, she had to use her fingerprints and voice analysis to enter. The shift commander from the overnight watch laughed to himself.

"Always makes you chuckle, doesn't it, Robinson?" Quinn sat behind the computer station and put her folding cane in the desk drawer. "Something about the computer do that to you, or is it just amusing watching a blind woman?"

"Oh, ease up, Quinn. You'd think after all this time, they'd have found a way to check you in, you know?" He downed the last bit of mess hall coffee before crumbling the paper cup. "You know as well as I do that your blindness ain't nothing to me. If anything, it makes your smart-ass comments seem almost endearing.

"And why's that?" Her hands floated over the console, fingers detecting the electrical charge that let her feel the Braille." The haptic technology allowed the spots on the glass to vibrate ever so slightly, much like on a touch screen phone. To look at the terminal, all anyone would see is dark glass with certain spots lit for visual access; when Quinn took over command, though, the lights didn't show, and the haptics kicked in.

"Because you can't see me roll my eyes," he laughed. "You ready for the change report?"

Lifting a small touch pad from the station, she readied her fingers to receive the status report. "Ready when you are."

"Reports in from most divisions, except Epsilon, Theta, and Gamma with fifteen divisions in the field. All the rest on high alert. Commanders from Upsilon, Iota, Eta, Lambda, and Psi requested backup between 0320 and 0540 hours. Still waiting for final reports from them. Two reports came in, although they're unassigned. One in Chile from local law enforcement, and one in—"

"Greece. East coast. Town… Litokhoro," Quinn interrupted, reading the intel gathered by local sources on the scene. "Pseudos sighted. Three vics. Locals reported seeing a large, black mass moving through the town, like a fog." *Pseudo*, short for Pseudo-Lifeform, was division jargon for something metaphysical or indistinguishable. "Cameras reported… nothing."

"You want me to send in Alpha, Psi, or…"

"No." Her fingertips flew over the glass screen. "I'll dispatch Gaea." Something about this report didn't smell right, she thought. "And then we'll finish the report."

At 0645, Quinn sent Aegis and his teammates to the coordinates 40.10°N, 22.50°E, in Greece. When Aegis asked what the mission was, Quinn replied, "It's six miles from Olympos."

On missions, the U.N. Task Force Division used code-names for its operatives. Traveling by way of sword was no problem for the team, as long as Aegis had been there before, and Olympos was certainly one place he had been. It didn't take long once they arrived in Litokhoro to find out what the commotion was about, police cars surrounding the home of the Ranopoulos family. Flashing Task Force Division badges got them into the house, a spider's web of yellow tape blocking off the kitchen and living room, both places stained and dripping with blood. Local law enforcement kept nosy neighbors from creeping over the crime scene, and few police officers stood hunched over outside, retching. The stench from inside the house could surely have done that to someone not used to the smell of putrefied bodies. Perfume from the rose bushes growing by the door couldn't hide it. Talon and Zodiak scoped out the crowd, looking for answers, but Aether and Aegis scoured the house for more of their own. Just as they were about to enter the living room, a room normally adorned with Greek icons, lacy curtains, and family photos, Aegis held out his arm in front of Aether instinctively, his eyes forever stained with the sight. He had smelled decaying flesh before, but the visual was almost too much to bear. Aether knew he was trying to stop her, but she had to see and leaned over the tape.

"Great Gaea…" Her skin tingled with a chill, her eyes taking in everything.

In the center of the room lay the remains of two bodies, disemboweled, their entrails forming a circle around their corpses.

"Nico and Irene Ranopoulos, 67 and 65," commented a police officer from behind her.

Knowing their names didn't help. Their limbs, Aether noticed, were placed in what seemed to be a ceremonial position, something unusual. Photographers had already taken pictures, the officer added, so they could take a closer look as long as they didn't corrupt the scene. Aegis kept his eyes on the walls where a large circle was drawn in blood made up of three intertwining circles. Off to the side of the living room, Aegis saw an opening to another room and left Aether to investigate. On a side table sat framed pictures, a few dripping with blood spatter, but Aether cared more about the content. One white frame housed the wedding picture of Nico and Irene with others displaying what would seem to be their children. Three younger faces showed up in other photos, two girls and one boy.

"Aether, you need to come in here." Aegis' voice quavered.

Hardwood floors, aged with time and salty air from the sea, echoed her footsteps as they moved toward Aegis' location. Despite his tone, Aether moved into the room with a faster pace but stopped short and gasped, turning her head.

"You could have warned me."

"What words could I have used to describe this?"

Another eviscerated body lay on the floor, but only the torso remained. Ripped from the body cavity was the heart, now attached to the wall in front with a bone, presumably the ulna or radius. What remained of the arms sat in a heap with the other limbs, but the intestines hung on the wall in the same intertwining circular pattern as the blood in the other room.

"By the gods..." Aegis brushed his hair back with his hands. "Who could have done this?"

It took a few moments for her eyes to fall on it, but when Aether noticed the decapitated head, she gasped.

"Aegis, look." Looking up, she saw Theo's head, not even cleanly removed but rather pulled off, hung from the light fixture, his now useless eyes wide open.

"Do you sense any evil presence here? Being in touch with the spiritual world, sometimes you feel things, right?"

"I'm Wiccan, Aegis, not psychic. But, no, I don't feel as if anything else is with us. I mentioned one time that I had an intuitive feeling, and all of a sudden, I'm psychic." Her dry humor fell a little flat in this environment, although Aegis' silent smirk was enough of an acknowledgment.

They heard familiar voices in the kitchen and then Zodiak and Talon turned the corner.

"Holy hell," Zodiak turned away.

"What did you find out?"

"No one knows what happened, Aether, but what they do recall is a sense of extreme fear that night washing over the town, like a tide. We need to find out a name," Talon said.

"Whose?"

"His, Zodiak," Aegis pointed to the severed head.

He crouched down a little to get a closer look at a dark spot on the carpet. "Aether and Talon, go upstairs and see what you can find. Zodiak, check this out."

"What is it?"

"Not sure. Looks like a scale," Aegis poked at it with a pen.

"Fish scale?"

"Take a closer look. More like a snake scale, a black one."

"How did you even see that?"

"I noticed a slight shimmer on the carpet. I'll take it to show Quinn. Maybe she can make something of it."

Aegis showed Zodiak the rest of the crime scene, but the police were having difficulty keeping the neighbors away. With a shout upstairs, Aether threw a whirlwind around the house, just enough to keep people from being able to get close. Zodiak took pictures of his own, not knowing whether the local police shared their findings. About ten minutes later, Aether found them in the kitchen.

"The guy, or pieces of a guy, in the other room was Theo Ranopoulos, according to a phone bill on the desk. Talon took off out the window to ask around town. She said she'd be back as soon as she learned something. An officer radioed he needed to enter the house, so Aether reduced the winds long enough to give him entry.

"So, have you folks gotten what you need? My commanding officer wants to know if there's anything else we can do?"

"How long have you known the Ranopoulos family?" asked Aegis.

"Ever since I was a kid. I went to school with their two girls, Isme and Phoebe."

"And did you know their brother, Theo?"

"Who? They didn't have a brother."

Aegis picked up a few framed pictures from around the house and put them in front of the officer, each picture showing Theo at various ages.

"You mean to tell me you don't know who this guy is? He's in almost every picture in this house."

"Trust me. If the girls had a brother, I would know. I've lived here all my life, and so have they."

A short time later, Talon flew back through the upstairs open window, but she descended the stairs with wings hidden.

"You want to hear something weird?"

"Let me guess, Talon. No one has any idea who Theo is." Zodiak pointed to the officer. "The cop here doesn't know who he is either."

Talon held a photo. "I showed this all around town, and some of the locals said he had gone into a bar, but no one knew him. They said he claimed to know everyone there. At a café, when I showed his picture, one of the servers said she'd found a picture of him in her wallet, but she had no idea who he was. You know what's weirder? The back of the picture said, '*S'agapo me oli mou tin kardía, Theo*'."

"'*I love you with all my heart, Theo*'." Aegis examined the photo. "I'd say she was hiding something, but if no one in town has any idea who he is, I'm beginning to think we have a special problem."

"I have an idea." Aether returned upstairs.

Within a minute, she came down with a laptop computer.

"Check this out. I did a search for Theo and up came social media sites and blog posts for local businesses. This guy seemed to exist here, but no one knows him."

The police officer folded his arms. "I'm telling you. He's not from here. Nico and Irene only have two daughters."

"And they're not in town?" Talon's impatience was showing.

"No. They both live in Athens, but I can get you their number. Hold on." The officer reached for his radio.

Aether continued to browse the Internet for more on Theo, but nothing more came up other than what she had already found. His social media site was open, and she could see pictures of him all over town in restaurants and bars. And, then, she clicked on an album labeled 'Good Times'.

"Guys, we have a problem."

The officer returned with a slip of paper. "Here's Isme's number. We could get you Phoebe's, but she's not listed. It would just take some time." He noticed they were all staring at him. Aether turned the computer screen around toward him, and, when he looked, his face grew pallid.

"That can't be. I don't know how that's possible." He backed away.

About ten photos showed Theo, some random people, and a man named Markos Pellemides, the young officer who stood in the kitchen.

"Officer Pellemides, care to try again? We have three dead people here, and now, you're the only one we've talked with who actually has had contact with the deceased Theo." Aegis' patience was waning.

Aether browsed through the list of friends Theo had, and one young woman caught Talon's eye.

"She's the server at the café. Ianthe Galanos. But, she said she didn't know him. In fact, she looked genuinely surprised to see that photo."

Aegis and his team decided they needed to talk, but

43

they all agreed the fetid smell was overbearing. Officer Pellemides suggested another café on the other side of town, but he feared people might get through the barricade and allow their curiosity to damage the scene. Aether assured him they wouldn't. Just before they walked away, she gestured, and a dome of earth covered the small house; even with shovels, no one would be able to get inside for hours. That would give them enough time to figure out what they were dealing with; in the mean time, Aegis made a call.

For a few hours, Café Athenia had more customers than it had had all month. Sunset brought the usual patrons, but then one entered who had never been to this place, although the region was not entirely unfamiliar territory. A taller man with short, sandy blond hair found the back booth.

"Thanks for coming, Mr. Fairmont." Aegis always hid his father's true identity as a default.

"How can I help?"

Aegis explained what had happened, making sure to speak without any bias so his father could do what he knew how to do well—discern the truth. Officer Pellemides had arranged for Ianthe to meet them there as well, and Aegis questioned them about their knowledge of Theo. Apollo's answer didn't really help them, however.

"They're telling the truth, the truth they believe. From what you've told me, this is a fantastical tale, Aegis. An entire town has forgotten one of its own, and I don't really know how to help you. I would, though, like to see this crime scene, if possible."

"Of course. Aether, why don't you and I take my father there? Zodiak. Talon. Catch up with us as soon as you wrap up here."

Nightfall reduced the number of curious people around the house, but a few dozen remained. Like scavengers, they lingered, hoping to get a picture of the devastation. Litokhoro had never known so much excitement. Apollo scrutinized the scene, even with the faint electric lights. The sun god's eyes could discern everything perfectly, since illuminating through godly means, or even with Aether's help, would draw more attention, and they didn't need speculation of a curse or a haunting. Despite his Olympeian lineage, he found himself just as stumped as the others. It had been a while since he'd seen a crime scene like this.

"While it would seem that this symbol should be something I would know..." Apollo hesitated. "It's just not familiar to me. Three intertwining circles could be a cult symbol, perhaps. We're not far from Olympos. It's certainly possible a traveling cult to one of the other gods, or to me, thought Litokhoro as good a place as any to perform a rite. I'll keep my eyes open."

When Aegis and Aether couldn't handle the stench, they thought it was a good time to leave the house. Apollo remained, however. That symbol did indeed look familiar, but he wanted to protect Aegis, Aether, Zodiak, and Talon as long as he could. They would figure it out when they needed to, anyway. If he gave them all the answers, they wouldn't trust their own skills. It could be related to that entity hunting the gods, he thought. Would this foe be so blatant, or was it just possible some mortal faction did this? Olympeian Resurrectionists? They were always trying to tap into whatever residual godly power flowed through the world. Apollo had other concerns, though, and he trusted his son and companions to do their job. Aegis asking for assistance was well timed; Apollo had wanted to know how Brandon was doing, but he didn't want to seem too obvious. The palpable tension buffeting them both would soon give way to some kind of confrontation, but until that time, Zodiak would have to make sense of the situation in his own way.

No immediate resolution emerged from this, so Task Force: Gaea returned to Boston with new information for Quinn to process. Perhaps her computer knowledge could reveal something they could use to solve the puzzle. Sadly, Markos Pellemides, Ianthe, and the rest of Litokhoro had questions that no one could answer, and the local police department, under advisement from the United Nations, placed a permanent guard around the Ranopoulos residence until more answers surfaced. With the house sealed, no one could properly bury the remains of three people inside, and no one would mourn the loss of a young man whose life no longer resonated with anyone.

7—NO QUARTER

A hurricane, its gales whipping the already chaotic world into a frenzy, knocks even the mightiest off their feet. Heracles himself would find standing up to that force of nature a task more daunting than facing all the twelve labors combined. Catastrophic winds have no compassion, no mercy, no emotion and their aftermath shames those whom they have devastated—they were impotent in the face of such raw power. Leaving Litokhoro unsatisfied, the dark cloudlike form of *The Nebulous One*, with enough power to dwarf any hurricane, moved toward the scent of Zeus once more, this time fueled by deep rage. One mortal man, even one descended from Olympos' king, held not enough energy to sustain her. A rolling black fog with a singular mindset, she picked up an even stronger energy from a place in the south, far past Larissa and Lamia, toward the west of the Peloponnese by the Ionian Sea. Even with her voracious hunger, she avoided most of the populated areas, not wanting to be distracted from her journey, and her presence raised such fear in mortals that she would take notice and need to feed off them. Despite her solitary efforts as she flowed over the landscape, she brought madness to

47

cities and villages in her path as she also had to the healer in Megara when she was born, caused traffic to stop, overcame people so that they fell to the ground nauseated; violent tendencies overtook even the youngest, prompting them to attack random people — side effects of *The Nebulous One's* own visceral and primary emotions.

Passing Patra, she smelled her father's presence even more strongly and oozing like black pus, she moved toward Pirgos, where she could detect it in the very earth itself of a place most sacred — Olympia. Like a tiger catching the scent of a fresh kill, *The Nebulous One* lunged onto the ruins, sucking up every iota of Zeus' energy that lingered from millennia ago. Fractured marble columns, weathered by time, and statuary no longer recognizable, their faces eroded away by the wind, fell beneath her touch and became powder. The ground withered and cracked as she passed over it, so completely did she suck the last bit of Olympeian energy — all life — from the ancient shrine. Her hunger ignited, she turned toward the northwest, seeking more. Citizens of Pirgos felt the wave of cold blow through their streets, an icy harbinger of the horror that would befall them. As the temperature dropped to that of the underworld, *The Nebulous One* fell on the town, creeping her way through alleys, windows, open doors, and even air vents, seeking out life. In this moment, she no longer needed someone connected to Zeus; any form would satisfy her. When she passed over someone, she would find their face and gaze into their eyes, generating fear. Then, while she burrowed into their soul, she extracted their warmth, watching as their body fell limp; then, she took the electrical energy generated by their brain. Like a shark with the scent of blood, her primordial darkness ripped skin, muscle, and sinew away, leaving moist bone before discarding the remains.

A mother of three, walking home from the market, didn't stand a chance before she and her children, all under the age of ten, were no more. A son returning from the pharmacy with prescription medications for his ailing father made it to within a block from his house. A teenage girl on the phone with her sister never had the chance to say goodbye before being overtaken. One by one...

Some who could muster a scream found themselves silenced as parts of the body were removed until, they, too, were nothing but a bare skeleton. Men, women, children, and infants — it mattered not. All succumbed to *The Nebulous One's* insatiable appetite. Within a few hours, not only had Pirgos fallen, but neighboring Amaliada, Gastouni, and Vartholomio, too. In total, approximately 150,000 innocent people fed *The Nebulous One* before she set her sights on Zakynthos, an island to the west, and its population of 40,000. In the midst of her frenzy, however, she felt the presence of one far away, one whose connection was like Theo's, a weak yet direct link to Zeus. The fire of her vengeance knew no limits, and the people of Zakynthos should pray to whomever they worshipped that Nyx's daughter spared their island for one young man in India.

After a few days, ferries from Zakynthos ventured to the mainland filled with tourists returning to catch flights home or business owners looking for supplies. As soon as they arrived at the dock, ferry-goers found hundreds of scattered skeletons, ultimately drawing the attention of the local law enforcement and the Task Force division. Preliminary investigation suggested that Task Force: Alpha should come in, but this didn't truly seem like a natural disaster, and then Task Force: Beta seemed like a logical choice, but no trace of any infectious disease registered with initial scans. No investigating agency could logically explain how hundreds of thousands of people could mysteriously meet this fate, and the Greek army and navy, coupled with the Task Force divisions, set up a perimeter of armed vehicles stretching thousands of square miles surrounding the northwest corner of the Peloponnese. In response to this horrific situation, the Greco-Italian Alliance instituted a 9 p.m. curfew; anyone out past that time would be jailed, and resistors would be shot on sight.

Quinn dispatched Task Force: Gaea, but their investigation brought nothing. The destruction of over a hundred thousand people would be marked as an open case, and local authorities were welcome to continue their investigations; Aegis and his team instructed them to sample the remains and send it to the Task Force main laboratory in Boston for future analysis. Mortal instruments wouldn't detect anything metaphysical, though, and the deceased would never receive proper burials. Apollo's prophetic dreams solidified more, but he was still unable to see anything else.

8—CONVICTION

A ri lay with his chest against Dan's back, his left arm draped over his sleeping boyfriend. Having only met a few months prior, they felt an immediate bond for many reasons: both originated from Greece, were highly spiritual, and valued truth. Ari credited Dan for having rescued him from a more mundane life when he arrived in Boston, Ari having left home because he had seen Dan where he never expected him to be. He would have had to follow in his father's footsteps, and that was a position he couldn't bear, filled with too much loneliness and isolation. Life hadn't moved in any direction he could ever have planned for himself, and even having this man in his apartment seemed like an impossibility; he wasn't used to things working out for him.

Certain commonalities crossed over frequently, and each recognized something in the other that just drew him closer; as the moon moved the tide, so did their chemistry ebb and flow over the past weeks, eventually solidifying enough aspects of their relationship to form something unique. Aside from those intangible connections, Ari liked the little things like how Dan's black hair was just long enough to brush against his shoulders; Dan liked how playfully sarcastic Ari could be. Both enjoyed how each liked black licorice or spirituality—the little things made all the difference.

Being a research archaeologist and lecturer at Boston University kept Danelos' schedule filled with meetings, dig debriefings, classes, and other extracurricular activities that Ari had just become aware of. Every so often, when they were watching television or drinking coffee after dinner or about to meet friends, Dan would excuse himself, give his boyfriend a quick peck, and vanish for hours, sometimes days. Even with what they had in common, Ari tried to understand, but he couldn't help but feel jealous of the others in Dan's life who took up so much of his time: Aleta, Brandon, Sarah, hydras, Stymphalian birds, and chimerae—the usual suspects. While lying next to Dan, Ari propped himself up on his right arm and picked up Dan's arm bearing the Earthsteel manacle. His thumb brushed the etched metal, the Olympeian glyphs making his pulse jump. Ari tried not to wake him, but he was curious about the details, so he gently rotated Dan's wrist to look at the rest of the symbols. He wrapped his hand around the metal band and squeezed, although he didn't know why he felt the need to do that. Something about the etchings felt good against his palm, bringing him back to his former life ever so slightly. It was the closest he would get to the Olympeian language since he left home. Dan rolled to the left, his groggy eyes focusing on Ari.

"Do you want to know what they say?" Dan yawned.

Although Ari spoke Greek, he didn't speak the language of the gods. Eyes locked, and Ari nodded like a curious child about to learn something only certain people should know.

"Okay," Dan grunted, sitting up, gave Ari a peck on the lips, and leaned against the headboard. "These glyphs refer to Olympos, Gaea, and Olympeia." He pointed at the three largest symbols. "This line that runs around the band reads, 'To honor and protect with my life, this I swear by Potamos Styx.'"

Danelos looked at Ari whose eyes were locked on the manacle.

"And you are okay with being bound forever?"

"Yes." Dan didn't hesitate to answer. "I made that decision a long time ago. To break my oath, a Stygian Oath, would mean being cast out of the world for nine years. Well, not literally. I would lose my birthright for nine years, be cut off from anything Olympeian, even communicating with my father. And, other horrors I won't talk about."

Ari leaned his head on Dan's shoulder. "When I was a child, my father told me that those who broke an oath to Styx lost their voice as well. I couldn't bear not hearing your voice."

"Well," Dan started, "you won't have to worry about that because that won't happen." He stared out the window across from the bed out into the morning sky, a pale blue sky illuminated with faint orange and yellow of sunrise.

"How old were you when you received this," Ari asked, taking hold of the metal once more.

"Twelve."

And the story began.

Mt. Graylock, northwest corner of Massachusetts.

Turning points and milestones tend to fall at certain ages, and each event holds such weighty significance. It came time when Danelos was 12 that he and his father go on an outing, a special one. According to ancient tradition, one that Apollo regarded as sacred, fathers took their sons to a high place, the highest in the area, wherever possible, a place absent of others for a rite of passage. In this place, the father would pass on an aspect of kinship to his son that would not only bond them more closely, but also would enable the son to rise in responsibility. In this case, Apollo had taken his son on a camping trip to an austere campground on Mt. Graylock, the highest point in Massachusetts. While Apollo, in mortal guise of Paul Fairmont, was setting up the tent, Dan wandered nearby collecting firewood, the dryer the better. For Apollo, this was more than just a chance to bond with his son; it became one of the rare opportunities he would have to use true Olympeian magic. With the gods distant during this modern era, he had no other family around. Alkinoë preferred he not be too active with his godly power while around mortals, especially Bostonians, who could be especially cantankerous when confronted by things they didn't understand, didn't like, or both. Apollo would refer to them as "a proud people," mostly tongue-in-cheek, but he wasn't far off. In any event, this would be an experience young Danelos would not forget.

During late afternoon, when the sun's rays streaked the sky with shades of purple and gold, pink and blue, Apollo sat on a log before the fire having just finished their dinner. Next to Apollo was a leather pouch tied shut. To see him, sitting in his denim jeans and t-shirt, one would never know he was the son of Zeus, the caretaker of the sun chariot, and the god of music, healing, and prophecy. Here, in the world of mortals, he was just that, and the father of a young man whose time had come.

"Come over here and sit next to me, Danelos," He patted the tree trunk.

The boy, who had just gone to retrieve his sweatshirt, joined his father. Sitting facing west, Dan felt the glaring sunlight push back at them like a wave, something he noticed whenever his father was around; light felt alive.

"There's a reason why we're here, and it's not just to go camping."

"Yeah. Mom said something about it. How come she's not here? Is everything okay?"

Apollo chuckled. "Absolutely. This is just for you and me, though. I need to tell you some things and also give you some things. I need you to listen carefully, though, and if you have questions, just ask."

Dan nodded, eager to find out what was in the leather pouch.

"When I was a younger god, about your age in mortal years, Zeus showed me the trappings of my position: my horses, Mount Helicon, where the Muses resided, and even introduced me to my bow. He had had Hephaestos make it for me, too. I learned quickly what it meant to be a god of things like music, prophecy, and healing. Now that you're at the right age, I need to pass some things along to you. When I chose to walk the path of a mortal man, I wore a manacle on my left wrist so that I was constantly reminded of how limited I was being human, but also to remind me that I was a god. I chose to give up all my godly power for one year, and that band kept me focused on trying to be the best human I could be. After my journey, when I returned to Olympos, I opted to keep the manacle."

Apollo rolled up his sleeve to show his son the metal wrist cuff on his left arm. Ancient markings etched into the surface glistened in the later afternoon sun. Although he had worn this cuff for a few millennia, it shone as it did when the blacksmith first crafted it.

"I normally keep it hidden with what's called a glamour, a simple incantation that hides something behind a field of light."

Untying the cord on the pouch, Apollo removed another manacle, showing it to his son.

"I had this made for you before we left Arkadeia. Your mother was pregnant with you when we arrived here. She lost her immortality when she came to the mortal realm, a sacrifice she knew she had to make, but it meant that you were born mortal. Even though you weren't born in Arkadeia and never had the proper upbringing of a prince, as the heir to the throne, you should have royal insignia." He had originally had it made for Brandon, but Dan didn't need to know that.

He handed it to Dan to examine.

"It's not as heavy as I thought." He turned it around in his hands. "Are these markings the same as yours?"

"The metal is called *Gaeatsáli*, or Earthsteel. Its strength comes from how it's made, and nothing can break it. Your glyphs show that the wearer is of royal status, specifically Olympeian, and he pledges his life to the ideals of Gaea. By wearing this, you would be making that pledge. Not sure if you knew this, but, technically, she's your great-great grandmother."

Danelos smiled as he thought about the family history, and he always enjoyed knowing more about his lineage. Exploring the manacle with his fingertips, he could almost feel the power of the Earthsteel flowing through it. Wanting to be just like his father, he asked how he could put on the metal band. The idea of being a prince in more than just name only made him giddy.

"Okay, but there *is* a catch. Once you put this on, it cannot come off. You and it become bonded, Dan. There's no backing out. Do you understand?"

Nodding without really paying attention, Dan was enrapt by the idea of being Prince Danelos, heir to the Arkadeian throne—for real. Also, wearing the same band his father did made him feel even more connected. Apollo watched his son lose himself in the grandeur of the idea, but he had to make it clear that, if this decision was made lightly, the *mania*, or madness would come. Dan would have to believe that he should be wearing the manacle for the right reason.

"Wearing this manacle means you are forever changed. No longer can you sit idly by and watch people suffer, Danelos. You are duty bound to protect those who cannot protect themselves. Even at the cost of your own life."

"Why can't I just be the prince of Arkadeia, Dad? If we can't even go back, why can't I just wear this to remember where we're from? What difference does it make?"

Apollo understood now, and he knew what he had to do.

Shortly before they went to sleep, the rising hazy coin of the moon hanging in the sky, Apollo asked Dan to find some dry logs for the fire while he put their food away so bears wouldn't find it. Flashlight in hand, Dan would only have to go about fifty feet from the campsite to retrieve a log or two. He had been gone about ten minutes having moved beyond the guarding glow of the fire, and his father's scream shot above the darkness. It was a sound he had never heard before and, without thinking, he ran back to the campsite, dropping the flashlight. In the shadows of evening, he saw the tent had been shredded and the campsite had been destroyed with no sign of his father. Calls into the young night echoed back at him, but he refused to give into fear. *My father's a god,* he thought. *How could this happen? Maybe it was an animal sound?* Once he put some of the wood on the fire and it brightened, his eyes took in the damage. Then, it hit him: his father really was gone, and he was alone in the dark woods. He instinctively chose the best place near the fire so he could see the most of the surrounding woods, but he knew the fire would need to be fed. All of the wood he had gathered might last an hour at most. After adrenaline stopped pumping through him, his emotions took over, and that gnawing fear grew in his gut. He knew if he went into the woods at night, whatever took his father might take him as well, and he wasn't a god or even immortal.

Unseen bats flapping in the sky startled him, and rustling branches in the trees had his eyes darting about. He had pulled his knees to his chest and wrapped his arms around them to keep warm; the fire couldn't quite take the chill out of the air. It was the fear. Danelos could do nothing, and that just made him fidget. He tried to muster the courage to stand up and look around a little, but every time he moved, something moved in the darkness. Could he just sit there until sunrise? What if he fell asleep? He did feel a little tired now that he had calmed down a bit. Eyes drooped a little, but then the breeze would wake him. Or was it something else? If his head bobbed slightly toward slumber, he felt something inside that prompted him to stay awake, as if the ground moved.

Paranoia and fear of the unknown brought back the anxiety, but then he felt it again. That peripheral nudge. An hour or two passed — he couldn't clearly tell — but then he remembered something his father had told him when he was very young:

"She who is the earth itself is mother to all. Trust her. Gaea will always look out for you."

That's it, he thought. *That's who has been keeping me awake, with the breeze or that feeling in my gut.* His father called her his great-great grandmother. Once he understood, he knew he would be safe. Even though Gaea didn't intervene actively, she provided nurturing and inner protection. That helped him push back the fear long enough to stand up. He knew he had to find it now, that which his father had told him would connect him to Mother Earth. But, even she had to be sure he was ready. One didn't make an *Asilos Pistis*, a sacred pledge, without understanding all that it entailed.

In the distance, to the west, he heard his name in his father's voice, a weak voice at that. With his recently kindled courage, he grabbed a stick from the fire as a torch and started off in the direction of his name when a shadowy form stood before him and blocked him. Waving the flaming stick, he hoped to make himself look more formidable, but the shape didn't move. It seemed almost bearlike, but Danelos couldn't focus on it long enough to tell. If he moved a little to the left or right, so did the shadow. Again, he heard his name, but this time his father sounded in pain. Knowing he had Gaea with him, he stood his ground and held the torch before him, but the intangible thing before him moved closer. He had to get to his father, to stand with him no matter what it was that had taken him. Danelos moved around the fire to find another way around this creature keeping him from his father, dancing around the fire, taking courage from it. Halfway around, he kicked something toward the campfire. It was the leather pouch, and it kindled. Grabbing another stick, he quickly pulled the pouch away. As he knelt down, he kept his torch aimed at the looming darkness, hoping to keep it at bay just long enough. Pulling the manacle out, it burned his fingers a bit, but he couldn't worry about that: his father needed him. He tossed his torch into the fire, causing the flames to rise slightly, and he pushed his left hand through the manacle. The seam sealed, locking the band onto his wrist, but sending searing heat into his arm. *It doesn't matter*, he thought, *burns heal*.

He didn't feel any different, except a surge of confidence. That would have to be enough.

"Gaea, help me find him," he uttered, pressing forward toward the darkness. "Thank you for your faith in me."

His back felt a little strange, like something was weighing him down. When he reached back, his fingers brushed something metallic, and he instinctively grabbed hold and pulled. From its scabbard, he had released *Thyroros*, the sword PortalBearer, Gaea's gift to his father. Once in his hand, it didn't seem that heavy, and he gripped it tighter. Where his father could hold it in one hand, it took both his smaller hands to grip it. Standing right in front of the only obstacle between him and his father, Danelos swung the sword without hesitation, walking through the darkness and into the woods.

"Dad! Where are you?"

With moonlight painting the forest silver, Danelos scoped the area, his sword ready. When he heard his father's voice calling him back near the campsite, he headed that way, severing any branch before him. Back at the site, he froze—everything was as if nothing had happened. Sitting on the log, leaning toward the fire was his father, perfectly fine.

"It's okay, Danelos. You can put the sword away now."

But, the 12 year old couldn't be sure this wasn't a trick. "How do I know you're really my dad?" The sword's power pulsed through him, compounded by more adrenaline. Unknowingly, he had taken a defensive posture, something his father had never shown him.

"Dan, seriously. It's me. This was just my way of showing you that the manacle, as well as the sword, is not a toy or a symbol. They have great power."

No. This didn't feel right. Danelos looked carefully around, noticing if anything were out of place. Courage became layered with anger, because he just knew that something had happened to his father, and he would find out what.

"Dan, before you hurt yourself, or me, put the sword away. I'm sorry I had to deceive you, but I was afraid you wouldn't take me seriously."

The boy recognized that feeling he had had by the fire—Gaea. She was with him; he felt it from his feet. His connection to the Earth gave him strength, fortifying his own courage. Surely she wouldn't trick him. He had to trust her implicitly. And, then, he saw it.

His father, seated in front of the fire, cast no shadow. In human form, mortal laws bound even Apollo.

"Who are you!" His own voice surprised him. "You're not my dad. What have you done with my dad?"

In his mind, Danelos had received instructions from his great-great grandmother. Even though she wouldn't tell him more than he needed to know, she showed him one thing.

"What are you talking about? I *am* your—"

"No! You have no shadow. Shadows don't have shadows." He had been paying attention. "I know what you are, and I'm not afraid of you."

His father smiled. "Oh, but you should be."

As soon as Danelos saw his father stand, he held the pommel of the sword toward the moon, its beams activating the enchantment, enabling the sword to live up to its name. Electricity pulsed in the Earthsteel, and when Danelos saw his father was close enough to attack, he jumped forward, slicing through reality, opening a portal. Lunging toward the boy, the man fell into the hole, and it sealed. Contrasted against the recent noises, the sudden silence filled the absence. Sensing he was successful, his sword replaced in its sheath, he sat on the dirt, putting his hands through his hair. Again the adrenaline receded, and this time tears replaced it.

"Where did you send him?" The voice seemed to come from everywhere.

Danelos jumped up. "Who are you? Where are you?" He didn't know if he had it in him to fight this time.

"The sword opens portals to places you have been," the voice spoke again. "So, where did you send him?"

"Dad?"

Out of the tent came his father, and Gaea confirmed for Danelos that it was truly the son of Zeus who stood before him. Just to be sure, the 12 year old checked the ground; yes, there was a shadow. Danelos hugged his father hard, not willing to let go right away.

"I'm sorry I had to deceive you, *evgení polemistí mou...* my noble warrior." Apollo kissed the top of his son's head. "Taking on the responsibility of being the prince isn't just for show. You have to be willing to protect those at any cost who cannot protect themselves. Are you upset?"

Danelos stood back from his father and shook his head, but didn't raise his eyes. Apollo lifted his son's chin.

"I would have let nothing happen to you. Understand that, okay? And, I'm proud of you. You have much to learn about being a prince and a warrior, but your courage and concern for me I won't soon forget. Now, let's get some sleep. We have some hiking to do tomorrow."

"I'll be in in a minute. There's something I have to do first," Danelos said.

He took a seat by the dwindling fire and took a good look at his manacle. Even though he didn't fully understand what it meant yet to make such a pledge to Gaea, he was starting to realize how important it was to trust her. His hands touched the ground, the closest he could do to embrace her. Before he entered the tent, he whispered,

"*S'agapo, Matêr Pantôn. Sas efkaristo.*" He wanted Gaea to know that he loved her, and that he was grateful for her.

Just before they fell asleep, Apollo realized that Danelos had never answered the question of where his son had sent the shadow he had created as a test. It didn't matter, since the energy would dissipate, but what place could Danelos think of that would hold something like that? Alas, he would never know.

"Were you angry at your father? Did you truly understand why he did what he did?"

Dan was now sitting on the edge of the bed with Ari next to him, both aware of the brighter sky.

"I don't remember being angry. I do remember, though, having doubts early on, but I was still young and immature. The idea of being royalty didn't sink in fully until I was about eighteen, just as I was about to go off to college. I researched ancient Greece and even tried to find Arkadeia on old maps, but I could only find an occasional reference in old scrolls or books at the museum. The city of Tegea was gone, and it was almost as if the cosmos didn't want me to find it. That was when I decided to become an archaeology major. I fell in love with my own history."

"So, did you get teased much for having this on your arm?"

"Well, not for that, but sure, I was teased like most kids. My father used the same enchantment on my manacle that he had on his when he appeared in mortal form. Only those who knew about it could see it, and if I were to be engaged in battle, or feeling the need to defend myself, it would appear. I wore long sleeves quite a bit." He chuckled.

"I can't imagine you being teased. Why would they do that?"

"Ari, I was a diplomat's son with privileges, and that

made people uncomfortable. Kids usually act on what their parents say, and those who might not have liked my parents said things, whether they realized the consequences or not, that would come back to haunt me. I defended myself, though. By the time I was in tenth grade, I had shown them I was just like them."

Something dawned on Ari. "So, why is it that I have always been able to see the manacle? You hadn't told me about it until I asked you earlier, but I've been able to see it for months."

"Think about where we met," Dan replied, his eyebrow raised. "The first time. That's why. Okay, we both have to go to work. Go ahead and jump in the shower. I need to check my email and make some coffee."

Later, while Dan showered, Ari got ready to go to the construction site.

New to the country, Ari didn't have any resources, so Brandon had been able to get him a job working with a local construction company alongside the architect since that was Ari's schooling. Before his father had expected him to follow in his trade, Ari had studied architecture and mathematics on his own. It was a menial, low paying job to start, but it was enough to pay bills and allow him to stay in the American Conglomerate. Immigration laws had become tougher over the years, and since Ari had no identifying paperwork, Dan asked his father to pull some strings through the Greco-Italian Alliance creating, in essence, a birth certificate. As soon as Ari had an identification card, Apollo arranged for him to have his initial retinal scan and fingerprints taken so he would be on file. Depending on where someone was in the city, some police gave immigrants a hard time if they were 'old school', that is, from the early years when the immigration riots all but destroyed major cities in the Conglomerate. A staunch military presence in most major cities, as well as meticulous record keeping of citizens and their whereabouts, squelched most of them, but pockets of resistance existed up until the early 2000s. Ari would eventually become a citizen, if he chose, but bureaucracy swallowed people whole, as Kronos had done to his own children to prevent their rise to power. Paranoia clung to Boston, as in most cities, and those in control continually worked to stay that way.

When Dan and he met, the second time officially, Ari lived in what the Boston city officials called 'reconstructed neighborhoods', pockets of housing where those who had little to no income could live, for six months at a time, as long as they promised to remain employed. Once they no longer had a job, they would have to live in retention centers, group homes where residents would serve the community by acting as gardeners, sewage maintenance workers, street cleaners, and other arduous, yet necessary, jobs — without pay or food — but they would live on government assistance. Fortunately for Ari, when he first arrived, he found the City Office of Immigration, or rather he was escorted there since he spoke no English, and they put him through a battery of tests. One of these assessments was physical endurance, and when Ari could outperform even the strongest, they brought him to their Public Health Office where they checked his vitals. He couldn't articulate to the doctors who examined him why he was so strong, but his highly developed musculature implied he had been trained somewhere.

A few months earlier, when Dan was sitting at The Beanery, an outdoor café, reading, a city worker moving large boulders into a neighborhood garden caught his eye, but not just because of his appearance. Something about his face triggered a memory. While he watched the man carry the rocks, in his arms, something uncharacteristic of city workers he had seen, he went through his mind to see where he might have met this man before. Other garden workers used wheel barrows to move the larger rocks, but this man lifted them with great ease and walked without trouble a hundred feet or so. Not since childhood stories of heroes from his father's time had he even seen such strength. On his way back to the dump truck, the worker glanced over and caught Dan looking at him, but neither looked away. In fact, the worker brushed his hands off and slowly walked over. As soon as he recognized Dan, he hopped over the wrought iron gate that divided The Beanery from the sidewalk and got down on one knee.

"It is an honor to see you again, Your Royal Highness. I hoped I might find you."

Dan looked around to see who might be watching this display and then softly told the man to stand up. It was then he realized he had been addressed in ancient Greek. He still couldn't place the man, who introduced himself as Aristeides. They spoke briefly until Aristeides' supervisor yelled at him to return to work. Danelos stood up. Aristeides held up his hands to the man he claimed was royalty as if to say, 'It's all right', genuflected once more and hopped back over the gate. As he left, he looked back and said, "*Ávrio. Edó.*" *Tomorrow. Here.*

Dan, as if by reflex, nodded, and then Aristeides returned to work.

Not knowing when he needed to be there, Dan arrived at the café as it opened, took the same seat, and waited. He prepared some documents for the university on his laptop, his eyes scanning the street with every passing car or voice he heard. Finally, exasperated with his own lack of concentration, he slapped the computer closed, sat back, and crossed his arms. Two hours later, Aristeides returned, this time dressed in street clothes, and sat down at the table.

"How do I know you?" Dan asked. "Why'd you address me as royalty?"

"You are," Aristeides answered, not looking up. "When we first met, you saw me while I was tending to my duties."

Images flashed through Dan's mind, but he couldn't really make sense of them. He did remember something about this man, but from where?

"Can you be more specific? And, please, look at me," he said, lowering his eyes to get Aristeides to lift his.

"A few weeks ago, I was doing my job, when I saw a flash of light in the forest. Where I work sits at the edge of the Grove of Persephone, at the outskirts of Tegea. Coming from the forest, I saw a man—you—bearing a sword, dressed in nightclothes, I believe. You passed by me and continued toward the city. Hours later, you returned down the same road, under the cover of Selene's moon, and entered the forest. I heard what sounded like sword strokes, two in fact, and then nothing. This happened a few more times that week. The last time you emerged from the forest, moonlight showering upon you, I saw your eyes, those of our king, Apollo. Even though you were not born in Arkadeia, I knew you had to be his son, our prince, even after all this time. Where you came from was a mystery to me, but when you entered Persephone's copse once more, I followed you to where you unsheathed your sword, *Thyroros*, the blade I had seen in my king's hand. I followed you through the portal, eager to see where my prince would go, and ended up on a street in this city. Before I could return to the shrine, the portal closed, and I would be forced to remain here. And now, after all this time, I have found you once more."

Dan processed what Aristeides told him, but he had no words to reply.

"I know not why you traveled to Arkadeia, or how you could have, since you had never seen it, but I assumed it was an act of Apollo or some enchantment of the sword. I mean no disrespect, my prince."

"Okay, first, stop calling me that. Yes, I *am* Apollo's son, but you can't keep bowing in my presence or people will get suspicious. It's just weird... Aristeides." He didn't know this man, so he needed to tread carefully. His story sounded incredible and impossible... almost. "Second, I don't really remember going to Arkadeia, or how I could have. You said it yourself. I've never seen it, and the sword only opens portals to places I've been to. That's not my issue, though. What do we do now?"

"That, my prince, I do not know."

City noises filled the silent void opened by this conversation. Something about the shimmering morning sun illuminated Aristeides' face, the face of a man who held nothing but loyalty and admiration for the dark-haired man sitting across from him—loyalty he had neither asked for nor earned. But, Dan noticed, he had a kind, gentle face. Aristeides explained where he was living, to the best of his ability, since words for places he didn't understand how to translate into Greek sounded strangely pronounced. Once they figured things out, as much as they could under the circumstances, Dan felt the urge to give Aristeides his cell phone number and instructed him to call him should he need anything. Living with Brandon, he couldn't just bring Aristeides home to stay on the couch, even if he was technically one of Dan's subjects. For the moment, Aristeides had a place to stay and a job; that would suffice. The young man's resourcefulness, despite his abrupt transplant into a world he couldn't possibly understand yet, gave Dan a little more confidence about Aristeides' ability to survive. The man was, like it or not, an Arkadeian, and they were a clever people, according to his father, their absent king. They parted, and Dan realized he was late for work, but it was well worth the grief he would receive from his colleagues for missing the morning meetings.

In the weeks that followed, the two grew closer, and ultimately, Dan introduced Aristeides to Brandon, his best friend and roommate. In his short time in this modern world, perhaps because of where he lived and his daily interactions, Aristeides picked up the English language slowly, but spoke in a thick Greek accent. Soon, he told Dan to call him Ari, since that would be easier for everyone to say. Unspoken emotions surfaced more and more as they saw one another, enabling Ari to whittle away the barrier of royal fealty he had for Dan and reveal feelings for him: he was falling in love. This situation became the foundation of a wholly different relationship, one that Dan enjoyed because it meant he didn't have to worry about

Ari's origin—for the moment. For reasons he couldn't completely wrap his head around, he wouldn't tell his father yet.

Dan had just gotten dressed when he received a call from Quinn that Brandon needed his help, in Kanpur, India. Just as Ari walked in the bedroom to bring Dan his coffee, he saw the portal close. In that instant, he remembered that Dan was a bit more than just his boyfriend.

9—RAGE

Kanpur, India.

Five-year-old Bakura had wandered away from his parents. With hundreds of people at the Naveen Market, it wasn't that difficult for him to lose his way. Vendors and musicians provided distractions even for adults, never mind children. He would pick up a toy from one booth, but see something else and walk over to another. Other children ran through the crowd, chasing each other with toy ray guns or balloons, but Bakura didn't seem to care. At his eye level, too many other things caught his interest. At the end of the market, he was at least a block away from where he last saw his parents, but he couldn't see his mother or father anywhere. Crying out for them didn't help, since the musicians and crowds made much more noise than his little voice. Confusion gave way to fear, and he just wandered about, not noticing the black fog creeping down the street and over the houses like an army of dark ants. A few teenagers approached him to help, but the icy wave that preceded the fog splintered a mind-numbing fear into them, causing them to flee as soon as they saw it. Bakura stood alone, crying. A few blocks away, a young man turned the corner and shouted something unintelligible before running away. She saw him at last, and soon she would have what she needed. As the cloudy entity slipped over the pavement, the man turned around a few times, but then he stopped. She wasn't after him.

Before *The Nebulous One* could reach Bakura, the young man fought against his fear and his instincts kicked in, prompting him to save the child. Even with the paralyzing horror in his mind, he ran toward the boy, but he was too late. Her tendrils had surrounded Bakura, and her eyes held him still, mesmerized, while she removed from him what she was drawn to. Not far away, the man heard the sound of raspy breathing, but he didn't think it was coming from *The Nebulous One*. Louder and louder it grew. His eyes moved from one alleyway to another, but he saw nothing. His ears, however, grasped a sound his mind couldn't comprehend, and when he turned around, razor sharp claws swiped at his throat, removing his ability to shout for help. He put his hands to his neck, writhing, and fell to the ground, his blood pooling. A raspy tongue flicked at the body, removing chunks of flesh, until nothing recognizable remained. *The Nebulous One's* Hadean entourage had followed her to India, and this monstrous goddess had but one thought—rage. Skulking back to the shadows with no other prey to dispatch, the creature waited until another opportunity where she would feed on human flesh.

Receding, *The Nebulous One* left Bakura's small body only a few blocks away from where his parents suddenly had stopped looking for him, wondering why they had been running around the market. Kanpur Police found the boy, in a coma, and brought him to the local hospital. *The Nebulous One* had moved on, a small piece of her lineage within her.

Nothing scared people more than waking up to see fighting in the streets, the uncertainty of who was on what side and what they were fighting for, but it worsened when it was one man who fought against the goddess of rage and a daughter of Nyx, Lyssa. A few miles from the airport, from a fissure in the earth, she had pushed her way into the mortal world from Hades, attracted to the chaotic energy left behind by *The Nebulous One*. Aegis had been engaging Lyssa since just after she left the Naveen Market. Standing about ten feet tall, she shredded everything her four taloned arms took a swipe at: human, building, or automobile. Unfortunately, the citizens of Kanpur didn't speak much English, and Aegis' body language didn't translate. Curiosity won out, with terrible consequences. Lyssa wasn't alone.

From all over the city, the sound of growling dogs echoed, as if from the shadows, and then the sources stepped into the sunlight. Dogs of all breeds, strays or domesticated, from diminutive Chihuahuas to Great Danes left alleyways, houses, and pet stores, their mouths foaming. Lyssa had been the one, at Hera's bidding, to drive Herakles to madness; now, Lyssa turned Kanpur's canines against their owners.

Without hesitation, Lyssa's bronze claws ripped through passersby, those unlucky enough not to get the message, leaving corpses like shrapnel. Aegis tried to hammer her off the main street, but he underestimated her mass, and that she had wrapped her massive tail around a tree. When he tried to disengage her, he couldn't get a firm grip on the scales, a slick substance like pus or mucus oozing from beneath them. Striking the tail with *Thyroros* only made her angrier, if that were even possible, and she caught him by the arm with a claw, flinging him across the street. Brute strength wouldn't be enough; he'd have to outsmart her, but her unpredictability made that almost impossible. He'd fought Hadean creatures or even angry goddesses before, but something about her was different, but he just couldn't figure out what it was. For as much as he wanted to help the citizens who needed rescue from the dogs, he knew that taking out the source would be much more beneficial.

Lyssa slithered down Jaipuria Lane, heading for the Ganges River as something near the river had caught her one red eye. *The train*, thought Aegis, *she sees the train tracks*. The Innercity Express would be within striking range soon, and then she would have her fill of hundreds of unsuspecting people. The slimy substance on her tail allowed her to move fluidly down the street, and Aegis would need to pour on as much speed as he could just to get close to her. More civilians left houses and apartment buildings, nonplussed by any of the noise or destruction they had seen just a few blocks earlier. *Perfect*, Aegis thought. Now, he needed back up.

"Quinn, I need help. I'll open a portal, but I need someone now!" He shouted into his wrist communicator under his manacle.

"Roger that, Aegis. I'll give you Zodiak in two. Quinn out."

Growls and screams in the distance, he wanted to help Kanpur's citizens, but he had two minutes to delay Lyssa, since he didn't think he could stop her by himself, and that concerned him. He should be able to take her down, but she seemed smarter than the average goddess-monster. Two minutes seemed like an eternity. Even with *Thyroros*, when he could open a portal to anywhere he had been, he just didn't think it would be enough. Sending her back to Tartaros wouldn't work; she'd just find another exit point. He kept an eye on her movement as she slinked along the street, her flaming hair leaving a trail of acrid smoke like sulphur. Aegis had to stall her for a few more moments, no matter what. Using a lasso made from Atlas' hair hanging from his scabbard, he caught Lyssa around the throat, dug his feet in, and stood his ground. Once taut, the rope kept her from moving forward, but she writhed around and smashed into cars along the street, using her own claws to loosen the black cord. With every heave, his feet sank a little further into the earth when she pulled back, and playing tug-of-war with her distracted her from the civilians. Aegis tightened his muscles, found his core, and reminded himself of his connection to Gaea and Olympeia — he would use their strength to augment his own.

Canine growls came closer. He didn't have to look to see that Lyssa had summoned some of her rabid allies. Flipping around, Lyssa caught Aegis with her one eye, wrapped all four clawed hands around the rope, and pulled. He didn't move. As long as he could keep his concentration, he could anchor her until help arrived. The problem would be, once back up was ready, he'd have to use his sword and time it just right. Collateral damage was inevitable, now that he'd managed to anger the goddess of rage even more, but he had no other option. No matter what he heard, even the shrill screams of children all over the city, he couldn't stop trying to defeat this goddess.

"Portal!"

As soon as he heard Quinn's signal, Aegis took Lyssa to the ground with one massive pull long enough to get his sword. Through the portal jumped a centaur, arrows at the ready.

"Good to see you!" Aegis pulled harder on the rope. "Now, help me take... her... down!" Lyssa had managed to drag him about twenty feet before Aegis released the rope. He leaped to his feet, picking up his sword.

"Intel. Who and how?" Zodiak started galloping down Jaipuria Lane toward the bridge.

"Lyssa. Rage goddess. A daughter of Nyx that oozes pus. Don't underestimate her. And... the train's coming."

"Got a plan?" Zodiak put his quiver away until he could get a clearer shot.

"Stop her. That's the plan."

Zodiak, channeling the zodiac sign Sagittarius in centaur form, rode faster than most horses could on a good day, but with Aegis on his back, he couldn't maneuver as quickly. Aegis resisted the urge to make jokes about needing a saddle. Random dogs appeared from nowhere, growling and snapping at Zodiak's hooves. A few kicks knocked them out of the way, but more came out, and Zodiak was already distracted enough. Lyssa left a trail of bodies behind her, some in pieces, and as she moved even closer to the bridge, local law enforcement had blocked off Tagore Road on both sides to keep any other civilians away. With the body count rising, the citizens of Kanpur lost most of their curiosity and stayed in their homes, but dozens had already been killed. Rabid dogs continued to ravage people, too, and Zodiak and Aegis could do nothing. With the river in view, Aegis asked Quinn for some reconnaissance of the area so they would know what to avoid. Using his sword, he scooped up the discarded rope as they rode by.

"Aegis, just over the river on the right is the Shivam Convent School. To the left, housing."

Just before the river, Aegis lassoed Lyssa's two right arms and pulled, turning her to face them. If they could make themselves the target, it would give the authorities time to stop the train, but it would take too long to evacuate the residential area and the school. He and Zodiak would have to take her out by the river, and he had the makings of a plan. Leaping off Zodiak's back, he somersaulted mid-air and landed on her torso, knocking her to the ground, but she maneuvered away between a bakery and a bicycle shop. Zodiak continued down toward the river, looking around for something, anything to use to help them. *If only she had been a hydra or that two-headed canine, Orthros,* Zodiak thought, *something that could actually be killed.* He resumed human form just as Aegis exited the alley, chasing Lyssa toward him. He hadn't had the chance to get a good look at her earlier, but she truly would make any normal man wet himself. He felt the fear rising, but he gritted his teeth and pushed forward. Things that slithered just drove him crazy, too, and he had no real persona that could hold her, not with her oozing pus. His only hope was that Aegis would send her somewhere else, but he knew that if she had found one way out of the underworld, she would find another one at some point.

Loops of black cord encircled her once again, and Aegis pulled her in such a way that she gained momentum around him. Firmly planting his feet, he grabbed with both hands, swinging her around and around, until he just let go in the direction of the Ganges. Bound by Atlas' hair, it would take her a little time to release herself, especially under water, so that would give him and Zodiak a few extra minutes to plan.

"Smart. What now?" Zodiak scanned the area. "How do we defeat this one? I mean, come on, a goddess?"

"The best I can do is send her to Tartaros, but she'll find her way out again. And then we're back where we started."

"But, that gives us time, right? Next time, we get Aether and Talon to help."

Aegis caught a few passersby and told them that they should tell the Shivam Convent School to hide in the basement. Fortunately, one of the people knew enough English and had seen the results of Lyssa's actions up the street to believe him. If nothing else, that might keep them alive a little longer. In the mean time, Zodiak knelt by the water's edge.

"I'm going to try something."

Putting a hand on the water's surface, he placed the other on his Earthsteel talisman. With eyes closed, he focused on the constellations that formed in his mind; the ones that stood out most were the water signs: Cancer, Scorpio, and Pisces. *Those won't work*, he thought. He needed something stronger. Each constellation came into his mind's focus, and each dissolved just as quickly, until he found the one that resonated.

"*Hudrokoos*... Aquarius... The Waterbearer."

In ancient days, Zeus kidnapped the comely youth, Ganymede, and made him his lover and also cupbearer to the gods. The boy would walk around the Hall of Tribunals on Olympos, refilling the chalices with sweet nectar. As a reward for his service, Zeus eventually released him, but gave him the task of containing the might of the rivers, should they flood, keeping mortals from harm. His power allowed him to keep whatever was in the river within the water's grasp.

Both hands on the water, Zodiak summoned the power of Ganymede through the Ganges, and a mist formed on the surface, but the containment followed the bottom of the river, enveloping it, until the mighty river was held. As he was a mortal, Zodiak drew will power from the heavens though the *Ophthalmos Ouranou*, the Eye of Ouranos, in the center of the talisman.

"By the gods," Aegis whispered, seeing his teammate. "I had no idea you could do that."

A few minutes later, the water rippled, and just beneath the surface, Lyssa was trying to leave the river. The containment held. It was as if she were beneath a sheet of ice on a lake with no way out. As she thrashed about, Aegis could see Zodiak grimacing a little, but maintaining control. Concentration was key. This probably wouldn't hold her for long, seeing as she was a daughter of Nyx, but the power of the constellations was as old as the heavens themselves. Ouranos held great sway over the stars before Kronos struck him down, so all Zodiak had to do was continue to channel that primordial energy for a little while longer, and Aegis could use his sword to send Lyssa to the depths of the underworld.

"If only we had some help, like Aether, who would use her elemental power, or even Apollo."

At the mention of the sun god's name, Zodiak's mind drifted for a second back to that day when Alkinoë told him who she was. Just one second. Lyssa struggled harder beneath the surface, forcing a clawed arm to pierce the containment.

"She's broken through!" Aegis has his sword ready.

Clenching his eyes shut, Zodiak focused more will into the containment, and the scaly arm descended beneath the water's surface again, but his mind kept slipping. The more he pushed, the more those thoughts surfaced and the emotions attached to them, almost as if they could no longer be held back. This time, Lyssa herself surfaced, and Aegis could see she was still tangled in the black cord. Using that opening and hoping she would be too distracted, Aegis dove into the river, grabbing the cord that dangled freely under water, and pulled her beneath. Without light to trigger his sword's power, he couldn't open a portal, so *Thyroros* was useless. He didn't have the agility in the water that he had on land, being a descendant of Gaea, so his attempts to contain this rage goddess were losing their impact. If Zodiak could just focus on the containment spell, the water would keep them both submerged long enough for him to subdue her again. The murky Ganges wasn't helping, though, and Aegis had to be careful not to let one of Lyssa's claws get to him. As soon as his arm felt air, he knew Zodiak wasn't able to keep up his concentration. Within the water, Lyssa's fiery hair sizzled, boiling the water around her head, making it harder for Aegis to get a hold on her. Also, her agility increased, and her scaled tail thrashed about, bringing up mud from the bottom. That gave him an idea.

Meanwhile, on the shore, Zodiak's anger at Apollo and frustration over his lack of control made it all but impossible to regain his original command on the containment. Knee-deep in the Ganges, he pounded his fists into the river, losing the mental battle he was having. Slumped over, he just propped himself up and sat there. He'd let Aegis down, and he didn't know how to help.

Dan used the muddy water to keep Lyssa from seeing him, and he tied her four claws together behind her back as quickly as he could. She had landed a few blows on him, and his chest was bleeding. When he felt the riverbed rumble, he knew the train was passing overhead. *At least they'll be safe*, he thought. With the free end of the cord, he secured Lyssa's tail. Cord in hand, he brought her to the riverbank and dragged her to the shore. As soon as Zodiak saw Aegis, his shirt shredded and bloodied, he came out of his reverie.

"What the hell—"

"I'm fine," Aegis grunted. "I was counting on you, you know. Do you think you can help me do one thing?"

Zodiak couldn't look his friend and teammate in the eye. "Yeah. What is it?"

"I'm going to send this bitch back to Tartaros, but I need you to retrieve the lasso. As soon as I toss her through, follow, quickly untie her, and come back. Preferably in one piece, okay?"

He had never disappointed Aegis like this before. Eventually, it would be okay, but right now, all Zodiak wanted to do was scream. Nodding, he stood ready. A portal to Tartaros was unreliable, as the realm constantly shifted, but Aegis used the last place he had seen as the drop off point: the Cavern of Woe. With the doorway open, the fetid smell of rotting souls came through; not even a Dumpster filled with dead fish that had been sitting out in the sun for a month had as permeating of a stench. As Aegis tossed Lyssa through, Zodiak went after, and moments later, emerged with a slimy, pus-covered black cord. With the portal shut, the saline smell of the river and the train's exhaust were all that remained.

On the walk back to the center of Kanpur, they didn't speak: Aegis, because he was still so angry that Zodiak had let him down, and Zodiak, because he felt ashamed. Two blocks later, someone broke the silence.

"I have to tell you something… It's the reason why I crapped out back there."

"Okay, so tell me."

"When we get back to the apartment."

After a quick portal trip to Boston, both showered and put on clean clothes, regaining some sense of humanity before Brandon explained every detail of what had been told to him. It took a while, with stops and starts, but eventually Dan knew the truth.

"I don't even know what to say." Dan paused. "But, I have a question. Why are you so upset at Apollo? You find out you're his son, but you don't really seem all that happy about it."

"I have parents, Dan, remember? Parents who love me. I've been having nightmares ever since I found out. But, I think they're more than nightmares. More like memories. They're just too identical every time they happen. I think finding this out triggered something in my mind, and now I'm trying to make sense of all sorts of stuff."

"What's in these nightmares?"

"I have this vague recollection of being in a shopping cart, and I distinctly remember seeing Alkinoë... my mother... our mother... And, I also know this makes us brothers." He smiled. "I just need time to absorb this."

Dan moved next to Brandon on the couch. "Look, of course it'll take time. Don't rush things. I still don't know why you're upset with Apollo, though. He told you that you were kidnapped."

Brandon shook his head. "I don't think I've heard the whole story. As weird as this sounds, I think Apollo isn't being completely honest."

A DNA scan of Bakura matched Mahavir and Radha Diwan, and birth records confirmed the connection. Neither one had ever heard of the child, but when the authorities arrived at their home, suspecting foul play, they found a child's bedroom complete with toys and clothing. Family photos showed all three together. They had no explanation. Police arrested the Diwans under suspicion of child neglect, a crime punishable by up to five years in prison. A social worker contacted family and friends, and they corroborated that Mahavir and Radha had no children. The charges were brought up to kidnapping, but then a worker at the hall of records noticed that the online birth certificate was dated five years earlier and the last time the record had been accessed was indeed five years prior. All evidence began to prove that the Diwans did indeed have a child, but they had no recollection of Bakura. Baby pictures and other memorabilia muddied the circumstances further.

Local Kanpur authorities decided to hold the Diwans for questioning indefinitely until they could investigate further.

10—LIGHT AND SHADOW

Sometimes the Internet provided a bevy of answers to the most meaningless inquiries, memes, e-cards, and fan pictures at the top of the list, and people could get sucked into the online mire, almost like a virtual Charybdis, a whirlpool of data providing links to more data. For the hours Brandon had spent online, he had come to few answers about the intertwining serpents. Picture after picture revealed just how common snakes were in online clip art, design work, and amateur graphics, but the exact design of the three snakes he had seen in Theo's house didn't show up. He hadn't spent this much time on the computer when he was in graduate school, but the urgency of the situation motivated him. He needed to do something to distract him from his personal issues, but his conversation with Dan the week before did help. Having his brother know made him feel more grounded. Brandon thought it might be awkward for Dan to be his younger brother, but they had been best friends for years — this just seemed like a logical extension of that relationship.

Disemboweled almost beyond recognition, Theo's parents, at least according to birth records since memories held no definitive proof at all, sat in pools of their own blood, their eviscerated remains heaped together like the remains of a bird of prey. Their intestines woven together in a circle on the floor to imitate the symbol on the wall, the young man's parents would not be the last victims of the Erinyes. Brandon rubbed his eyes and sighed. Two hours into his search, something got his attention. As he scrolled further down the repetitious list of images, he saw something resembling the symbol he was looking for, but not in clip art or modern renderings. On old photographs of ancient pottery were these interlacing snakes, and something eerie about them blew over him like an icy wind; a distant memory, perhaps, or maybe a more recent one—he couldn't be sure—but he had seen this image somewhere else. Sitting back in his computer chair, he brushed his hands over his head and laced them together. The longer he stared at the old photograph, he could swear he saw the snakes move, but perhaps only in his imagination.

He saved the image to a folder on a flash drive and clicked on it, opening a new page. Brandon scrolled mindlessly, letting his weary eyes fall on words hoping something would fall into place. The pictures came from archaeological digs throughout Greece and Italy from as early as the mid-1800s, specifically in Attica, Lokris, Boeotia, among others. Explorers in the 19th century found unending supplies of artifacts to fill their personal coffers and sell to museums and collectors, eager to grab onto a remnant of the past. One location—Arkadeia—pushed vague memories forward for him, bringing back clouds of thought that he couldn't readily decipher. At the bottom of the web page, the text links he saw had nothing but repeated news stories from early discoveries, outdated biographies of archaeologists long gone, and references to research proven wrong or updated. Upon a closer look, however, all of the text was black except for one period at the end of the second to last sentence. It was blue, and that meant it was also a link. Another page opened entitled *Cults of the Erinyes, Goddesses of Vengeance.* Beneath that lay a larger color picture of circular intertwined serpents from part of an ancient kylix, a bowl used for rituals, and the picture was dated 2005 from an archaeological dig.

"That's it," Brandon muttered, bookmarking the page. "That makes more sense."

A quick text message to his team updated them to his find, and then he grabbed a protein drink and stepped out onto the balcony, a star-speckled sky blanketing Boston. When his phone buzzed, he thought it was Dan, Aleta, or Sarah, but it was from his mother, Evelyn Jeffries, the woman who had changed his diapers, nursed his illnesses, and comforted his bad dreams; she asked him to stop by during the week. With the heavens as his confidant, he wondered aloud whether his relationship with the Jeffries, the people who given him so much, would change once they knew that their adopted son wasn't left with an agency by a reckless youth looking to make some money. They loved him and treated him as if he were their flesh and blood, and finding out who his birth parents were shouldn't change anything, but his idealism had been whittled away long ago.

He played with the phone in his hands mindlessly. Sitting down, he dialed. The ringing on the other end while he waited for someone to answer was like a harpy's shriek.

"Hey, Mom. Just wanted to return your call...Yeah, I'm fine. Sorry to call so late...Listen, I'm going to stop by on Wednesday for dinner.."

The *Moirae* busily spun the threads that would forge his future, and Brandon knew that nothing stayed their hands. Once he had spoken with the Jeffries, he would next need to talk to Apollo and Alkinoë. With so much power at his disposal, Brandon could dispatch armies of drakones or demons, perhaps even a demigod or two, but he couldn't wrestle any more with his own inner demons. Those had to be eradicated or he would be no use to his team as the events in India had shown him. He needed Apollo to tell him the entire truth.

Back at his computer, he continued to read more about the goddesses of vengeance and what they did in the past since they, or those acting on their behalf, had apparently resurfaced. Preparing for battle was a lesson he had learned through many injuries and rash decisions, so he printed pages, took notes, and prepared to debrief Quinn at headquarters, too. As good as she was, she hadn't actually seen the serpent symbol, so she would have nothing to go on. He didn't trust email, since the government tended to check random IP addresses, even though Quinn assured him his Internet connection was secure through the Task Force server. He had become accustomed to trusting his own paranoia.

After a few days of arrangements, a TF-18 airlifted the team to Arkadeia, Greece, a site from antiquity, weathered and whittled to a dusty field from what was once an ancient megalopolis. Aegis knew of this place from family history, but the others had no real emotional stake. Just beyond a copse of cypress trees in the shadow of Mt. Parthenion not far from Tegea, the ancient capital city, sat a temple once consecrated to Apollo, ruined by age and befouled by three whose touch brought decay and disease. What was once a lush valley, originally named the Valley of Truth by ancient priests of the sun god, filled with life and verdant landscapes, wildlife, and peace, later came to be known as the Valley of Despair. Gleaming marble columns and colorful, painted façade gave way to a crumbling structure, infested with mold and ooze, giving off a stench of death. Animals did not venture too closely out of fear, and flora ceased to grow within half a mile, layers of dust allowing nothing to thrive. This now desecrated shrine, shadowed by cypress, was the Temple of the Erinyes.

Zodiak led the others into this maw of rot and squalor, followed by Aether and Talon, with Aegis taking up the rear. Walking down the eroded path, Aegis couldn't help but remember part of his nightly, dreamlike visits to this place, taking in the grandeur of this honeyed city of his ancestors. Zodiak, on the other hand, now having partly realized his past, had actual memories of this place, when he used to go for walks with his mother, Alkinoë, and pay homage to Apollo in the temple: wisps of the past—a past he wasn't sure he wanted to remember. He could still smell the sandalwood incense in the air wafting from the braziers in the temple, a faint memory that brought him little comfort, however. When they walked through the broken opening to the temple, weathered stone stairs led down into the earth toward a gateway to Hades. Aether struck a match and maintained a handful of flames to lead the way. Even the fire seemed to fear where it was going, and it flickered wildly as if trying to free itself from her control. Talon kept a tight grip on her javelin, ready to bring thunderbolts, if need be.

Just before the steps ended, on the left wall was the same entwined circle of snakes, only larger. Each of the three serpents had distinctive markings. Here they would find the three sisters.

The path opened into a large chamber with a vaulted ceiling of rock, dilapidated columns embedded in the walls that were alight with rusted torches, their flames carrying an ominous hue. Shadows danced in rampant patterns on all surfaces, living entities that shared the space. Zodiak made sure the others stayed with him; here, his power would provide what they needed more than any other. Simultaneous hissing came from all over, echoing throughout the tunnels that led off in myriad of directions, all headed toward somewhere in Hades. From a cave opening above the chamber descended three female figures, on bat-wings as black as night. Each had dark snakes slithering up and down her arms, serpentine attire, and threadbare tunics adorned with tarnished chains around each waist. Hands bore glossy talons, ready to shred the living or the dead.

"Visitors we have," hissed Tisiphone.

"Aye," replied Alekto, "shall we welcome them?"

All three took off in different directions around the chamber, hovering dangerously close to their guests, trying to take one of them off guard. Megaera flew toward Talon, but bolts of lightning crackling around her javelin deterred the black winged Fury momentarily. Tisiphone and Alekto aimed for Aegis, but his manacle generated an invisible impact shield that protected him from their septic claws; the attack wasn't meant to hurt him, though. A weak spot would show through his defenses, and they hoped they would find another opening to try again. Aether drew a flame from a torch on the wall and grew it to encircle the three long enough to demonstrate her power.

"Where is *The Nebulous One*?" Zodiak's eyes darted about. "We know you've been hanging around your sister lately."

The Erinyes flew around like angry hornets, each flap of their wings washed a fetid odor of decaying flesh around the chamber.

"Shall we just give her to thee?" screeched Alekto, lunging at them. Aether put a wall of earth up to block the attack.

"That would be nice." Aegis assessed their surroundings. "I enjoy gifts."

Megaera flew behind them, but Aegis swung around, sword ready.

"Guess not." Aegis passed *Thyroros* hand to hand.

Aether brought her palms together in a protective stance. "Do we have a plan, guys?"

"I'm good with fried Furies." Talon arced lightning between her hand and the javelin.

"We don't have time for games. I'll just carve out their hearts, one at a time." Aegis flipped his sword around by the hilt. "Of course, they'll grow back, but I can just keep doing it."

The winged sisters screeched and flew down, but Aether's earthen wall rose up once more. When she concentrated hard enough, she could make the wall as tough as steel. Earth was the easiest element to manipulate since it was always beneath her feet, but she also found it the most frustrating at times. Having spent most of her time connected with Gaea, her link was the strongest with the goddess, but *Æther*, the god of the upper air, gave her balance. They had come for information, however, about the connection between the Erinyes and *The Nebulous One*, and leaving wasn't an option until they had it. Aether dropped the earth shields to access the torch fire, placing a ring of flames around her companions. Goddesses of torment didn't enjoy fire, least of all Hesteian fire. It had a protective quality that resisted their power.

"Thou shalt not find her on the lighted path, either," hissed Megaera. "When 'tis thy time, she will appear." She flew to where the shadows hid her.

Tisiphone and Alekto followed her. Aegis tightened his two-fisted grip on *Thyroros*, his senses attuned to their raspy breathing. Of all the members of the team, only Zodiak had not taken a defensive stance. Aether kept up the fire ring while Talon kept her raptor's eyes where light met shadow. Occasional hissing from above reverberated off the walls, masking the exact location of Nyx's daughters. On white wings, Talon leaped up, keeping the wall behind her just in case, and cast a small bolt into the shadows, momentarily illuminating their adversaries who cackled their amusement. Aegis nodded to her, and she soared to the other side of the chamber, repeating her task. Once the four had a reasonable location, Aether drew from all the torches, sending a fireball into the darkest part of the ceiling, but the Erinyes had moved. Initially, she thought such a feat was impossible, but then she remembered that these were daughters of the Night, and they could move in shadow like air. Zodiak stood still, arms at his side, but his eyes darted around. Talon leaped up to a stone ledge, ready to blast the first bat-winged goddess she saw. From within the stone, however, black serpents emerged, surrounding her, and she dropped the javelin.

Held fast against the wall, she couldn't scream. Aegis was about to leap up to try to free her, but he couldn't move. More serpents had come through the dirt floor, wrapping around his legs and constricting. One traveled up his torso and around his mouth, forcing him to drop his sword. With bodies about four inches thick, the serpents were not easily moved, especially when they tightened their hold. Aether surrounded herself with a wall of fire, but more black serpents dropped from the ceiling, extinguishing the torches on the wall: no fire, no wall. Before she could move the air, other serpents had bound her hands behind her, squeezing until her hands went numb.

Zodiak sat cross-legged on the floor, his palms over his knees. Tisiphone descended, and he felt her breath on his face and neck; it smelled of decaying flesh and made his eyes tear. Then, Megaera and Alekto surrounded him. He couldn't see them, but he felt them. He had given some thought to what he might do should this meeting not go as intended. Of course, he could draw strength from some of the zodiac, or perhaps endurance, and even combine a few signs together — although that would weaken him — but, no... he wouldn't attack. Even though he hadn't committed a crime against nature that they could punish, he knew they had no conscience and wouldn't hesitate to drive him to the edges of insanity and back over and over and over again.

"What shall we do with this one, dear sisters?" asked Tisiphone. "Eat his heart? Devour his limbs one layer of skin at a time? What say you?"

Licking Zodiak's cheek, Megaera replied, "I want his lungs, or perhaps his brain."

As the sisters amused themselves deciding how he should meet his fate, he went deep within to a place where he could access the only zodiac sign he had never used before. His mind opened, revealing the path to that one sign of the twelve he had protected more fiercely than he had any other. This was not a zodiac entity he could use much, for experience would taint it, but now he knew this was the time to release it. In the thick, inky blackness within the temple, a faint light grew within him, growing larger and larger until it filled his entire body, radiating, pushing the accursed sisters back from him. His thoughts flew to protecting his brother Aegis, to his friends Aether and Talon, and the light enveloped them all, liquefying the snakes that held them. The Furies pushed toward him, and he felt himself shudder, but the sign within pushed back, not willing to relent. He felt connected to the heavens in a way he had never experienced, but he also felt the most vulnerable. Raising his hands, he joined them above his head, creating an unending loop. Light within began pulsing from him, like ripples in a pond, attuned to his heartbeat. With each thump, the physical light pushed back the darkness, and he controlled the rhythm of his heart. The Eye of Ouranos in the center of his amulet was ablaze, as if the sky itself had entered the chamber, and repelled the daughters of Nyx, pushing them back into the shadows. This was the strongest constellation in the sky, and it would always protect him when he needed it. His purity of spirit had put him in touch with Virgo, also known as the *Parthenos*—the Nurturing One. Just as the heavens watched over the earth, so would Zodiak watch over his team. While all the other signs manifested themselves physically, this one was spiritual, grounding him much like the god *Æther* did for his teammate Aether. Virgo was the keystone of the zodiac.

Aegis touched his brother on the shoulder. "I had no idea you could do that."

"Me, either," Zodiak replied. "We didn't get the answers we needed, but I did learn one thing: we have to remain true to each other. We have this sacred trust, all four of us, and we have to be completely honest for this to work. That means I have to talk to Apollo." Aegis felt the gravity of his brother's words revealed a seriousness he hadn't heard much; channeling Virgo brought out a rational side to him.

"Do you want me there?"

"Yes, but I'll talk with him first. You need to know the truth as much as I do. We all do, but some things need to hit my ears first. Deception and lies keep us in the dark. Truth will help us defeat *The Nebulous One*."

"What about the Erinyes?"

"We haven't seen the last of them, Aether. Trust me. However, we need a better strategy for confronting them. They're goddesses, so we can't kill them."

Talon grunted. "Then what?"

Aegis headed for the exit, the others following. "We make sure this primordial bitch goes back to Tartaros, once and for all. All the rest will fall into place. Until then, we fight back. Oh, and Zodiak?"

"Yeah?"

"Another word for Virgo is *Parthenos*, the Virgin. Is there something you want to tell us?"

They laughed, but it would be a long while before they would again.

The Nebulous One learned of the encounter, prompting her to ascertain more about these four flesh-bound creatures, as they were becoming impediments to her undertaking. She wanted to think they were insignificant. The Erinyes, however, insinuated they might be more, and *The Nebulous One* would do well not to disregard her sister goddesses of torment.

11—FILLING THE VOID

Dan yelled from the shower, "Ari will be here any minute. Can you just let him in and have a seat until I'm ready?"

"Sure," Brandon replied. "And this would be my first time letting someone in, so if you want to tell me how to open the door, feel free." He smirked at the anticipation in Dan's voice. For a man 31 years old, standing six foot two, with an almost Herculean build, Dan was a giddy teenager.

Brandon, who hadn't dated much, was actually excited for his brother. For as long as he'd known Dan, he had never truly known him to have a social life. Going to The Beanery for a latte didn't count, either. And, lately, with the revelation that they were indeed family, tension had grown within their team. It wasn't anyone on the team's fault, really. Had Brandon thought for a moment that he would be thrust onto this path for his life, he didn't know if he would have gone down it. Fate had a funny way of intervening, like that annoying friend you tried to ignore but always showed up when you least expected it. With his career stagnating a little at the university, he had come to accept Task Force: Gaea as a welcome distraction from the everyday drudgery. Going up against *kakodaemons* or one of the rabid dogs of war let loose from its Hadean prison by a faulty portal to the underworld gave his life that heart-pounding, adrenaline-pumping diversity that rock climbing or running hadn't. Brandon knew where the tension really lay—between him and Apollo, his birth father. The dreams he had been having about the day he was kidnapped would replay in his mind for weeks on end, but something wouldn't make sense, and he couldn't figure out what. That day in India, when Dan could have been hurt or worse, reminded him that he needed to confront his demons, and not just the ones from the underworld. He would have to talk to Apollo soon, and then he'd have that dreaded talk with his adoptive parents. Even though they supported him finding his birth parents, they wouldn't understand the reality of the situation. 'Hey Mom and Dad, I found my birth parents. He's an Olympeian god, and she's the queen of an ancient race.' *Yeah, that would go over well*, he thought. All in due time...

The doorbell saved Brandon from his reverie. He could hear Dan was out of the shower, too, so he wouldn't be left making awkward conversation too long.

"Hey, you must be Ari. Come on in. Dan'll be ready in a sec," Brandon said, gesturing for Ari to have a seat.

"It is a pleasure to meet you, Brandon. Dan has told me much about you." Ari's accent took Brandon off guard.

"Well, he's been talking nonstop about you. And that's a good thing, too. Can I get you something? A drink?"

Ari shook his head. He couldn't stop looking at Brandon's face. Something about his eyes. Brandon must have noticed because he excused himself to check on Dan. While he waited, Ari walked around the living room, looking at pictures. One photograph in particular struck him, of both Dan and Brandon in Rome when they were on vacation a few years back. Glancing back and forth from face to face, Ari unconsciously smiled. It was a smile of comfort, as if he knew something. The two were standing in front of the Forum, Dan's arm over Brandon's shoulder, both grinning, as if someone had snapped the picture candidly and caught them in the midst of something. It was then that Ari's smile faded. He looked closer at Brandon's face. He recognized that smile. Those eyes. As Dan and Brandon entered the room, neither one expected what happened next.

Ari genuflected.

"Ari, we've talked about this. I'm technically royalty, but I don't want you bowing before me. Come on and stand up." Dan thought Ari was being playful.

"Dan, I think he's crying," Brandon crouched down. "Hey, are you okay?"

Ari muttered something without looking up. Dan knelt down, gently lifting Ari's chin. "What's wrong?"

Slowly standing, Ari walked over to Brandon and put a hand on his shoulder.

"I... I never thought I would ever see you again, Your Highness. Praise the gods. I thought you were dead."

Then, Dan realized, and he went pale. Brandon didn't know what was happening.

Dan leaned over and whispered to his brother, "He knows who you really are."

"Ari? Tell me..." Brandon started.

"I used to visit the royal palace when my father did not need me to assist him," Ari began. "The aroma of the food and flowers in the agora cleansed the dust from my nose, and the sounds of life, and children, and laughter... It erased the dirges that I heard every single day. My father always told me it was a great honor to serve the gods. He had, and so did his father. I was to follow him, but I kept telling my father I was not ready. Day in, day out, laboring from sunrise to sunset with no future of my own became tedious... May the gods forgive me. I brought a clean tunic with me to Tegea, and I would bathe in the river to wash the stench of death that covered me. I wanted to enter the city clean. Sometimes, the children would want me to play with them, or the merchants would engage me. During one of my visits, I found the courage to visit the palace, to meet Lord Apollo and his queen, Alkinoë. The guards did not stop me, which intrigued me, but I also did not pose a threat. I did not know until later that Arkadeians could always visit the royal family. That trust comforted me. One rainy afternoon, while I sat on the marble steps that overlooked the city, I heard a child crying. When I found the source, I saw it was a little boy, and he had accidentally broken his toy sword. I ripped a piece of cloth from my tunic and repaired it for him, and he laughed. He ran away, but when he returned, he had a ball of string and handed it to me. He wanted to play. We tossed that ball of string back and forth for hours while Zeus' storm raged outside. Eventually, the queen, drawn by the laughter, found us in the Hall of Tribunals play fighting with his toy sword and stick I had found. At first, I thought she would be angry that I was engaging in such behavior with a two year old, but she simply laughed and said, 'The prince has found a worthy instructor. His father and I had been drawn away, so I am glad he was suitably entertained.' She extended an invitation for me to come whenever I was not needed in the temple since the prince was not usually fond of his nursemaids. For a few months, I returned when I could. Then, one day, I was told that the royal family had left Arkadeia, and no one knew when they would return. From that point on, I never left the temple unless necessary."

Whispers of memories floated through Brandon's mind. Insubstantial scenes, smells, the feeling of a wooden sword, the texture of twine... Glimpses of a past he had forgotten. He tried to resurrect them, but something blocked his memory.

Ari knelt again. "It is good to see you again, Prince Kidemonas."

Brandon would find Apollo and demand the answers he wanted — needed, in fact. No longer would he swim in murky waters of the past, a past denied to him. The god of truth would tell him what he had to know.

12—UPPER LIMITS

Quinn always gave the team as much intel as surveillance cameras could relay, and every surface, external and internal, had multiple lenses trained on key areas of entry, whether it be a fast food restaurant, a hospital, a cemetery, or even out in the vast deserts. Such was the nature of the world. A surveillance system of the highest order kept its many eyes on the world's citizens, much as the one hundred eyed giant Argus of ancient days watched those whom the gods wished guarded. Encrypted via satellite and sent to computers all over the globe, digitized photographs made their way to many places, including the Task Force Division data collection units so that any task force could use them in its missions. In Quinn's case, she used her haptic control panel to send each member small pictures visible on arm wrist receivers. So fine tuned were the identification algorithms of United Nations computers that they could distinguish what was in each picture and apply a few to a dozen keyword tags so that Quinn would know where to funnel the information. Task Force: Gaea's metaphysical opponents, however, required more attention from Dan and his teammates. Not many people knew what a centaur looked like, or two-headed Orthros for that matter, so the team would add their own tags into the system. When pictures of a green-scaled dragon standing approximately 600 feet tall with eight heads, six legs, and a tail as long as a football field showed up on the monitor, Quinn heard the beep of new information, but felt no tactile keywords.

"Oh, crap," she muttered, pressing the button to alert her team. "Guys, unidentified nasty by the Rock of Ages granite quarry. Height: think Washington Monument. Damn… Coordinates sent. Graniteville, Vermont. There's something else interfering with our cameras, too, so be on guard. TF-18 will pick you up in two minutes at the usual rendezvous. Good luck."

When a TF-18 stealth copter arrives to take a team on its mission, it makes almost no sound, at least not like a traditional copter — it has no blades. In place of them, electromagnetic field generators put out invisible "blades" of energy that act in the same way. Smaller engines attached to the side of the copter help regulate it during stormy weather or enemy fire. Flying at 300 mph, the TF-class copter can go from Boston to Graniteville in 30 minutes; driving would take almost three hours. The TF-18 arrived at the quarry at 0600 hours, and as they made visual contact with the dragon, Talon jumped from the copter and flew around the quarry, making sure to keep her distance; they didn't know if it was a fire or acid breather. While in contact with Quinn, they used their codenames until the completion of the mission. Layers of white granite, like large sugar cubes, lined the walls of the quarry, and metal scaffolding stood along the walls, more for the stonecutters than to hold up the sheer tonnage of rock. Stark green scales like roofing shingles showed up more against the bleached granite, making the dragon look even larger than it really was, if being as tall as the Washington Monument wasn't tall enough.

"What the hell is that?" Aether looked down into the quarry. "I think we're in trouble, guys." Her voiced quivered a bit.

Zodiak caught a glimpse of it over her shoulder. "Damn. I think that's the largest thing we've gone up against. Aegis?"

"I see it," he said, assessing it from the other side of the copter. "You're right, Zodiak. Let's get on the ground. And that's Ladon, so yeah, I'd say we're in trouble."

Ladon — son of Ekhidna, mother of all monsters, and Typhon, another monstrous dragon but with one hundred heads — guarded the golden apples of the Hesperides, sacred to Hera. What could have brought this beast from its post was a mystery, but nonetheless he towered up over the granite canyon's walls. Aether glided to the ground on the air currents, while Aegis and Zodiak just jumped to the ground when the copter was close enough. Talon returned from her aerial reconnaissance without much to tell.

"So, no people. I don't think there were any to begin with. It's just us, and that."

"What's the plan?" Zodiak realized it was more rhetorical. He knew the answer: either transport it somewhere, or kill it. "A head-grower, right, Aegis?"

A head-grower was a dragon that grew two heads when one was cut off, like a hydra. Only one head of the eight would be impervious to weapons; *that* head would be a challenge.

Aegis nodded. "This doesn't make sense. Why would Ladon be here of all places? No human prey, either."

"Let's speculate later. You ready, guys?" Zodiak needed no answer.

They moved closer, hearing the roaring heads below, not noticing the dark cloud looming above them, like a thunderhead before a storm. Ladon's sneer vibrated the air around him. Taking a running jump, Aegis landed on the back of one of the heads, grabbed onto a green scale, and positioned *Thyroros*. Another head opened its mouth, spewing fire, but Aegis threw his manacle up, and the impact shield kept him from being incinerated. Unfortunately, he let go, bounced off Ladon's back, and landed on the floor of the quarry. He didn't have time to get his bearings when the dragon's tail swept him into the granite wall, cracking the stone, chips flying everywhere. Aegis sheathed his sword, ran toward a massive leg, leaped up and did a somersault, landing on Ladon's back. Smooth scales made it almost impossible to get a strong foothold, but Aegis balanced his way to the base of the eight necks, clenched his hands together, swinging them down hard. Most of the heads turned, some spewing acid while others spat fire. Drops of acid landed close enough to eat away some of the leather on Aegis' black boots. He looked up and saw Talon flying in an attack formation, her javelin at the ready. Even if he could get his sword out, he could only get one, maybe two, necks severed before Ladon's other heads would attack. He would have to time his sword strikes just right and signal Talon. Withdrawing *Thyroros* once more, spinning it over his hand, he slashed into the six-foot wide scaly neck. Earthsteel went smoothly through dragon flesh and bone, and as soon as the head and neck fell to the ground, he signaled above and a meandering bolt of lightning came down and cauterized the wound before it could grow two more heads. One down, seven to go. Roaring loud enough to shake free some of the granite blocks from the side of the quarry, Ladon turned three of his heads toward Aegis, ready to shower him with both acid and fire. The son of Apollo knew he couldn't make another strike without giving the dragon a tactical advantage, so he leaped to the ground to find a better position. The cloud that had hovered above them descended slowly, but went unnoticed.

At the top of the quarry where she could see Ladon from a safe distance, Aether gathered her strength, silently found her focus, and sent blocks of granite on him, one after the other, but his heads were fast enough to shatter them. One of the first tactics when encountering a new foe was to test limits; she now knew that granite blocks measuring in the tons wouldn't affect the dragon, but she had a few more maneuvers to try. Before she could, however, a spray of acid headed toward her from below, and she brought up a wall of granite to protect her from the blast, although the caustic liquid ate right through it. She would have to be more careful, she thought, since she had no idea what Ladon's upper limits were. With no water handy, she only had the fiery dragon breath, earth, and air — they would have to be enough. To try what she had in mind, she would have to get closer to the dragon, but the unpredictability made her hesitant. Ladon's own fire wouldn't hurt him, so she ruled that out. Leaping to the quarry floor, she landed on a cushion of air behind some granite blocks. The quarry shook as the six-legged monster lumbered over toward her location. Her hands flat to the stone floor, she drew upon her connection to Gaea, but her concentration was shattered when Ladon's tail came crashing down on the block she had hid behind, smashing it to dust. Momentarily blinded, Aether whirled some air around her to remove the powder. She would have to try something else, and it was at that moment she thought perhaps Ladon was testing *her* instead.

To eliminate all possibilities, Zodiak shot his Sagittarian arrows, but they either shattered on impact or bounced off green scales. Most of his powers came from signs that offered strength or agility; the archer was the only one with projectiles, and they had proven ineffective. Taking a running leap off the quarry edge, and channeling Taurus and Cancer, he somersaulted midair and crashed into Ladon's front leg. That only distracted the dragon for a moment, and three heads came in close, spewing fire. Zodiak had positioned himself behind the leg just in time, but he felt the fiery breath close enough. Using his heightened grip, he climbed the scaly leg to where the necks all converged, climbing further up one of the necks near the head. If he could confuse the head enough, maybe he could use its own strength against it. The closer he got, the more the serpentine neck whipped around to loosen him. A few of the other heads moved toward him, but he just needed to hold on a little longer. An acid-breather lunged for him, fangs ready to clamp down on Zodiak's soft, human flesh, and he released the neck just in time to see Ladon's fangs sink into his own neck. The acid would have no effect on Ladon, but wounding himself might be enough to disable that head. Black, pus-like blood oozed from the gouge, crystalized, and then fell away, revealing a healed injury. From the ground, Zodiak saw Aether being flung across the quarry, smashing into the granite wall. He wanted to help her, but he saw she was undamaged, and her eyes glowed yellow—she had connected with Gaea, and the Earth mother would protect her physical body from harm. For the first time in a very long while, he felt a shiver of fear. What if they couldn't defeat Ladon?

Keeping to the edge of the granite canyon, the dark cloud meandered toward a niche where it could remain undetected.

Using her javelin as a shield, Talon deflected the fiery breath, but it knocked her lower in the sky. Unseen, a head moved to snatch the winged woman from behind and caught her in its mouth, the teeth and fangs like prison bars preventing her escape. She felt the mighty mouth inhale, ready to push out fire, so she called down a few thunder strikes. Again. Again. The black cloud entered between the fangs, encircling Talon, who felt another presence with her. The immeasurable power of this terrifying nebulous entity, combined with being imprisoned, caused Talon to summon a bolt of lightning bigger than she had ever used before. Ladon's mouth opened just enough, and she squeezed through, her wings singed by the fire that burst forth. Once Talon was far enough away, she glimpsed the smoky form move back toward a rocky alcove. Whatever that was, she thought, it could be a larger problem than this dragon. It didn't harm her, but she felt power, ancient power, and that made her doubt whether or not they could indeed defeat Ladon if he had such powerful allies.

Hurtled against the walls again by a mammoth scaled foot, Aether tired of being treated like a ragdoll. Her hair sooty and tangled, she brushed it back while dusting off her Emma Peel-style black catsuit. *I'm not getting bounced around again*, she thought. Ladon's powerful legs needed to be contained. By funneling her emotions through her ring, she had more control over the elements. At the north end of the excavation, Aether could see the expanse, and visualizing the two stone walls in her mind, she reached out to Gaea. Her arms outstretched, she held her hands with palms facing each other, and slowly brought them closer. When she crossed into the world of an elder god, she gave a part of herself over to him or her, and her raw anger transformed into energy; her Atlantean ancestry provided the conduit of elemental control. With teeth clenched, she saw herself pushing the quarry walls together in her mind, moving the tonnage of stone. Every muscle in her arms and shoulders tensed as if it were really pushing against granite. She could see Aegis and Zodiak attack on different fronts, distracting Ladon, and Talon's lightning attack was pushing the dragon into a frenzied state. What Aether didn't see were the tendrils of darkness rising from the chasm beneath her and winding around her legs, but Gaea tried to warn her. It was no use. Through a cacophony of voices in her brain, Aether fixed her attention on squeezing Ladon between the walls, and it was working. Nyx's daughter, entwined like a coiled serpent, felt the visceral power channeling through this young woman, and *The Nebulous One* knew instantly this mortal would be a threat to her. Gaea again tried to warn her, but the connection was too strong. Aether screamed, providing a release of the pain she felt moving that much earth at once, but her goal was to trap the dragon, and she would do it, or die trying.

Aegis figured out what Aether was doing and redoubled his efforts to decapitate as many of Ladon's heads as he could. He had managed to get four in total, the lifeless heads strewn about, oozing black pus. That still left four, and one of those was immortal and impervious to his sword. The rumbling of the rocks ceased, and Aether separated herself from Gaea's consciousness, releasing her hold on the earth. That would be the best she could do for now. Aegis did notice a snaky presence around her legs suddenly untangle itself and head back into a recess. Zodiak's voice brought him back into the moment.

"Hey, I found the immortal head, and I have an idea. I told Talon to keep our friend distracted while we try something."

"What's the game plan?"

Zodiak led his brother to the south side of the quarry far enough away to show him something.

"See that head on the left, the second to last one? Look underneath its chin."

Just beneath where the jaw met the serpentine neck, Zodiak saw it, a scale that looked a little different than the others.

"I think that's the immortal head, the one you can't sever. But, I have an idea." Zodiak laid out his plan.

Aegis disappeared through a portal and emerged carrying a black cord: an unbreakable lasso made of the hair of Atlas, the last of the Titans. If the Titan could hold up the heavens for eternity, then certainly a rope fashioned of his hair had strength as well. Both brothers helped each other get into a position where they could mount Ladon's back and managed to get to the right neck without being eaten, incinerated, or corroded. Aegis wrapped the cord around the thick, scaly neck and handed his brother the other end. An unseen swish of the massive tail knocked Aegis into the wall, and tons of granite buried him to the quarry floor. A fire-breathing head lunged at Zodiak who then back-flipped out of the way, but the tail snapped again, swatting him like a fly to the floor and pinning him there. The black cloud stayed close to the ground, and in serpentine fashion, watched the pile of rubble covering Aegis, waiting for movement. Talon was about to send a thunderbolt down to shatter the granite when she saw a ten-ton block rise from the ground. At first, she thought it was Aether, but then she saw it was Aegis — he rose to his feet slowly, lifting the mass, his fingers embedded in the stone. Like Atlas, he shrugged, launching the granite into the air. Just before it landed on him once more, Talon heard the clang of Earthsteel, and two five-ton blocks fell away, revealing their team leader. With a growl, Aegis leaped up and rammed into the tail crushing his brother. Jaw tightened, he snatched the reptilian tail away. Both brothers climbed back to the base of the immortal neck, the one no blade could remove. Zodiak and Aegis, paying more attention to the remaining heads, wrapped the neck in the black cord and pulled as hard as they could, constricting the lasso tighter and tighter. Sensing what they were trying to do, *The Nebulous One* darted through the stones and moved her cloud-like form toward them. She couldn't let them destroy him. Aether, working with Talon to keep the other dragon's heads distracted, saw *The Nebulous One* making her way toward the men.

"Don't let her touch you!" Aether wasn't sure they could hear her. "Move away!" But, they couldn't hear her over the din. When *The Nebulous One* had touched her, Aether felt the depth of her power.

Tighter and tighter they pulled the cord, and gradually the long neck swayed as their tactic began to work. Zodiak drew strength from Taurus, Leo, and every other sign he could muster while Aegis used his formidable Olympeian and Arkadeian strength — together they watched as the eyes of Ladon's fanged, immortal head shut from lack of black blood, and then the neck slackened before crashing to the ground. *The Nebulous One* would be on them in a matter of moments.

"Move away!" Aether tried again to warn them. Talon heard her and went into a dive, swerving around heads striking out to devour her. One head, however, crashed into her, sending her plummeting to the ground. The men turned to see her just before she made contact with the stony floor, shouting one word at them, "*Pyli!*" 'Portal' — a last resort code word. Aegis and Zodiak leapt through a portal just as *The Nebulous One's* cloud-like tendril lashed out for them, but she was too late. They were safe.

Just as Herakles had squeezed the life from the Nemean lion during his labors, since the beast was immortal and couldn't be killed by any weapon, so too did the brothers use this tactic on Ladon. With his immortal head strangled, the rest of the beast lumbered to the ground and ceased moving. *The Nebulous One*, not willing to face Aether and Talon directly yet, dissipated into the air. Aether extended her arms before her, clenched her fists, and pushed them outward. The ground, following her command, rumbled, opening into a vast chasm, and the dragon's body fell into Gaea's embrace and disappeared within the earth. Talon brought down lightning to incinerate the severed heads, leaving only ash.

Back in their Boston apartment, Brandon and Dan lay crumpled on the floor where they landed, catching their breath, recuperating on the sweat-laden carpet. This had been their most physical encounter yet, and they knew that, despite their otherworldly powers, they would need time to rest and heal, emotionally as well. Brandon was the first to stand, patted his brother on the shoulder as he went to his bedroom. Dan hobbled to his own room with his cell phone. A half hour later, Ari sat nestled in the corner of the couch, Dan asleep in his arms, and rested his cheek on Dan's head.

Although he had no magical weapons or military training, at this moment, Ari would be Dan's protector, keeping him safe from the nightmares that would latch onto his soul and try to shake his resolve.

13—THAT WHICH DEVOURS

The *Nebulous One* never even attacked her or Aleta, Sarah thought. Either she saw no tactical advantage in doing so, or she had another motive. Sarah brushed herself off, feeling a bruise forming on the back of her head, and saw Aleta. Her wings had vanished, as had her javelin. With the mission over, they could stand down from alert status.

"You okay?"

Aleta's expression said it all. "Fantastic. We just got the crap kicked out of us by Ladon, then *The Nebulous One* crawls all over us. Bitch. I want a piece of her. Just saying."

"I wish you'd open up more," Sarah smiled. "You're always so reserved."

Aleta smirked. "You seriously kicked butt, though. Didn't know you could do that." She rubbed her left shoulder. "I felt the earth move under my feet."

"Cute. Sort of scares me a little when Gaea gives me more control."

Along one of the paths at the top rim of the quarry, they found a chunk of granite small enough to sit on. Sarah saw Aleta rotating her shoulders, so she sat behind her and put her hand on the left one. A few seconds later, the

105

pain vanished. Not only could Sarah move the earth, she channeled Gaea's power to restore, although it took more energy to do it.

"Quinn, we need a lift," Sarah gladly informed their liaison. "Talon needs to rest, so can you get a fix on us and get us back to Boston?"

"TF-3 will be there in an hour, ladies," Quinn replied. "We have a brief delay at Fitzgerald AFB. Hang tight."

Sarah lay back and sighed. "Okay. We have some time to kill. Now what?"

"I need a nap. Wake me when our ride comes," Aleta stretched. "Maybe tonight I'll have a good night's sleep."

"I know what you mean. Ever since we came across the Erinyes, I've not slept more than an hour or two."

"Dan once told me that even a brief encounter with them could mess someone up. I think they did exactly what they intended to do."

"Nightmares," Sarah started off, a combination of her thoughts and fatigue. "Almost every night."

Aleta knew that feeling. "Sometimes our inner demons do more harm. My grandmother used to say that. What're you dreaming about?"

Sarah took a minute before she answered, the words rushing through her mind wanting to burst out. No one else knew about what happened. Every time she had wanted to talk about it, it was as if a powerful hand clamped over her mouth. That was her guilt, she thought, and the Erinyes tormented people who committed crimes against their parents. Maybe they thought she should have been able to do something to save her mother. Even if she couldn't have, immortal goddesses of vengeance had planted seeds, and over the past few weeks, gnarled roots of guilt and self-loathing had grown, choking her from the inside out.

Aleta was like a sister to her, the sarcastic, mouthy sister she never had. Seventeen years had passed, and perhaps it was time to pry that hand away from her mouth.

"My mother's murder." Her casual tone surprised

Aleta.

"When did this happen? Not since I've known you, right?"

"No. It was my twelfth birthday. The day I got this," she said, holding up her ring. "I've been holding onto this for way too long. I need to tell someone."

Sarah's words eroded the years, almost two decades of repressed memories aching for freedom.

"Happy birthday, angel!" Roger Jacobs said to his daughter. "We're about to begin."

Twelve-year-old Sarah, her red hair pulled back into a ponytail, sat in the center of the prayer circle. Roger and his partner, Mark, had planned quite the birthday celebration for their daughter, having reached the age of ascension, her Fourth Triad. Both of Sarah's parents were Wiccans, and when they divorced, Roger took custody, but they both decided to be a part of their daughter's life as equally as possible, and that included their spiritual beliefs. Today was that special day they had planned since her birth, the time when she decided to become part of the coven.

Roger and Mark had invited some of Sarah's friends, but a few parents didn't think a Wiccan ritual was the best experience, so they kept some of their children home. A handful of teenagers, some with their parents, attended to give Sarah support during this ritual, a time when she would become part of the inner circle. Even though she had been surrounded by her parents' beliefs, she was never forced to participate in any prayer rituals or other services. In fact, she had to make the decision on her own to participate. Friends who were there for support sat in chairs around the prayer circle, a ring of white candles, their flames moving in unison to the movement around them. As Roger was the father, he was the one to call the quarters, or invoke the four directions:

"Those of *Aer*, of the living Air, Eagles who guard the Eastern gates, we call on you to be present at this ritual. Those of *Pyr*, of the living Fire, *Drakones* who guard the Southern gates, we call on you to be present at this ritual. Those of *Hydor*, of the living Water, *Naiads* who guard the Western gates, we call on you to be present at this ritual. Those of Gaea, of the living Earth, *Leimakides* who guard the Northern gates, we call on you to be present at this ritual."

Mark performed the invocation, "I call upon the *Tetrastoikheia* — O Mistress of Fire, *Hesteia*, we call upon you to bless this day. O Mistress of Water, *Thalassa*, we call upon you to bless this day. O Mistress of Earth, *Gaea*, we call upon you to bless this day. O Mistress of Air, *Kha-os*, we call upon you to bless this day."

Outside the Victorian home on Massachusetts Avenue, no one noticed the breeze pick up slightly.

Sarah took a white candle from her father. Her voice shaking, she began the ritual. "May my strength give this candle the ability to take away all darkness and negativity from me, making my path to success clear. May the light attract all goodness to me and purify me."

Her mother, Annabeth, dressed in a white robe with her blond hair braided down her back, took the candle and placed it on the altar. She handed her daughter an athame, a sacred ritual dagger.

Sarah's friends looked on, barely blinking, not wanting to miss one part of this ritual. A few of the teenagers present had already started thinking about how they could do this as well, even though their parents more than likely wouldn't agree. Waving the blade in small circles in front of her, she said, "May this blade remove all my sins, all my ill thoughts, and may its edge remain sharp and powerful, just as my inner strength should be, from now until the end of time."

Exchanging the athame for a piece of parchment and a quill, Sarah wrote down her three worst qualities and her three best, holding the paper over the closest candle.

"May the flames burn away all my weaknesses while they give my strengths an anchor," Sarah continued, holding the parchment until the fire consumed the very last corner, catching the ash in her other palm. A small cauldron within the circle received the ash.

"On this, the anniversary of my birth, may my power be made bold. May the *Tetrastoikheia* watch over me and keep me from harm."

Roger, Mark, Annabeth said in unison, "As above, so below. May the stars and the earth guide our daughter."

Wicca had been a way of life for the Jacobs family ever since Roger could remember, but Mark was newer to the practices. Minor spells and meditations made up most of their practice, and they also ascribed to the axiom that what you send out, you receive threefold. Sarah embraced these ideas, and sometimes she feared if she was too angry with her fathers or her mother that her emotions would be revisited upon her; even with her beliefs, she never did experience any actual mystical experiences, although she respected the elementals. Now that she had completed her induction ritual, she had a place in the coven, and she had a say in how coven business was handled. Others would guide her and instruct her in the old ways, since she had never been involved as much, but deep within her, she felt that something had become awakened this day.

While her guests enjoyed the birthday sweets, she held her paper cup of iced tea close to her lips as she gazed out on the street below. She didn't notice her mother's presence.

"Blessed be," Annabeth used a Wiccan greeting, giving her daughter a peck on her head. "You're a special girl. Do you know that?" It was more rhetorical, but Sarah wanted to answer, "Yes, I think I *am*."

"Mom, have you ever," Sarah uttered, her eyes not leaving the cars and pedestrians below. "Did you ever feel really connected?"

"To what?" Annabeth answered, her arms gently embracing her daughter, resting her chin on Sarah's head.

Both had eyes aimed outside, but Sarah also looked inside herself."

"Them. The *Tetrastoikheia*."

"I suppose I did. Why do you ask? Is this because of the ritual?"

Sarah turned to face her mother and nodded. When she looked into her mother's eyes, she saw green hazel eyes flecked with brown. That was it. No energy, so special gift.

"Mom, after the ritual, I felt like my mind was opened. Like I could see things around me that I had never seen before. Did that happen to you?"

Annabeth, cradling Sarah's cheeks in her hands, kissed her forehead. "We're all connected to the natural world, sweetie, but some do feel more connected than others. During my twelfth birthday, my grandmother and mother led me through the ritual, but they hadn't warned me about what it means to be a witch. I didn't really take things as seriously until I met your father. Our coven grew from that."

That wasn't really the answer she wanted. Her mother took her hands, brought them to her lips, and whispered, "You will learn what you need to know. Your father, Mark, and I will make sure of that."

Annabeth hugged Sarah tightly, and Sarah could smell the sage smoke on her mother's dress. That herbal perfume comforted her and reminded her of days when life was so much simpler.

"Oh, before I forget..." Her mother reached behind her neck, unclasping a silver chain.

Sarah couldn't help but see clouds moving a little more quickly, gathering together as they would before a storm. It would figure, she thought, that on her birthday, it would rain. Something about the world beyond the window seemed electrified, but she couldn't see anything out of the ordinary. Her mother's voice broke her reverie.

"Sarah, are you with me?" Annabeth smiled. "You seemed lost for a moment. I need you to do something."

After she spoke with her mother, Sarah brought the objects her mother requested back to the window, putting them on a small wooden table. She couldn't understand why her mother wanted the cauldron and the candle.

"I need to tell you something, and I need you to listen carefully, okay?" Her words conveyed seriousness, but not the type to worry Sarah. "Our family history goes way back into the ancient days, did you know that? Back before written history, we descended from *Æther*, the Upper Air. His daughter, Leukippe, and her husband, Euenor, ruled an island kingdom."

Stories from her childhood usually comforted Sarah, ever since she could remember, but the more she listened, the more she realized this wasn't simply a story to distract her or lull her to sleep like those bedtime stories she had heard. Under the words, Sarah felt the threads of truth her mother used to weave together this tale. Atlantis, Annabeth told her, was an island brought about by the Ancient Ones, the sacred mountain gods whose power touched the earth in so many ways. Unlike her husband, whose devotion was primarily to the sky god, Leukippe held in divine reverence the *Tetrastoikheia*, the guardians of the Four Elements: she was their High Priestess. A reward for her loyalty came to her in the form of a ring, one of golden Earthsteel, adorned with four gems that could control Earth, Air, Fire, and Water, respectively — emerald, diamond, agate, and moonstone. As Leukippe was mortal, she could manipulate the elements but not create them. With this gift, she could aid her husband and her people in times of war. When the Atlantean High Priest of Zeus offended the sky god, storms of vengeance swallowed the island, but not before Leukippe could escape to the Greek mainland with one daughter, Syra.

"Syra received this," Annabeth said, holding the ring up. "And so has every daughter since then. My mother gave it to me on my twelfth birthday, and now, it's yours."

Sarah then realized the connection: Syra, Sarah. She scrutinized the ring, lingering on the gemstones. "Why did you need the cauldron and the candle?"

"You may have reached the age of ascension, but I still have my gift to give you. You need to claim the ring as your own, Sarah. Call on the elements."

Even though she was a smart girl, Sarah, at twelve, had difficulty deciphering her mother's cryptic comments occasionally. Annabeth wanted her to call on the elements, but she didn't understand what that meant. Did she mean literally? Was there a ritual she was supposed to know? Sarah's forehead wrinkled while she worked things out, but a few minutes later, as soon as she had the answer, her smile grew. She peeked over her mother's shoulder to see where her father was, since she was enjoying her mother-daughter moment, but he was drinking coffee with a few members of the coven on the other side of the room.

Dipping her hand in the cauldron, Sarah said, "I invoke Thalassa and Gaea with water and ash." Moving the lit candle in a circle, she continued, "I invoke Hesteia and Khaos with fire and air. Bind me with this ring, this from my mother, from Syra, from Leukippe, from *Æther*."

Putting the ring on her right ring finger, she rubbed the ash and water on her right palm, followed by touching the candlewick to the same spot.

Annabeth was proud of her daughter; this was her first official incantation. "Blessed be," she said, embracing Sarah. Out the window, she saw the sky darkened by the horizon, the growing cloudbank moving closer, and felt her heart skip a beat.

"Sarah, honey, let's move away from the window," she said, looking over her shoulder toward the oncoming tempest as she guided her daughter toward the guests. She remembered those skies as well as what they brought, so she thought.

The *Tetrastoikheia* didn't act without purpose, and they needed to make sure the initiate was pure — *Æther* demanded purity. In ancient days, the initiate would go off into the wilderness to face the four powers, to be tested for her worth. If she returned successful in her task, she kept the ring and her sanity. Weaker minds couldn't contain the power, melting like a glacier in the afternoon sun.

Sarah was showing the ring to her friends when the first attack came hurtling through the window. As the shattered glass settled after having sprayed window shrapnel across the room, Mark, a nurse, helped Roger tend to the wounded. They, too, knew Sarah would be tested, since Sarah was the fifth in line to receive the ring. Annabeth was the first born of five sisters, and the fifth in line as well. It was always the fifth, since that initiate housed the fifth element, the embodiment of the Upper Air, the Æther. Only she who was the fifth could control the other four elements. Sarah, knocked to the floor, brushed herself off, tiny shards of glass embedding themselves in her hands. Unconscious to her left lay her mother, and she could see one or maybe two of her friends who looked like they were dead. Her father and Mark had removed most of the remaining guests, but a few wounded remained. In front of her, though, was her greatest concern, and this concern had a voice. This wasn't the test they had expected.

"Oathbreaker," the voice whispered, hoarse, like escaping air. "Oathbreaker."

Whimpering from both the pain in her hands and her rising fear, Sarah pushed her feet back, trying to put as much distance between this disembodied voice and her. The best her eyes could tell her was this was a thin, old man, cloaked in shadow, with eyes that hurt her soul when she looked into them. Like a wild animal finding its prey, he leaped onto Annabeth, opened his mouth to reveal unnatural fang-like teeth, and seemingly unhinged his jaw like a snake. As the jaws snapped shut, the teeth ripped away chunks of her mother's flesh, and all Sarah could do was scream. Her heart wanted her to move, to try to help, but her mind restrained her, the fear pulsing through her like a disease. He looked at her, his mouth dripping with her mother's bodily fluids and pieces of flesh, and then returned to feed. Moments later, her desecrated corpse lay in a heap, unrecognizable to anyone.

"Who are you!" Sarah cried out, her voice shaking. Her limbs felt numb as the blood drained into her body — shock had begun. "Leave my mother alone!" Futile words, but she had no other ones to say.

"Oathbreaker," he muttered again. Walking on all fours, his tongue licked away the last remnants of her mother.

Backed up against the wall, she wanted to turn away, but she couldn't take her eyes off this creature or man, whatever he was. Where her hands had pushed against the floor, streaks of her blood marked the wood. She had moved beyond pain at this point, and her panic was giving way to control, a strange kind of control she had never experienced. Edging closer to her, this monstrous man-like animal heaved his breath, wafting the fetid odor of Annabeth's flesh on Sarah. Without really thinking about it, she lifted her hands from the floor, turned her palms up and flexed her hands open. At first, blood trickled from the tiny holes in her hands as all the glass shards exited her skin. But, slowly, she wiped her hands together, using her own blood to remove all of the debris.

Seconds later, the creature lunged over to her, and instinctively she put her hands up in a defensive move and closed her eyes. She could still feel him near her, his body heat radiating inches away. Pushing forward abruptly, she felt a strange sensation around her hands. As soon as she heard the crash, she looked up. A pocket of wind had entered from the broken window, coalesced into a denser shape, and was pushing him against the wall. Was she doing that? Closing her hands, the winds ceased, and he fell to the floor, dazed. Again, he charged at her, and again she pushed forward, using the pillow of air to press him against the wall. Catching a glimpse of the ring, she noticed the diamond was glowing. He noticed she was distracted by something and pushed against the winds, taking her off guard.

This time, when he lurched forward, he managed to

place his mouth near her throat, leveraging himself above her with his arms.

"Burn in hell!" This time she felt radiant heat emanate from near her hands.

Roaring, he fell back, writhing, giving her a chance to stand up, leaning against a table as she did. The agate had just stopped glowing when she glanced at the ring, and she noticed the candle that had been lit earlier had burned to its base. A wave of calm flooded her, allowing her a moment to process what she had been doing. With her shock fading, and her eyes glued to where her mother's body had once been, the presence of a primordial god within her mind gave her subconscious the time it needed to understand. It had to be her actions, her decisions, but he was her ancestor, and he would stand by her. *Æther* embraced her soul, and that gave her clarity. No longer did she care what happened to her, something unlike what a twelve year old would think; but, no longer. Repeating her oath to the *Tetrastoikheia* she had made with her mother, making it a mantra, she grounded herself.

"I invoke Thalassa and Gaea with water and ash, Hesteia and Khaos with fire and air. Bind me with this ring, this from my mother, from Syra, from Leukippe, from *Æther*."

Her attacker rose, having recovered from his flaming distraction, and for the first time, Sarah didn't fear him. And — she finally knew who he was. Only one individual sought out those who had broken their oaths or made false ones, only one could even make the Erinyes cringe. She remembered her mother's story, the one from Sarah's childhood and how it terrorized her. But, her mother reminded her that knowledge had tremendous power. She remembered something else as well — names had power, too.

"I know who you are, Horkos, god of oaths. My mother told me all about you." This time when she spoke, she wasn't shaking.

"Oathbreaker," he repeated. "Oathbreaker."

He wasn't making any sense. She had repeated the oath, so surely she wasn't an oathbreaker. What could he mean? And, why did he kill her mother? What oath did she break? She had been standing by the window when her mother gave her the ring, the one she knew she would receive on her birthday. Her father had told her to expect the ring, since she was the next in line to get it. On her birthday. Sarah noticed that her father and Mark were no longer in the room; she hoped they were okay downstairs. She wasn't sure how she would explain any of this, but this was definitely the most outrageous birthday she had ever had. This calmness that allowed her to think rationally made more sense, too, and she knew it was more than *Æther*. A strong female presence was within her, too. She had hoped it would be her mother, although she knew her mother would always be with her. This aura was stronger, deeper, and much older.

"You don't have any power here, Horkos. I understand why you came for my mother, why you're here for me. My mother swore an oath to give me my ring on my birthday, but I haven't turned twelve yet. I'll be twelve later today, so she made a bad oath. And since I'm not twelve, I can't make the oath, either."

Horkos wouldn't leave without Sarah's body in his gut, her soul festering for all eternity just outside the gates of Hades. He needed to punish her, the way he had punished her mother and so many others before her. She was an oathbreaker, and that was unforgivable. Just as he would punish those who had broken Stygian oaths, the most sacred one of all, he would make an example of her. Her tender, young flesh would rip so easily, so smoothly.

Elements were hers to control—she had figured that out—and she had already seen what fire and air could do. Swirling her hand around, she thought about the water in the cauldron, the water mixed with ash, an earthly aspect. Calling them to her, she pictured a liquid ring surrounding Horkos, and fueled her will with rage. Circles hold power as unending shapes, and using a circle as a binding force was self-replenishing. The more Horkos fought against it, the tighter it became, but Sarah was an initiate. Her control ebbed and flowed with her emotions. Her mother couldn't help, and her fathers were downstairs; calling for them would endanger them. Rage surfaced again, and she could taste the sourness of adrenaline--the ring tightened. She felt she would fail, though, since she didn't have the mental strength, not like her mother or grandmother who had had time to perfect their craft. Feeling her mind wander, he pushed back against her, but she recovered, closing her fists. Both knew it was a matter of time before he would devour her.

As each wave of rage fell on Horkos, he growled louder. "Oathbreaker will die. Like her mother..." His ochre eyes fixed on her heart.

Æther could help ground her, but he wouldn't intervene directly. But, she knew what to do, even for a twelve year old. Making oaths was a part of her Wiccan background, and she now remembered something from prior rituals she had witnessed. It was a long shot, however. If her bad oath brought out Horkos' fangs, she would defang him, taking away his power. Soon, she would have to lower her aching arms, though, so she put all her faith in one more thing before succumbing with all of the eloquence of a twelve year old.

"Ancient Ones, I need the one who is in charge of oaths! I've made one and need it approved. Helios, I know you're out there. Just so you know, I'm related to *Æther*, if that helps. I promise, on my mother's soul, to uphold the *Tetrastoikheia* forever!" She said this two more times, just to make sure it fit the Rule of Three. This wasn't the time to offend an Ancient One.

Nothing. Perhaps calling on older gods only worked if you were an experienced witch, she thought. Why would Helios come to her aid anyway? She couldn't concentrate anymore on that, though. She'd push all of her will toward him, but Horkos was proving stronger than she was, regardless of her growing ability to manipulate the elements. Instantly, her concentration faltered, and he reared up to pounce, his jaw already unhinged. Drops of saliva left scorch marks on the wood floor as his hunger superseded all else; he would indeed have her. After pinning her down, his acidic fangs moments from eviscerating her, spots of her cheeks turned black from the drops of bile falling from his teeth. A long, bile-coated, scaly tongue with a serpent's head slithered from Horkos' mouth, it's own tongue flitting just about Sarah's right eye. He meant to devour her piece by piece.

The snake-headed tongue recoiled to strike, and then Sarah heard a deep whisper say, "Dechomai." *I accept.*

Two words. With her oath now sanctified by Helios, Horkos had no claim on her. Having heard Helios' voice, he whimpered and backed away, melting into the floor. Offering her silent prayer of thanks, Sarah slowly got to her feet, brushed herself off, and surveyed the damage.

All that remained from her mother was a stain on the floor from where her body once lay, and now Sarah could mourn, after the danger had passed. Kneeling, she rubbed her hand gently on the stained wood, hoping for one last connection with her mother, and wept. As she leaned over, freeing her grief, she felt warmth on her back and sat up. Sunbeams, pitying Sarah's loss, touched her gently, but she loathed them. Although she was grateful for what Helios had done, she hated him for what she had had to do. As the light hit the floor, the stains faded.

"Don't you dare take them," she said. "Leave my mother alone. I want to remember."

The floor regained the pale crimson blotches, a forever reminder of Horkos and his actions. She curled up over the spot where her mother once lay, her anger mixed with her grief, and Sarah swore to herself that she would never let anyone take someone she loved ever again.

Aleta gently squeezed Sarah's hand. "Honey, you did

nothing wrong."

Barely nodding, Sarah replied, "I know that now. But, I had carried the guilt of a twelve year old with me. When we get home, I need to go back to that house."

"To pay your respects?"

"No. To burn it to the ground."

Ten minutes later, TF-18 airlifted them from Vermont. Sarah held Aleta's hand again, this time more for solidarity than comfort; she knew little of Aleta's background, however, but that might have been by design. Sometimes, secrets were best left alone, even if they became like infections rotting one's soul. Aleta hadn't wanted to burden her friends with her earlier life, a time that she had come to accept begrudgingly, over many years. This darkness seemingly had no end, and she wanted to be free again. Her sleepless nights must have come from the Erinyes, too, but unlike Sarah's nightmares, Aleta had already buried her past, literally.

"Vermont's very beautiful." Sarah's eyes, looking for peace, rested on the landscape. "Too bad it took a demon to bring us here." The rolling hills and tree-dotted landscape gave her a chance to unwind, even though she knew Quinn could call at any moment with another disaster. She thought Aleta was also staring out the window of the helicopter, but her eyes were looking inside. "Hey, what's up?"

"Your story got me thinking. So did the Erinyes, I guess."

"You're fidgeting, too. Did you want to fly back on your own?"

Aleta shook her head.

"You know, I just noticed something. The white stripe down your hair. When you have your wings, the white hair—"

"Turns to feathers. Yeah, I know. That was a gift."

"How so? Who gave it to you?" She knew to ask.

"Zeus, actually. This was before the gods went into

119

hiding… about 1997, I think. I can tell you want to know," Aleta said, "but I don't want you to tell anyone. Promise me."

Sarah nodded.

"Okay. Well, I'm from Colorado originally."

The words left Aleta's mouth and coalesced into a story she never told anyone else.

1985 — Off Route 550 in southeastern Colorado, near the San Juan National Forest, in the shadow of Cloud Mountain, sat Oak Grove, a quaint hamlet of just under a thousand people. Pressed dirt roads led from the center of town, with its main street of small businesses and vendors, coffee shops and groceries, separating into other gravel roads leading to individual homes and farms. Heady mountain air blanketed the community, and wispy clouds sailed on by. Down Treetop Lane, a street with only two farmhouses was the home and office of Dr. Sheila Halston, veterinarian, her aging mother, Rebecca, and her 12-year-old daughter, Aleta. One of a few black families whose history went back to the 19th century in Oak Grove, these three women lived an uncomplicated life, relatively free of bigotry and hatred, with people who just let people live their lives. Being so remote from other towns, this hamlet enjoyed being sequestered from big city life, sitting about 25 miles from Durango, the closest town. Despite the tranquility, however, the shadow of mistrust and paranoia had even reached this place, its buildings on Main Street housing surveillance cameras and identity card scanners, not quite as sophisticated as their modern counterparts, put up by the government, but even that didn't prevent the citizens of Oak Grove from being a strong, cohesive community. A rarity among the surrounding towns, this one seemed almost protected by things unseen for a fate unknown, and this mystery provided a strange comfort to its inhabitants, even though none ever spoke of it.

On the front porch of 2 Treetop Lane, with its yellow balustrade, Rebecca Halston, known to everyone as Granny, sat in her wicker rocker, lost in thoughts of how much she appreciated the cool breeze and the smell of musky grass, while her granddaughter Aleta read one of the many novels she always had with her. Finishing a chapter, she put the feather in the book and closed it, taking a deep breath.

"Granny, why haven't we moved to a bigger city? Wouldn't Momma have a better chance of more patients if we did?"

"'Your Momma grew up in Oak Grove, and so did I. In this house, in fact. We don't see a reason to leave. You eager to go somewhere?"

Aleta stood up and leaned on the porch rail, her pale green sundress ruffling. She wore her long black hair in two braids, each wrapped around the back of her head.

"No, ma'am. I do want to travel the world someday, maybe fly to Europe or somewhere exotic, but I'm not really ready to leave. I was just curious."

"Come sit by me, and I'll tell you a story, since you're so fond of them." Granny patted her lap.

Aleta pulled up the other rocker next to her grandmother, a woman in her 70s, her white hair pulled back and tied with a thin leather strip. Granny spoke about a time long, long ago, when the Ancient Ones existed, and how they helped shape the sky and the earth. She didn't refer to them as gods; they were more like entities that embodied forces of nature, albeit powerful forces. Sometimes these entities showed up as animal forms, sometimes as people, but their natural state was simply pure energy. With the skill of the *Moirae*, Granny wove the words into a shimmering tapestry, wrapping itself around the wide-eyed girl hanging on every word. Events unfolding in Aleta's mind, the clouds sailed across the sky. The breeze picked up slightly.

Granny spoke of magic and strength, power and intrigue, mesmerizing her young granddaughter—these words could move the earth, hide the heavens, and could overshadow both. Words had power. A few hours later, Dr. Halston arrived, her Ford F-150 rumbling, and she grabbed two paper sacks of groceries from the back. A hawk flew overhead, squawking high above.

"Go help your momma," Granny clipped the story she was just telling. "We'll talk more later."

"Rain's coming, 'Leta. Why don't you help Granny in and then help me with supper?" Dr. Halston handed her daughter a bag.

All throughout the meal, Aleta couldn't help but linger on Granny's stories of the Ancient Ones whose power controlled everything, and she just knew deep down that she was a part of that. Her mother talked about the peregrine falcon she had been nursing back to health, a victim of an amateur archer's arrow, and occasionally Aleta caught some of that story. The idea of someone shooting at something as majestic and powerful as a falcon made her angry, and she blurted out that if she ever saw someone hurting an animal, she'd stop him—somehow.

"Now, 'Leta, we can't go around hurting people who hurt animals. We're part of the natural world, too, and we wouldn't want someone to hurt us, now would we?"

"No ma'am." She felt her cheeks get hot. "I just hate seeing any of the earth's creatures come to harm. Like you, Momma, I need to teach people how to respect life."

Granny wiped her lips with a linen napkin. "We're all part of the electricity that flows through the world. Your momma has a gift, a gift of healing."

For the rest of the meal, Aleta just kept looking back and forth at her mother and grandmother, hoping that someday she'd have those gifts, too, of healing and wisdom. One of the stories that Granny had told her a while back was about the Triple One: the maiden, the mother, and the crone. Each had a special gift that came from the earth and the sky, and these gifts brought understanding, something that Aleta wanted so she could make her mother and grandmother proud. She wanted responsibility.

With dinner over, Granny sat by the fireplace doing her needlework while Sheila thumbed through some veterinary journals, sipping chamomile tea. Aleta stood out on the front porch, looking out at Cloud Mountain, its snowy peak watching over everything below. Summer tended to be cooler so close to the mountain range, and the breeze brought the perfume of lilacs to Aleta's nose. She found herself inhaling the incense-like scent deeply, letting the breeze and the smell take her to other places in her mind. She would travel someday, she mused, and her future would be certain. With the sun setting, the soft hues in the sky finished the meditative scene. Down the dirt road, she spied a deer with her fawn, and Granny always said that to see a mother and her child in nature was a good omen.

"'Leta, honey? Could you go into the attic and bring down my basket of yarn?" It always amazed her that she could hear her grandmother clearly no matter where she was in the house.

In many homes, the attic becomes this catch-all place, filled with dusty boxes of seasonal clothing or holiday decorations — dark, stagnant, and avoidable. Other times, this place becomes the stuff of nightmares, haunted by the imagination and paranoia. To Aleta, though, the attic room above her bedroom housed her family's memories, its soul, and sanctuary from the mundane. In one corner, she had a blanket, a pile of her favorite books, and a small trunk with random objects she'd collected over the years. Her prized possession was an eagle feather she found while hiking around Cloud Mountain. A small, octagonal window looked out over the front yard, giving her a clear view of the mountain, and — on especially clear nights — the moon. Behind some wooden boxes, Aleta retrieved the basket that housed her grandmother's assorted yarn, a collection of strands she had accumulated over the years she had lived in Colorado, but it was stuck on a purple fleece blanket that covered a few assorted boxes, one of which was wooden with metallic adornments. Almost like silver appliqués, the shape looked like a bird of some kind, elongated to fit on the cover.

Five feet long, the box had thin, rusty hinges and was sealed shut with a unique padlock. Aleta felt almost magnetized to it, but her grandmother was calling for her, so she threw the blanket back where she had found it and descended the ladder, never taking her eyes off the place where the box sat.

Midnight rose, and while Sheila and Rebecca Halston slept, the youngest Halston could not. It could have been from the echoing thunder that rolled over the horizon, the harbinger of a summer storm, or perhaps the lingering thoughts of the box in the attic. Moving about the house was risky, since the wooden floor had creaky spots, but Aleta knew how to avoid them. With great aplomb, she skulked up the ladder, snatched the box, and tiptoed outside, careful not to let the screen door slam shut. Winds increased, pushing storm clouds closer and closer, but she couldn't be bothered. Something shared the darkness with her — something with purpose. Running with box in one hand and a shovel in the other, she stopped about a quarter mile from the house. In the middle of a dusty field, her flannel nightgown fluttering about her, Aleta picked up the shovel and put all her strength into striking the padlock. Not a traditional lock, it had no discernible keyhole, and looked more like intricate woven metal. With each strike, she could swear the storm was getting closer.

Dry grasses whipped around, and Aleta's hair mimicked them, getting in her eyes. With each successive strike, she grunted more openly, her desire fueled by the thunder thumping around her. Finally, the next blow brought success. As if it realized it had no choice, the lock fell away.

Even though she had been so eager to open the box, she used the shovel to lift the lid. Wrapped within white linen, a silver javelin, unmarred by time, caught her eye. The great power of the approaching clouds, moments away, could do nothing to distract her. At one end of the javelin was written something in a language she didn't understand, and holding it in her hands felt so natural. She was unaware that something watched her from within the darkness itself.

As if by instinct, she held the javelin up toward the black clouds. Whatever lurked out in the field was drawn by this awakened power, and it moved one silent step at a time; gateways to the underworld existed all over Gaea, even in places like Oak Grove. This entity sensed a connection the moment Aleta saw the box in the attic, kindling an ancient memory she didn't know she had. Cloud Mountain, Colorado, near this tiny hamlet in a vast world, once went by another name long ago — Jupiter Mountain.

Aleta's eyes scanned the sky, which grew darker by the second, and she kept her arm outstretched toward it. *This feels so right*, she thought. Rain began pelting her, like needles of water, almost piercing her skin. That which watched her from the darkness edged in closer, unsure of what would happen next, but the power beneath the moment allured it. Electricity, rising from the ground, charged Aleta's body, until a determined bolt of lightning from the sky met its earthbound counterpart. So much power running through a human body would probably kill the person, but the javelin protected her.

Moving over the earth under the cover of the storm, what hid in the shadows felt a magnetic attraction to the magic coursing through the air. Once the lightning subsided, Aleta needed to expel all of the energy she had absorbed and clumsily threw the javelin toward an old oak tree on the side of the house. The moment the silver touched the trunk, the lightning did as well, blasting the top third of the majestic tree to splinters. Of course, thunder followed, shaking the tree, the ground, and the house. Convinced that this object had connections to Olympos, the eager lurker moved toward the shattered tree only to find nothing in the wooden debris. Turning its attention on Aleta, it moved through the grasses, until it was within striking distance. This underworld creature could take what it wanted, leaving behind a tattered corpse. With such a ferocious storm, Aleta never saw or heard it approach. Darkness makes no sound. Rising up behind the girl, the presence was ready to strike. Aleta felt a chill, like part of her was being drained away. Falling to her knees, she cried, her hands wrapped around her torso. Heaving and shaking, she didn't know how to make it stop. Her thoughts went to the lost javelin, and she was afraid she had lost it forever. Soon, she heard screaming, and it took her a moment to realize that she was the one screaming. Flashes of her mother and grandmother in her mind helped keep her focused briefly, long enough to reach up, and then she cried out a word she had never heard before:

"Nephoskizetes!" *Cloudsplitter.*

The silver form miraculously materialized in her hand. One dark, hairy limb whipped out, but a thunderbolt crashed down, striking the silver once more. Repelled by the energy, the two-headed canine Orthros jumped back, an echoing growl hidden by the rolling thunder. He could not get to her as long as she had the javelin, but he smelled more human meat not far away.

Aleta made out the sound of her mother's voice over the wind and rain, and took the box and its contents back to the house. Orthros, brother to three-headed Cerberos who guarded the gate to Hades, moved through the night like a stale wind, ending up on the porch just before her, but his matte black fur kept him from human vision. She scurried through the door and managed to hide the box in the downstairs closet before her mother stepped off the landing. Orthros looked through the porch window, his fangs showing.

"Girl, what are you doing out in the rain? Are you trying to get sick? I went to check on you when I heard that thunder, and you weren't in bed. Storms like these are nasty."

"I went out to watch it from the yard, Momma. But, I didn't make it back in time when the rains came. You know how much I love thunderstorms." She hated lying to her mother, but right then, she knew it was best. How would she explain what happened? And, what did she feel out there? Something was with her, but she didn't know how to put it into words. Perhaps, after she thought more about it, she might be able to work through it all.

Sheila smirked. "All right, well, go put some dry bed clothes on and go to sleep."

"Okay, Momma." She headed for her room. "And, Momma, storms aren't nasty. Granny says that they're just how the Ancient Ones communicate."

"And just what did this storm say to you?" her mother asked, her hand on her hip.

Aleta didn't answer. While she lay in bed, she watched the shadows on the wall of her room flicker in and out with the lightning, something she had always feared but had come to have respect for in such a short time. She slept, dreaming about dancing with the clouds.

One set of canine jaws turned the worn doorknob, and Orthros walked across the wood floor making no sound. An underworld creature only knowing death and decay, he salivated smelling the fresh human meat that lay asleep on the second floor. At the top of the stairs, he turned left toward the grandmother's room, taking up most of the hall. He was about to dine on elderly flesh when he felt a sharp pain in his hind leg. Aleta stood in her nightgown, javelin in hand, her eyes never leaving the four-legged dog as he slowly turned, his four eyes on the twelve-year-old girl. She said nothing, but Orthros knew that face, the one worn by a protector. He could dispatch everyone in the house before she even saw him move, but something about the javelin had him at bay.

Aleta knew it, too. In a low voice, she said, "Back off."

Orthros moved in closer toward her, but she wasn't going to back down.

"Leave my grandma alone," she said, waving the javelin toward the stairs. "I'm not afraid of you."

That wasn't entirely true, but she wasn't going to let anything happen to her grandmother or her mother.

Something about the javelin gave her the strength of will to stand her ground. Orthros' eyes glowed red and both his heads growled. She shoved the silver rod forward again, nudging him toward the staircase. The twelve-year-old girl inside her shook, but the brave girl protecting her grandmother felt empowered by the past somehow. She didn't expect what happened next, however. The canine creature dispersed into a gray fog and went under the door of her mother's bedroom. Before Aleta could reach the doorknob, she heard the snapping shut of powerful jaws and the crack of bone, stopping her in her tracks. A few seconds later, dark blood seeped under the door into the hall. Without thinking, Aleta threw the javelin at the door, a lightning bolt disintegrating it. Through the haze, she saw two sets of feral eyes at floor level. The blast had shattered the bed, her mother's headless body next to a stunned Orthros. She reached up and the javelin coalesced in her hand once again. This time, with point blank accuracy, she sent the silver rod into the dog's body, lightning ending its existence. Burned fur combined with scorched wood and flesh, and Aleta ran to her grandmother's room.

"Grandma," she said, her voice shaking. "Grandma, please wake up."

Waking to her granddaughter's tear-stained face, the old woman listened to Aleta try to tell her what happened, although shock had set in and adrenaline faded. All she could muster was, "Momma's dead. Momma's dead." Rebecca Halston held her granddaughter for a moment, and then found her daughter's body on the floor. Orthros' body had vanished, but the puddle of blood and the debris remained. She had seen much in her long life, but she had never seen something like this. Even though she held the family's history in her mind, no stories of the ancient warriors who made up their lineage ever ended up with such a horrifying display. Rebecca knew that this was the work of a primeval power drawn by the javelin and its connections to the Ancient Ones. She drew her strength from the stories her mother and grandmother had told her. The next day, she would bury her daughter according to the old ways. This night, however, she would comfort her granddaughter.

A week later, Sheila Halston lay buried behind the house, next to her great-grandmother. Rebecca and Aleta hadn't talked about what happened that night, but soon they would have to. Aleta spent much of her time in the attic wrapped up in the purple blanket, staring out the hexagonal window into the sky. She only went downstairs to eat when Granny called her, to do her chores, and then she returned to the attic at night to sleep. Rebecca gave her granddaughter a few more days before she climbed the rickety ladder.

"It's time to tell you, 'Leta," She sat next to the girl who lay staring off into the sky.

Aleta turned toward her grandmother. "Are you mad at me for taking the spear? Mom would still be alive if I hadn't..."

"Don't you talk nonsense. Your momma and I should have told you about the box sooner. We didn't know it would attract... evil.... No one knew. Don't go blaming yourself."

Rebecca lifted Aleta's chin, her eyes peering into those of her granddaughter. She kissed her forehead.

"You were drawn to the box. Had we told you, maybe we could have helped you understand more. But, now, I just need you to listen.

"In ancient days, long before we came here, long, long ago...," Granny began, lingering on the word 'long', "we lived near a great river, by the Black Sea. Our tribe was proud, so proud, and we found sisterhood. It was a simpler time, a life uncomplicated. We and the earth were one. We and the sea were one. Some of us hunted. Others were plant-gatherers. But, we all shared a common love for one another and the Ancient Ones. I don't remember all the names."

She paused a moment to concentrate, giving Aleta time to absorb the little she had just learned.

"Tribes like ours found sacred many things, and they adopted different symbols to represent parts of the natural world. Our sisterhood revered birds of all types, and they chose the sky god as their guardian. He took the form of a white eagle at times, soaring high above them. Some say he still does watch out for them, but the signs are murky now.

"And, it's a javelin," Granny muttered.

"Granny?"

"You called it a spear. A spear's a weapon, but a javelin's a tool. You'll see."

Aleta had so many questions, but she was afraid to ask. She had never been afraid to ask questions before, and that bothered her. One thing she needed to know.

"What happened to that tribe? Are any of them still around?"

Nodding her head slowly, she said, "You, your mother, and I. We're the only ones came from that line. We're the only ones left. Now, it's just you and me. As time passed, so much time... but, they left us a legacy. Something that only one of us could use to protect the sisterhood. Only one."

"The javelin," Aleta whispered, feeling a tingle go up her spine. "If it belonged to you, Granny, or to Momma, I'm sorry for taking it. I am so, so sorry, since I didn't know who it belonged to. When I went to get your yarn, and I saw the box, I couldn't help myself. Whoever it belongs to, I'm really sorry—"

Granny put her hands on Aleta's face, looking into her eyes again.

"'Leta, honey, it didn't belong to your momma or me," Granny interrupted. "It's yours."

"Aleta, I am so sorry," Sarah squeezed Aleta's hand. "I didn't know you lost your mother, too."

"Years later, I learned that Granny meant Amazon

tribes," Aleta added, "and then Zeus came to me in a dream just after I got my wings. He told me that, back when my tribe existed, tribal leaders wore headdresses made from discarded eagle feathers to show their status. Since I had inherited *Nephoskizetes*, he wanted me to have my own headdress, so he gave me the ability to hide my wings, and said the white stripe would become feathers.

"I think I need to back up a bit. Early in my career as a geneticist, I planned on trying to fuse animal DNA to human DNA to strengthen them both in a prototype genetic transfer apparatus. An albino eagle came in for treatment, but I thought if I could enhance it genetically, it would be stronger. My research partner, Jack Forrester, had reservations, and the fact that there was a storm coming convinced him we should wait. I was naïve and eager, a bad combination, and decided to try the procedure anyway. I got locked in the chamber, so when Jack went for help, I tried to summon my javelin, thinking the lightning would trigger the release mechanism. Instead, it shorted out the machine, initiating the transfer sequence. When I awoke, the room was on fire, the chamber was destroyed, and the eagle was gone. Again, I called for my javelin, but the lightning tore through me and acted like a catalyst for the DNA to fuse. I felt a strange tingling all over and passed out.

"When I came to, I tried to stand. The lab was destroyed. Jack came back in, muttering something about an ambulance coming, and stopped as soon as he saw me and pointed. I turned toward a window and saw my reflection. I had grown large, white wings. My body felt different, too. Lighter. And, my hands and feet had gnarled like the taloned feet of a bird. I had become genetically fused with the eagle. I turned back toward Jack who had found a chair that hadn't been destroyed by the blasts. The paramedics found me wearing a lab coat surveying the damage. I felt fine. Either my wings didn't really show under the coat, or no one really noticed. Jack told me he wouldn't reveal to anyone what happened, and the official story about the machine would be that the storm had damaged it. I assured them we were fine, so they let us go. It was a few weeks later, after my dreams had pushed me closer to the edge, that Zeus visited me.

"My grandmother passed away never knowing what had become of me."

Once they landed, they debriefed with Quinn, but left out the story that Aleta had told Sarah since that was technically not part of the melee scenario. Both were sure to iterate that *The Nebulous One* seemed to have no interest in attacking women, but that, too, felt like one more of the unanswered questions heaped upon them.

14—COLLATERAL DAMAGE

Reverberating down the white cement brick halls of Centro de Salud Mental Arganzuela, a mental hospital in downtown Madrid, the screams of Esteban Reyes, a 20-year-old college student, carried the words, "Ella viene." *She's coming.* Each time he said the words, either he sang them or simply blurted them out. The guard, Rico, a burly man in a white shirt and white pants, peered in the small square window on the door to Esteban's room and saw the young man huddled in the corner, his arms wrapped around him in a straitjacket. The hospital usually kept its more unstable patients in padded cells, but Esteban responded better to having his hands bound. He told his therapist and the doctors that bound, he could give himself to her, but they didn't understand what he meant. Normally, when a patient acted out, Rico rapped on the door with a wooden stick and told him or her to be quiet, but when he saw Esteban rocking back and forth in the corner, he knew the young man's mind was all but gone. Besides, the hospital had so few mental patients that it really didn't matter how much shouting Esteban did; no one else would hear him.

"I know who you are," he uttered, his eyes staring off. "You steal from people. Ladróna." *Thief.*

Whoever she was, Esteban spoke as if she were in the room with him.

"It will be so much better when you're here. They will never know. They must never know."

Rico used to bring the therapist to the door to record what Esteban said, but no one could make sense of the words, and when he was talking to himself, he wasn't shouting down the hallway.

"A dark, dark place. You want to take me there, to this dark place. So dark. Dark dark dark."

The night nurse, Juana, who sat at the end of the hall often told Rico that Esteban reminded her of her son, from his age and his black hair, but her son died when he was ten. Whenever Rico would take his cigarette break, he would tell her not to go down the hall, that Esteban would be fine until he returned. But, she never listened. Once at the window, she'd look in so he couldn't see her, but he always spoke as if he knew she were there.

"You want me to go away," he would say, nonchalantly. "You're ashamed of me, mamá." These words weren't meant for Juana. Deep down, she knew that, but she needed to connect with Esteban since he did remind her of her lost son. She would cry at her desk, silent tears, wishing in her heart that her son were with her still.

"Ella viene!" he shouted while Rico watched through the window. "Ella viene viene viene…"

Having been a night guard at the hospital for ten years, Rico looked like he had been to prison, his hard-worn face, lashed by the emotions of the patients, barely showing any expression, his muscled arms tattooed and scarred, and his eyes colored by despair. He had come to this job by an ad in the paper; back when he started, the job paid poorly, but the work was consistent. Now, a decade later, he made enough money to rent a two-room apartment on the outskirts of Madrid. Life wasn't what he would call good, he would tell his friends, but it was enough. Keeping an eye on patients like Esteban gave him perspective, he thought.

"I want you to have it, ladróna... Tú vienes." *You come.* He used the familiar form, feeling an intimacy with her.

Rico raised his voice a little. "Quién viene, Esteban? Who's coming?" He used to think Esteban was insane, but he just wasn't certain that was true anymore. He told Juana he was going for a smoke.

Esteban began squirming, almost with pleasure, like a worm. His eyes glazed over, and he laughed. "I know why you come... to satisfy a hunger," he said, licking his lips. "From deep inside the earth you come, and you feel—" As if he heard something, he looked around.

Within the hallway, the temperature dropped, but Juana just put on her sweater and continued reading her email. Her desk sat at the end of the hall, and from her position, only the lights within the occupied cells shone through, leaving small square patches of light. Since bedtime had come and gone by two hours, few of the fluorescent lights glowed down the corridor. Past her desk lay the stairs going up or down, and Juana wasn't looking at them, but she felt the fear approach. Her eyes scanned around, and she called for Rico, but he didn't respond. Like an army of ants with purpose, the fear climbed over her. Even with the chill, sweat trickled down her neck, and her eyes twitched.

Esteban smiled and leaned his head back. "Ella está aquí." *She's here.*

Juana didn't know where to go, but soon it wouldn't matter. Flowing up the stairs, the black gelatinous cloud rose over the last step and poured down the hall, clinging to the walls. The nurse tried to scream, but a tentacle of the darkness encircled her, covering her mouth, entering her pores, filling her veins and arteries, and draining her of her bodily fluids. Both skin and bone dissolved simultaneously. All that remained of Juana was her uniform, a white dress lying in a pile on the white floor. But, she was not the intended victim.

"I will feed you," Esteban laughed. "I can give you what you want."

From all around the door the blackness seeped in, puddling around him. He didn't fear her.

"You have come for me. I know why, too. You want to embrace me, don't you... Lismonia?" He smiled at her.

And, he knew her *true* name.

No one had ever addressed her before. All felt fear around her, but not him. She rose up, this amorphous form that was both cloud and ooze at once, and formed what would be her neck, her red eyes surfacing.

"Let me look into your eyes. I will let you in."

As he was so willing, she didn't need to wrap herself around him, but he kept asking her to do it. He sat up in the corner, preparing himself for her, and then she looked through his eyes inside him. His body went slack inside the straitjacket as he felt her push her consciousness into his, searching for what she wanted. Surrounding everything was the pervasive madness, that thick, mucous-like part of his mind that could understand who she was and why she was coming. He had been preparing for this moment for weeks. Meandering around within him, she found what she was looking for and extracted it, but she had to take more than she wanted. Esteban's mental illness was so interwoven with everything that, when she withdrew from his psyche, she had no choice but to remove some of the madness as well. Lismonia sank back through the doorway, leaving the hospital a little less satisfied than she had with her other prey.

Esteban awoke hours later and found he couldn't move. He didn't know why he was in a straitjacket. Foggy memories swirled in his head, with glimpses of something dark around him, like a thick blanket, smothering him, and then he had become conscious. Shouts for help, saying this must be a mistake, went unanswered. The more he sat on the floor wriggling in the buckled jacket, the more he thought he must be in prison or worse for reasons passing understanding. Waves of fear rippled through him, forcing tears to come, and through clenched teeth he began to hyperventilate. Closed eyes kept him from seeing the cell walls, the padding stained and torn. His last complete memory was being in his Comparative Literature course, arguing with Dr. Riviera, the professor. That was a week ago.

Esteban realized he wasn't alone.

"The Nebulous One has left me a plaything." The voice was gravelly, and it knew better than to use her true name since it might draw her back. As Esteban opened his eyes, he saw a black snake's body coiled in the corner—the body was almost two feet thick. Raising his eyes, he saw two leonine arms extending from each side of the serpentine body. The head looked like a lion, but in place of a mane, snakes wriggled, much like the head of the Gorgon, Medusa. Over the head sat a rusty helmet. Metallic armor covered the creature's shoulders and across its chest was a rusty breastplate.

"Who... what are you?" Esteban tried to back himself even further into the corner. "What do you want with me?"

Slithering closer, the lion-serpent leaned in. Esteban could smell the rank, rotted smell of decayed flesh on its breath, and the slick looking black scales glided across the floor in fluid, deliberate movements.

"Phobos, mortal." He sniffed Esteban. "You smell of flesh. She took what she wanted... I can have the rest." Phobos growled before sliding around the room.

"She who? What did she..."

The tip of the tail curled beneath him, and Phobos dragged him to the center of the room. As each black coil wrapped itself around, it tightened slightly, just enough to keep him secure. Panic controlled Esteban now, and he screamed for help so loudly his voice became raspy. The god of fear laughed.

At shift change, Eduardo, Rico's replacement, swiped his ID card on the first floor. Before passing through the door, he put his left eye in front of the DNA retinal scanner, and the computer replied in a female voice, "Identity Confirmed: Eduardo Gaspardo." At the second floor, he heard the screaming. Normally, he would get the shift report from the prior guard, but Rico wasn't there. Nyx's daughter had taken him during his cigarette break so the custodians would only find his clothes in a pile outside by the garbage. Eduardo didn't remember a male patient being on the floor, and Celia, the nurse for the next shift, didn't notice the pile of Juana's clothing by the desk. The name on the door, *Esteban Reyes*, didn't look familiar to either one of them; they had thought the room vacant for months. Celia put in a call to the doctor to see if perhaps he had authorized a new patient and had neglected to share that knowledge. They waited outside Esteban's room for the doctor to arrive, listening while this patient they didn't know cried out as if being tortured. Without approval from a doctor, they weren't going to do anything.

Dr. Duarte arrived an hour later to find that Esteban had stopped crying out and found the young man in a catatonic state in the center of the room, but without any knowledge of his condition, he was reluctant to treat him. He did enter the cell to check for vitals, though, and found the man to have elevated blood pressure, higher than he should have for a man in a seeming catatonic state. Celia showed him a file on Esteban she had found on the nurse's desk that showed he had been admitted for acute schizophrenia... a month ago. Clearly, the records didn't show any catatonia, but the most disturbing part of this discovery was that Dr. Duarte had been Esteban's doctor since his arrival; he didn't understand how that could be since he had never met Esteban before. He had even signed off on medication, too. Notes taken about what the young man spoke of, aloud to himself, revealed that he was expecting something to happen. Baffled, Dr. Duarte took a business card from his wallet, flipped it around in his hand, and ultimately called the number. If anyone could help him in this dilemma, it would be a doctor he had met years before; this man knew how to heal all sorts of maladies.

Just after sunrise, only a few hours after the phone call, a tall, blond, older gentleman found Dr. Duarte in Esteban's room, seated on the floor in the other corner.

"Dr. Duarte. It's good to see you again," the man said, shaking the doctor's hand and pulling him up.

"Thank you for coming. Here's the file. No one here knows who this young man is, but I'm the doctor of record. I've never seen this patient before. Neither has the guard nor the nurse."

"May I have a moment with him? In private?"

Nodding, Dr. Duarte left with Eduardo and Celia. Once the door was closed, the man knelt down put his hand on Esteban's forehead. Concentrating, he entered the mortal mind, but not to take, as *The Nebulous One* had done. He merely wanted to know the truth.

"You are in no danger," he thought. "What..."

Flashes of memory staggered along, giving him answers to questions he hadn't even asked yet. Screams brought on by terror surrounded the inner mind, and the voice he heard was Esteban's, even though another was present. Even with his power, he was unable to unravel all the images. Some powerful barriers lay in place, but he needed to push past them to determine the problem. Pictures floated by that held images of Juana and Rico, and even Dr. Duarte; these scenes undeniably placed Esteban Reyes as a patient in this hospital. In the background, the screams grew more erratic, as if something were being torn from Esteban. Then, other images surfaced, as if rising through fog, images known to elder beings. The fear rose within him, crept through the thoughts of the man Dr. Duarte had called, the one in contact with Esteban's inner psyche. He felt the vacuum of thought, the helplessness that Esteban had hidden deep within his mind, even when he wanted that other presence to enter him. He saw the void of memory, all that *The Nebulous One* took. The familiarity of the disembodied presence made him jump back. He knew who she was now, and that empowered him. Confident for the first time when dealing with her victims, he spoke to Esteban in a soft, soothing voice.

"You are twofold safe, mind and body."

The man wanted to look further, but he felt another ethereal presence—something not human—in the room but didn't want to let on that he knew. This wasn't his fight. Backing out of Esteban's mind, he opened the door.

"Dr. Duarte, could you please send in my assistant?"

Dan Fairmont walked in. "What did you find, Dad?"

The man, known to Dr. Duarte as Dr. Andrés Paolo, whispered, "We're not alone," and looked toward the far corner. "I'm going to step out and talk with Dr. Duarte. I trust you will handle this."

Sword drawn, Dan spun around in time to see Phobos, his tail wrapped around Esteban. The god of fear showed his true form and leaned toward the young man's face and licked it, keeping his eyes on Dan.

"*My* meat."

Two fists gripped the hilt while the blade's tip was inches away from Phobos' head.

"Think again. Let him go."

One of Phobos' clawed arms swung down to swat Dan away, but Earthsteel met godflesh first. The arm made a dull thud upon hitting the floor. Phobos slapped back with the remaining arm, knocking Dan into the wall.

Dan smiled. "So, we're going to play *that* way. Good."

The serpentine tail, having released Esteban, pushed the catatonic man into the corner; Phobos was protecting his meal.

"You do not fear me, do you?"

Dan shook his head, smirking. "I know who you are."

Phobos undulated his body, slithering around the room. He brought his face closer to Dan, trying to force him to doubt himself just for a moment. The greatest weapon against fear, knowledge, could be weakened by doubt, and that would leave Dan vulnerable. The son of both a warrior race and an Olympeian god, Dan didn't have much doubt about what he could do or about his opponents. As lion jaws snapped close to his face, and venomous fangs from the serpents on Phobos' head hissed in his ear, Dan whirled around, dropped to one knee, and swung his blade upward. When he felt no resistance, he knew he had missed, but that wasn't possible. He never missed. For a god of his size, Phobos moved with the agility of a smaller serpent, and his armor didn't impede his slithering. Rising up on his tail, he loomed over Dan, but he didn't expect what happened next. Rolling across the floor, his arms still bound behind him, Esteban knocked into Phobos wildly, catching him unaware. Despite that his mind wasn't entirely with him, he instinctively knew this wasn't right and lashed out. The god of fear lunged his gaping mouth at the young man, intending to tear away hunks of flesh, but Dan knew what to do and brought *Thyroros* up toward Phobos' torso. This time, Earthsteel made contact. Without making a sound, the upper chest and head of fear lay on the floor, its serpentine hair ceasing to move. Wisps of Phobos then melted into the air, leaving only an unconscious Esteban on the floor.

Dan's father re-entered and sat the young man upright. Even though his pulse had resumed a normal beat, Esteban's mind still raced with thought and torment. With a mental gesture, Apollo brought him from his catatonia, but the result wasn't what he expected.

"Get them off me! Oh my God! No!" Esteban wailed, flailing around although limited by the straitjacket.

"What do you see?" Apollo asked.

"Snakes! There are so many of them! Help me!"

Dan walked over to his father. "Can't you do anything to help him?"

"I wish I knew what to do. When his mind was ravaged, part of his madness left, too, but I fear that it was

actually protecting him. His healing is beyond my means."
Esteban's shrieks became unintelligible, filled with fear.

"Then Phobos won, didn't he?"

"Dan, I would hate to say so, but I think he did...
somehow." Apollo crouched down by the young man. "I
can do one thing." Soon, Esteban's wailing ceased and his
breathing returned to normal. His eyes, however, became
fixed and glazed over.

"What did you do?"

"I put him back in a catatonic state. It will suppress his
mania. He will have to remain like this for the rest of his
life."

Dr. Paolo spoke one last time with Dr. Duarte before
he and Dan left. Eduardo locked the door to Esteban
Reyes' cell. Now, a different type of patient care would
begin.

Outside, in the courtyard of the hospital, Dan sat on a
marble bench overlooking the city.

"Phobos isn't gone, Dad. I could tell he was just toying
with me. Can he mess with Esteban anymore?"

"No. I put up some boundaries to prohibit further
tampering. Phobos and I will meet again in a different
place, though. Truth and fear always find a way to battle. I
didn't want Dr. Duarte to see me do anything that I could
as a god. He knows about the Task Force Division, which
is why I thought to ask you along."

"I figured. My team and I need to figure out a strategy
to deal with Nyx's daughter. I feel like we're always a few
steps behind her, dealing with the aftermath of her actions."

"I'd try to scry for you, but I'm afraid there's a bigger
problem for me."

Dan didn't quite know how to respond.

"She's immune to prophecy. I can use my scrying pool
to see glimpses of the future, but with her, I just see darkness. Maybe because she's part primordial, part god... no
idea."

"Then, we'll have to try to outthink her."

"I do know one thing that will help you," Apollo said. "When I was inside Esteban's mind, I found out *The Nebulous One's* true name."

Dan turned. His eyes hungered for that knowledge.

"Lismonia."

"That's Olympeian Greek for *Oblivion*." Dan understood the true meaning of that word. "I need to get back to my team."

Apollo nodded, dissolving into mist.

15—PAST IMPERFECT

Brandon found the spot where Apollo was waiting at the ancient site of Delphi. When interacting with mortals, Apollo found it best to appear like Paul Fairmont, although, at this point, the difference between the two was marginal at best. The son of Zeus had given up on the grandeur and gold and much preferred the Oxford shirt and jeans—the mundane suited him more and more, although he wasn't giving up the Olympeian side of his life. Where a golden garland of laurel leaves once adorned his head, now a pair of Ray-Bans did, and the latter was much more practical. On his left wrist was a manacle, much like the one Dan had, and its etchings also spoke of allegiance to Olympeia and Gaea. Most mortals who saw it just assumed it was trendy; he had long since abandoned the glamour. He leaned against a ragged pillar, staring off toward the horizon where his chariot would descend soon. He missed those days.

"You asked to see me." His eyes embraced the sunbeams. "I'm intrigued why you picked this place of all places to meet."

"It's supposed to be where truth is paramount, as you once told us," Brandon replied, stopping a few feet away.

"I thought it fitting that we talk here."

Apollo turned to face him and saw the frustration he radiated. He nodded, but couldn't look Brandon in the face.

Brandon moved to where he could look the man, his father, in the face. "Why did you abandon me? Once I found out who you were to me, who Alkinoë was to me, and then Dan, it left a lot of questions."

Apollo sighed. "I know. But, if I tell you everything, you have to be willing to understand everything. There is so much to this, Brandon, and I don't know if you can handle it all. But, I will tell you what I can, and we'll go from there."

"Fair enough."

"When you, Alkinoë, and I came here, to the mortal realm, I knew that a great evil was hunting the gods, but I thought if we left the *Ge Theôn*, I could protect you both. I was wrong. As a god of prophecy, my dreams told me of this... thing... this monstrous evil, and it even frightened Gaea and Olympeia. For a primordial being to be afraid, well, that doesn't happen. In thousands of years of living, I have never known Gaea to fear anything, even when Ouranos had imprisoned their children in Tartaros. She might not have acted, but she wasn't afraid. Knowing nothing about when this evil might attack or who, I took you and your mother and made a life in Boston as close to a mortal family as we could. I had spent time here for a year, on my own, to see what mortality felt like. I had made connections during that time, so taking you both here was the natural thing to do. As an Olympeian, I retained my immortality, but since you and your mother were not Olympeian, you lost your immortality. I knew then that I had to do everything in my power, and I have quite a bit of that, to protect you."

"Why were you so concerned for me? Why not Alkinoë, or yourself? What was so special about me?"

Apollo smiled a little. "You were—are—my son. The first one I had ever claimed. I had many, many children from many, many women and goddesses, but when I married your mother, I forsook all the others and vowed to be loyal to her."

"And to me?"

"Yes. And to you." He turned away. "Your mother is an Arkadeian warrior, a woman who had seen more combat than almost all of the heroes of the past combined. Athene trained her, Ares tested her, and being the queen of Arkadeia showed her at her best—diplomat, warrior, negotiator. If anyone could hold her own, mortal or not, against what was coming, I knew your mother would. Or, she would die trying."

"You're not telling me something. What are you leaving out?" Brandon rarely ever raised his voice.

"Whatever was coming wanted the gods, or those descended from the gods. Back then, Zeus knew little about this threat, so he didn't fear for his safety. His arrogance prevented the gods from doing anything, so they lived in constant fear. Yes, in fear. It wasn't until recently when Lismonia found a path to Olympos that the gods needed sanctuary in the *Ptinotrofeio*. When we came here, I thought I could handle what might come. We had left the ancient era of Olympeian magic and jumped through time to thirty years ago in this mortal realm. I hoped that might keep us safe. But, you, Brandon, were a two-year-old child with no means to protect yourself!"

Brandon had never heard Apollo raise his voice, not once. He wondered what an angry god would sound like, especially when facing him alone and stepped back.

"I'm not proud of what I did, to you... to your mother. I bear my shame every single day, and knowing that I will live a very long time, means that I will carry this burden forever."

Now Brandon was confused. Something about Apollo's comment ran deeper than just putting his son out of harm's way. Apollo saw his son's expression, and he knew it was time.

"I need to tell you the whole story. May Gaea forgive

me, gods... may Alkinoë forgive me." He took a deep breath and sat on a bench near the tourist path to the shrine of Apollo. Events of years before played back in his mind, and he could no longer hold back the tears of guilt.

"What whole story?" Brandon sat beside him.

"I feared for your life, Brandon. Although, back then, you were Kidemonas. Do you know what that name means? I'd imagine you don't. It means 'guardian'. As crown prince of Arkadeia, you were so named because you would have taken over the responsibilities of ruling the country when your mother and I would step down. You used to play with wooden swords, even at two years old. We knew you would grow up to be *our* guardian.

"The day you and your mother went to the Stop-N-Shop, I told her I was going to New York to meet with the United Nations Security Council. In my role as liaison between the Greco-Italian Alliance and the American Conglomerate, I had helped bring out the Task Force Division on my first trip to the mortal world back in the early 1960s. My title was Ambassador Principal. Your mother had grown accustomed to shopping at markets, after she learned how to use the currency, and she also enjoyed meeting with others from our neighborhood, including other parents and their children. If I had told her what I intended to do, she would never have let me do it, especially since I hadn't told her how extremely dangerous the situation was. I was there in the store."

Apollo had to stop himself for a moment. This memory was a curse to him every day of his existence, but he needed to tell his son the story.

"Your mother turned away, and I took the opportunity to take you from the cart. No one knew. After I had you in my arms, I materialized around the corner from an adoption agency in Newton. I had one more task to perform, and this one tore away a piece of my soul. To protect you from that hell spawn coming, one who I now know was focused on the offspring of Zeus, I had to... I... I had to remove your connection to your mother and to me.

There could be nothing in you that remotely would reveal your lineage. I had a vial of water from the river Lethe, in the underworld, the river souls drank from to forget their past lives before being put into new human lives. I knew just enough water would remove whatever memories you had, but not enough to hurt you. It was then I went to the adoption agency, in another mortal guise, and put you up for adoption. To the lawyer I spoke with, I appeared to be a younger father. They asked no questions, and then I left. I transported myself to New York where I was told I needed to call my wife... that it was an emergency."

Brandon had no words; he barely had thoughts. He did have tears, however, that had started somewhere in the middle of the story. Apollo broke into sobs.

"I'm so sorry I had to do that. That memory has tortured me."

For a few moments, Brandon began to understand. The idea that his father tried to protect him from something he couldn't have fought seemed to placate him. It made sense, and the tears stopped. He reached out to embrace Apollo, but then something else rose to the surface.

"What about Dan?"

"What do you mean?"

"You protected me, and I understand that, but when Dan was born, why didn't you do the same thing?"

"I didn't know your mother was pregnant when we left Arkadeia, so when she was showing, and I had seen what your absence had done to her, I couldn't do it to her again. I couldn't rip out her heart a second time. So, I made a silent vow that I would just do everything, everything I could to protect him."

That answer didn't make Brandon feel any better. "So... you kept him all the while knowing your other son was somewhere out there with another family. If you were going to protect Dan, why not just do some godly magic and bring me home?"

"At that point, you had been adopted by the Jeffries. I used my power to peek in on you from time to time, to make sure you were okay. Your adoptive parents treated you so well. They loved you. I couldn't shred their hearts, either."

"So, you left me with them! You had Dan and left me with strangers. Sounds so easy. One son leaves and another enters. You don't lose."

Words spoken in anger, but Apollo knew that it was true at some level, but he wouldn't let Brandon get away with saying it was so easy to lose one son. The winds picked up and clouds rolled in, thunder echoing in the skies. Zeus wasn't the only one who could control the weather. Darker and blacker the sky grew, and Apollo gripped the handle of the bench to where it melted in his grip.

"How dare you! How dare you minimize my love for you! You have no idea what I've lost." He stood and even seemed to grow a bit taller to Brandon, who leaned back against the bench. "There's more to this story, so you need to listen carefully before you pass judgment on me. During that other timeline, the one that no longer exists, my son was named Demetrios. One consequence of the destruction of the Scales was that two souls began to emerge within one person, and that could not be. The gods were unaffected, but anyone who was not fully divine was in danger of losing his or her soul, both actually. With Gaea's help, we created an exact duplicate of Earth in another dimension where the godly Olympos didn't exist, and all the second souls were sent there to live out their lives, not being the wiser. I needed to escort Alkinoë and my son's soul to this *Oikoumene Broteios*, the land of mortals, and my wife lost her immortality. Demetrios' soul, however, had a different path. He was reborn through Alkinoë, as a mortal mother, making him mortal. It was part of a prophecy, and that's another story for a later time.

"So, I had one son, the crown prince of Arkadeia, living out his life ruling that nation, while my son Danelos lived out a mortal existence. To fulfill this prophecy, Danelos was sent, with Morpheos' help, to Arkadeia in the *Ge*

Theôn, the past where the gods still ruled, where he ultimately had to kill Demetrios and reclaim the other half of his soul."

"What? Danelos killed your son? I don't understand."

"No, Danelos killed his other self. Remember, two souls for one person. Each man had lived out his life separately, in a different time. I arranged for Danelos to kill Demetrios without him knowing he was going to do it, although I think he knew, and then Danelos claimed the other half of his soul that included all of Demetrios' memories and experience. When Danelos returned to the modern world, he was immortal and whole."

"I'm not sure I understand where this is going. You still had your son."

"Brandon, I had *Danelos* in my life. But, the son I had reared from birth, the one who Zeus tried to take away from me, the one who ventured to Tartaros to retrieve Ares so he could provide balance on Olympos... that son was gone. Even though Danelos remembered those things, he was not Demetrios, if that makes sense. They were in fact two distinct people leading two distinct lives. Try to understand that it was painful for me in that timeline, and as I am the only one who remembers it, my dreams torture me that I lost my son, even though that person never existed to anyone else. Those two decades of Demetrios' life will haunt me for as long as I live."

"Alkinoë doesn't remember?"

"No — only I do. I don't expect you to understand. But, now you know the truth. Do with it as you see fit."

Brandon felt how difficult that must have been for his father to share, and even though he didn't fully realize the depth of Apollo's emotions, he would forgive him. Apollo walked toward the ruins of Delphi, his hands in his pockets.

"I can only hope that the truth will provide you the comfort you seek, Brandon."

The young man sat for a while, putting these pieces together in his mind. He had enough trouble balancing one calendar; he couldn't imagine trying to remember two, or the challenge that must be, even for a god. Looking back in his life, the Jeffries had been wonderful parents to him. He had wanted for nothing, and they gave him unconditional love. Max Jeffries wasn't always around, since his job had him traveling, but when he was there, his wife Evelyn and Brandon were the only people that mattered. If Brandon had suffered at the hands of neglectful parents or had lived with tremendous hardships, he could hate Apollo for what he did. But, in reality, his life was good, and now he had his brother back.

"I have questions. And, I'm still angry."

Apollo turned around. "I know. We can handle that in due time." The skies cleared, and the evening returned to its star-speckled normalcy. "Before we head back, let me show you around. You won't get a better tour guide."

This would be an opportunity for the two to have time together without Brandon's teammates or his brother, and although it wouldn't replace the years they had lost, it would start the road of healing, and this was one set of wounds Apollo couldn't fix by means of Olympeian magic. Only time would do that.

16—BETWEEN WORLDS

Alkinoë thrust her arm under Apollo's throat, her knee pushing into his abdomen as she slammed him into the wall; drywall cracked behind him. She had lived in the mortal world for thirty years, but she hadn't entirely forgotten what it was like to be the warrior queen of Arkadeia and leader of the Royal Army, to be a finely honed weapon. And now, Apollo was reminded of that as well.

"You kidnapped… our son?"

Under any other circumstances, Apollo would have flung his adversary across the room with a mental gesture, but at this moment, with his wife's eyes stabbing his soul, he turned his head in shame. Nothing he could say would be a balm to her wound.

"Do you know…" Tears caught in her throat. "Do you remember how many heart-wrenching nights I wept myself to sleep, wondering if my son had been mistreated or lay dead somewhere?"

Apollo knew she couldn't hurt him physically, but he did feel the pressure she applied to his neck and abdomen. Had he still been mortal, he would have broken ribs and a collapsed trachea. He knew this moment would come, preferring any other punishment the gods could give him.

"I don't even know what to say to you," she said to her husband, every word a dagger.

Apollo opened his mouth to respond, but she cut him off.

"Say nothing. I know you did this to protect our son, deep in my heart. But, you did not seek my counsel in this, and that deception sits on that same heart like a stone."

She stepped back, turning toward Brandon; cupping his chin, she missed his cheek.

"Your father is lucky, Kidemonas. His torment will be short-lived compared to the agony of my soul."

Alkinoë looked at that moment like the fervent ruler of the Arkadeian nation, standing tall, shouldering her burden better than Atlas ever did his. Embracing Dan, she said,

"You have your brother now. Take care of each other, Danelos. For the love of Gaea, protect each other."

"I will." He squeezed her.

She stopped at the doorway of her townhouse with her hand on the knob. From the back, they saw her black hair hanging to the middle of her back, reminiscent of the warrior helmet she wore in battle, a barrier between the raw emotions pulsing through her and the others in the room. Her chest heaved as she contained her tears within, but her sons knew her pain.

"Apollo, I need time. Don't look for me."

The click of the door as it closed behind her triggered the sun god's tears. In his mind, this felt like when Ares had taken her from him, in that other time, so long ago. Apollo could bear much, but losing his Alkinoë had no equal.

Finding out the truth of what happened to his brother, Danelos left his apartment unsure of what to think about his father. He knew Apollo had done what was necessary to save Brandon, but he didn't think he would feel such unsettling emotions. He wandered Boston for hours, which wasn't easy to do when the police checked identification every few blocks; he just kept his card handy, flashing it as he passed the inquiring officers. Seeing a man in a full-length leather coat tended to arouse suspicions, especially when he was wandering around in the middle of the night. His mind was elsewhere, however, so he didn't realize when he ended up by the Charles River. Across the water were hotels and businesses, their checkerboard lights glowing like larger than life stars in the darkness. A slight breeze cooled the air, but Dan didn't really notice. Shimmering on the surface of the river, the waning moon cast a pale haze, and the distant stars that he could see seemed so inconsequential. Apollo had been a good father to him, even though he wasn't always around to be with his son and wife. The only Olympeian god to exist in the mortal world, he had taken a great liking for the simple and mundane, and that type of solitude had been a comfort to him when he thought about his past life as a younger god, when his actions and their consequences seemed as trivial as the pin-pricks of starlight did in the heavy blueness of the heavens. Dan thought about how much Brandon had never learned, how much he had never understood about the willing sacrifices Apollo had made for his family. He could have chosen to live an immortal life on Olympos, but that wasn't his destiny. His earlier taste of a mortal life, a choice the gods never understood, had made his decision so easy when he left Arkadeia to sojourn through time and space to this place, this *Oikoumene Broteios*. Living a mortal life never bothered Dan, even knowing his brother had been immortal in another place. The labyrinth of his thoughts kept him from hearing footsteps until they were only a few feet away.

"Why did you leave?" Brandon asked, sitting beside Dan. Only his hooded sweatshirt guarded him from the chilly air, and he had his hands in his pockets.

Dan replied, keeping his eyes on the river. "I could ask you the same question."

"We were friends long before we knew we were family. Apollo can fend for himself."

"And our mother?" Dan said.

"As Apollo often reminds me, she's a tough woman. Either she'll go back to him, and they'll talk it out, or… Whatever. They'll figure it out. You're more important."

"Thanks. I thought you told me that after you and he met at Delphi, you understood what happened and why."

Brandon sighed. "That was before I knew he hadn't told Alkinoë. He let her think someone else kidnapped me. He let her think I was gone forever."

Dan put his arm around his brother's shoulders, giving him a gentle squeeze. "You always told me you thought he wasn't being honest with you, and you were right. The question is, now what do we do?"

"What do you mean 'we'? He didn't put *you* up for adoption. You and he and Alkinoë got to live a happy little life together."

At first, the words stung, but Dan knew that Brandon was upset. They both knew Apollo had his own personal agony to go through, but now Alkinoë had to relive that horrible day in her mind knowing that her son wasn't gone forever, and that her husband had stolen him away. Both Brandon and Dan wondered if she would ever trust him again.

It'd be nice if we could go to Arkadeia and see just what kind of person Apollo was, you know? Brandon said. "Too bad we don't have a time machine. We might even find ancient knowledge to stop *The Nebulous One*."

Both sat, looking out at the Charles River, the silence providing a cocoon from their recent wounds. Dan replied, "I've actually been there a few times."

"What? How?"

"I was experimenting with my sword… I still don't entirely understand its power. I had never been to that ancient Arkadeia, but I tried to imagine what it would have looked like. My father… our father… talked about quite a bit when I was a kid, and I had a pretty good picture of what I might see if I were to go. Sarah once told me that the mind constructs better realities than we think. One night, during a waxing gibbous moon—I think that's what Sarah called it—I was concentrating on the gemstone in my sword. Not the one that opens the portals, but the Eye of Gaea. Another power I don't entirely comprehend. Well, anyway, I thought about Arkadeia, the one we had seen when we encountered the Erinyes, but when the portal opened, I saw the original place. I didn't stay long, but I did find out a few things. I'll have to tell you sometime." Some things would have to wait for a while, however, things that Brandon wouldn't understand. It was better not to think about them.

The mirror of the Charles reflected the moonlight, and Brandon became uncharacteristically quiet.

"I don't remember it at all," he whispered. "And I lived there."

Dan looked over at his brother with raised eyebrows and a certain look he gave when he didn't even have to ask a question or say anything; Brandon just knew.

"No, I won't ask him to help."

"Why not? He may actually be able to help us."

"Right now, I'm not inclined to care what he can or can't do."

"Then, I'll ask him," replied Dan. He crossed his arms and sat back.

"You're infuriating sometimes."

"I know. Look, I don't know if you could even travel with me since it's a time thing. Portals are funny like that. There's no harm in asking."

His brother's eye bore through him, but he knew Brandon would relent. His curiosity would get the best of him, and he'd want to see his ancestral home just as much. Two police officers patrolling the park approached and asked for identification and a reason why the two were there so late. Boston hadn't instituted a curfew like other cities, but the police frowned upon late night carousing. Dan told them he had burned a late night snack in their apartment, and they were letting it air out. Strangely enough, that appeased the officers. The cocoon of silence returned for a bit, and Dan sat there smirking to himself.

"If we *did* ask him for help," Brandon started, "I want to be the one to ask."

An hour later, after Dan grilled his brother about life with the Jeffries, they returned to their apartment to find Alkinoë hadn't returned, but Apollo lingered on the balcony overlooking the river. Brandon begrudgingly asked the sun god how to allow him to travel with Dan through a time portal, not a spatial portal. If Apollo suspected why, he didn't let on.

"You each have the key," he answered, lost in his own thoughts, and then shimmered away into the night.

Four a.m. skulked up on them: Dan lying back on the couch, one arm behind his head, the other flipping *Thyroros* back and forth. Having wielded this blade in battle dozens of times, he knew every inch of the Earthsteel weapon. Eyes whose color mirrored the metal followed the contours of the blade, reading the Olympeian Greek inscription etched into it over and over again: *He who bears Thyroros holds the key to Boundless Vision.* The key to boundless vision. That was the sword's power. If he wanted to return to Arkadeia by himself, he probably could when he was asleep, but that wouldn't help his brother. Across the room, Brandon had positioned himself on his head, against the wall, meditating. His arms supported his muscular frame, and he regulated his breathing and pulse — this was his favorite pose when he was musing. In the right frame of mind, he could remain like this for hours.

"Brandon, where's your amulet?" Dan asked, sitting up. He placed the sword on the table gently, the inscription facing up. On the other side of the blade Gaea had etched other glyphs and symbols tying the magic to the sword itself.

"Hanging on the wall. Why?"

"Isn't there an inscription on it?"

"Yeah. Zodiac symbols. Why?"

"That's it?"

Brandon lifted one hand from its handstand and reached for the amulet. Unlike Dan's sword, the amulet responded to its owner's call. One-handed, he looked all around the disk, seeing something for the first time engraved around the edge. "Here, Dan. Catch. There's something in Greek."

"He who bears the Kyklosdodeka holds the key to the Zodiac."

"So, this amulet actually has a name. Who knew?" replied Brandon. "I think even I can translate that. Circle of Twelve, right?"

"I just thought of something. Your name, the original one."

They shared a look before Brandon spoke. "The irony's not lost on me. I am the Guardian of the Circle of Twelve. Makes you wonder if Alkinoë and Apollo knew that when I was named."

With both weapons on the coffee table, now the trick became how to use these keys they had discovered. Back and forth they looked, but the meaning wasn't jumping up at them. Four thirty a.m. came, and they both decided it would be best to sleep on this and tackle it in the morning. Quinn hadn't given them mission specs for anything, so it was possible that they might actually get a full night's sleep for a change. Dan was thankful that, for this night, Ari had other plans. If there was one thing he didn't want to do was get his boyfriend involved, especially since Ari came from Arkadeia. Sleep came quickly to both brothers, and soon the apartment returned to silence.

Three nights later, Dan was up late on the phone with Ari and noticed a waxing gibbous moon in the sky.

"Let's go," Dan shouted, waking Brandon.

"Dude, a little warning next time," Brandon yawned. He grabbed his amulet off the nightstand and met Dan in the living room. The portal was already open.

Neither brother had really given much thought to what he was wearing when he stepped through into the past. Brandon's Led Zeppelin T-shirt and sweat pants would get some looks, but Dan was only wearing running shorts.

"Where are we?"

Dan said, "You can't tell me?"

Brandon shook his head.

"The Grove of Persephone. Don't worry. It'll all come back."

"I guess the Eye of Ouranos let me come with you. Where do we go now?"

"I need to go to Apollo's shrine. We'll pass the Temple of Hades soon, and then we'll be in the city. You just wander around and get your bearings. I'll find you later."

A waxing gibbous moon, just like the one in Boston, hung in the sky, and Dan figured it was maybe a week or two since he visited last. This temporal incongruity really threw him off, but traveling between eras was unreliable. Dan had no idea what he would say if people saw them, especially since he had a scabbard over his shoulder, a pair of running shorts, and nothing else. Both men couldn't see more than a few feet in front of them, and the dense pine forest muffled sounds from the distant city. Off to the right, the faint torchlight from the Temple of Hades showed through the branches. Dan suggested that Brandon check out the shrine while he go into the city, even though his modern clothing might arouse suspicions from the caretaker. Gray light from the sky gave the black marble an eerie cast. The temple offered those who mourned a place for solace and comfort as well as a chance to offer up tribute to the god of the underworld. The door to the cella, or main chamber, was ajar, and the cloying smell of incense poured out, adding an odd perfume to the stale air. Brandon poked his head inside, but no one stirred. He expected to see the caretaker performing his ritualistic duties, but all that moved were shadows. Ari had told both him and Dan that his father kept the shrine clean and catered to the mourners by offering prayers on their behalf to Hades, known most commonly as *The Unseen One*. Using the torch he found at the entry, Brandon made his way through the empty chamber, a stark coldness pushing against him, a temperature drop that felt like winter. A faint moaning came from the corner, but not the type one would hear from the bereaved; this was a muffled cry of pain. It was then he looked up.

Keeping to the shadows along the dirt road into Tegea, Dan stayed behind every tree he could find until he reached the gate. He would arouse too much suspicion the way he was dressed, even though some no doubt would remember him from his prior visits. It was best that he not have too many people aware of him. The sword could place him in a few spots within the walls, but not only did he not have enough light from the moon, but he also couldn't be sure that he wouldn't end up where people could see him. If he could get close enough to the wall, he could climb over it, but the goddess Athene had trained these guards who would hear him approach. Most of the city was asleep, with only a handful of citizens out walking around, so he couldn't blend into any crowd, either. His only choice was follow the walls until he saw a place less fortified, but when he moved behind the next tree to cover his movement, he felt a cold blade on the back of his neck.

"Put your hands in the air and turn around," said a gruff man's voice. "Make no sudden moves."

He wouldn't hurt a kinsman, even though this man's voice was unfamiliar and wouldn't know him. In another place and time, he might have ruled Arkadeia, so it was in his best interest to keep his identity hidden for as long as possible. He laced his hands on top of his head and walked in front of the sentry toward the gate. As they approached the city, the soldier noticed Dan's attire.

"Surely you would not attempt a siege on Arkadeia's capital without armor. Who are you?"

He had three choices: he could run for it and hide somewhere in the city, he could admit who he was and who his father was and hope the man would believe him, or he could just give him his name and see what happened next. Before he could respond, he heard another man's voice.

"What have we here, sergeant? Another thief?" That voice sounded familiar to Dan, but he couldn't place it. Unless he could assure himself safety, he wasn't going to risk anything.

"He was skulking about just outside the gates, captain. I am not sure what to make of his garb, though. And, he came armed."

The captain, a man in his thirties, bore the sun and earth insignia on his breastplate. He held his helmet at his side, but his other hand rested on his sword's pommel. Dan had indeed met this man before, but he didn't know if the captain would remember. The captain lifted Dan's sword a few inches out of the scabbard to check for any markings, and he withdrew the entire blade when he recognized it.

"Sergeant, I shall take care of this intruder. Return to your post."

With a quick salute, the lower ranking officer left. Dan was about to fabricate an explanation of who he was when the captain interrupted.

"We have met before," he said, looking into Dan's eyes. "You carried this sword last time as well, and either you are of the Royal House, a royal emissary, or…"

"Take a good look at my face. What do you think?"

Five masses adhered to the ceiling with skin that, depending on the shadowy light from the torch, resembled dark blue or black silk. Brandon could see movement, too — probably shallow breathing. The shape furthest from him fell to the marble floor like a drop of oil, and it was then that he could tell he might be in trouble. No humans he knew stood seven feet tall with eyes that glowed like fiery embers. What bothered Brandon most was they made no sound when they touched the floor. At once, the rest descended. He saw each had two large limbs that ended with a black spur, probably meant to hold down or shred their prey. Five against one seemed like better odds if he had armor, and he wouldn't find any in the temple, that was certain. They gradually moved in on his location, leaving slug-like trails of mucus, but he knew they had to move faster than that. His best guess was that they found their way through a passage to Hades beneath the temple — hence the icy air — something he didn't want to fathom further.

From where he stood up to the ceiling was about twenty feet, he figured, and leaped up with all the might Taurus would give him, using Cancer's power to grip into the marble itself. Dangling from above by one hand with the torch in the other gave him a slightly better view, but even if he managed to leave the temple, these creatures might follow, and he couldn't imagine the damage they would do in the city. Plus, he had to investigate the moaning he had heard earlier. The five blue-black entities glided under him. *If they got up here once, they can do it again*, he thought, and dropped the torch in the middle of them. As he thought, they shunned the flames, giving him a few moments to drop down, reclaim the torch, and once again leap into the air, managing a somersault before he landed by the one he had heard groaning. Torchlight revealed the reason.

The captain could size up someone during battle based on his word choice, dialect, or even stance; a man entrusted with the capital city's security had to know how to deal with potential threats in just a few breaths. Dan's Greek did sound different than an Arkadeian's would, but his confidence showed he was either willing to take a risk or he was a fool. Kleisthenes discovered something else in Dan's eyes, something that put him at ease, and that made him uncomfortable because he was rarely at ease. He had to wonder why his king, who had left not long ago with his wife and son, would give this man the royal sword. The captain of the Royal Army saw something in this scantily clad man's bearing of the king he admired more than any one. He didn't know how Dan was related to Lord Apollo, since Dan had dark hair and a heartier build, but the more he looked, the more Kleisthenes wanted to trust this complete stranger.

"I think I need to trust you." The captain returned *Thyroros*. "How did you come by the royal sword?"

"It belongs to me. Do you know Lord Apollo well?"

Kleisthenes sensed a test. "Yes. I serve as Arkadeia's guardian in his and the queen's absence. I thought he had left the sword in the armory. It appears I am mistaken."

"Then, he trusts you completely. And, yes, you are."

Dan stepped to the side of the road by the gate, outside of earshot of other guards, gesturing for Kleisthenes to join him. He noticed that the soldier's hand never left the pommel of his own sword.

"I need to trust you as well. What I have to tell you may seem unreal, but since you're a man Apollo trusts..." He held up his left wrist. "Do you recognize this?"

How he hadn't noticed it earlier, Kleisthenes couldn't say, but he had only seen that manacle on the wrist of his king. Unlike people of Dan's time, the captain could read a little Olympeian Greek, enough to know that this man had pledged his life to Olympos. Finding out that he was also the son of Apollo didn't surprise him. Learning where and when Dan had come, however, seemed a bit more of a challenge.

"I live in the year 2009, some 3200 years from now, in another country far beyond Greece. I can't explain everything right now, but when Apollo took his wife and child, he knew time passed differently here than in the mortal world. He once told me that time in mortal perception raged like a flooded river while here it trickled like a glacial stream. When he crossed the threshold, what was the age of powerful gods, the *Ilikía Olympios,* became the age of mortals, *Epoki Thnetou,* an age that's shamed most of us who consider ourselves mortal. Anyway, Alkinoë was pregnant when she left Arkadeia, and a few months later, I was born. My father gave me *Thyroros* when I reached the age to pledge my loyalty to Gaea and Olympeia, and I have been its custodian ever since. I'm here with my brother now looking for scrolls in my father's temple that could potentially help me in my time."

Kleisthenes, having grown up in the world of immortals, susceptible to their whims and fancies, blessings and curses, understood enough to know Dan spoke the truth. Apollo had moved within realms many times over the years, and he had disappeared once for a great period where his queen never left the palace except to venture to Gaea's shrine to pray for his safe return. Perhaps time would allow Dan the chance to explain himself further, but his quest sounded vital. If nothing else, having the Sword of Gaea helped Dan's cause as well. He bowed his head.

"I serve the Royal House, Your Majesty," Kleisthenes replied, handing Dan his cloak. "This will serve you better when you walk around the city. Wait… your brother? Do you mean to say—"

"Thank you, Captain."

Dan promised to return before he left the city, saluted the captain, and went off to the Temple of Apollo, hoping he would find something he and his friends could use.

In the corner was a man, probably in his fifties, lying in a pool of his own blood. Even though his robes were black, Brandon could see they were soaked through. Swinging around, he extended his torch arm, keeping the dark ones at bay for the moment, but he realized that wouldn't last long. Their slow approach scared him more than their razor sharp barbs.

"Can you get up? We need to leave," he said, but the man didn't move.

Without any light but the torch, he couldn't even tell what was nearby to use as a weapon. Even with the zodiac, he didn't know if he could take this man from the temple safely. An empty iron brazier stood against the wall behind which hung a tapestry depicting some ancient symbols and designs. Aside from that and the food offerings by the altar, the austere surroundings didn't inspire him with much hope. He needed something to give him some time. The man reached up to him, his arm shaking, but Brandon knew as soon as he made himself vulnerable the monstrosities would take advantage of that. He ripped the tapestry from the wall, wrapped it into a ball, threw it in the brazier, and lit it. A pillar of fire rose for a few seconds, casting enough light to give him a brief pocket of time. He grabbed the man by the arm, lifted him over his shoulders, and used his torch to repel those things that would relish ravaging him. After only a few steps, the brazier light dimmed, however, and darkness pushed closer once more.

"Any idea who or what these things are?" he asked, not expecting a reply.

The man whispered, "*Eurynomoi…*"

"That doesn't help me, but thanks." Brandon was stuck in the corner again.

"They eat corpses," the man coughed. "Just let them have me." For some reason, Brandon could understand this man, and he hoped he could communicate back.

"Not part of the plan, my friend. Hold on."

"Light from above will protect us. Light from above…"

"As you can see, we don't have any. Next idea?"

"*Asterismos…*"

Brandon assumed the man had lapsed into muttering

phrases from his loss of blood, so he placed him back on the floor behind him, resting the torch against the wall. The iron brazier extinguished, it could at least provide him with a suitable weapon. The strength of Taurus filled him as he threw it into the shadows where he knew the Eurynomoi to be.

"*Asterismos...asterismos...*"

"What does that mean?" Adrenaline coursed through Brandon, and he was losing patience. "Tell me what that means!"

Barely able to lift his head, the man looked up and gestured. "*Asterismos.*"

Somehow, Brandon had been able to understand some of what the man said, but this one word didn't register with him. He looked up, but saw nothing but the marble ceiling. Incoherent words and phrases came from the man, now in shock, and when he saw Brandon's amulet, he stared.

"*Asterismos.*"

"You mean this? Aha. *Asterismos* has something to do with the stars. But, light from above? We can't see stars in here."

He felt the presence of the Eurynomoi behind him. The man grabbed Brandon's amulet, flipped it around, and collapsed. Brandon had never noticed that the gems in the amulet went all the way through the Earthsteel disk. *Light from above* — of course.

By the time Dan reached Apollo's temple, only one priest kept the ceremonial hearth lit inside. Golden tapestries depicting stylized sun images and arrows adorned the walls, and the bronze braziers contained glowing embers. In the central chamber stood a marble likeness of his father, carved with verisimilitude to the god's body, albeit a younger one. Hours until sunrise, the temple had no supplicants, and this gave him the chance to see what a

temple to his father really looked like. Dan was an archaeologist by trade, so he had only seen the time worn ruins,
abraded by the winds. Unlike some depictions in history
books, ancient cultures did indeed paint their temples
with bright colors; rarely were they simply plain marble.
His bare feet touched holiness, since it was said that Apollo visited every temple consecrated to him. Dan had lived
a mortal life with no Olympeian dreams, so his accelerated
pulse truly reflected what an everyday man would feel in
the presence of immortality. He had a mission, though, so
that would require calling upon his knowledge of cultures
long gone. His mother used to tell him stories that the
gods hid what they didn't want mortals to see in plain
sight. Other than the polished altar that held baskets of
fruit and bread, the fiery hearth, and the statue, nothing
else took up space. Scrolls could be hidden anywhere, especially if they were flat, and Dan knew that priests of
prophecy never revealed to anyone where they hid scrolls
entrusted to them individually. No one priest knew the
whereabouts of all the prophecies.

Warmth from the fire coupled with the golden hues of
the fabrics and paint made him feel protected, as if the
color itself could shield him from harm. The only weapon
allowed in the temple was his sword; otherwise, soldiers
would have to leave their arms outside, entrusted to the
priests. Behind the cella, or main chamber, the adyton of
the temple sat, protected by enchantments only the priests,
or Apollo himself, knew. Not even Zeus could enter the
adyton of another god's shrine without knowing how. In
fact, Zeus could destroy the entire shrine with a barrage of
thunderbolts, and all that would remain would be the one
room, unscathed. Dan found the outline of the doorway
into the sacred room, no thicker than a piece of thread, and
traced it with his finger. *No*, he thought. *The prophecies
wouldn't be in there.* On the altar sat woven baskets atop
delicate silks and linens woven specifically for this purpose. As Dan's eyes floated around the marble platform,
he caught a glimpse of something that made him smile. He

had found some of the prophecies, and it was the flickering light from the hearth that had given them away.

It was simplicity itself, Brandon thought, removing his amulet. Holding it against the torch basket, he wrapped the chain around the torch itself, and then he saw it: firelight shone through the gems, casting a circle of colors, a prism of constellations. He heard movement from the darkness and held out the polychromatic lantern. The *Eurynomoi* had retreated to the corners where the light didn't go. Unlike regular torch fire or brazier fire, this light had been filtered through the gems, the central one specifically. Brandon lifted the man up with one arm, crouched down, and put him over his shoulder, blood trickling from the man's wound. The five blue-black creatures from the underworld didn't move at all, as if paralyzed, but Brandon kept his eyes on them until they were outside the temple. Plunging the torch into the dirt, he kept the circle of stars projected at the entrance to the Temple of Hades while he attended to the man whose breathing had become raspy.

"We're out. Who are you and what happened?"

Sitting against a poplar tree on the other side of the road, the man put his hand on Brandon's.

"Thank you." Every breath was a labor. "I am Timaios... the caretaker."

"Why did the *Eurynomoi* attack you?"

"I..." He coughed up some blood. "I summoned them."

"Why? So, you did want me to leave you there."

"My son vanished a few weeks ago. He was not in the city. No one had seen him. I could not live without him."

"Wait. Did the *Eurynomoi* hurt you at all?"

Timaios turned away, his left hand falling from his body, revealing a bloody dagger.

"You did this to yourself, didn't you? You wanted to

die so they would just devour your remains."

"I love my son. And he is gone." Tears dripped down Timaios' cheeks, clearing away soot and dust from the temple.

Brandon didn't know what to say. The anguish of losing a child and not knowing where he was had brought this man not only to commit suicide but also to desire nothing remained.

"If I can no longer give my heart to my son, then I no longer want it."

He coughed more blood. Brandon caught a glimpse of the torch; it still burned, although a little dimmer.

"Promise me that when I die, you will leave me to them."

"I can't let you do that. But, I will try to find your son. What's his name?"

Timaios' eyes fluttered a bit, and his body fell limp. "Aristeides."

Shadows and light hit the baskets at such an angle that the lining became translucent. Dan gently removed the contents and stretched out the parchment and examined the slightly frayed edge. One of the projects he had done while in graduate school was to examine old papyrus and parchment scrolls found in tombs. When kings or priests wanted to hide their contracts, maps, or — in this case — prophecies, they would hide one piece of parchment between two others. Even though some would do this to throw people off the trail for treasure, others took advantage of this technique, hiding the documents where people would least expect to find them. In this case, Dan found them sitting right on the altar. A quick scan of the text confirmed that this was indeed a prophecy.

A past life who lives among a mortal age
Shall be a key to Gaea's strength
To face One of night and sky,

Suckled on Hate and Memory
Who will cleave the Namesake
Of a Scythe-bearer from Thought and Time.
When the corners of the world
Come together as one,
Then shall She who rips existence apart
Be caged.

Too tired to play with the enigmatic language, Dan folded the parchment and tucked it into the elastic of his shorts. He would have more luck talking with his father about this when he returned. Surely other prophecies lay hidden in the temple as well, but they would probably say some version of what he just read. Cloaked, he descended into the agora, the quiet city market that would soon have throngs of citizens setting up their wares, but instead of heading back to find Brandon, he left word with the priest that should a man coming looking for him, he should check the steps to the palace. They wouldn't go back until Brandon could learn more about his father, and what better place than the city where he ruled. Sunrise would come in an hour or so, and he had some things to do.

Brandon had gone against the wishes of Timaios and carried the man's lifeless body to the city gates. The same sergeant who had stopped Dan earlier stepped onto the road before the city, but seeing no weapon on him, he had no reason to detain him.

"I need to find the Temple of Gaea. Can you please point me the way?"

The sergeant saw that Timaios was dead but didn't recognize him.

"Why would you bring him to Gaea's temple? Surely, the Temple of Hades would be a better place."

Brandon continued to walk toward the gate. "Not for him."

"Tell the caretaker you wish to honor your friend, and

he will see to it." The soldier blocked Brandon's path.

"This *is* the caretaker. Arrest me if I've done something wrong. Otherwise, tell me where the temple is." He looked into the city and saw the highest dome. "Never mind. I see it. I need to use your cloak."

Whether it was his imperious tone or his desire to honor the dead, Brandon was not followed, and he carried the sergeant's cloak with him.

At the base of the steps that lead to Gaea's temple sat a fountain, a place for supplicants to bathe their feet before climbing to the zenith of the city. Brandon had never prepared a body for burial, but he wanted Timaios to enter the shrine clean, physically anyway. As he entered, he smelled the sweet incense wash over him, and he carried the cloak-shrouded body to the altar. His first time in a temple, he had no knowledge of protocol, so he left the caretaker's body there and went to find Apollo's temple. At the very least, he could see what his father's shrine looked like before he located his brother. Walking through the streets, merchants had begun setting up for the day, and local farmers had already unloaded bushels of fresh fruits, vegetables, and flowers. Tegea wasn't what Brandon expected, although he really wasn't sure what to expect. From history books and movies he had seen taking place in ancient Greece, he had always thought life was more challenging. He did find, though, that streets had no litter like they did in Boston. Even with cameras on street corners and a military presence, people had enough hubris to throw trash anywhere they wanted. That just proved to Brandon that the government had bigger issues to deal with, and it couldn't bother with smaller issues unless those issues fed into larger ones.

A fisherman had fish wrapped in wet burlap, ready for his daily customers, and Brandon watched in amazement how much the man did by himself. One of the baskets looked as if it was going to fall off the wagon, so he reached out and caught it. In Boston, the fisherman would have used inappropriate language and gestures, but this man, a slight, hoary man in his sixties, smiled and nodded without fear.

"Seems you have a nice catch this morning. You must have been out for hours." Brandon leaned against the wagon. The elderly man noticed the T-shirt and lounge pants but said nothing.

"Aye, praise Poseidon, although this day's catch is less than it used to be." He arranged the fish by size order on the cart.

Not wanting to linger and make the man uneasy, Brandon just continued some casual conversation.

"Rumor has it that Arkadeia's ruling family has disappeared recently." He paused for a reaction. "It's hard for me to believe they truly cared about their people to just run off like that."

Less than five feet tall with barely enough strength to push his cart, the old fisherman stepped right up to Brandon, pointing a bony finger in his face.

"No one speaks ill of our king and queen as long as I can draw breath! I came here from Athens, and I can tell you that Pandion didn't do half as much for his people. Not a day passed when Alkinoë wasn't helping out in the provinces, or bringing her son, Kidemonas, to play with the children by Triton's Well. It can't have been easy for Apollo to give up his Olympeian throne and live among mortals, but he got his hands dirty. Why, he helped me dig a well a year ago. He said to me, 'Philemon, when your first catch comes in from the river, you let me know. My wife and I will bring the wine, and we shall come back and celebrate your bounty.' Not truly caring indeed. And, when I came back with a few sacks of fish, he showed up with our queen and their son."

Philemon muttered more, but Brandon gently thanked him for his hospitality and continued on through the market, more and more filled with locals. He would occasionally stop to speak with merchants, getting much the same response when he brought up his father. Only a few people seemed less than pleased by something Apollo did, but nothing Brandon heard sounded that terrible. Near the well, in the center of the agora, sat an old woman, her face marked with a virtual map of experience. Her chair placed her near a spinning wheel, but she wasn't using it. A basket of yarn sat at her feet, a tangled mess of wool with grasses mixed in; a few kittens had gotten a hold of a small ball and played. As he walked around the well, brief flashes of memory surfaced, and he saw a little boy running around with children his age, a small ball made of leather in his hand. Laughter got caught in his ears, but he came out of his reverie when one of the kittens had batted the ball of yarn near his feet. Scooping the kitten up in one hand, he nestled it against him, but it squirmed to be put down.

"She's a feisty one." The old woman rocked back and forth. "Best put her down and let her play before she scratches you."

Brandon put the tiny cat down by the basket so it could join its playmates. "I have a soft spot for animals, especially babies," he said, squatting down. He dangled a loose piece of yarn to get the kittens' attention.

"You're not from around here, are you?" Her hazel eyes danced over him. "I'd remember you."

He chuckled. "No, I'm not from here." He had a hard time lying to her, but she wouldn't understand.

"Those eyes of yours look familiar, though. Strong eyes."

Their conversation had no pattern of reason, mostly because time had addled her mind a bit. Topics changed as easily as the breeze that pushed through the valley, and then she got silent. He took in a deep breath, and the perfume of the rose bushes mixed with the dusky scent of the earth gave him a chill. The longer he stayed in this city, the more he remembered, each glimpse from the past more specific, more emotional. And then, she spoke once more, but she looked past him into a place only she could see.

"They left in the middle of the night... a dark, painful night. We hated to see them go, but we knew they had to leave us. We would be safe, he said. Our king always put us first. A gentle man, he pushed us to be better than we thought we could be. The love he had for his queen... oh, how he adored her. She empowered us... spoke to us with respect and love. And their son, young, brave Kidemonas, how they cherished him. He was their shining gift. Apollo brought him into the market a few times a week, usually midday, and the little prince would chase the kittens. The morning of the day they left, he sat right here and the little balls of fur scampered over him, one nestling in his lap. He had a gentle touch. A gentle touch."

The time had come to find his brother.

From the steps into the Temple of Gaea, one could see the entirety of Tegea — the busy agora, the gleaming palace, and even the farmlands just outside the main walls. With the sun rising, the snow-capped mountains at the pastel horizon looked like silver armor, a protection against the troubles of the world. Arkadeia had garnered a reputation as a land of peace, a peace hard won by bloody battles against hordes of armies sworn to the bloodlust of Ares, their warlords dedicated to erase Apollo's favored city from Gaea's verdant face. The sun god himself had worn battle-stained armor in the early days of this land's existence, and his queen fought by his side. He had brought Arkadeia into existence with Gaea long ago, when mankind had yet to explore all of the earth mother's land. Their offspring grew from the earth, trees of oak and birch, maple and poplar, as diverse as snowflakes. Each at his or her heart drew strength from the goddess, trained with Athene in strategy and skill. The sun's rays bathed them in immortality and courage, making them counterparts to the Amazons of the river Thermodon, the Spartans, and the Athenians — races born of the gods but tested in the crucibles of war and love. Apollo was the only Olympeian to serve as a king of an earthbound race, and his experiences with mortality had burnished his soul into one who could teach his people how to survive. In his absence, he knew they would prevail. Heirs to Apollo's throne, two brothers stood in this holy place, surveying what might have been theirs.

"This is our home." I'd only seen a little of the city in my nocturnal visits, but now..."

Brandon nodded. "Yeah. I've learned a lot in the past few hours. We have to talk about so much."

Dan put his hand on his brother's shoulder. "I know, and we will. I had left word at dad's temple for you to find me at the palace, but I wanted to come here. I was drawn here."

"She wanted us to see this together." He spoke of Gaea. "I heard her, too. You know, from every sci-fi movie I've seen, isn't it supposed to be a bad thing to go into our own past? Doesn't that mean we change the future?"

"All I have is a scroll to take with me that I don't think anyone would miss. You?"

"I did talk with some people in the market. Learned a lot about the city, the royal family... our family." Brandon then remembered when he arrived. "And something else. Have you been inside the temple?"

Dan shook his head. "Why?"

The shrouded body still lay where Brandon had left it a few hours earlier.

"Who is he?"

Just past midday, the market's friendly chaos having subsided, they found Kleisthenes at the guard station by the gate, and the captain bowed his head when Dan introduced his brother; both of Arkadeia's princes stood before him, one he had seen a few months prior as a toddler was now fully grown. With the austere composure of trained soldier, Kleisthenes absorbed the revelation quietly, torn inside that he wouldn't see his king or queen. A silver urn in Dan's hand brought him back to the current moment. Without much explanation, Brandon told the captain to explore the temple during the daylight hours and seal any breaches found. The five *Eurynomoi* he had fought earlier would have retreated to Hades with the sunrise, but they would return when they smelled the decay of corpses within the city gates, and no amount of martial training would defeat them. The urn contained the remains of Timaios, the caretaker, a sacred pyre having consumed the man's mortal remains. Kleisthenes didn't ask why they would take the ashes, but he knew if the princes of Arkadeia needed them, that was all he had to know. As they turned to leave, Brandon felt pinpricks at his heel; an orange and gray kitten had tried to climb his lounge pants. He nuzzled it before handing it off to Kleisthenes who promised to find it a home.

Walking away in silence, they reflected on the events of the visit to their ancestral home, a place they didn't know if they would ever see again. An inner voice told Dan he had found all he needed, and his brother had found what he never expected to find. He reclaimed his amulet as they passed the dark temple, Brandon lingering a moment before they entered the sacred grove.

17—ORIGINS

Ari and Dan had just shared a rare dinner together, and one story that Dan hadn't told was how Task Force: Gaea first came to be. After a swig of wine, he leaned back in his chair.

"Sometimes, Fate just plays with the right strings in the right ways. Four years ago, I was in Greece during my internship for an archaeological dig on the island of Naxos, something I'd worked hard to get, but I was on a probationary contract with the university. My job was to document anything that the archaeologists found, no matter how trivial. Trust me when I say, I didn't sleep much that entire semester. I'd like to say I spent all my time working, but being in Greece was always a distraction. As soon as a few of the interns and I had earned some leisure time, we grabbed a rucksack with a few days worth of clothes and supplies and decided to rough it around the island. With a limited budget, I could eat bread and cheese, and not much else. No matter how good Greek feta cheese and pita bread were, they're still bread and cheese. Anyway, I had just enough bus fare to get me to Naxos, a port city on the northwest part of the island.

"The Aegean has many mysteries, some that even archaeologists haven't even discovered yet, and a place I had to see was the Portara, all that's left of a temple to Apollo. It's just the stone doorway, actually, and it faces the island of Delphi, where Apollo and Artemis were born. Unused doorways end up getting used... somehow.

"Maybe forty or so tourists come out per day to see it, if that many. While everyone else seemed interested in taking pictures of it, and the ocean view, I was more intrigued by the stonework and the dirt surrounding it. It's only about 26 feet high, so once you've walked around it once or twice, you've pretty much seen it all. After taking notes and a few pictures when I sat down to admire it, I felt the ground tremble a little. A puff of smoke came from the opening in the arch, but I dismissed it as either someone's cigarette or maybe some dust. Again, the ground moved a bit more, and this time, a bigger puff of smoke came through. Then, the earth heaved underneath me, knocking the journal from my hands. Screams from other visitors made me look back toward the arch, thinking it was about to fall, but I jumped back at what I saw. Through the Portara came a green serpentine head on a long, scaly neck, its mouth open just enough to show off its fangs. Before I could do anything, it screeched, moved its head back and spewed forth fire at a group of American tourists. Four didn't make it. That's when all hell broke loose, literally.

"I reached behind my back and pulled out *Thyroros*, drawing the creature's attention. I noticed it didn't move through the opening, though, so I stepped to the side to get a better vantage point. That was when I learned quite quickly that serpentine necks were quite agile, and I leaped out of the way of a fiery blast, but I dropped the sword. Thankfully, the rest of the tourists had evacuated to the city via the causeway. Every time I tried to get the sword, flames stopped me. I couldn't seem to get close enough to the creature to do anything. I decided to go for broke and jumped toward the blade, but *drakon* breath almost took me out. I had remembered, though, to hold up my manacle, and that invisible shield it generated kept me from harm. I was tiring, and the creature took every advantage to strike at me, as if it knew. I miscalculated a bit, and the head rammed into me, sending me about twenty feet back. As I caught my breath, I heard a few whistling sounds above me and noticed that a cluster of arrows had landed on the underbelly of the serpent. Man, did that make it angry. But it was distracted enough that I could get my sword. I'm the son of a god, but I didn't expect to see a centaur leap into action, firing volley after volley of shafts. I saw an opportunity and lunged at the flailing head, severing it from its body.

"For my first centaur, I wasn't sure what to expect, but I noticed he was bare-chested with a large silver amulet around his neck. Unlike the mythological half-man, half-horse I had seen with long, dark hair on pottery or artist renderings, this guy had short blond hair, more of a military cut. He resumed his human form, fully clothed, too, and came over to check on me, and that was when I met Brandon, who had been taking classes in Athens but chose to sightsee in Naxos. We didn't quite know what to do about the serpent head or the neck that extended into nothingness within the portal. Neither one of us had any explanation for what happened, but we had a brief, yet awkward, conversation about centaurs and swords. A sound like ripping fabric echoed around us, and when we looked back toward the Portara, what had been one serpentine neck had become two, and each had a new head. Brandon and I then realized this was a hydra, but neither one of us had actually ever seen a real one. If what we both knew about how to kill it was true, we realized we had an even bigger problem.

"I didn't know at that point that Brandon could channel the zodiac signs, but I could see he could become a centaur and that he was almost as strong as I was, something I later learned came from a few different zodiac animals. We spent about twenty minutes dodging scorching discharges and leaping out of the way of fangs since we couldn't do much but prevent creature's heads from hurting anyone, including ourselves. I spotted a young woman running toward us, a redhead who wouldn't turn back. At first, I thought she was just a tourist in shock. While I was yelling at her to move, she put her hands out, pushing the air toward me, and it wasn't until I felt my back getting hotter that I realized she was pushing back the hydra's breath. Both Brandon and I leaped into the fray, hoping to buy some more time, but then the woman told me to get the hydra to breathe fire again. I told her that I didn't think that would be a problem. Brandon threw a boulder at one of the heads, and it shook it off as if he'd thrown water on it, spewing fire back at him. I thought he was done for, but the woman caught the fire, held onto it, and shouted to me to cut the heads off. I was way ahead of her.

"As the hydra's heads hit the ground, she pushed the fire at the severed stumps, cauterizing them closed. They wouldn't be able to split again. Two questions came to mind: if the hydra could push its head through the Portara, why didn't it just step on through? And what do we do with three hydra heads and the hydra's necks? Since the fire had gone out, the woman, named Sarah, couldn't bring it back. Apparently, she could only manipulate elements, not create them. Holding the sword in front of me, I waved at Brandon to come with me. He had no idea what I was doing, but we were able to walk through the opening, only to find ourselves in a cave in Hades standing next to the carcass of a dead hydra the size of a blue whale. My guess was that the portal had been weakened enough for it to smell a food source, so it must have been simply exploring its options. Between the both us, we dragged the hydra's body further into the cave, drawing the necks back with it. Passing back through the portal, we were blinded by a flash of light and peal of thunder. When my eyes adjusted, I saw a winged woman hovering over us, waving a silver staff in her hand. She had apparently summoned thunderbolts to obliterate the remains. It turned out that Aleta was a friend of Sarah's, and they were traveling the Mediterranean together. About fifteen minutes after everything was finished, the local police showed up to see what the fracas was about; the only evidence that remained was some scorch marks on the rocks and a few unlucky tourists who had been incinerated. We had forgotten, though, about the surveillance cameras everywhere that had caught everything we did, and local law enforcement brought us to a detention center for debriefing. We knew better than to resist, and the last thing I wanted was for anyone to be afraid of us. Before any Alliance officers could ask questions, a Task Force representative seemed to appear out of nowhere and took over the investigation, giving us one day to get our affairs in order before escorting us to New York. My father, who worked for the Greco-Italian Alliance, and apparently helped establish the Task Force Division of the UN, stepped in, telling us that, for our security, we should join the UN Task Forces or both the American Conglomerate and the Alliance would investigate every aspect of our lives, something my father had no control over. The TFD assigned us a liaison, trained us over the course of a few months, and then we met with my father as a team. He explained that, because of what the world now knew about our abilities, and us we might be called upon to handle the metaphysical threats to the planet, and since he and I had connections to Gaea, we should use our abilities to defend her. After a bit of a rough patch, since Brandon and Aleta were a hard sell, we settled on calling ourselves Task Force: Gaea."

Ari sipped his glass of Merlot, enrapt by the story, one that brought out an animated side of his boyfriend he hadn't seen. The more he learned about Dan, the more he realized just how much the *Moirae* wanted them together. Although he, too, was an Arkadeian, he didn't have anything to offer the team, although the thought of being a hero made the hair on his arms stand on end. Dan reached across the dining room table and took up Ari's hand.

"I can tell you wish you were part of something more, Ari. Trust me when I tell you, this isn't glamorous. You will find your own path, and it will be something you can embrace as your own."

"Even being…"

"Yes, even being stronger than most people, you're not a trained warrior. Your path isn't the same as mine. My fear is that you'll want to prove yourself, because I know you're a proud man, but you may just end up getting yourself hurt or killed. Now, if you want to spar with any of us to keep up your skills, I know the others would be happy to oblige. And maybe someday you will find a way to be a part of what we're doing."

Ari looked down at the table and squeezed Dan's hand. He knew Dan was right. Taking unnecessary risks wouldn't help anyone, and he had already lost his father. He finished his wine with a hard swallow. Dan had that look where he furrowed his eyebrows and pushed up his lower lip.

"I do have an idea," he said. "I'll have to talk to Quinn about it." He looked Ari in the eye. "How would you like to be a consultant for the team?"

"What does that mean… a consultant?"

"You have knowledge of the Olympeian world. You lived in Arkadeia, saw creatures and monsters, probably a few gods. The monsters of legend were part of your life. Quinn has little knowledge of these things, and we don't always have the time to explain everything. You could work with her to develop files on all of the magical aspects you know. Who knows? You might be able to shed light on our missions as well. What do you think?"

"You are serious."

"As Medusa's stare."

Dan took Ari's smile as a yes. This, he thought, might just be a part of the prophecy: *'A past life who lives among a mortal age shall be a key to Gaea's strength to face One of night and sky.'* Maybe Ari was this past life whose knowledge could help them deal with Lismonia.

18—SIMPLICITY

D ays later, Dan and the team arranged to meet with Quinn at the Boston headquarters to start putting things together. Ari had some hiring paperwork to do, even as a part time consultant, but he wanted to offer what he knew. Getting there constituted taking the subway to Park Street, about a twenty-minute ride from Brookline. While Sarah and Aleta tapped into social media on their phones, Dan read a copy of the *Boston Times* he bought at the station, while Ari read the discarded pages so he could improve his English. News from many of the Task Force Division's recent incidents, excluding those of Task Force: Gaea, had made it to the front page. Quinn knew how to handle the press. International news outlets had published pictures before showing the Gaea team in action, but the American Conglomerate always tried to downplay the activities of the United Nations, in effect, undermining much of their work. Too much publicity showcasing the world's social or political issues shone a spotlight in corners where certain people preferred shadow. The less attention given to these events, the fewer the questions asked. Despite the best efforts of the UN, the actions of their task forces had long since lost their covert ability, too. With surveillance equipment everywhere, covert operations were laughable at best, and the best they could hope for was that people were too uninterested or unintelligent to care. "Covert Ops" became "Damage Control" to minimize the exposure—such was the nature of a paranoid world.

Flanking the entrance to the black glass structure in the shadow of the State House that housed the Task Force Division stood plainclothes military officers, reminiscent of the marble telamons, male figures used as columns, and their gaze, poorly hidden by mirrored sunglasses, inspired the avoidance one might have to Medusa, the Gorgon, whose stare could petrify even the most stalwart warrior. Their surreptitious observation of passersby actually aroused more attention, but most just walked past them without regard. Ubiquitous cameras jutting from every surface motivated proper behavior, so most of the time, the guards could have vanished for a time and nothing would really happen. Local law enforcement kept a close enough eye on citizens that the overcurrent of fear was simply a way of life for the majority.

The United Nations preferred secrecy, but Brandon didn't care if people knew why he was there, so he flashed his ID card with zeal while noticeably leaning forward to have his retina scanned. Photos on these cards showed full body shots and kept a DNA sample in a sealed spot just in case of technical difficulties. Dan followed, tapping his foot and fingering his ID card while his brother entered— this was the demigod in him, feeling inconvenienced. He joked with Sarah every so often that he would just love to carry his sword openly through the door and challenge the security detail to stop him. Ari's ID card, arranged through Apollo, worked to get him in, but the guards did keep scrutinizing his face and his photo. Sarah, on the other hand, saw herself as Mrs. Emma Peel, the partner of John Steed from *The Avengers*, walking with a wry sly smile and awareness that she looked striking in her catsuit, one of her 1960s-style standard outfits. Just to be different, and because she felt much like Dan did in her contempt, Aleta would flirt with the guards — whether they were men or women — flashing a smile, winking, or wearing low cut blouses just to elicit a response. Also like Dan, she thought of walking through the door with wings and javelin.

The elevator down to the Task Force Division hummed, the fluorescent lights flickering ever so slightly. Ari got off two floors down so he could go to Human Resources, assuring Dan that he would be just fine and would meet them in Quinn's office if and when he finished in time. At the lower level, even more security checks with passwords interrupted them, and the directors sent daily emails to the every department changing the passwords. Each team used its own email server so no one could read email from another department unless coded accordingly, and every morning, the team liaisons would receive a briefing on current projects as well as the new daily password. Utilizing the most complex technology of any UN department for obvious reasons, the Task Force Division had access to software and hardware not even available to the public, especially when it came to security. No one could bring in any recording equipment, and any computer, flash drive, or electronic device had to go through yet more screenings before they could enter or leave the building. Breaching protocol brought with it prison time or a more severe consequence, not limited to exile.

Down a corridor of more glossy black glass, walls like obsidian, they went until they reached the office of Quinn Reynolds, their liaison.

"Hey, guys." She caught a new sound. "New boots, Dan?"

"Nothing gets past you, does it?" Dan smiled. "Yeah, just last week."

"And if something does, that's why I have you guys. So, you scheduled this meeting. What's up?"

Sarah began. "We need your techno-wizardry to help us fill in some gaps. We're hoping you can enter some info and spit out something we can use for this ongoing search we have for a nasty."

"I'll do my best." Quinn's fingertips tapped the haptic keyboard. "What's the info?"

"The names Theo Ranopoulos, Bakura Diwan, and Esteban Alarico Reyes." Sarah spelled them, too.

Fingers blurred over the glass panel. "Usual searches, to start."

Less than a minute later, a report popped up on Quinn's keyboard. "Hang on. Let me show you."

Most of the information contained other names, addresses, telephone numbers, school information, and anything accessible through public access. Immunization records. Hospital records. DNA samples.

"Hmm, nothing too different from the ordinary," Quinn said. "Let me broaden the parameters." Her fingers tapped in a fury again. "This may take a moment."

While they waited, all five got caught up. Sarah had a pottery show coming up in a few weeks, and Aleta had received a grant for some DNA and RNA comparative research. Quinn was headed for Ireland to meet up with some family. Brandon had planned to go to a conference in San Diego on zoological research methods, and he'd have the chance to see a few college friends. Also planning to travel a little, Dan was going to take Ari on a cross-country trip. All of these plans were contingent on their team's agenda, however.

Quinn's screen lit up. "Okay, now that's more like it. I ran the gamut of analyses, including cultural, socio-economic, genealogical, etymological... Take a look and see what sticks." She handed each a tablet computer with a copy of the entire readout.

Fingers flicked the screen, bouncing back and forth between pages. At first, they looked at the cultural report, but a Greek, an Indian, and a Spaniard had nothing in common. The Ranopoulos family was upper-middle class, the Diwans, upper class, and the Reyes, middle class. No age connection existed, either. Other reports offered random facts that didn't have an obvious bearing on the individuals. And then Brandon saw something that made him pause.

"Etymological analysis, Quinn?"

"Hey, I ran everything I could, Brandon." Coffee in one hand, she tapped the screen with the other.

They all flipped from report to report, but Brandon couldn't get past the names. Something was right there but he couldn't put his finger on it. "Dan?"

"Mmm?" Dan was in the census data.

"You're the language specialist here. Take a look at the etymological report."

Manipulating the data almost as well as Quinn could, Dan found it. His eyes lingered for a moment on each name and the meaning. Then, he sat up.

"I'll be damned. It threw me a little, though. She's a clever one."

"Lismonia? That's not the word I'd use, but Quinn doesn't know me *that* well." Aleta winked at Quinn.

"Guys, look at the report. Anything strike you?" Dan groaned at the regrettable pun; Aleta snickered.

Sarah said, "The only connection that I don't get is with Theo's last name. I mean, I get it, but how does it fit?"

Quinn had no idea. "Someone want to fill me in?"

"Look at the etymologies." Dan was tempted to reach over to point to Quinn's monitor but thought better of it.

ETYMOLOGICAL ANALYSIS

THEO	GREEK...	GOD
RANOPOULOS	GREEK...	DERIVATIVE OF OURANOS, GOD OF THE SKY
BAKURA	SANSKRIT...	THUNDERBOLT
DIWAN	....	
ESTEBAN	SPANISH...	CROWN
ALARICO	SPANISH...	RULER OF ALL
REYES	SPANISH...	KINGS

"I think I understand," Aleta pursed her lips. "They all have one commonality…Zeus."

"But, Ouranos?" Brandon asked, nodding toward Sarah. Then, he worked it out. "Ah… god and sky."

Dan remembered a conversation he had had with his father not too long ago about the gods and their hasty departure to the *Ptinotrofeio*. Pieces started to fit together.

"Lismonia wants the gods, at least that's what my father told me. But, all the Olympeians except for Apollo managed to go elsewhere where they could be safe while they took mortal forms on earth. If she was after the gods, she would have gone after Apollo."

Sarah scrutinized the other reports, looking up every so often to stay in the loop.

"So, since she can't get the gods, she's going after people whose names have some loose connection to the gods? That doesn't make much sense to me."

"I don't think that's the situation, though, Aleta." Dan leaned over to her. "Why would Lismonia want to kill the gods? And, if she were going to destroy them somehow, why go after ordinary humans? That has no effect on the gods. And, like I said, they're in hiding. If she knew where they were, she'd be there."

Sarah tried to get their attention, but they were caught up in their own frustration.

Aleta sat back and threw up her hands. "There's something we're just not seeing here. Either that, or I'm just that stupid." Brandon laughed a little.

Again, Sarah tried to interject, but she couldn't seem to get a word in.

Brandon handed Quinn the screen. "Have I mentioned lately that I hate puzzles. What are we not seeing?"

"Guys!"

"No need to shout, Sarah. We're sitting in the same room." Aleta shot her a look.

"Anyway, I found something." Sarah glared back. "I scrolled back a few dozen reports to the genealogies and found that all of these victims are not only male, but they're also the youngest born of their families."

"Why does that matter? So what, they're all guys."

"Aleta, I wasn't done. According to these records, each family can trace its lineage to an ancient family tree, and then it drops off. That can't be a coincidence. If they're all male, the youngest of their families, and their names have connections to the gods — "

"It's not the gods she's after. It's just Zeus,"

"And because she can't get to Zeus, Dan, I'm guessing these three are his descendants. She's exacting revenge through those related to him." Sarah added her last piece.

Brandon and Dan just looked at each other. Either Apollo wasn't telling them something important, or he hadn't figured it out himself. Even though they couldn't communicate telepathically, they had become experts at reading each other's facial expressions. Dan pulled Brandon into the corner of the office.

"Are you thinking what I'm thinking?"

"That Apollo should be one of Lismonia's victims?"

Dan nodded.

"Not that I want that, but you would think that the youngest son of Zeus would have been first on her list. And then, me."

"Brandon, think about it. Apollo wiped away your memory of your past. Even though you're regaining it slowly, you're not connected to enough people who know who you really are. That means Lismonia doesn't know. Our parents, Aleta, Sarah, Ari, and I know. Six people."

"Why should that matter?"

"Every other victim that we've found was known. Theo had connections all over Litokhoro, Bakura had parents and probably extended family who knew who he was, and Esteban was a student in a large university and a patient in an asylum. The community knew them well. Tie that into being first-born males descended from Zeus, and she wouldn't be coming for you."

Brandon had an epiphany. "You're right. My *true* name is Brandon Jeffries, the son of Max and Evelyn. According to my friends and colleagues, I'm not Olympeian born. Too few people even know I am Kidemonas, son of Apollo, to attract Lismonia. She's coming for *you*."

"How do you figure?"

"Think about it. Something about Apollo has kept him from harm. He should have been her first victim, but she's never tried to attack him. Since another family adopted me, you've become the true first-born son of Apollo and Alkinoë. Technically, since you were born here in Boston, you are their first-born."

"Why hasn't she tried to attack me?"

"She did. Remember when we were fighting Ladon, Sarah shouted a last resort code word, *"Pyli."* That was meant for you, not me, since only you can use portals. I think Sarah knew Lismonia was gunning for you and wanted to save you."

Dan brushed his hair back with his hand and paced in small circles. He kept shooting looks over at the women.

"What do we do? If Lismonia's looking for you, it's only a matter of time before she does. She's both a *Protogenos* and a god—you wouldn't be able to hide anywhere."

Brandon watched Dan's expression change and shook his head vigorously.

"No! Absolutely not!" he shouted.

Aleta and the others turned. They kept hearing Brandon repeat himself, "No!"

"Hey, what're you two yammering on about over there, and why's Brandon about to lose it?"

Brandon glared at his brother. "Aleta, he wants to use himself as bait to get Lismonia." They needed to know.

Sarah jumped up from her seat. "Are you crazy? We don't completely understand what she does to people, and you just want to throw yourself at her? Have you lost your mind?"

The cacophony of voices, some loud, some calm, attracted the attention of other liaisons across the floor, but it was one voice that silenced them all.

"No!" Ari had returned from Human Resources.

"Ari. How much did you hear?" Dan said.

"Enough." He took a deep breath. "The other night, when we talked about me joining this group as a consultant, you told me it would let me contribute while keeping me safe. And now you want to go off and throw your life away? Do you know what she will do to you?"

Dan put his hands on Ari's shoulders. "Ease up. I didn't say I was going to do that. It was just an idea. You have to have faith in me, Ari. I know what I'm doing, if that's what I decide to do."

"No, you don't. *The Nebulous One* doesn't just steal your soul or dissolve your body. Do you know what her *true* name means?"

"Oblivion."

"Yes! She doesn't just destroy you. In fact, she will sometimes leave you thinking you escaped her power, but then…"

His voice trailed off a bit. Dan and the others had never seen Ari get so upset. But, he wasn't finished.

"Then, she reaches inside you, traps you with fear, and removes something from you."

Sarah cringed. "What?"

"She takes away the memories of you from those people who knew you. They no longer remember who you ever were. To be in a state of oblivion is to be forgotten by everyone around you. It is irreversible. Is that what you want? Danelos, I cannot bear the idea that I would not know who you were. It would be as if we had never met. You would remember, but you would be the only one. You would be alone."

Ari sat down and put his head in his hands, and Sarah sat next to him, her hand on his back. The others argued back and forth about whether or not Dan should even consider this act. What would it even accomplish? It might delay Lismonia from attacking Apollo for a little while, but eventually, she would. Quinn had the task of squelching the debate long enough to point out to Dan that Ari needed some reassurance. He was, in fact, the only one among them who had lived in an Olympeian realm where magic and monsters predominated. Dan held out his hand to Ari, who cautiously took it, and the two went down the hall to talk. Brandon and the others had other ideas to discuss.

In the coffee break room, Dan and Ari sat facing each other on a small black couch. Ari took Dan's hand and covered it with his other.

"Please do not be angry with me. I just cannot see you sacrifice yourself to something so evil just to delay another attack."

"I'm not angry with you. But, tell me something. How do you know so much about Lismonia?"

"*The Nebulous One*. I grew up in the Temple of Hades. You hear things from the penitent and the mourners as they pass through. Sometimes, I swear the walls talk. So many times, I went down to the stone door beneath the temple that my father said opened into the underworld. I studied every symbol, every crack, every shape, just to see if I could learn what was behind that door."

"You were that lonely?"

"Lonely enough to want to commune with the dead. My father had stopped talking to me when my mother died and focused on being the caretaker. I was three years old. Going to that door... I did not wish to die, but I was so close to that cold, oppressive realm, and all I could do was yearn to see it. Every so often, a spirit or underworld daemon would pry itself into the mortal world, and I would try to learn as much as I could from it before it dissolved away. That was how I learned about *The Nebulous One*. I use that name because the other is her true name and might summon her here."

Dan hugged him tightly. "I'm sorry you had to endure that... I love you, Ari. I don't want you to suffer." He put his hands on both sides of Ari's face. "I promise you that I won't make any decision that will jeopardize my life needlessly. Can you live with that?"

They returned to Quinn's office to find the others in a vibrant discussion, mostly about whether or not Dan and Ari were splitting up. When the men walked through the doorway holding hands, Brandon said to Sarah, "You owe me a twenty."

Ari and Quinn talked about what he would be doing while the others went home. Dan rolled up a print out of the report to take with him, but a guard wearing a black suit and mirrored sunglasses silently stepped in and snatched it out of Dan's hands, handing it to Quinn. No Task Force paperwork could leave unless cleared by the liaison. She simply initialed it and returned it to Dan so he could leave, smirking at the guard.

Ultimately, the team of Task Force: Gaea felt a bit more informed, as did Quinn, but as individuals, they had their doubts, unspoken and unverified. Lismonia — whimsical, petulant, precise — didn't think about her victims beyond their lineage. Since she couldn't have Zeus, then Zeus' descendants should quake with fear.

19—CLARITY

Wandering the rain-moistened streets of West Roxbury at night, with crime statistics on the rise, could be hazardous to one's life, let alone one's health. Despite the round-the-clock surveillance of plainclothes police, assault and battery, robbery, and even the occasional murder stained the streets. The ever-present cameras from Argus Monitoring festooned building façades, giving an ornate, oftentimes Gothic, silhouette to even the starkest structure. Even shadows couldn't hide the surreptitious, ill-intentioned activities of the desperate, greedy, and sometimes unbalanced. A woman in her early fifties, her long black hair braided down her back, wearing a light blue t-shirt with a gray zip-up sweatshirt, Z. Cavaricci jeans, and running shoes seemed a bit out of place walking in such a dilapidated, poor neighborhood. Her hands in the pockets of her sweatshirt, she moved on autopilot, her mind elsewhere; she seemed unaware of the small group of young men who had been following her for a few blocks, hidden by shadows and the occasional bushes. Three broke off and circled around toward the intersection she was headed while the other five took up the rear, keeping an eye out for police or even the occasional Task

194

Force patrols: *Theta* units looked for drug activity, *Lambda* worked alongside police or SWAT teams for other criminal activity, *Tau* watched out for hate crimes, and *Phi* for racism. Much of that activity had been stopped, but then the random group would surface.

The woman walked at a casual pace, no underlying anticipation or fear prompting her to move faster through such an economically depressed area where unsuspecting passersby had been known to disappear. Truly, whatever was on her mind had made her vulnerable to those skulking about in the dark. Her reverie could certainly be her undoing. The three who had moved ahead leaned against the bank building, smoking their Marlboros and keeping a peripheral eye on her. At 2 a.m., no traffic drove through town, so the only sounds were her moist footsteps and the occasional whispered comment from the men. Those who followed acted as if they were caught up in their own revelry, and their laughter and conversation didn't seem to have an effect on the woman, who would be passing the bank in about a minute.

A Yellow Cab stopped at the light by the bank, so the three men tried to look busy, one lighting a cigarette, while the other two pretended to be on their phones. The driver gave them a curious look, but when the light turned green, he drove on. As soon as he was gone, they resumed their anxious stance. This would be an easy pick, said one of the men; she's not from this neighborhood, so she won't know what hit her, said another.

She reached the corner, turning her head slightly, but moved on. A hand reached out, grabbed her arm and flung her into the alley between Middlesex Savings and the Laundry Express. The three men turned into the alley while their companions went around the other side. Leaning against the trash bin by the bank, she said nothing but her breathing quickened a bit. Each of the three men swaggered around, smirking, eyeing her.

"Not too shabby. Mama wanna give me some lovin', dontcha?" The man made an obscene gesture.

"She's real nice." His friend winked at the woman. "I like 'em older."

The third one said nothing, but cupped himself and smiled. He looked past her and saw his other friends were taking up the rear.

"Hey, boys. Look what we got here. Wanna piece?" He gestured at her. "We can share. My momma always told me it was good to share." He spat off to the side.

Her eyes bounced from one to the other, and she knew the others were behind her, like sharks waiting to strike. Two stepped up and grabbed an arm, holding her still. She didn't move. One of the first three strutted up to her, waving a switchblade.

"If you behave, you might even like it." He leaned into her face and made a biting gesture.

She smiled and lifted her knee faster than he expected until it made contact between his legs.

"Bitch! I'm gonna kill you." He hunched over. "I'm gonna make you bleed!"

"Doubt it," she replied. The two men holding her had been laughing at their friend and didn't hear her say anything. Swinging her legs up over her head, she broke their grip and landed behind them. Before they could strike, she lifted one with her left hand and tossed him into the trash bin. The other one tried to grab her, but she caught his hand, bent it back, breaking it in three places. A roundhouse kick knocked him into the wall, unconscious. One of the five behind her ran when he saw that, but the other four brandished their weapons and wanted to finish what they started.

Now taking a more defensive posture, she playfully avoided their knife swipes or iron bars, always keeping an eye on where they were. One threw his blade at her head, but she caught it and returned the gesture, lodging it in his thigh. Bent over in pain, he muttered some obscenities and pulled a 9mm Browning from an ankle holster, firing two shots. When he looked at where she had stood, she wasn't there. He felt two taps on his shoulder and turned, only to have his face meet up with her fist. Just before he passed out, he wondered just how she managed to get behind him. After all the commotion, only one man remained. She snatched up some discarded computer cable near the trash bin and wound him in it before he could realize what was happening.

The man who had received her knee slowly hobbled over to her, lead pipe in hand; she was facing the other way. As he brought his hand down to crack her skull, she reached back, caught the pipe, and disarmed him. About to do something foolish, his eyes widened as he saw her bend the pipe with her bare hands. His footfalls echoed out of the alley.

Brushing herself off, she heard the whoop of a brief siren and saw flashing red and blue lights approach just as she stood at the streetlight. The officer rolled down his window.

"ID, please. It's kinda late for you to be out, especially in this neighborhood. We've had reports of gang activity nearby. Have you seen anything out of the ordinary?"

"Hmm. No, officer, no, I haven't." She handed him a plastic card. "I was just out for a breath of fresh air. I'm heading home now, but if I see something, I'll report it."

He returned her card. "Okay. I suppose the cameras would have caught something anyway, so we'll find out if anything happened. Have a good night, Mrs. Fairmont. Stay safe."

"Indeed I shall, officer."

As she walked on, she smiled, remembering how good it felt to be a warrior once again. Alkinoë mused how much she enjoyed taking out her frustrations on those who deserved it, since she couldn't take them out on her husband — one of the downsides of being married to an Olympeian god. She had been sleeping on her friend Sheila's couch ever since the fight with Apollo, but with her adrenaline rush fading, she thought it might be better to try to face her anger and go back home. The seven-mile walk would give her the opportunity to word just what she would say to him. Not quite ready to forgive him, she was gradually coming to terms with the difficult position he had been in.

A crow flew off into the cloud-streaked night sky. The alley cameras had been broken long ago, so the police would never know what happened, but Apollo would. He always made sure those he loved were safe.

20—TURNING POINT

Matsuyama, Ehime Prefecture, Japan.

On most mornings, just before the sun poked its fiery form over the horizon, Rakurai could be found in his simple garden, pinching weeds from the soil around his eggplant and string beans. Surrounding the living garden were meticulously placed rocks and ponds, a testament to his patience and obsessive personality. Although he and his wife lived in the heart of Matsuyama, a bustling city of over half a million people, they created a place of solitude and meditative silence, a symptom of their acute agoraphobia. After moving to the city, they found people were friendly enough, but so many wished to encroach upon their privacy, wanting to visit spontaneously and linger. Rakurai had no patience for lingerers. He and his wife, Kujaku, both in their eighties, had developed a routine that worked for them, and deviation from that just made Rakurai bitter. He found solace while grooming his garden, tending to those leafy companions that asked nothing more from him than love, care, and silence. He always longed for rain. Most neighbors had come to accept this ancient couple as a feature of the community, despite the fact that neither Rakurai nor Kujaku actively sought their friendship. Once in a while, if Kujaku felt magnanimous, she would leave parcels of homemade treats, like red bean dumplings, at the Buddhist temple, Hōgon-ji. In exchange, the monks would offer some of the lanterns they made out of scrap wood they found throughout the city; these luminaries had the workmanship of almost godly inspiration, with the ascetic hands of the monks training many years to perfect their craft. In random parts of Rakurai's garden, wooden poles jutted from flower beds or vegetable patches, carved wooden lanterns casting their pale illumination. With the delicate and fragile beauty of the garden, along with their house, enclosed within tall stone walls, Rakurai and Kujaku Saro wished to live out their days with few of life's intricacies.

Once a week, Rakurai would wrap himself in his well-worn shawl and visit the local market to supplement what he didn't grow. Both he and his wife had eschewed animal flesh long ago, finding the idea of consuming meat disdainful and impure. Only having lived in Matsuyama a few months, he had tried different markets throughout the city to see which farmers and merchants had the best produce. With a hunter's eye, he scoped the freshest goods, bartering with each merchant for the most amenable price. As he shuffled from booth to booth, he sniffed each item, paying for the ones he wanted, and gently placed all the vegetables in a wicker basket that hung over his arm.

The cabbage seller, Hiroyuki, saw Rakurai approach through the crowd and selected a few of the best cabbages, putting them on a weathered wooden block, anticipating his customer's discerning eye.

"You're late, my friend." Hiroyuki adjusted his baseball cap. "I almost sold my best cabbages to the widow Yang."

Rakurai grunted, spying the chosen produce on the block. His wrinkled hand picked up one, felt its weight, and put it down. The second one felt better, and he nodded his head slightly as he placed it in his basket.

"You don't want to check the last one, eh? You might be missing out on the best of the lot." Hiroyuki chortled and adjusted his hat.

Walking away, having left the correct money on the board, Rakurai muttered something about a worm. Hiroyuki snatched up the last cabbage, turning it around, and saw a tiny cabbage worm he hadn't noticed on one of the leaves. Shaking his head and smirking, the merchant rinsed off the tiny intruder, rechecked the cabbage, and put it back on the pile.

A short time later, about midday, the old man stopped by a noodle shop a few blocks from home, nodded at the woman behind the counter who brought a steaming ceramic bowl of soup to Rakurai's table on the patio. He always had the same thing: miso broth with sea vegetables, tofu, and shiitake mushrooms. While slurping his soup, he noticed a few small children playing with a ball in the street, noticing how they always knew when cyclists or cars approached. One of the little girls, Shin, waved at him, and he broke into the slightest smile, just enough to discern amusement. Every so often, Shin's father would help Rakurai with woodworking projects and, in turn, the old man would give Shin a small basket of sesame candies he had made. Rakurai had an insatiable sweet tooth. With soup finished, he left a few coins on the table and headed home.

He turned onto Okaido Street, a mild uphill climb that always provided him with the most trouble. One step at a time he lurched forward, careful not to drop his basket. A flock of pigeons flew above him, making more noise than usual, causing Rakurai to look up, and that is when he felt the chill, like a wave. His old bones wouldn't let him go any faster, but he managed to rewrap his shawl around him, but the air felt much colder than it should. Normally, he knew when a storm front was coming because his canary wouldn't stop singing, a sure sign of rain or maybe a monsoon. He only had to go two more blocks before he turned onto his street, so he gathered his resolve and pushed forward.

One more block to go, he thought, and then he could have some tea with Kujaku and rest a bit. Approaching his turn, the chill of the air became the chill of his bones, and a fear climbed into his body, something he couldn't shake off. The sidewalk before him felt different, as if what were around the corner was affecting the concrete itself, but a part of him dismissed it as arthritis or fatigue from the climb. *Maybe that's all it is*, he thought, *this body isn't what it used to be.* Turning onto Nikkuna Street, his heart raced the moment his eyes fell on the black, shapeless mass gurgling from the alleys between houses, pouring into the street like an overflow of oil. He tried to fight back the terror, but soon his mind gave way to it, the basket and its contents tumbling onto the sidewalk. Rakurai used every ounce of will to stay focused, but the pulses of energy from this ebony mass pushed further into his thoughts. As soon as he thought to move, his legs compelled him away from Lismonia, but an aged body could only move so fast. As she moved closer, her serpentine swaying forcing him to watch her, not knowing what part of her might move next, Rakurai fell backward into the street. A creeping paralysis took over, fueled partly by his realization that he didn't have the speed to outrun what he perceived as a demon before him.

He simply gave up.

Crashing down upon him, Lismonia encircled Rakurai's frail body, drawn by his scent — yes, something about him was different from the others. Elongating part of herself, her red eyes appearing, she caught his tired gaze. Yes, something was definitely not like the others. It wasn't that he just gave into her while others fought back as much as they could. No. The moment she made contact with his soul, leeching out what she needed, extracting his memories with the precision of a primordial surgeon, she felt a faint connection, hardly even there.

Zeus. This *man* was her father? But... how?

The longer her embrace lingered, she wondered why so little power existed, only the whisper of a whisper. Wasn't he the king of Olympos, Lord of the sky, the son of Kronos and Rhea, grandson of Gaea and Ouranos? *This* was the god who seduced her mother in the bowels of Gaea? He must be tricking her somehow, she thought, because, surely, the god who ruled all gods and mortals alike wouldn't be such a shallow well, and then... she felt it: he had no immortality. Not one spark. Pity for this ineffectual husk of a god but also anger for being her betrayer battled within her. This was not how she imagined it would be, if the daughter of Nyx could even imagine. Lismonia was no longer an immature, singular entity as she had been when she first left Tartaros; she had learned about frailty and weakness, both human and divine. If Zeus was indeed trying to mislead her, as betrayers do, then she would take it all. She would leave almost nothing of him behind, just enough to breathe... barely. The mortal world could have him.

When she usually left her prey, they would either eventually go mad at the hands of the Erinyes or see the futility of their empty lives and find the end. They always did something that didn't really affect the world, but this time, there would be repercussions — for her and the rest of the cosmos. Even with her vast power as the daughter of a *Protogenos*, not even she was immune to that which was greater than she. She didn't trouble herself to think about the world — the entirety of the universe — forgetting about Zeus, the god whose energy had shaped the world. Why would she? Uncurling from the husk of her father, she let him slump to the sidewalk like excrement and, for a second, she hesitated, before retreating into the shadows.

His descendants would continue to pay, however. She would see to that.

In the deep, in the dark center of Mother Earth, extracting Zeus' memory from Gaea, from Olympeia, and from the *Moirae* who weave the tapestry of all things would leave a void. Unlike so many of Lismonia's other victims who had never really left such an indelible mark on the world, Zeus was inextricably linked to all things. Voids had a tendency to collapse in on themselves, and what would be left would be an unraveling, a dismantling of creation.

Just as Nyx, in another time, had acted rashly to punish Zeus, ultimately punishing all that existed, her daughter, Lismonia, had acted without considering consequences, and the curse of memory is that once it's gone, nothing takes its place. This all-encompassing void would indeed need to be filled.

Lismonia, *The Nebulous One,* whose true name means *Oblivion*, would seek to fill that void.

PART TWO:

AFTERMATH

21—ELEMENTALITY

E arth, fire, air, water, and the all-encompassing spirit that allows these sacred elements to exist comprise the entirety of the cosmos. Nothing can exist without their presence, and the absence of any one of them would unravel the world. Each of these represents intricate facets of a larger, more complex, world created when Khaos first emerged millennia ago. They ebb and flow through the universe, just as divine ichor surges within immortals or blood does within mortals.

To tamper with such primordial forces is to throw off a delicate equilibrium, once that even the *Hieros Zugos*, the Sacred Scales, cannot set aright, despite their power over order and chaos. Layered next over this basic foundation come the *Protogenoi* and the gods themselves. Each of them is an element that, once removed, fractures and changes the very nature of life itself, for each immortal being has touched, and continues to touch, all that exists.

With surgical precision, Nyx's daughter plucked the memory of Zeus from all. Even though the modern mortal world knew little of the Olympeian king, at some level, this absence would be felt as time moved forward, and thought and action might be altered even just an iota in a direction it might not have gone had it been for the knowledge of Kronos' youngest son.

With each passing moment, the world would evolve, and the cosmos itself would never be predictable again.

The first to feel the tug of loss would be the *Moirae*, the three Fates whose power put fear into even the king of the gods, although they themselves had no control over the events that unfolded in each thread they wove. Some magic was even beyond them: the maiden, mother, and crone. Without their knowledge of Zeus' majesty and decisive influence, they would look back at the tapestry they had woven and reflect upon the choices they had made to cut short the lives of heroes and demigods that some charlatan named Zeus had induced them to perform. Given even more time to ruminate, since they have forever, they might even consider repairing the shorn threads for some, feeling that this interloper to their domain had ensorcelled them to perform misdeeds. The unknown effect these decisions would have on the Sacred Scales could be foretold by none, since no supremely omniscient god existed who could see into time yet born. Elements were simply tools of man and gods, and the consequences for altering would indeed be dire.

υδωρ
WATER

With the Lord of Olympos' presence gone, the souls of the underworld felt the absence of their lord, Hades, *The Unseen One*, even more. While he, unbeknownst to them, sojourned across Gaea in mortal form, they hovered across the dark realm, visiting the judges of the dead, hoping for an eternity in Elysian Fields among the souls of heroes. Some would indeed get that wish, while others would enter everlasting torment in Tartaros. Even though the judges of the dead, Aeacus, Rhadamanthys, and Minos, arbitrated without supervision, the governing of the rest of an entire otherworldly realm took great energy, more than one god could supply. Using his divine authority kept most of the dominion in check, but Hades needed to draw an ongoing source of energy from a place of holiness, a well of power that would last eons. After the *Titanomachia*, after Zeus defeated the Titan lord, Kronos, the three brothers — Zeus, Poseidon, and Hades — divided up the spoils of a tumultuous war by drawing straws, brooding Hades drawing the short one and becoming sovereign of souls. He linked his own Olympeian power to that of the barely living Titans in their stony encasements, and he shrewdly generated a net of control. In his absence, although that was rare, his wife, Persephone, would assume the sovereignty, keeping a tight rein on her half-year home.

Without its king, the realm named for him lost the balance he had worked so hard to attain, even with his wife on the throne, as she didn't have the same presence, the same heavy eyes of the dusky son of Kronos and Rhea.

Monstrous Cerberos, the canine guardian of the gates, kept souls from entering the realm unless they had an obolos under their tongue, and Charon, the ferryman, continued to usher the spirits of the dead across from the land of the living. The most loyal of Hades' subjects, they would serve him and his wife unceasingly; others, however, saw an opportunity to wrest his authority.

Meandering through the sleepy poppy fields and past the meadows of asphodel, around the borders between the land of the living and regions that had never been kissed by Apollo's sun, ran five rivers, each embodied by a god. These *Potamoi Haidou*, the Rivers of Hades, themselves had pledged their fealty to Hades long ago to keep the underworld from harm, but also to keep the living as far away as possible. Times had indeed changed. With Lismonia having drained so much energy from the Titans in Tartaros, more than Hades would have over many years, the presence of the god of the dead waned. Each of the river gods rose from his or her respective fluid homes and built five thrones that circumscribed the underworld, comprised of lost souls who would never see Elysium. The five filled these royal seats, as tall as mountains, and thus seized the power they felt had been denied them.

Akheron, whose robes consisted of dank waters and tattered funeral shrouds, took his throne, his crown of bones seated upon his hair of decayed water grasses; his eye sockets were empty, yet they echoed with shrieks of pain and woe. To his right sat Styx, adorned with swirling, fetid waste combined with animosity, her eyes pools of flat blackness. Dead flowers, reeking of hate, from the field where Persephone was abducted sat on her head. Cocytos sat next to her, black, decayed leaves crawling with larvae on his head, covered by a gauzy shroud of unrepentant souls. Eyes of jaundiced ochre looked out over the vast underworld with disdain. With hair of souls on fire and eyes smoldering with a mixture of anger and the First Fires, Phlegethon sat, wrapped in watery robes, teeming with wickedness and muck. Lastly, with her eyes empty of emotion yet filled with wisps of thought, pale Lethe reclined, her hair consisting of souls of the lost adorned with memories of the past, and gray fog hovering around her. Waters flowed into one another, yet remained distinct. This ruling confluence had no need to change the current order of things; rather, it asserted its dominance simply because none could stand before them without trembling. Even Persephone stayed in her ebony, jewel-encrusted palace, with shades and spirits as companions.

Keeping his vigil on those who debarked from Charon's skiff to ensure only the dead entered, Cerberos noticed the change in smell pervading the already foul air; looking back toward the iron gates, his three heads let out a soft growl of discontent, and then returned to his duty. The ferryman, too, was instantly aware. No matter, he thought. As long as it didn't upset his role, he would bide his time. Hades would reclaim what they had taken, and perhaps Tartaros, with many of its recesses hotter than Apollo's sun, would receive and torment the rivers.

As yet another consequence of Lismonia's acts, this shift already yearned for *issoropia* – equilibrium. Tartaros had relinquished his rule of the underworld to Hades long ago, such was the order of things, so he had no way to prevent the liquid coup, nor did he care. The Sacred Scales would provide balance in time, and only the *Moirae* knew when and how.

DAVID BERGER

γαεα
EARTH

I magine having an arm or an eye or heart, something essential, ripped from one's body without warning. Now, think about the pain, feeling one's own sinews shredded, compounded by shock. A human body could only withstand so much before shutting down. When Lismonia stripped memories from a human, she circumvented his will; a human mind had no recourse against the daughter of an Olympeian and a *Protogenos*. However, when Lismonia erased the memory of Zeus, the king of the gods, from all of creation, the Mother of All felt as if a vital organ had been extricated from her thousands-year-old primordial body, and Earth's voice echoed within every living thing.

Gaea writhed as filaments of Lismonia's form reached inside and found any remnant of memory, entwining themselves about those thoughts, ready to extract them. She fought back with all the power a *Protogenos* could. Normally dormant on the mortal plane, since she had he-roes guarding her in the modern world, Gaea had become acquiescent. All she had ever concerned herself with was replenishing the earth. For every wound she suffered at those who strip-mined her, gouged out chunks of her flesh, soiled her waters, and poisoned her, she would re-bound in silence, repairing the damage over time. Zeus provided a stable Olympos and, in turn, a stable world for this happen. Without him in her memory, she feared for the survival of mortals. As she resisted this heinous extrac-tion, random earthquakes rattled in places where no fault lines existed, magma-spewing volcanoes pushing their way through the upper crust, showering the surrounding areas with fiery rock—a testament to the Earth's will. Animals, rivers, even the smallest of plants responded to her agony, offering up their own life energies to fortify her. This daughter of Khaos held on, pushing back, and drawing strength from those who relied upon her, staving off the extraction. If she were to let her guard down, to relent for a second, those memories would be gone. The second oldest *Protogenos*, she would triumph.

Now both the mortal and immortal worlds would see what happened when ancient gods interfered with the natural order. Gaea had disregarded Lismonia as simply another primordial god, one whose power could cause turmoil for others, but now she knew the threat Nyx's daughter posed to all who lived, even herself, and she wouldn't be submissive anymore.

αηρ
AIR

Separated from the world in the *Ptinotrofeio*, a place beyond Lismonia's reach, the avian forms of Olympeians left their crags or branches jutting from nowhere and flew in circles above a gnarled oak branch on which sat a white eagle whose keen eyes had become aware of something beyond the impenetrable boundary through Hesteia's flames. Although untouched by the events outside the aviary, he scanned for any breach in the clouds that protected this sacred realm of Ouranos for a way out—he sensed his mortal form had been compromised, and he needed to find it before humans would mistreat the king of the gods. Every attempt to fly through the cloud barrier failed, and the majestic white bird squawked, sounding an alarm that confused the others. Only with the sword *Thyroros* could they leave the aviary; the avian form of Zeus wouldn't be able to summon his thunderbolt, either. Whatever had happened in the mortal world would have to wait until the year transpired. Enervated and once again on his knotty branch, the eagle slowed its flapping until its wings were folded back. Unrest would burden his remaining time in this celestial place.

πυρ
FIRE

San Francisco. A midnight among midnights.

Who knew the absence of an Olympeian god few mortals even gave much credence to could cause so much chaos in the modern mortal world, a world that had largely little to no knowledge about the ancient world? Olympos was like a whisper of a memory for most humans, and the idea that gods existed was ignored—not by all, however. Groups of believers, some who had connections to ancient magical power, had formed what the press had called Olympeian Resurrectionists, groups seeking to bring the worship of the gods back. Some proclaimed to be related directly to the gods themselves, although that was almost impossible.

Just a few blocks away from Corona Heights Park, a Resurrectionist group called the New Attic Conclave, a re-imagined cult of Zeus, was performing one of their daily rituals in an abandoned warehouse to avoid local law enforcement and Task Force: Delta intervention, since the Conclave had been targeted for insurgent behavior. The American Conglomerate government and the United Nations Security Council had deemed Resurrectionists as subversives who, on occasion, had caused metaphysical disturbances when summoning entities. Task Force: Gaea had been unsuccessful in disbanding the Resurrectionist groups as they were too small or met too infrequently to watch. Most times, conclaves would summon a chimaera or a small dragon into the mortal realm, something easily contained, but just before Lismonia wiped Zeus' memory away from others, the New Attic Conclave were beginning a ritual to summon the essence of Zeus to give themselves enhanced physical power. Even without godly ancestry, mortals could invoke the gods, although it took a burnt offering and complete devotion—not one member could waver. In possession of a stone that Zeus' thunderbolt had struck in ages past, they believed it would connect them even further to otherworldly magic. Dust covered shipping crates towered around them while hazy windows covered in cobwebs allowed pale moonlight to illuminate the space during their incantations. Most mortal magic required will power that exceeded the limits of most average humans, especially those without a mystical lineage, so undisturbed concentration was necessary. In the middle of their chant, their resonant voices in unison and growing louder, a ripple passed through them, wiping from their memory the god who inspired them to return the world to Olympos. As their minds adjusted to the change, they looked around, not knowing why they were there in the first place. Fear crawled onto them, like unseen spiders in the dark, and their concentration faltered. The expanding energy they had started to invoke needed a conduit into the world and burst forth in blue fire, an all-consuming one that fed on its catalyst, moving like a swarm of incendiary piranha. Bits of flame devoured human flesh, the followers of a forgotten god crying out in agony as their skin singed and fell away, as their blood evaporated, and their bones charred. When all was gone, the stench of burned flesh and blood clung to the musty air, and scorch marks marred the concrete floor.

αἰθηρ
SPIRIT

Millennia ago, not long after Kronos fell under Zeus' scythe, the three sons of Rhea met in the underworld to bury their father, a final act of respect toward the one who had devoured them as newborns, or tried to, in Zeus' case. As all three stood above the rocky pile that encased their father's body in the deepest cave of Tartaros, they drew straws to divide the great kingdoms of the world among them: the mysterious underworld, the boundless sky, and the mighty oceans. Joining hands that could rend the world if necessary, they invoked Gaea and Olympeia, earth and spirit. The brothers would hold dominion over the world together, supported by the other gods, with Olympos as its foundation.

Gaea had faith in Zeus and his brothers, but Olympeia had a price. Having given the Titans her mountain based on trust of Gaea, she felt betrayed that the Titans could not defeat those who rose against them with her power as their anchor. An icy wind filled the cave and brought them to their knees. At first, they thought Tartaros or Thanatos approached, but then they saw her. Garbed in white, her head and face covered, she spoke to them.

"To rule from Olympos, sacrifice there must be of something held most dear. Zeus, slayer of Kronos, I take from you... your first-born son, the Shining One. He shall serve me. Poseidon, I take from you the last year of your life. The Moirae will cut short your thread, however long it shall be, by one year. Hades, I take your heart's desire — to sit on Olympos itself. The underworld shall be your domain forevermore. Upon burying

your father, you will inherit Olympos and my protection."

Without hesitation, Zeus raised his hand and called down a thunderbolt that coursed through the caverns beneath the earth, striking Kronos' tomb, sealing it and carving the glyphs into rock, creating the Olympeian Pact.

And, now, when Lismonia carved the memory of Zeus from the world, Olympeia didn't have her sister Gaea's resolve, and that memory evanesced. Without it, the pact of three gods ceased to be valid. Who was this third name etched into the tomb of Kronos along with Hades and Poseidon? What deception had Poseidon and Hades tried? The Olympeian Pact was no more, and Olympeia rejected the gods themselves. Olympos would not allow them to set foot on that sacred ground.

That which Lismonia had sought, the destruction of her father and his descendants, would not be woven into the *Moirae's* tapestry. For the first time ever, inexplicable gaps would exist in the temporal cloth, and they would bring about change that no prophecy could ever foretell.

PART THREE:

UNITY

22—GAEA'S RETURN

L ismonia returned to the Tartarean niche that once served as her nursery, cascading more confidently over the craggy cavern floor and the enchanted stone encasements of the Titans, her gelatinous cloudlike form seeming more like a young adult than the infant primordial that she had been not long ago. She had feasted on humanity—its flesh and bone, its blood and sinew, and its souls—but nothing appeased her appetite more than the power she leeched from Gaea's bound offspring. In the rocky mausoleum where a now-forgotten god once helped his brethren to commit a glorious coup, *The Nebulous One* surged like black waves over the Titans, but something wasn't right. She could feel no such energy, weak though it might have been, beneath the rocky skin. She tried again to drain that life force, but... nothing. And, then, she felt the presence of another. At first, she thought it was her mother, Nyx, but this was another entity, one whose power rivaled her mother's, perhaps even outshone it.

Gaea.

Ignoring the presence, as she had since her birth, an act of proud entitlement, she again poured herself over the tombs of Rhea and her brethren, but no power, not even

221

one iota, was there. Once more, Mother Earth asserted her presence. Nyx's daughter gathered herself, forming a riotous, undulating mass of darkness and energy, posturing for the mother of all. All around her she felt the manifestation of Khaos' firstborn, and in her mind, she heard a voice. *Impudent fool*, it said. *You are nothing before me, and you have no power over me. You took the memory of Zeus from the world, but you cannot extract it from the Earth.* Lismonia recoiled at this. How could anyone resist her power? Not even Olympeia could.

Nyx's daughter swirled around the cavern, a primordial tantrum, but everywhere she turned, Gaea was there. She felt that ancient source of growth and healing all around her, and she winced. The voice returned. *I shall not deal with you — that is not my destiny. Others are prophecy-bound to contain you.* Lismonia replied that none could contain her... none could stop her. None could hide from her. She would take all that she wanted, as her mother had told her she could.

No longer. Gaea's voice rang through Lismonia's mind. *I am the world, the force of life and death. Even Night cannot exist without me.* The gelatinous cloud of dark power quavered with rage. No one would speak of her mother — the hubris! Again, she tried to extract the Titans' power.

Gaea spoke. *My children reside within me, and I shall protect them from you. No longer will you steal their essence.*

Lismonia flung herself on every wall, clinging like leeches, to suck power from the Earth itself, to weaken her, to show her who truly had supremacy. If she couldn't have the Titans' lifeblood, she would take what she needed from the Earth. Foolish indeed. Gaea repulsed her, generating the curative strength that allowed the world to heal itself. This power wasn't what Lismonia wanted, and it burned.

Nyx's daughter left the cavern to return to the world of Humanity to feed, but Gaea's voice followed her. *Know that I shall see all you do, child, and nurture those who devote themselves to me.*

Lismonia said that the world of mortals would suffer for Gaea's actions, but the Earth Mother's fury should not be discounted.

I shall reclaim my sister, Olympeia. Take heed, little one.

None can resist the power of Gaea.

23—VOID

Apollo awoke to a gray skied morning, and he saw that Alkinoë had not slept in the bed. He was glad when she returned home, and he took a little pleasure in the beating she had given those men who tried to assault her. She hadn't lost her warrior side.

This tension between them was one of a few times since they had met that they couldn't resolve the issue before they went to sleep. His actions had ripped out her heart, and the worst part was, he had no remedy — ironic for a god of healing. Such a betrayal he had never done to anyone before, but his reason was sound: he was protecting his son from evil. He hoped that, in time, she would understand and forgive him, but he didn't really think it would happen soon. As he passed through the living room, he noticed his wife asleep on the sofa, the blanket pulled up to her eyes. Even though the hazy daylight didn't cascade like sunbeams, the light was still too bright. He knew she was lying there awake, but he said nothing and went downstairs to get the newspaper. As soon as he opened the glass door to the outside, a chill passed through him, one that caused his head to ache a little. Automotive pollution, he thought. Mortals should just use chariots.

But, it felt like something more.

He read the paper in his home office, mostly not to disturb Alkinoë, but he heard her get up and go into the kitchen. Minutes passed, and he smelled coffee brewing. It was one of the few mortal trappings he had become accustomed to over the years. After getting himself a cup, he commented aloud as he walked back to his office that police officers in San Francisco found charred human remains in an abandoned warehouse the night before while sweeping the area for squatters. No response from his wife. That affirmed they were still fighting. Continuing the article, he saw photos of the crime scene with Greek graffiti on the walls.

"That's odd. Some of these pictures show Ancient Greek words on the walls. I think that one of them is Zeus. Strange…"

From the living room, Alkinoë asked, "What is that?"

"What? You mean Zeus? You're kidding, right?"

"No, I wouldn't have asked if I were. Why would someone write the word 'Zeus' on the wall? What does it mean?"

Apollo sat next to his wife on the sofa.

"Why do you look so perplexed? And, for the record, I'm still angry with you. The story just seemed intriguing."

"Zeus is my father, Alkinoë. Surely you remember the brooding, silver-haired thunderbolt-bearing god who rules Olympos."

"Apollo, I have no idea who that is. Seriously. Doesn't Hera rule Olympos? Hasn't she always?"

She wasn't lying. He could tell if she were, and she truly believed what she was saying. He called Brandon, but hung up just as perplexed. Brandon had no idea who Zeus was either. Dan wasn't answering his phone. The next call was to Quinn.

Lismonia must have found Zeus somehow. Why did Apollo still remember his father then?

"Dad, why did you call this meeting?" Dan rushed into Quinn's office. "You said it was urgent."

Everyone else had already arrived.

"Thank you for coming." Apollo sounded calmer than they expected. "I have to ask you all something, and it's quite possible you may think I'm crazy." He scanned their faces to make a mental note of their expression. "Who is Zeus?"

Quinn was the first to respond. "No clue, Apollo. Is this someone you know? Someone connected to this case?"

"I already told you my answer, Dad." Brandon leaned back and folded his arms. "Who is this person, and why do you seem so off?"

Both Sarah and Aleta shook their heads.

Apollo looked at his son. "Dan?"

For a moment, Dan said nothing, but then he shook his head. "Never heard of Zeus. Why do you want to know? Does this have something to do with Lismonia?"

Ari turned toward Dan. "What are you all talking about? Zeus is your grandfather, Danelos. The king of Mount Olympos. Why are you playing games? Can you not see this is important to your father? It is obvious that *The Nebulous One* found him. Right?" He looked right at Apollo.

"Ari, I have no idea what you're talking about." Dan had never seen that side of Ari. "Are you and my father in on some kind of joke?"

Apollo sat back, speechless. For some reason, though, Ari remembered.

"Never mind. Sorry to have wasted your time." His aberrant monotone got Quinn's attention. "Ari, may I have a word with you?"

The young man couldn't help but look puzzled at Dan as he left Quinn's office with Apollo. They left the building and headed for the Public Gardens, one of the few spaces where they could talk more openly than other places in the city. Apollo said nothing until they found a bench near the Swan Boats.

"Okay. Tell me how you remember Zeus and they don't. It's obvious that Lismonia found him somehow, his mortal form. Even I didn't know where he was."

Ari rubbed his hands together. He had never had a private audience with Lord Apollo, as he knew him, the king of Arkadeia and god of Olympos.

"It's okay, Ari. It's just me, Dan's father. Don't think of me as anyone else."

"Did Danelos ever tell you how we met?"

"He just told me you met at a café. That you and he struck up a conversation in Greek and hit it off. Why?"

Unable to look Apollo in the face, Ari told the story of how he had come to be in Boston. Judging by the look on Apollo's face, Dan hadn't told his father about his many nightly trips to Arkadeia. He only knew about one time, when both Brandon and Dan asked how to get there, but Apollo had dismissed them by saying they each had the key. They had never mentioned anything since then, so he had assumed they were unsuccessful. Ari told him about his father and how he died, and Apollo remembered Timaios, the caretaker of the temple. He had never met Ari, known in Arkadeia as Aristeides. Things started to come together.

"You're from Arkadeia's past. Of course. That's why you still remember Zeus. Lismonia can't sense you here. You're a man out of his time, so your memories are somehow protected."

"If *The Nebulous One* has found Zeus, how is it that you remember? The same reason as me?"

"I don't think so. I've been carrying two sets of memories of my life with me, one from another time that no longer exists. For some reason, that's another anomaly Lismonia can't detect. Only you and Task Force: Gaea know about this. Not even my wife knows. We may be the only ones who remember my father, Ari."

Apollo felt a gentle touch through the ground, a pulse of energy through his feet, something he hadn't felt in a long time. She was reaching out to him, wanting him to know. He clenched his eyes shut.

"She remembers," Apollo whispered.

"Who?"

"Gaea. Somehow, she managed to retain the memory as well. That makes three of us."

Overwhelmed by being in the presence of one of his gods, although in mortal form, Ari felt even more humbled to know that Gaea's presence was with them, too.

"What do we do?"

Apollo put his hand on Ari's shoulder. "We hold onto that memory. It may be one of the only ways we can save my father."

Mother Earth spoke again, and Apollo instructed Ari to go home and say nothing. He had somewhere to go.

Unable to go to Olympos, Apollo went to Delphi, the seat of all oracular power, and there, Gaea told him about the Olympeian Pact. Olympeia felt betrayed by Poseidon and Hades and had nullified it, reverting control to the Titans, despite that they remained imprisoned in Tartaros. Even though only three remembered Zeus: a *Protogenos*, a god, and a mortal, the enchantment imprisoning the Titans would hold. Gaea would see to it now. While the gods' avian forms remained in the *Ptinotrofeio*, they would be safe; that vault belonged to Ouranos, not Olympeia. Unfortunately, Apollo knew of no way to restore Zeus' memory, and without access to Olympos, he wondered how long he would remain a god. What would happen when the gods' avian forms reclaimed their mortal bodies and tried to enter Olympos? What exactly could Olympeia do to them?

24—FLUIDITY

D an found it especially intriguing that Task Force: Gaea hadn't been sent anywhere in a few weeks, and he wondered if perhaps Lismonia had found the gods somehow and had exacted her revenge. She could have simply become much smarter and had been ravaging parts of the world they hadn't considered. All of her attacks had been motivated by anger or revenge, but they could never track her. Plotted on a map, her movement had no rationale. She sought out those who had descended from the gods, which didn't explain to Dan how he, his brother, or his father had not been attacked again. Apollo had told them that his prophetic visions didn't work on Lismonia because she was part *Protogenos* and part god. Perhaps they were looking in the wrong place.

Dan met his father at The Beanery to discuss what he thought would be a keen strategic move, and he wondered why they hadn't tried it before. As a god of prophecy, Apollo had the ability to see part way into the future, but only for specific reasons. Instead of looking for Lismonia, what if Apollo could focus his scrying for potential victims? They had all the parameters, according to Quinn, and somehow that might help them narrow down the search.

Apollo heard his son's proposal, but he wasn't sure exactly what Dan wanted him to do.

"Dad, you told me when I was a kid that you used your scrying pool to seek prophetic visions and shared them with your high priests. Couldn't you use the same enchantment to locate male, first-born sons who had descended from the gods?"

"Theoretically, yes. But, that's not who we're looking for. I would need to locate male, first-born descendants of Zeus. You know, my father?"

Dan shook his head. "I wish I knew what you were talking about, but I don't. If you don't want to help me, then just say so. I'll figure something else out."

"Danelos Demetrios..." Apollo only used his son's first and middle names when he was angry or frustrated. "You obviously don't remember your grandfather. Fine. But, the scrying enchantment you want depends on connections to Zeus, but since the world no longer remembers him, I cannot scry for just descendants of the gods. Do you have any idea how many gods there are? Not all immortals are Olympeians. So, I don't believe Lismonia wants *them*."

"Well, do you have any suggestions since we seem to be at an impasse?"

Apollo sat quietly for a few minutes, tracing the edge of his coffee cup with his finger. "I have something." He explained, enunciating his words, that, even though Dan didn't remember Zeus, it would be pretty hard to explain how Apollo existed if Zeus hadn't. The key was that Dan didn't remember; it wasn't that Zeus never existed.

"Every human being has electromagnetic fields that help run the body's processes, and these fields have a distinctive energy signature, like a fingerprint. One of the ways hand scanners work when you enter buildings is by scanning your fingerprints, but also but reading your energy signature. Immortals have something similar, a certain aura that surrounds us, like metaphysical DNA. Both you and your brother have this aura, for lack of a better term, through me. Since we gods exist as energy, but choose to live in more finite forms, the energy we embody has its own wavelength, if that makes sense."

"Okay, that helps a little. But, how do we find that wavelength? We mortals use technology to scan for energy. What do immortals use?"

"At the height of my power, I could simply scry for those who were related to me, but with Olympos off limits, I can't get to my scrying pool in the Hall of Prophecy. Only there do I have unlimited vision."

"Wait... Unlimited vision. What about *Thyroros*? Through the sword, we have access to Boundless Vision, but is that limited to places only?"

"Let's go back to your apartment. I have an idea."

Apollo had Dan hold the hilt with both hands so the tip of the sword pointed toward the floor.

"As my son, you have that aura of Olympeian energy, but you channel it more as strength and stamina. Instead of using the gemstone to power the sword to cut open a portal, focus the stone's energy on tracking those like you. If what I'm thinking is correct, you should be able to visualize the locations of those potential victims."

Dan closed his eyes and focused on the blue crystal, concentrating on his breathing. As the son of an Olympeian, he did possess some mystical power, but as his mother had given up her immortality when she moved to this place, he didn't have the ability to draw from that well of energy like a true *hemitheos*, or demigod. Gradually entering a meditative state, he channeled his own aura through the stone. In his mind, the aura looked light blue and crackled like lightning. He willed the light to find other light sources like his, but the light didn't move. Perhaps he wasn't strong enough to do this, even being the son of Phoebos Apollo. Dan pushed harder, but all he felt was a headache building at the base of his head and radiating through his skull. He had to stop.

"I can't do it. I can access that energy, but I can't get it to move beyond the crystal and find the potential victims. Maybe if Brandon and I..."

Apollo shook his head. "I don't think that will do it, and I figured out why. You're an immediate descendant from me, as is your brother, so your energy signature is strong, but the others are generations away from their divine source. Basically, their signal is too weak. Plus, even if we find them, we can't protect them. Lismonia can go anywhere."

"So, we're back where we started."

"Maybe. Assemble your team, I have another idea, but it might be another dead end. I'll contact you when and if my idea will work. In the meantime, do me a favor... think about why you didn't tell me how you met Ari." Apollo wasn't angry as much as he was disappointed, but before Dan could say anything, his father left in a burst of light.

Two hours passed, and Task Force: Gaea, plus Ari, sat in Dan and Brandon's apartment. Concrete tension lingered in the room, especially because Ari felt odd being the only one in the room who remembered Zeus. He had come to terms with the effects of Lismonia's power, but that didn't remove the irritation. Dan and he simply resolved not to talk about it. Aleta wanted to know what they were waiting for, but Dan said his father would contact him when he knew something. Sarah, having been pulled away from finishing some pottery she was going to show in an upcoming gallery exhibition, sat cross-armed next to Brandon who tapped his fingers on the arm of the couch. With a subtle gesture, she pulled some fire from the votive candle flickering on the coffee table to her, holding her fiery hand menacingly near his face. He stopped tapping.

Apollo materialized before them.

"I'm glad you all could come. I'm sure Dan explained

to you what we tried to do earlier, but with no success. We should try again, using both Brandon and Dan, but Sarah and Aleta, you're needed, too. I find that I do many things on my own, mostly because I'm used to acting as a god. Olympeians don't usually play well together. But, you're a unique team, and by simultaneously tapping into all your powers, you can anchor each other."

"Even if we find these potential victims, how can we protect them?" said Sarah. "Lismonia has no limits. Like Gaea or Khaos, two *Protogenoi* I know well, she has unlimited power. But, unlike them, Lismonia has doesn't care about cosmic rules or balance."

"True, she's already shifted the scales. But, she focuses her attack on removing memories of her victim from those who know him. Mortal minds, as fragile as they are, can be strengthened to withstand that attack. She uses the victim's memory of those he knows to link to those minds and erase that person from them."

"How do you strengthen memory?"

"Well, Sarah, that's where you come in. You and Aleta need to run an errand. Suit up, so to speak."

As the TF-18 departed into the night, the silhouette of Mount Olympos loomed above. Aether and Talon found the entrance to Hades just where Apollo said it would be, marked by a stone block fifty feet tall leaning against the mountain. Judging by the plant growth, no one had tried to move this door in a long time. Talon readied her javelin.

"Are you crazy? There's a reason why this stone is here. If you atomize it, anything and everything waiting on the other side will just come out to play," Aether snapped, her hand on Talon's arm.

"Good point. I'll provide defense while you move that rock."

"When I move it, you go. I'll be right behind you."

Talon nodded, standing ready with *Nephoskizetes*.

Extending her arms, Aether made her connection with the tonnage of stone and moved her hands to the left.

Earth rumbled as the seal came loose, and the stench of decaying souls leeched out into the night air. Nauseated, Aether turned her head, but she kept her control on the stone. As soon as the opening was big enough for Talon to squeeze in, Aether followed and quickly sealed the doorway. Talon's javelin sparked, giving them a little light to see by, but it didn't extend far. If she called forth a lightning bolt, the door would indeed shatter, so she only used what little power the javelin contained. And then their journey began.

Being an elemental put Aether in touch with all five sources of power, but Gaea's influence dominated here. In the underworld, her power worked differently, so she stayed alert without tapping too much into the surrounding energy. When Talon's javelin sparked again, Aether saw the pathway meander left, but saw something attached to the wall.

"Talon, can you control the sparking?"

"Depends. Lightning doesn't like to be controlled. Why?"

"I think I saw iron torches on the wall, covered in gods-know-what. If you can spark near a torch, maybe we can get a little more light."

Aether moved her hand along the wall, not thinking about the slimy substance she grazed over, and when it hit an iron torch, she asked Talon to spark by her hand. A little tendril of lightning made contact with the torch basket, igniting the contents. Then, something miraculous happened—every torch simultaneously ignited along the walls.

"Something tells me that's going to be the last good thing to happen here," Talon muttered.

Shadows along the wall played tricks with them, but when Aether reached out to the torchlight, she could manipulate it. That might come in handy. Aegis had warned them that traveling in the underworld could take a while, months even, or maybe just moments, but they needed to take that risk if they wanted to stop Lismonia. After what seemed like hours, or it could have been days, they saw a stone staircase descend toward an open area blanketed in a living gray mist. Gradually, a vast river spread before them.

"Styx?"

Talon corrected her, "Akheron, actually. Common misconception, according to Aegis. Charon, the ferryman, won't be coming, either. Look."

At the water's edge, a shattered wooden skiff lay like driftwood, and the shrouded remains of the ferryman sat in a pile of bone.

"Apollo mentioned that Hades' power over this place would have diminished since the river gods had usurped control of the underworld in his absence. I'm guessing these same river gods got rid of *anyone* loyal to Hades."

A resonant howling echoed over the river. In fact, it was three distinct howls, mournful ones.

"Cerberos. He doesn't sound happy."

Talon laughed. "Not sure a hellhound would ever be happy. We have to cross the river, though."

She jumped up, flapping her wings. Aether grabbed her ankles firmly.

"Whatever happens, don't let go." Talon had experience with this. "You don't want to take a dip in this river."

With a raptor's strength and grace, Talon carried her friend over the river of pain. From above, they could see the tormented souls stuck in the murky water, forever tortured with soul-shredding agony. Yes, Talon was correct: mortals shouldn't swim in Akheron's waters.

"We don't have any wine-soaked cake, so I'm going to have to do some fancy flying to get around the dog. Hang on."

At the other side of the dark river, the monstrous son of Ekhidna crouched, each of its three heads howling into the misty air. Keeping an eye on the fanged jaws, Talon soared as high as she could, but she noticed that Cerberos had no interest in either her or Aether. As they landed on the other side of the iron gates to Hades' realm, one of the heads turned toward them, his eyes looking as forlorn as a dog that had lost his master. Even though Cerberos could disembowel a dragon, his plaintive howls evoked sympathy in the two women.

"We need to find the white poplar by the edge of the river Lethe." Aether then remembered she couldn't touch that water either.

Talon pulled out a piece of folded white paper from her waistband. Apollo had given them a rough map to find the river of forgetfulness, but the poplar was the real goal. Whispering shades, souls who had passed beyond the iron gates, hovered like hummingbirds over the fields, one minute they were there, and the next, somewhere else, with no pattern to their movement. Aether approached a spirit, but before she could ask anything, the misty form melted on the stale breeze. Power over the elements afforded her no great advantage with the dead; they no longer cared about the constructs of life.

Talon broke the silence. "Just beyond the Grove of Persephone, we'll find the river's edge. This way." She couldn't bear to walk on the ground, its bleakness sucking away part of her energy, so she climbed higher, soaring around the dreary landscape of monotonous fields of gray asphodel. Aether concluded she was all but useless here: the earth barely brought forth any life, its dusty surface unable to hold a root or plant; rivers embodying raw emotions held no draw to be touched; the air, stagnant and stale, clung to her like leeches; and, perhaps worst of all— no fires burned here. The First Fires that Dan and Apollo spoke of must be further down in this netherworld, probably closer to Tartaros.

Through Persephone's forest, a dusty path ambled, the trees bereft of any leaves, and winged creatures they had never seen before perched on withered branches. The sound of crunching in the distance put them in a defensive stance, but sound traveled differently in this place, so they couldn't locate the source. Talon, like her teammate, felt impotent. Before them, a thick fog sat, as if ready to hatch something horrendous, unfathomable, something beyond their imaginations. Aether extended her hand and tried to move the air, but it felt like she was pushing her hand through gelatinous ooze. Walking further into the grove, silence that absorbed sound clung to everything. Feeling unsettled, Aether stopped.

"I need a moment."

Talon understood and kept her raptor eyes ready. Aether sat on the path, cross-legged, her hands palm up on her knees. Controlling her breathing, she closed her eyes, calling quarters.

"Those of *Aer*, of the living Air, *Aetoi* who guard the Eastern gates, I call on your strength. Those of *Pyr*, of the living Fire, *Drakones* who guard the Southern gates, I call on your energy. Those of *Hydor*, of the living Water, *Naiads* who guard the Western gates, I call on your presence. Those of Gaea, of the living Earth, *Leimakides* who guard the Northern gates, I call on your nurturance."

Her intonations took on a serenity Talon hadn't heard before. Hearing Aether call upon the *Aetoi*—Eagles—made her feel included, too. This was Aether's grounding ritual, the one she repeated in her mind when she felt uneasy or challenged. Now, in this realm of death, she needed to voice the words aloud. After a deep, cleansing breath, she stood, brushing herself off.

"I'm ready. Let's go."

Apollo had told them to be ready to encounter a whole bestiary of Hadean creatures in this place. So far, they had been lucky, but that luck had just run out when they reached the end of the path. Before them, flat stones led down toward another river, one whose waters moaned. To the left, a gnarled white poplar grew from the riverbank, its roots forming an enclosure where a fountain bubbled. Entwined around the twisted branches, slithering through the wooden maze, was a fifty-foot serpent with bright green scales that glistened like prisms. His head moved in mesmeric ways, shimmering and undulating.

"Look away," Talon said, turning toward Aether and

spreading her wings as a visual shield. "It reminds me of an Ismenian drakon."

Cadmos, a legendary hero, slew the Ismenian drakon that guarded a spring near Thebes. He planted the teeth at Athene's behest, and they grew into fearsome warriors.

"What are you talking about?"

"Ismenian drakones guard fountains and springs, but this one has a defensive posture. It won't leave the tree unless we get too close, but we need to get that water. Plus, I don't think we need to plant any teeth." Talon had paid attention to Aegis' stories. "Never mind."

Glancing over Talon's wing, Aether saw the creature almost gliding through the branches, its fluidic moves drawing her gaze, but she quickly looked toward the base of the fountain, bleached bones strewn randomly about. Evidently, they belonged to the victims of curiosity.

Aether pulled something from a waist pouch.

"Distract it while I draw the water from the fountain into this vial."

Lowering her wings, Talon leaped up, flapping her way around the riverbank, keeping only a peripheral eye on the green serpent. Aether was only about twenty feet away, but she had to get closer to be able to see the water in the fountain better. Inching her way down the bank, she kept glancing at Talon's location.

"Don't worry about me! Just do what you need to do," Talon said.

Swooping closer to the poplar tree, she had to get almost too close to the drakon to draw its attention away from Aether, now fifteen feet from the fountain. The serpent lunged at her above, snapping its fangs within inches of her foot. She couldn't use lightning here, not full blasts anyway, or it would tear a hole to the outside world. Arcing the electricity through the javelin, she shocked the drakon back, but instead of backing down, it smoothly uncurled itself from the tree, encircled the fountain, coiling its massive body to block Aether's view while keeping its eyes on Talon above. A cylindrical barrier of iridescent scales looked more like the impenetrable walls of Troy to them; but even mighty Troy eventually fell. Their original intention was to take the water without incident; that apparently was no longer an option.

Talon swung around, dipping and turning, wings at the proper angles, and flew close to the riverbank behind the undulating head. Anticipating her moves, the drakon snapped its tail, knocking her to the bank. Muttering a few obscenities, Talon took off once more.

"Grandma, forgive me, but I need to use the javelin as a weapon, not a tool," Talon said, getting closer. Taking a hard left, she flew around, jabbing the silvery point just under the jaw until the point emerged through the top of the serpent's head. Flailing about, the green-scaled head couldn't open, and Talon crashed into it, knocking it to the ground. Before she could move, the scaly tail wrapped around her, constricting her movement, and every time she breathed, she felt the coils get tighter. Without access to the javelin, Talon had no means to escape.

Aether, seeing the opening she needed, witnessed Talon moments from being crushed. She reached out her hand and drew forth enough water to fill the vial, and then hurled any rocks on the bank toward the serpent, but they had no effect. Touching both hands to the sand, Aether opened the ground beneath the serpent long enough for its head to fall in, and then she closed the crevasse, squeezing the head long enough for the coiled tail to release her friend. Her wings and ribcage crushed, she barely had a pulse. Aether gently put her friend over her shoulder, not an easy task with the weight of proportional wings, and made her way to the iron gate. Without Talon to fly them over the river Akheron, Aether had to do what she dreaded the most. Improvising, she solidified the river's surface. Shuffling along, bearing Talon's weight, she broke into a sweat concentrating so she didn't fall into the river of pain. Touching the water in solid form under feet connected her to the agony of the spirits of the dead trapped in the befouled Akheron. Sharp, stabbing pains in her feet shot through her entire body, but she held control the best she could. Gaea couldn't help her — not even Thalassa, a water elemental, could. Thousands of years of agony had tainted these waters.

With only ten feet left until the bank, another shooting pain triggered her memories, and she released some of her mental control, falling into the river. Crying out, Aether had no choice but to swim the distance, pulling Talon along. Akheron's waters tastes like ash, and each unfortunate swallow forced a shrill wail that even made Cerberos cower. Every second felt like an eternity, and her tears stung her eyes. She crawled onto the bank and, eventually, the pain receded. Talon was unconscious, thankfully.

Once at the other side, Aether formed an earthen platform upon which she placed Talon whose breathing had become shallow and strained. It was easier for Aether to move the platform along the ground than it was to carry her friend, and adrenaline pumped through her so that with one sweeping hand gesture, she slid the stone door away, bringing them back to the land of the living.

The TF-18 arrived with a trained medical team, and Aether stayed next to Talon the entire flight back to Boston when she could have easily slept. Looking down at the vial of water in her lap, she silently hoped it was all worth it because being in the underworld, and that river, even for a brief period, changes you; she contemplated what she had felt not only in Hades' realm but also touching the agony-filled souls of the damned forever cursed in the river's clutches. Nothing humbles one more than being in the land of the dead.

25—WING AND PRAYER

On the sacred ground where the Delphic oracle used to prophesy, Apollo placed a small brazier of iron into which he layered poplar, laurel, and bay branches, dried by his own power, the command of the sun. Ritual always demanded fire; in fact, it demanded all of the elements, which would give Sarah great purpose here. It had been a week since Aleta had been released from the hospital, and it had only been a few days before that they both traveled to Hades to retrieve some water, but Apollo hadn't told them anything about it or why they would need it. Encircling the brazier was laurel ash, leaving a perimeter of ten feet. Without access to Olympos and the sanctified holy ground, he chose Delphi, a temple sacred to both him and Gaea. Since his great-grandmother had decided to participate in this, he wanted the location amenable to both of them.

Dan, Aleta, Brandon, and Sarah would perform the ritual, and he gestured for them to sit around the brazier, but they would need someone to observe and protect them from outside forces, if needed. Even though he dressed as the mortal man, Paul Fairmont, he allowed his Olympeian aspects to show; none who saw him at this moment would ever mistake him for a human being. He held out his hand to Dan who gave him *Thyroros*, and then he pushed the sword down through the brazier so that only the hilt showed. None seated noticed that crows had perched themselves on the trees surrounding the shrine.

As the sun sank, the natural world took on a reddish hue, as if the world had been dyed with blood. Sarah poured the contents of the vial into a bronze chalice and placed it on the ground by her legs. Crows cawed behind them, signaling the approach of night.

Seeming to them as Apollo in this place, the god of prophecy stood where they could all see him.

"Tonight, you perform a ritual designed to strengthen the power of memory in those who would be Lismonia's next victims. Each of you represents the cosmos and its vast power, pieces of a puzzle that form a complete idea. Sarah, your elemental powers will be the focus of this enchantment, since your spiritual beliefs and ancestry tie you to ancient Atlantean magic. You represent the earth, the seas, the sky, and the First Fires that Khaos used to create all.

"Dan, your overlapping ties to the earth will sustain Sarah's connection, and your ties to Olympos will sustain *you*, even though the mountain's spirit has abandoned the gods. You represent part of Arkadeia's legacy, too, which anchors you to the world.

"Aleta, your tie to the vast skies, and the lightning of the Cyclopes, shall fuel the ritual and your teammates. As an elemental creature yourself, you overlap with Sarah, thus providing her spiritual support. As a descendant of the Amazons, you bring with you strength and courage.

"Brandon, your connection to the heavens and the fiery stars above, while overlapping with Aleta's gifts, will also connect with Dan's ties to Olympeia. As part of the same Arkadeian legacy as Dan, you fortify this circle.

"Tonight, you no longer act as four to create one unit. Your unity shall fuel *Thyroros*. Waters from the fountain of Mnemosyne in the chalice will be the vehicle. Once these potential victims have been reinforced, Lismonia will not be able to take anything from them, hopefully giving us time to find her. Let the rite begin."

Apollo stepped back, and Sarah took over. After each elemental invocation, the others repeated in unison.

"Those of *Aer*, of the living Air, *Aetoi* who guard the Eastern gates, we call on you to be present at this ritual."

After she finished repeating the words, Aleta's wings outspread, the white stripe of hair down the middle of her head transforming into white feathers. Her eyes looked like two small stars shining in the darkness, and lightning striated the heavens, providing a percussive background to their choral voices.

"Those of *Pyr*, of the living Fire, *Drakones* who guard the Southern gates, we call on you to be present at this ritual."

With the last word, the brazier ignited, its dancing flames swayed around the sword, embracing it. Thunder cracked all around them.

"Those of *Hydor*, of the living Water, *Naiads* who guard the Western gates, we call on you to be present at this ritual."

Brandon's eyes glowed like Aleta's, and his amulet lifted from his chest while each of the constellation jewels sparkled with the newly kindled fire. The chalice rose before Sarah.

"Those of Gaea, of the living Earth, *Leimakides* who guard the Northern gates, we call on you to be present at this ritual."

His eyes like the others, Dan extended his arms, and all four created a circle holding hands. A circle of friendship within a circle of laurel, the wood of heroic deeds. Apollo stepped back. He had no idea how powerful they were, but his skin bristled, the ichor pumping through him. *This* was Olympeian power, old power.

Again, in unison, their voices spoke:

"Waters of memory, fires of life, fuel Gaea's blade that it may find divine blood, protect them with Mnemosyne's gift."

Twice more they uttered the words, invoking the triad charm. Fire flew from the brazier, surrounding them—a third ring to accompany the others. Brandon's amulet shot forth with colored streaks, the power of the constellations swirled above them, a prism of starlight. The sun god wanted to turn away; he had never seen such power, not even from the gods.

Shadows dashed across the black sky, hidden by lightning, looking like nothing more than clouds pushed around by the wind. Apollo sensed movement all around them, a fluctuation in the air that was so subtle that he would have missed it had it not been for his dark-winged minions. A murder of crows had been his eyes and ears while he ministered to the four seated around the fire. Beyond the electricity woven across the heavens, he felt another presence, or maybe three. *Not here*, he thought. *Not now.* He had to protect them.

"I can smell you, Tisiphone. You and your sisters. You will find no vengeance here."

The hissing of serpents, many of them, filled the night silence, while the flapping of bat-like wings roared around him. Apollo felt a claw scrape his arm, and his blue eyes blazed. Swinging around, his eyes shot a bolt of sunlight into the darkness, but it did nothing more than singe a few trees. The god of archery actually missed. Another swipe of a claw grazed his cheek, ichor dribbling down his face. He took a defensive posture, one that Athene had taught him, his hands ready to blast the Erinyes into atoms. Wings whooshed past him, and a third time a claw struck, this time piercing his arm. He healed instantly, but he was finished being the bull's-eye for the Furies' target practice. Something he hadn't noticed before prevented him from focusing. He had taken it for granted that the darkness around him was the night, but once he tried a mortal technique—using all of his senses—he realized that he had been duped. It looked, sounded, and even smelled like night, but it felt thicker, almost sentient. That was why his crows didn't continue to warn him: the darkness itself wouldn't let them.

"Erebos." Apollo had had too many dealings with this immortal. "You're here at Nyx's behest. Surely, you must remember Zeus, the Olympeian god who seduced your beloved Night, from which union brought *The Nebulous One* into the world. The daughter who isn't yours. You serve Night as a dog does its master."

The darkness shuffled around him. Apollo had gotten to Erebos. *Protogenoi* could be so insecure, being so single-minded. His only purpose was the darkness. Whether or not he remembered Zeus was irrelevant; the tiniest shred of doubt in his primordial mind was all that would be needed to weaken him. Apollo again heard the rushing of wings and conjured his bow. Veering to his left, he shot a golden shaft, the twang of the string striking a discordant note in the air. Hearing the shrieking hiss of his target confirmed that he had indeed manipulated Erebos.

"Why do you shield the Furies, son of Khaos? These goddesses of vengeance serve *The Nebulous One* more than they do anyone else. She has given them leave to attack without cause, and that goes against our protocol of vengeance, does it not?"

Another pivot on his foot and a second shaft plucked into the darkness, a darkness that seemed to be fading. Once more a dull thud and cry of pain reaffirmed the sun god's confidence. Apollo needed to get back to his sons and their companions to make sure the enchantment would work.

"I tire of this game, Dark One. Retire to Tartaros, or I shall be forced to let loose the sun's might. And, take those three with you. Heed me."

To show his seriousness, Apollo conjured a ball of radiant sunlight the size of a basketball. Viscous darkness melted away, allowing the true night to show, and two bat-winged goddesses trailed behind. In the shrouded melee, Apollo had moved about a quarter of a mile away from the circle, but he materialized back to where he had stood to find the incantation halted. Alekto, the only sister Fury not wounded, stood behind Sarah, her ebon claws resting on Sarah's shoulders and the black serpents from her arms moving about the girl's head. Each fanged mouth slithered dangerously close to Sarah's neck. Apollo's eyes burned, and he aimed his bow at Alekto's head.

"Make no mistake. I will endure the eternal wrath of your sisters by taking your life, since killing one of your kind brings a terrible price." He pulled the bowstring tighter.

Alekto's black eyes showed no mercy and stared back at the sun god. A dozen serpents moved over and around Sarah's head, the only sign of agitation in the vengeance goddess.

"I'd tell you to say hello to Hades for me when you arrive in the underworld, but he's indisposed." He locked his eyes on hers. Why was he hesitating?

Sarah hadn't released her hands from her companions, so the circle had stayed intact. They had indeed become one unit, one mind, and their will was decisive. Fire that burned in the brazier grew to where it could almost not be contained anymore, and it initiated the sword's magic. All four said, in one flawless voice,

"To Tartaros you shall go, Alekto, daughter of Nyx. So shall it be by *Khaos*, by *Hesteia*, by *Thalassa*, by *Gaea*, and blessed by *Æther*. Bound by the *Pentastoikheia*, the Elements Five, until the Sacred Scales no longer move."

Thyroros' gemstone in the pommel glowed red for a moment, and then Alekto melted into mist. Apollo lowered his bow. He was right to have put Sarah in charge of this ritual.

Five crows left their perches and circled the heads of Sarah, Dan, Aleta, and Brandon. The water from the bronze chalice, from Mnemosyne's fountain, split into five spheres. This time, only Sarah spoke:

"As of the heavens, so of the earth. As of the water, so of the fire. Sword of Gaea, find five souls linked the strongest to the line of Kronos. Imbue this sacred water with their spirit. As of the heavens, so of the earth. As of the water, so of the fire."

Again the gemstone in *Thyroros* glowed red, but this time the myriad of light from Brandon's amulet joined with the stone. One lone thunder strike kissed the stone as well. All four of them repeated, 'As of the heavens, so of the earth. As of the water, so of the fire.'

Apollo stared as five white sparks, like fireflies, flew from the gem and each settled in a sphere of water. Each of the crows carried a sphere aloft in its claws until the five lights twinkled in the sky. *Thyroros* rose from the fire, and Dan took it by the hilt replacing it in his shoulder scabbard. Sarah scooped up the fire with two hands and set it free as one does a bird that has been captive far too long. The Earthsteel disk settled to Brandon's chest once more, and all of the lights faded away. Reaching up toward the electric sky, Aleta reclaimed her javelin, her wings folded and then vanished, and her feathered stripe on her head became white hair once more.

The ritual was complete.

With nothing left to say or do, Apollo knew these four had earned well-needed rest, so he simply waved his hand over them, transporting them back to their respective homes. He had never been prouder of them than he was this night.

His last gesture brought a strong, warm breeze from the valley, wiping away the ashen circle and removing the iron brazier. Delphi resumed its quiet, prophetic silence.

26—SACRIFICE

Three weeks later.

Ari watched the sunrise from Dan's and Brandon's balcony, taking in the view of the Charles River. The Task Force team had a reconnaissance mission to run, and Quinn didn't really need any assistance, so rather than go back to his tiny studio apartment, Ari waited for Dan at his place. Even though he had been in this time and place long enough to get used to it, he still felt the rush of excitement looking out over Boston. Not quite the city of Tegea, he thought, although he hadn't seen Arkadeia's capital all that much growing up. Working in the Temple of Hades, watching his father as caretaker, had given him a perspective not many had—the darkness of death had a serene quality that grounded him. He didn't know that Apollo, ironically, felt the same way about the dark. As the sun god, one would think he would find solace in the brash beams of sunlight, but even they could be overwhelming. Ari's life had changed in ways he could never have imagined, and although he was helping Dan and the team working with Quinn as a consultant, Ari didn't feel as if he were doing the most he could do. Dan constantly reassured him that just his presence was enough, and he appreciated Ari's innocence and input. The son of Timaios never talked about his father, but not because he felt shame at being the *epistatis*, or caretaker, of the temple. It was in fact a great honor to be chosen by the high priests of Hades to serve in that capacity. Regrettably, the responsibility fell to the son or daughter should the *epistatis* die or be incapacitated. Ari could no longer perform that role, and he didn't want to, especially after what he had experienced in this new life. He missed his father, though.

He spent the morning and early afternoon cleaning the apartment a little, watching some television, even took a walk down by the river to take advantage of the beautiful spring day. Buildings along the river reminded him of the temples in Tegea, their majesty and presence giving him consolation. It was in this moment of meditation that he made his decision: he would help Dan and the others. On the walk back to the apartment, he visited the Stop-n-Shop for a few things.

Dan and Brandon walked through the door to see an organized, clean living room, something atypical with the schedules they kept. They found Ari in the kitchen packing a rucksack, and Dan embraced him around the chest and gave him a peck on the cheek.

"You going somewhere?" Dan squeezed his arms around Ari.

"I decided to take a few days and travel around Massachusetts. Quinn does not really need my help currently, and you have your hands full with work and your team."

"That's not a bad idea, actually." Brandon flopped onto the sofa. "You haven't seen much of the area."

"Any idea when you'll be back?" Dan already missed Ari.

"Not sure. But, I will not be gone that long, so you will not have time to miss me." Ari smiled as he tied the last cord on his sack. "I have enough money, and I have a map of the area. Do not worry about me, *Agapimeni*." Dan liked when Ari called him his beloved.

"I'll leave you two alone. I need to take a nap. Take care, Jas, and have fun." Brandon and Ari shared a fun handshake.

When they were alone, Dan turned Ari around. Short brown hair gave Ari a more contemporary look, as did his clothes, and his brown eyes could always stop Dan in his tracks no matter what he was doing.

"Are you okay? This just seems a little out of the blue. We're good?"

Ari smiled. "Of course we are. I just want to spread my wings a little."

After their kiss goodbye, Ari stood in the doorway. "*S'agapo*." He winked, something he had picked up from Aleta.

The passport, DNA card, and paperwork Dan had arranged for Ari just after he arrived in Boston to establish him helped him get to his destination: Epirus, Greece, near the border of Albania. The bus ride from Aktion Airport to Epirus was just under two hours, but from there, he would have to hitchhike to get to his next destination. He wished he had had more time to take in the sights of Greece, especially since this country looked vastly different from the place he had lived thousands of years ago. He double-checked his rucksack to make sure he had what he needed. He hated lying to Dan and Brandon, but if they had known where he was headed, he was sure Dan wouldn't have wanted him to do it. This desire to help went beyond just feeling ineffective; he knew the consequences of Lismonia's actions, and he couldn't allow Dan, or his friends, to fall prey to her. Some Greek rock music on the bus caught his ear, but he shook his head and smirked when he listened to the lyrics. *These are not the dirges heard in*

Hades' shrine, he thought. His experience with his father had exposed him to much, more than Dan even knew, and the music was just a small part of that.

Ari was the only one to get off when the bus stopped at his location, reassuring him that this part of Greece no longer held the same value for modern day mortals. He had a hike of an hour, maybe two, to reach his destination, and he prayed to the gods that they not only keep him from harm, but also that they watch over Dan and his friends. In the *Ptinotrofeio*, however, no prayers are heard.

Weathered signs pointed the way, and Ari noticed the absence of others on the path. *No life here*, he thought. *How ironic*. Ambling through a grove and some pasture land, he reached a cave near a river marked by an eroded stone plaque on the ground reading *Necromanteion*. The brackish waters seemed to have a life of their own and wouldn't resemble their counterpart beyond this cave. Steps moist with decayed leaves led down into the hole in the earth, and Ari tightened the sack on his back. He would need both hands free. Just before he stepped into the darkness, he turned toward the river,

"I greet thee Potamos Akheron, river of pain."

A cigarette lighter illuminated his way down the steps, but they only went about twenty feet below the surface where he reached the door to the *Necromanteion*—an ancient shrine to Hades and Persephone, devoted to necromancy, the magic allowing the living to speak with the deceased. Beyond this portal, he knew where he needed to go, but he had no illusions about reaching his destination alive, just his faith. He slowly unfurled a piece of lined paper and read the words,

"Waters of the trifold pass, hear my plea: allow me entry to the realm of Hades and Persephone. I beseech thee, O Akheron, O Cocytos, O Phlegethon, bring me through this stone to meet death."

Folding the paper and replacing it in his sack, he withdrew a knife he had purchased in town and dragged the tip across both palms. He pressed his bloody hands on the stone door and repeated the words.

Ari's pulse quickened as he felt the stone slide backwards against his hands. Once he could slip through, he turned to see the stone seal itself once more, dust swirling in the stale air; he had a twinge of regret. Before him now lay a path of bones that stretched out over the place where three Hadean rivers met. Fiery Phlegethon touched acrid Akheron, and they both touched Cocytos, the river of woe; all three rivers flowed into one pool beneath the bone bridge, and heat, wailing, and caustic mist brushed over him as he moved forward. This wasn't the true underworld, not yet, but simply a temple where he could commune with the dead. The bones ended at a round marble slab surrounded by columns at the center of which sat a shallow iron basin, etched with time and the acidic air. Ari stopped before the basin, realizing he could perform a rite to speak with his father... but he knew his time in the underworld would be short, and he had much to ask his father's spirit. Another time, perhaps. Beyond the marble slab lay a path, one of an infinite amount of paths that led toward Hades' realm. He had his reasons for taking this route through the *Necromanteion*. It was then he recited the enchantment he had learned as a boy, one that would keep him from harm. A powerful spell, it was known only to a few, and those who knew it were bound to secrecy. To speak of this magic would mean losing one's senses until madness came. Using his faith and his knowledge as a guide and shield, he walked for what felt like weeks until he reached an opening that led onto a different path, one of dead flowers that led right to the palace of *The Unseen One* and his pallid bride.

From his rucksack he pulled a tunic, sandals, and black cloak, similar to the one he wore in the Temple of Hades. Ari removed his mortal clothes, folded them, and placed them in a pile on the path, with a polished stone on top. He would enter the palace as a supplicant, and he needed to rid himself of his mortal trappings to do that.

Perhaps it was his training as a caretaker or perhaps his mind wrestled with internal conflicts, but he didn't notice the austerity of the underworld, the spirits wafting to and fro, or the wailing of souls from the distant pit of Tartaros. Hades' black marble palace, striated with white and crusted with gemstones, didn't radiate the grandeur it might have in ages past; the lord of the dead was elsewhere, and the palace, like a sentient being, knew this. Standing at the steps, Ari lowered his head and prayed that Hades and Persephone would be merciful and grant him an audience, not a common occurrence with the living. It was quite possible all of this would be in vain.

With each footstep up marble stairs toward the entrance to the palace, Ari repeated the phrase, "Praise be *The Unseen One*, He who guards the dead." It was a ritual his father had told him about, should he ever find himself in the underworld, alive, that is. Little did he know that he would ever need it. Curled up and asleep beside the entry was Orthros, a two-headed black canine related to Cerberos. Even lying down, the dog was taller than Ari. One of the heads stirred and sniffed, growling softly. Ari reached into his rucksack and put a piece of wine-soaked cake by the mighty jaws; Orthros ate it, looked at Ari, and then put his head back down. No other guards protected the entry, and the doorway, flanked with incense baskets, opened to his presence. Inside the main hall, Ari removed the cloak from his head. Adorning the walls were tapestries of the finest silk, gold and silver threads depicting intricate designs, symbols of mourning and meditation. Golden pots lined the walls on both sides of the entry hall, each growing a cypress, a tree sacred to Hades. At the far end of the chamber was a raised dais upon which sat two thrones. When he reached the base of the dais, he strew asphodel petals around him, a showing of respect to the one he had come to see. He didn't dare look up.

"You seek an audience with me, mortal." A honeyed voice flowed from the shadows. He began to weep.

From behind the thrones emerged a woman, tall and thin, her body wrapped in gauzy fabric edged in gold. Her blonde hair wound around her head was kept in place with a golden headband. Bracelets of different metals adorned her wrists, and they made a musical tinkling as she moved. In her right hand, she carried a thin torch, in her left, sheaves of wheat. Barefoot, she moved across the polished marble floor, making no sound. The wife of Hades reclined in her throne, inserting the torch into the arm and laying the sheaves in her lap.

Ari carried a pomegranate up to her, without raising his eyes, and placed the fruit by her feet.

"You knew to bring an offering." A faint smile appeared on her soft face. "Lift your eyes, mortal. I grant you audience."

When he saw her eyes, his tears stopped. Her face was a balm to his anxiety.

"Queen Persephone, thank you for your grace."

"Come, sit." She gestured toward a stool that materialized at her whim.

Once he sat, she reached over and placed her hand on his. He turned away instinctively, but looked back so as not to insult her. She commented that he knew the proper ritual, entering through the *Necromanteion*, something one would do who sought an audience with Hades' queen. Had he stopped to speak with the deceased, he would have diminished his intent. Persephone asked his name. He answered using the proper decorum.

"I am Aristeides, son of Timaios."

"Timaios. I know that name. He was the *epistasis* in my husband's shrine in Arkadeia."

As all knowing as he knew the gods to be, he was a surprised that she would know his father. As if responding to an unspoken question, she said, "Hades spoke of him, after his visits."

Ever since Ari was a child, he knew that his father took counsel with Hades; occasionally, *The Unseen One* would enter his own shrine, under the cover of darkness, and commune with his caretaker. The god of the dead adored his wife, and he had grown to care about the realm he governed, but when Persephone had to return to her mother, Demeter, during the springtime, he would leave the confines of the river-girded underworld and venture to the mortal world to connect with mortals who devoted their lives to the care of his temple. During those times, with those he trusted implicitly, Hades would share secrets, like sacred rituals or incantations. As Ari grew, he watched for the signs when the underworld king would visit and made sure to be within earshot of his insight and wisdom. Over the years, Hades would even let down his guard and make jokes or share jugs of wine made from grapes that only grew in Elysium, the place where heroes spent eternity. His father would tell Ari later that this wine was sweet with the goodness that those fair souls exuded. Timaios shared everything with his son, including information Hades had told him things about Nyx's daughter who nursed in Tartaros, making certain that Ari swore a sacred oath that he would never reveal what he had learned, unless it was to another Olympeian. Just as Danelos would swear to serve Gaea and Olympeia, Ari honored Hades with his own sacred pledge. It was Timaios' intention that his son should take over when he could no longer perform the duties of the *epistasis*.

"Your father's death was a loss that Hades himself felt, Aristeides. He would be proud to know that you honor his memory by carrying on the traditions of his station, even if you no longer reside in Arkadeia."

Humbled by her words, Ari turned away. He didn't regret leaving to follow Danelos, but he did wish he could have said goodbye to his father before leaving Arkadeia forever.

"Why have you come all this way to see me?"

"Your Majesty, I want to help my *agapimeni*, a brave warrior, and his friends defeat *The Nebulous One*. All my life, I have devoted my service to Hades, and I come now asking for aid."

Persephone's face fell into shadow. It had been eons since she had encountered a soul as innocent as his, a living one, and she desired to help him. She realized what she could give Ari. Opening her palm, she conjured a small gilded box. A gentle smile grew that warmed Ari's heart, but he instinctively knew that with any gift, there must be a price. Once, long ago, the box had been used to trick Psyche, who fell into a Stygian sleep, placed in the box by Persephone, when she opened the box intended for Aphrodite. The love goddess felt the girl wasn't worthy of her son, Eros. Now, Persephone would place something else in the gold box, but Ari must deliver it to Danelos without succumbing to curiosity.

"Alas, young mortal, I must exact a price."

Persephone offered him the box, and he received it, without hesitation, even once he knew what she asked of him. It was worth it if it would help Danelos and the others defeat this unholy entity. The queen of the underworld assured him that the contents of this box would indeed sway the scales in the favor of heroes. He thanked her and turned to go, but she asked him to stay a while, just like Hades used to do with his father. With the five rivers controlling the realm, and Persephone not having enough power to stop them, she would bide her time until her husband returned from his mortal sojourn. This allowed her more time to pursue other interests, including conversing with a mortal man who could tell her of the modern world. For that, she would return him to Boston. Travelling through Hades changed people, and she didn't want Ari to lose his humanity.

27—THE MURDER

A ri returned to Boston, and no one noticed that he seemed different. One doesn't have an audience with the queen of the dead without being affected by it. He understood her sorrow a bit more, now, especially when she would leave the underworld to be with her mother for half a year. They had talked for what felt like years, and it might have been, but his return only a week after he had left reassured his faith in the power of his gods. Even with Hades and the other Olympeians in another place, the ancient power that emanated from Khaos that had been passed down through the *Protogenoi* to the Titans and then the gods themselves still flowed like the lifeblood of the cosmos. That gave Ari hope.

Resuming his role as consultant to the team, he felt more at ease knowing he would play a part in what would come. His knowledge of certain magics and rituals, those he was not oath-bound to keep hidden, would certainly add to the arsenal of Task Force: Gaea. Also, his agreement with Persephone would ensure something positive would come from all this—he had to believe that or the price he was to pay would be more like torment than a willing sacrifice. He had done what he felt was best to protect those

he cared about, just as the team had done its best to augment the memory of five potential victims of Lismonia's
greed. Power older than the gods flowed through Sarah,
Dan, Aleta, and Brandon that night, and together they sent
five guardians. Each would find its way across the globe,
hopefully without incident. If the *Moirae* were kind, they
would weave a softer fabric for these five people, one not
stained with blood and fear.

Chengdu, China, Sichuan province.

Around Donghu Lake, a beautiful day brought out
families, many with children, to enjoy a little respite from
their daily routines, although the presence of the Royal
police, some plainclothes and some not, reminded people
just how much freedom they truly had. Like in Boston,
cameras glared into lives here, too. Children, however,
didn't pay as much attention to the officers or the cameras,
and many flew kites and played games by the water's
edge. Six-year-old Léi Wong frolicked with his friends,
and he held the string attached to a dragon-shaped kite in
his clenched fist. Light breezes brushed his black hair
across his forehead, and his infectious laugh made even
other families around him smile. Amid the bevy of kites
soaring in the sky, birds flew, seeming to compete with the
paper dragons. One bird in particular flew with purpose.

Léi had moved far enough away from his family that
they couldn't see him among the other kite-bearing children, and he got caught up in the gaiety, too. A few times,
some of the birds would try to attack the kites, but this
one, a black crow, circled overhead until it spied its destination. Swirling downward, it circled around, enticing Léi
to move into an open place. In its claws was a sphere of
twinkling water, looking much like a bubble, and the crow
descended on the breeze. Distracted by the glossy feathers,
Léi released his kite to reach up and try to catch the crow,
but the claws released the sphere into the boy's hands. For
a moment, he felt the ball of water against his palm and

fingers, and within seconds, it dissolved, imparting its protective power. To Léi, however, this was simply a game. Having completed its mission, the messenger of Apollo flew higher and higher, becoming one with the sunbeams once more.

To the west, a black cloud approached, its form unlike any other cloud. To those by the lake, it looked like an on-coming storm. They would have no idea. She had come for him, little Léi Wong, whose name meant *thunder king*, but she would find that when she ensnared him in her ten-drils, while others by the lake ran in horror, their minds unable to grasp this primordial form, she would stare into his soul with her red eyes, reaching inside him to take what she wanted. She would find his mind protected, however, not knowing the waters from the fountain of Mnemosyne had done what they were supposed to do. Recoiling from the boy, leaving him unharmed and con-fused as to why her vast power had no effect, she returned to the sky to find another.

One soul saved, and a myriad of minds she couldn't touch.

Kampala, Uganda.

Another of Apollo's feathered emissaries, empowered by Task Force: Gaea's magic, headed toward its target, a seventy-year-old man named Taji Atubo. Suffering from dementia and blindness, he had been homeless for five years, having wandered out of the elder care facility his children had arranged for him. Lost in a city he couldn't see, Taji had found a spot under an awning on Yusuf Lule Road. His brown, tattered coat held together by hope and tape, he sat in the same spot, day after day, holding his wooden bowl before him. Most days he would collect enough for soup, or maybe some stale bread — both, if he were lucky. The Kampala police, most of whom took bribes and turned away from crime, would leave Taji to the elements, so the old man would rely on the kindness of strangers, but kindness was rare here.

Only a handful of times since he had been in this spot on Yusuf Lule Road had anyone done more than put loose change in his bowl. If he had clarity, he might be able to remember when he last bathed, about two months earlier. A tourist from Spain and his girlfriend, a nurse, took Taji to their hotel, bathed him, and gave him a hot meal. He didn't have the means to thank them, but he offered the young woman a flower he had made from paper. Before they returned him to his spot, since they had not been able to find anyone who knew Taji or any place he could go, they bought him a brown coat to replace the threadbare sweatshirt he was wearing. Since that couple had helped him, he had been left to the whims of the *Moirae*. Spinning life's threads required neither emotion nor empathy.

Gray-feathered pigeons cooed all around the city, and if it weren't for the awning over Taji's head, he would probably be speckled from droppings. A crow had found the city of Kampala, and not many had seen birds with dark, glossy plumage before. Across the street from where Taji sat were some teenage boys taking turns throwing rocks at passing cars, but a few had taken to throwing them at the pigeons. Despite the electronic eyes above, the throng of boys didn't relent. Swooping over some trees, the crow flew, its liquid gift held tightly. Before it could make its way across the street, a stone thrown by one of the boys struck its claws, dislodging the sphere. The crow cawed loudly to frighten the boys and dove for the ground, clasping the sphere in its claws once more, just an inch before it would have been lost. The boys, amused by this spectacle, joined together to throw more stones, hoping perhaps to knock the bird to the ground and watch the strange ball of water splash to the street. Having to ascend away from its target to avoid the attack, the crow flew back around, making wide circles, cawing its frustration. An icy wind swept through the city, and the crow knew time was short. Coming in from the side, the black wings flapped into a blur, flying down under the awning and dropping the water on Taji's head. It dodged a few more stones before pursuing a trajectory far away from the on-coming black cloud. Again, Lismonia would find her quarry shielded and depart to find yet another she could ply with her power. But, she saw something that caught her attention.

Cairo, Egypt.

Malik Qureshi, a 44-year-old transnational business at-torney, stepped into a taxicab on Al Kasr Al Kaini Street around 5 p.m., cell phone in one hand and briefcase in the other. He gave the driver an address, showed his ID, and put his eye up to a scanner, and then continued his con-versation. Malik and his law firm had just closed a major deal with an Egyptian computer company, and all he wanted to do was get home to his wife and family.

Traffic in downtown Cairo was no different than rush hour in any country of the world, and the driver kept mut-tering in Arabic about how certain people shouldn't be able to have driver's licenses. Malik finished the call, but the phone vibrated again, and when he noticed the call was from his wife, his face brightened. The cabbie glanced in the rear view mirror, noticing how different his fare sounded on this call. *Must be his wife*, he thought. Before he turned his attention back to the road, his eyes widened. About ten blocks back, he saw a gurgling black mass move down the street. At first, he thought something had ex-ploded and that this was a cloud of dust and debris — terrorist activity was common in Egypt, especially from their adversaries in Asia and Mexico. He looked forward again in time to stop at a red light, but then he looked over his right shoulder. Fear penetrated his mind, and his psy-che began to unravel.

Lismonia had honed in on her target.

Not willing to wait at the light, he pushed his foot to the floor and screeched his tires. A high-pitched squeal broke Malik's concentration, and he noticed the driver was terrified. He couldn't get the man to slow down, and the driver kept muttering unintelligibly.

She was almost upon him. The cab weaved in and out of the lane; she was closing in on him and would soon feed. Twice before she had been thwarted by an unknown power, but not again. When her semisolid form spread through downtown Cairo, flailing tendrils lashed out in frustration, snatching up random people and dissolving them into her. Their fleshy bodies never resisted her touch, and a trail of bones picked clean and chunks of flesh remained.

Madness, like a festering parasitic virus taking root and feeding, had permeated the driver's mind entirely and causing him to turn the wheel abruptly to the left, and the car spun out of control. His mouth foamed, and his utterances spit bits of white all over the window and dashboard. Malik held on to the door handle, but he was being tossed about like a doll. Lismonia bided her time a bit since she knew she would reach him, and she retracted her dark, tentacle-like arms into herself and oozed her way down the street.

Those who had escaped her touch had fallen to the ground, like rabid animals, their mouths foaming as well. So strong was her power, so intense was her desire, that any creature within a two block radius would succumb to her radiant lunacy — all but one.

The cab lurched over the curb, hit the side of a parking garage, and flipped onto its side, windows shattering. The driver, now lying against the driver's door, convulsed in his seat, his eyes bleeding onto the glass. Malik had been fortunate that he had not seen Lismonia or he, too, would have met a similar fate, but the *Moirae* had other things in store for this mortal. He maneuvered so he could sit up a bit, reaching for his phone that had flown out of his hand

and had landed somewhere on the floor. The coldness frosted the window as she approached, and he felt his soul shiver. Nyx's daughter closed in on him, and she rose up, readying to strike when a black crow cawed from above her and looked for a way to get the sphere to its recipient. A flailing black tendril lashed out like a whip, severing one of the crow's wings from its body, and it tumbled to the earth, landing on the passenger door of the cab. Its brittle bones shattered and its life force waning, it had managed to drop the watery sphere through the broken window. Malik would be safe, but Lismonia had gotten closer; she would have to try a different tack.

Gaea smiled. She knew Lismonia's frustration would drive her to do something rash — most *Protogenoi* acted on raw emotion; even Gaea had in ages past.

Sitka, Alaska.

The village elders and other members of the Shee Ati-ka tribe who had gathered in the Tribal Community House had no idea what to make of the amorphous blackness that was Lismonia, moving across the Gulf of Alaska, except to think that it was an approaching thunderstorm. One of the shamans, a woman who claimed she was so old she saw the mountains form — although most thought that was simply hyperbole, had told everyone to go inside and just wait for instructions. She knew this was no storm.

Lismonia needed another way to find the one who bore that stench of Olympeian ancestry before the crow did. Ancient magic guided the bird, and Lismonia had no means to locate it beforehand. This deeply rooted grudge against Zeus' descendants had been her purpose since her birth, and it had indeed taken control of her. She couldn't see the irony. Before she made landfall, she dissipated, and the icy wind that most assumed was normal would hide her plan.

Diana Ravenfeather Boyd, one of the few shamanesses left in Sitka, had taken a headcount of all the people she had seen enter the Community House. Everyone knew her by her long gray braid and the leather thong around her head. A moon-shaped bead carved from wood sat in the center of her forehead. At only 5'3", she didn't have the most imposing stature, but anyone who went up against her knew that that was simply a bad idea. If she told someone where to be and when, they knew to be there at that time.

Less than an hour later, a Tlingit woman, about 25-years-old with long black hair, entered the House, but she went largely unnoticed by the others and moved toward the side of the great room where she found a chair. Diana noticed her, and their eyes met. They nodded at each other, and the young woman smiled faintly. It was clear to Diana that she was new to the community and didn't wish to introduce herself. As night fell upon the town, the mood of the great room became more peaceful, perhaps because the storm they had assumed would arrive hadn't. Families and friends took the opportunity to catch up, and volunteers put out potato chips and soda. The young woman stayed to herself, but she kept eyeing the room; she had no desire to draw any attention to herself. She saw a young boy, about 3-years-old, sitting on what seemed to be his mother's lap, but the woman could have been an aunt, cousin, or simply a friend. The next time Diana looked for the newcomer, she saw her seated near the boy and his family, and smiled—perhaps she would make some friends.

A little later, the young woman, having introduced herself as Coronis, was speaking with the family, and the boy seemed mesmerized by her long black hair. She learned that his name was Chaak, a Tlingit word for eagle, and her eyes danced. He was the one.

Coronis had little to tell Chaak's family, but she did tell them she had traveled far and was looking to make a connection in Sitka. Intrigued, the boy's parents inquired further, but she said she had reasons why she couldn't share more. At one point in the conversation, Chaak asked if he could play with her hair; she smiled and put him on her lap so he could reach more easily. Coronis was glad the boy had taken to her. It would make things easier.

Chaak had fallen asleep in Coronis' lap when the door to the House opened and a polar wind invaded the room. In the doorway stood a haggard woman, with two stark white braids down her back, and wearing a traditional Chilkat robe, its fringes hanging like gallows victims. The design on the back, while in the customary style, depicted an upside down white eagle, an atypical image. About as tall as Diana Ravenfeather, she had a wrinkled face and hollow eyes; to a shaman, they reflected a shallow soul and a mind not interested in the complex ideas of the natural world.

The woman's eyes scanned the room, unblinking, and when she saw Coronis, those hollow eyes took on a slight crimson tinge, so slight that only one up close would have noticed. She wrapped the robe around her and took silent steps through the throng of Shee Atika. Diana noticed her and moved to intercept; two strangers in the House in one evening had roused her suspicions. The woman with two braids stopped when she saw Diana, but looked toward Coronis, whose hand was gently stroking Chaak's head as he slept in her lap. The black haired newcomer looked up to see the older, hoary woman in the Chilkat robe, never once letting on anything was wrong. Diana sensed they knew one another. She took a few more steps to the center of the great room, her eyes bouncing back and forth. As soon as she saw the double-braided woman quicken her pace toward Coronis, she stepped forward. Words came from her mouth, and it was her voice, but the words came from someone else.

"You shall not pass."

The white haired woman stopped for a moment, but then moved forward. People closest to Diana saw this, and dispersed. They knew what it meant to cross their village elder; little did they know whose voice it truly was. Again, Diana moved between the two women; Coronis watched intently, making no change in her behavior. It wasn't time.

"These people are under my protection. You — "

Taking yet another step forward, the unnamed visitor began to extend a hand, one whose gnarled fingers bore claw-like, rotted nails. Diana stomped her right foot, and the Community House shook. In fact, the earth shook. At this point, the townspeople clamored against the walls, mothers and fathers holding fast to their children. They had never seen Diana Ravenfeather act this way before, and apprehension coated their whispers. Only Coronis remained, in her chair, Chaak asleep on her lap. Now the white haired woman knew whom she faced. It had been her curiosity to take human form to find her prey, a whim she found to be more of a hindrance. While it gave her a unique perspective, since she had been born through a mortal's womb, Lismonia's true form was more effective.

The Shee Atika shamaness raised her head slightly and earthen walls rose. She would protect these people, but it was not Diana Ravenfeather Boyd who manipulated the element of earth. Gaea had found a willing vessel for her essence, one who revered the earth and all that grew on it. Aged crone in Chilkat robe melted into gelatinous cloud, her dark red eyes feverish and eager to destroy the boy and the woman.

Coronis' eyes never left Lismonia's, but she lifted her other hand, one grasping a sphere of water, and just as a black tendril reached out to violate the boy's soul, Coronis dropped the water on Chaak's head, the mystical waters twinkling with the power of Mnemosyne. Nyx's daughter surrounded the chair, but she could not touch Coronis or the boy. Gaea.

Lismonia shot toward Diana Ravenfeather, but human body became intangible. Gaea wouldn't fight her here, not with mortal lives at risk, but she drew upon all her healing power, something that had repelled Lismonia in Tartaros. Lismonia writhed and churned, looking back toward the chair — Coronis had put young Chaak beyond the earthen wall, out of harm's way, and had taken her true form as well. Doing the bidding of ancient magic and being a mystical companion to the god Apollo, the crow had taken the form she needed to complete her task. It cawed her gratitude to Mother Earth and flew into the night sky, but not before Lismonia lashed out a tendril, splitting the crow in two. If she couldn't have Chaak, she would take Coronis.

Lismonia never had withdrawn before, but she had lost this battle and retreated back into the darkness. Gaea had injured her, so now her mission went beyond her revenge against Zeus; she wanted to make the earth pay. Diana's mind was her own once more, and the earthen walls crumbled, reforming the floor as if nothing had happened. Without hesitation, she did what she did best: nurture her people and help them heal.

The Mother of All who had brought forth the mountains, the rivers, the flora and fauna, and had even birthed the heavens knew Nyx's trifling child would lick her wounds and return with the hopes of revenge, but she had no idea what the Earth could do. Gaea had held back this time, and only she, and likely the *Moirae*, knew the outcome should Lismonia test her again.

Ísafjörður, Iceland.

Twenty-five-year-old Himinn, named for the sky, was an ice fisherman whose solitary life in the port city rarely changed from one moment to the next. The enchantment that sent five crows to protect the innocent had come from old magic, something Apollo hadn't seen in a long, long time. It knew no bias nor had any affinity for mortals, and it was not sentient. Not all its recipients were innocent, however.

Two years earlier in Reykjavík, in a drunken rage, Himinn had slit the throat of a boy who had stolen fish from him. Justice had been more merciful due to a few well placed bribes, and the ruling was to exile him to a more remote town where no one knew him. Not even the news of this atrocity had traveled to this northern town. In essence, he was already a victim of Lismonia's power — no one truly knew him.

He had chosen a life of isolation, bearing the pain and guilt of his crime. Every day, he took out his boat, cast his nets, and brought in his catch, but he didn't sell any of it. Himinn couldn't bring himself to slaughter senselessly hundreds of fish only to have them wasted. He kept a few for himself, and set the rest free. Others had been far more successful than he in fishing, and he couldn't force himself to socialize with anyone. He had relinquished most of the things he enjoyed, including drinking. If he returned to Reykjavík, he certainly would be sentenced to death.

A sunrise brought hope to many, with the prospect of fruitful catches or other undertakings, and Himinn did as he always did, wrapped in his layers, stepped out from his one room house and put his boat in the water. After thirty minutes, he returned to shore and sat on the beach. The few fish he had caught would be fine in the bucket until he returned to the house. An Icelandic morning sky had watery blues and lemon yellows, swaths of light orange, and even streaks of lilac. Himinn reflected on the promise such a visual offered and the peace of mind it could give him.

With outstretched wings, the sleek black feathers carried the crow aloft, over the Denmark Strait. As had its predecessors, this agent of Apollo headed for the mortal targeted by the daughter of Night, now pushed to the limits of her own rage by the earth mother. With its recipient in sight, the crow descended toward the beachhead where it saw young Himinn lying on the sand, his hands folded over his abdomen. Oddly, the wind was no colder than it should be in Iceland, and no dark menace loomed nearby. Hovering, the crow set down inches from his head and dropped its watery cargo before screeching back into the silent skies. It had no idea that the waters of Mnemosyne's fountain would have no effect. As the curative waters trickled down Himinn's face into the sand beneath, so too did his blood. Unwilling to face another day of silence and raging torment of guilt, he slit his wrists with his fishing knife, lay back, and allowed his life to ebb away. No maddening Erinye had prompted him, and no other force — human or other — had guided his hand.

Lismonia, preoccupied with planning her own reprisal against Gaea, had returned to Tartaros in lieu of seeking this fifth source of nourishment. While the enchantment meant to protect Himinn from Lismonia's power had been delivered in time, it only worked if the recipient were still alive. Just as the crow ascended to fly back to Apollo, a large expanse of wings followed. Lismonia had sent a minion to dispatch this messenger, and despite its best efforts, the crow wasn't as fast as its pursuer, and the shrieking harpy's talons made short work of the smaller bird.

Dan and his team had succeeded in denying their bête noire her ability to feed, and they would get word through Apollo when the corvine deed was finished. They didn't know, however, just how much time they might have before Lismonia would seek others again, and they each had unfinished business before they could face her.

28—FINALITY

Gaea hadn't directly involved herself in the affairs of humanity or the gods prior to her confrontation with Lismonia in Alaska. Before the *Titanomachia* eons ago, she was the reticent nurturer, reluctantly allowing Ouranos to imprison her children, the one-eyed Cyclopes and hundred-handed Hekatonkheires, in Tartaros. She had made her presence known to the gods, or some mortals, but more subtly, through dreams and using nature to show her support. She had never appeared in any other form than the earth itself. As the *Moirae* had always told her since she emerged from Khaos, her place was a source of healing and life, the womb of the world. It was for mortals and gods to engage one another, not *Protogenoi*, the First Ones. Her resolve had been strengthened, however; she had her champions in the task force bearing her name, and they would always be under her protection. The sons of Apollo and their team would be her first line of defense, but she would keep her eye on Nyx's daughter. In the meantime, since Apollo had assured the four members of the team of the crows' success, each had also come to turning points in his or her own journey, and individually sought resolution before the ultimate battle with Lismonia.

Brookline, Massachusetts.

Sarah felt the most grounded when she had her hands in moist clay, spinning the wheel, daubing the edges with the sponge. With her power to manipulate the earth, she looked at using her hands in this human way much more satisfying. This latest piece, inspired by some of her recent adventures, had a serpent's body entwining the curved vessel, but this serpent had multiple heads that felt alive beneath her touch. She never used her magical connection to work with clay; this experience was purely visceral and intimate. Of late, Sarah hadn't had much time to immerse herself in this passion, and this was to her what meditation or yoga was to Brandon. Bringing earth, fire, air, and water together with her spirit fulfilled her, but it didn't fill every gap within her. Some things couldn't be patched with wet earth and sponge.

Her foot-powered potter's wheel sat in the middle of an alcove surrounded by windows that curved around the walls, letting the morning light pour over her like liquid fire. On spring and summer days, she opened the windows, smelling the lilacs, and she could almost taste the perfume. During the fall and winter, she let the crisp air, laden with the scent of fallen leaves or fresh snowfall, wash over her. Sarah's respect for Gaea went beyond that of one who simply appreciated the natural world; she regarded the earth as her surrogate mother, especially since her own had been ripped from this world by claw and fang. She had been bearing that weight for far too long, and in the quiet moments, at night or when she looked at the handmade quilt on her bed, she was reminded of the woman who was a goddess to her. The wheel slowed without her concentration, and when it stopped, she made her decision. She needed closure.

Under her feet, the cement path to the front door of her childhood home on Massachusetts Avenue felt unrelenting, unwilling to let her sink into the earth. No—she would have to face the past head on if she expected to pacify the maelstrom of memories. The old Victorian house looked smaller than she had remembered, the paint having worn with the elements. No one lived there now, and the once vibrant and chaotic orgy of wildflowers that grew up around the porch had become a place for dandelions and invasive grasses. No longer did she smell the scent of roses or see the radiant panoply of colors. Sarah looked up to the window that let light into the room where she had first learned about her past, on her twelfth birthday. That was the day Horkos murdered her mother.

The porch boards creaked as they always had, perhaps more so since no one had replaced the ones cracked and weathered. Touching the doorknob, Sarah realized that this was the first time she had touched the house since she had left; the cool, tarnished metal was simply an austere reminder of the emptiness that would follow. Disregarding the sign from the police that read, "Do not enter. This building is owned by Boston Ministry of Housing. Trespassers will be prosecuted," she used her old house key to breach the first barrier and stepped inside.

By the time she reached the top floor and the room where her entire world had changed, Sarah had already cried a few tears, but just for a moment. Crouching down beneath the window flanked by sun-bleached sheers, the one Horkos violated, she touched the floorboards stained with her mother's blood. She remembered telling Helios to leave them. If she truly wanted to, she could speak with her mother's spirit; she knew how. But, Annabeth Jacobs was dead, and she needed to remain that way. Talking with her mother would just kindle a hope that could never become reality. Sarah looked at her ring, the four gems flickering in the sunlight as if each was a tiny flame. And, the band that bound them provided the connection to her primordial guardian, Æther, the upper air, the quintessence. This small Earthsteel ring could destroy mountains or flood deserts. The five elements of the *Pentastoikheia* were hers and hers alone to command. Staring at the gems, she had a revelation. Sarah now understood why she would only be able to control the elements, but never create them: they were sentient beings. She had seen the randomness of the fire, the whimsy of the air, the temerity of the earth, and the resilience of the water; they followed her command not because she possessed a ring. They did so because her humility in their presence showed the highest form of respect. Now, since the sun had set, she had to honor them and put the past behind her.

Locking the front door, she looked down the street that stretched before her. Miles away, she saw the skyline of Boston, its stalwart warriors of steel and concrete about to bear witness. Sarah pulled a matchbook and a candle from her pocket, placing the candle on the sidewalk. The candle, scented with lilac and sage, took the match's flame like a proud garment. Scooping up some of the fire, she let it frolic over her fingers a moment before casting it with a silent bidding. Strings of flame shot forth, finding and destroying the cameras along the street. Picking up another flame, she cupped it in her hands, said a silent prayer, and blew it toward the house. As if she were a conductor, she instructed the musical fire to consume the house, spinning around the whole structure, while she contained the conflagration. No other homes would be touched. Raising her hands, the fire followed, growing into an inferno whose heat instantly incinerated the old Victorian house. Then, she brought a wind to spiral around the house, containing the fire further, forcing it inward. She watched as the top floor turned to ash, forever erasing the bloody stains of her mother. Catharsis.

It took less than five minutes to consume the entire house, and Sarah's artful maneuvering of the nearby pond doused the fire, leaving nothing behind but a scorched plot of land. She was certain the neighbors had seen what she had done and had called the police, the fire department, or both. Sarah didn't care. A final gesture moved a layer of dirt over the lot, blanketing the ashen remains. Offering a silent prayer in honor of her mother, she walked the three blocks to the T station that would take her home.

Now, she could devote all her attention to Nyx's spawn.

Malden, Massachusetts. A few days later.

Aleta, already in her white lab coat, slid her badge through the reader by the front desk of BioCorps, formerly Genomics, and pushed her eye up to the retinal scanner. Three cameras, courtesy of Argus Industries, monitored the foyer, each catching a certain angle of the entry, all of which Aleta thought were unflattering to her. Glossy white walls lined the corridor to the elevator, the only entrance to the genetics laboratory. Even after being promoted to supervisor, Dr. Aleta Halston had to endure the rings of security, despite how long she had been with the company. After the chaotic activity with Task Force: Gaea over the past few months, she was looking forward to getting back to her real job, one that she had put in the hands of her assistant, Dr. Jack Forrester, without whom she couldn't do much of what she did. Gaea had told Apollo that Lismonia was back in Tartaros scheming. Until Aleta was needed, then, she wanted to get back to the tedium of her research.

At 5:30 a.m., no one else was in the lab, and Jack wasn't expected until around 10:00 a.m. Aleta had given Jack the task for clearing certain genetic samples for storage and certain ones for use, and now she had a chance to finish that work. The antiseptic perfume of the cleaners that helped keep the lab sterile smelled like fragrant incense to her, and she took private pleasure in a few deep breaths. She used to enjoy the smell of her plastic swimming pool when she was a girl; it was just something that brought her back to earlier time of innocence and being carefree. Slide after slide under the microscope reconnected her with her passion of helping animals, and ultimately people, survive disease and mutation. Aleta lifted her head, looking off into space for a moment, recalling briefly the accident that made her into the eagle/human hybrid she had become. Pushing back that memory, she put her eye back on the eyepiece. Most of the time, she would use the automated microscope where she would just insert a slide, wait a few minutes, and check the readout. Working with a more traditional scope forced her to use skills she felt had softened over the past few months; the haze and slight buzz of the fluorescent lights, however, forced her to find creative ways to stay focused. By 7:00 a.m., she had finished a sizeable chunk of her work, so she grabbed a cup of coffee from the lounge. Coffee — another thing she missed. It had been a while since she even had time to enjoy that. Come to think of it, she thought, she hadn't enjoyed much of the smaller things she usually made time for. That would have to change.

Enmeshed in the task once more, she heard the beep of an entry card and jumped a little. It was 9:30, and Jack was early. She had forgotten how nice it was to have someone who could do the same job, perhaps not quite as efficiently, but do it just the same. A brief conversation caught them up on one another's lives, especially since she had fabricated a story about working with a research grant. In her business, she could easily feign confidentiality since oftentimes the government asked individual scientists to participate in discrete projects. Aleta noticed Jack's hair had grown out a little so that his close-cropped brown hair had developed some waviness. It had definitely been longer than she thought since she had been at work. With his tortoise shell glasses, he reminded her of her ex-husband, but Jack wasn't an insecure, randomly unemployed slug. Maybe after her other responsibilities calmed down a bit, she might ask him for coffee somewhere outside the staff lounge. She didn't know what he would say, though, but before she could spend any more time pondering this, he excused himself to his office to finish some reports but offered to come back and help with the slides.

The distraction helped energize her a bit, but it wasn't long when her mind wandered again. Ever since her encounter with the Erinyes, and later Lismonia, she felt her mind gravitate toward other things, memories she didn't necessarily want to revisit. Aleta grabbed some files from her desk but caught a glimpse of a photo, one of her with her grandmother after she finished medical school. The once independent and headstrong matriarch of her family had the look of aging royalty with her short silver hair carefully coifed. In her eyes, Aleta saw her mother, and then her mind flashed back to that day when she was twelve when Orthros killed her. No, devoured her. This was something she and Sarah had in common, this barbaric loss of their mothers. Apollo would call it a sacrifice of a sort, but that always made her angry. Her mother wasn't sacrificed. One performs a sacrifice for a purpose, to obtain some sort of end, but this wasn't a quid pro quo—her mother was torn to pieces, consumed. Not long after, Aleta and her grandmother moved into a neighbor's house until Aleta went off to college. She pulled her eyes away from the photograph, holding back tears. No tears. The wheels of thought in her mind slowed, and when they stopped, she made her decision. She needed closure.

Aleta felt bad leaving Jack the note that she had to go, but she'd find a way to make it up to him somehow. She had asked so much of him. Maybe someday she would tell him everything. Entering the alley behind BioCorps, she knew just where to stand to avoid the cameras. Under her lab coat, she wore a long sleeve knit top with an open back; all of her shirts were open in the back. Reaching skyward, a lightning bolt deposited her javelin in her hand, and she stretched out her white wings. She would reach Oak Grove in about two hours flying under her own power.

Unlike Sarah, whose family home sat in the midst of other Victorian houses only a few miles from Boston, Aleta's childhood house sat on a few acres of land in a valley, not far from Cloud Mountain, Colorado. She figured out the irony of the mountain's name, originally called Jupiter Mountain, not long after she found the javelin in the attic. Touching down at the end of the dirt driveway, she could glimpse the oak tree she had blasted the night she learned how about her power. Sarah had called Aleta right after she had rid herself of the family house, and the two spent a few hours talking about closing old doors. She had told Aleta that she felt this calmness, this peace, while she did it. Without that old Victorian standing, her guilt about her mother and the residual anger just melted away. Aleta didn't feel peace. Her eyes burned from the inside as she stared up at the window of her mother's room, something Sarah had talked about, too, seeing the window of the upper room where Horkos had killed her mother. Aleta had been a helpless 12-year-old girl with no knowledge how to use the javelin; as soon as she heard the crunch of Orthros' jaws snapping shut on her mother, she knew she could do nothing. She wasn't helpless anymore. Someday, that two-headed canine would pay, but for now, she needed release.

Rising above the house, she flew in a wide circle to take in the view from a different vantage point. With each flap of her massive wings, she felt her heart cringe. A few vaporous clouds, unaware of how Aleta was about to shatter their tranquility, sailed above her. She gave no thought, no prayer. Casting the silver javelin toward the house, she grunted, and then a bright flash came. Without relenting, again and again she pummeled the farmhouse with white bolts. The wood didn't have time to catch fire before it received a lashing from the sky. Again. Again. Aleta's blood sped through her, her heart beating percussion in her head. Again. Again. Now the past revisited her, the sound of the canine jaws crunching through bone, and the sparks that flew from the lightning strikes showered the grass.

Her grunt had become a cry, her voice rising with each attack, until the human voice gave way to the screech of the eagle.

With no neighbors, the cloud-splitting thunder would echo around the mountain and dissipate before anyone in Oak Grove would have any idea what was happening. Aleta held the javelin with both hands above her head, titled her head back, and lowered her arms quickly. A last thunderbolt made contact with the remains of the house. Her breathing heaved from her lungs, and she let out one final screech before climbing higher into the sky. Sarah had performed her catharsis through ritual and control; Aleta released her fury, cauterizing the internal wounds closed. Nothing of her remained in Oak Grove, Colorado.

For the first time, she felt the predator's instincts surface fully, and Lismonia would be her prey.

Mt. Graylock, Massachusetts.

Ari awoke from a rough night's sleep and crawled out of the tent. He was unaccustomed to sleeping on the ground; even his cot in the Temple of Hades was more comfortable, but just barely. Having some time with Dan was just what they needed, Ari thought. So much was yet to happen, and the evil, ulcerous presence in Tartaros was plotting her next moves, but the sunrise over the mountains was hard to ignore. He had grown up in shadow his whole life, for the most part, and being exposed to a world he could never have imagined and a person who had changed his life had made him reassess his priorities. His visit to Persephone felt so insignificant and useless, but he didn't know what else to do. And now, he had to tell Dan about what happened.

When Dan emerged from the tent, he smelled coffee bubbling away over a campfire. Ari sat in silhouette on a log overlooking the valley as the morning sun had risen high enough to bathe their campsite in youthful light. Ari, dressed in a gray fleece shirt and jeans, handed Dan his coffee as he sat, and commented that he wished he could swim in the valley of sunbeams, to live in light. He no longer wanted to be in darkness. If he weren't going to be the *epistasis* of Hades' shrine, then he would choose another way. Dan replied that he would help him untangle himself from this dark-entrenched past. Ari smiled, but that would be harder to do, he said. He stood up to tend to the fire. The obscurity that clouded his life and had been his constant companion helped him make the choices he had made. Dan put his hand over Ari's on the stick pushing the embers around and said they would do it together.

Around midday, they were hiking around the mountain when Ari stopped near a flat stone leaning up against the mountain; it reminded him of the doorway to the *Necromanteion*, and he hesitated. Dan noticed, but said nothing. When they did finally stop to eat lunch in a clearing, Dan muttered a prayer to Demeter and Artemis out of reverence for the natural world while Ari deferred to praising Persephone. He looked at the man to whom he had devoted his life, who was both his sovereign and his love, and couldn't hold the truth back any longer.

In a cascade of words, Ari told Dan about how his father had communed with Hades, how they were friends of a sort, and that secrets were passed on through their conversations. Knowledge of *The Nebulous One*—he still wouldn't use the name Lismonia—had been shared, but neither Ari nor his father had had any comprehension of just who she was or what she was capable of doing. All Hades would say was that she was Night's daughter who had the power to melt minds and even souls. He never elaborated much, concerned that Timaios would become incapacitated with so much knowledge, but he did feel the caretaker of his shrine should know something of this atrocity. Ari got the impression that even Hades feared her, although he never said as such or let on in any way. Living with the knowledge of the dead and the underworld put a shadow over his life, Ari told Dan, a shadow that was all-encompassing and impenetrable. Silence flourished within him, the inner shadow germinating, even as the sun's luminous rays splayed across the sky and earth. Dan took his hand. No matter what, he told Ari, he would always protect him. The *Moirae* had brought them together, and he would go up against any god or mortal to keep that intact. Ari's next words might challenge that assertion.

Ari told him about the trip to Hades, when he was supposed to be traveling around Massachusetts, and how he had used the *Necromanteion* to visit with Persephone. Dan's expression went from peaceful to austere, but he continued to listen. He didn't tolerate lies, least of all from someone he loved. Ari took his time retelling the encounter and spoke of the conversation that he had had with Hades' wife in extraordinary detail. Then, he had to speak about the box. Dan's questions inundated his mind, but he let Ari continue. The history of Persephone's box was well known, especially to Dan, since he had been told these stories as family tales rather than surreal ones, but he could tell there was more to hear, and that made his arm hair tingle. Ari couldn't tell him what the box contained; that would have to come closer to when it would be the most useful, when they would face *The Nebulous One*. His eyes shimmered in nascent tears. This would crush Dan, he thought, but he had to know the price for the gift.

Persephone had told him that the five rivers had annexed Hades, and in doing so, had made enemies of those loyal to the god of the underworld. While some had chosen to remain compliant, others rebelled, incurring the direst consequences. One such individual who had initially been indifferent to the regime change, but later felt that it would impact his purpose was Charon. The five river gods had dispatched him, he who had ferried the souls across the river for eons, his undead remains sitting by the water's edge as a reminder to anyone who could see the consequences of betrayal. All things have purpose, Persephone told Ari, and the underworld would suffer for this loss. But, the Sacred Scales would balance. Once the gods returned, they could resurrect Charon and restore order, but that would take time — a year, to be exact. In the interim, Persephone revealed that, should Ari willingly accept her gift, he would have to replace Charon for that span of time.

He had agreed to it without hesitation.

Dan's expression hardened, and he instantly saw Ari through new eyes. With all the radiant light around him reflected off the dewy grass and the leaves of the trees surrounding them, he felt a darkness spark inside him. At first, he couldn't tell what it was, but the longer he looked at Ari, who had hung his head, he realized what this was: regret. He fought back words he knew would do irreparable damage, hammering them back inside. Dan wasn't sure what bothered him more, that Ari would lie to him, that he would risk his own life, or that he would be so willing to accept the price. A year would be agony without him. The silence that cocooned them in this sun-drenched meadow gave him time to form coherent thoughts. Ari, who had freely followed him into this world, giving up his own, had decided to jeopardize his own soul to cross into the underworld… he, who had no responsibility in the coming battle, would put others first before himself. That had to count for something, had to temper his actions somehow. Didn't it? He looked at Ari and saw a man hunched over, his face in his hands, probably wondering what would happen next. He had to be terrified, Dan thought, after having lost his father and his home. It was then that the blackness inside Dan shrank, retreating back inside. It would never truly go away entirely.

Dan lifted Ari's chin. A man who had known so much loneliness and had been surrounded by so much of death and loss had eyes that could take in the whole world. They didn't have to speak for Ari to know that Dan hadn't changed how he felt about him. A year wouldn't be that long, he thought, since he knew in his heart that Ari would come back. If nothing else, the gods kept their word. They finished their lunch quietly, not quite ready to engage in conversation, but they each knew the other would be all right. Ari spread a blanket out on the grass and lay back, one arm behind his head, wanting the sun to provide some sort of solace, having always heard that Apollo's sun could heal the soul of the willing. Dan joined him, resting his head on Ari's chest, a heartbeat thumping softly in his ear. Dan knew that as soon as the gods returned that Ari would have to go, but he knew he had two more months left before the year of the gods' self-imposed exile would end. In this meadow they drifted off to sleep, and they would be undisturbed. Morpheos would bring them some of the succor they desired, but time would have to do the rest. A warm breeze passed through the meadow; the trees seemed to stand a little taller, their branches seemed to grow a little fuller — Gaea also stepped in to watch over them. She couldn't heal them on the inside, but she would make sure they came to no harm otherwise.

Callahan Park, Framingham, Massachusetts.

Maxmillian and Evelyn Jeffries parked their black Mercedes S Class in the lot across from Baiting Brook Meadows in Callahan Park. Their son, Brandon, had asked them to meet him there at noon, but they had no idea why. Normally, he would just visit them at home, the place where he grew up in Newton, but his phone call sounded urgent. Max, who worked in international business, had a few days before his next business trip to the Sudanese Oligarchy and was able to make the time. With no other children at home, Evelyn volunteered often, but she had been a school teacher for almost 22 years with Boston City Schools. Brandon had grown up with a part-time nanny and hadn't spent as much time with his father as he would have liked, but they got along as well as a son and semi-absentee father could. His job as a zoologist through Boston University's Wildlife Preservation Society program had enabled him to get into a niche where he felt he could do the most good. Throughout his childhood, Max would return from a business trip with something for him, and when Brandon received his first stuffed bear as a toddler, his parents saw the magnetic hold it had on him; this was the beginning of his affinity for animals. A box filled with erector sets, action figures, and sports equipment sat in their basement while a bevy of plush animals lined Brandon's room until he was about 12 years old.

No one walked around the park — something Max and Evelyn found odd — so when they saw a law enforcement official trot by on horse, Max rolled down the window and asked if he had seen Brandon. The officer, wearing a Task Force insignia on his jacket, took off his sunglasses and let them know that Brandon would be by shortly. He said Mr. Jeffries had asked that this part of Callahan Park be closed today so he could use the meadow. In fact, the road into the park closed just moments after the Mercedes left the guard post.

For as long as Brandon had had his abilities to draw upon the Zodiac, he had been trying to find a way to tell his adoptive parents. Max was a 'cut-and-dry' sort of man with a business mind, so putting things in the simplest, and most efficient, way possible would be the best. On the other hand, Evelyn worked better with a gentler, subtler approach. Down the road past Baiting Brook Meadows, they heard galloping and saw a man approach, but the midday sun made it hard to see who it was. The officer left, stopped to talk to the other horseman, and then galloped further into the park. When the newcomer was about a half mile away, Evelyn took off her sunglass to get a better look. It had been a while since she had seen Brandon. At about twenty feet away, Max stepped out of the car and removed his own sunglass. It was indeed Brandon, but he looked different.

Rather than try communicating how he had come to become something—someone—different, he wanted to break the ice right away, but in this case, he probably shattered it into infinitesimal shards. Standing before the Jeffrieses was their son, half man, half horse, a silver amulet on his naked chest. Taking the form of Sagittarius seemed like the way to go.

Max and Evelyn smiled that uncomfortable smile one makes when he or she doesn't quite know what to say, but then Max commented how much he liked the costume and how it was so incredibly realistic. Evelyn got in close and looked for a seam; how else could a man wear such an outfit, she thought. They walked around him a few times; had their eyes had bristles, he would have been well groomed. Evelyn couldn't help but touch a hind leg, but winced when it moved. Brandon chastised her, though, when she looked underneath to test the veracity of the costume. Some things were better left underexposed, Brandon had mused, but he didn't have any solution to that problem. He invited them to follow him into the meadow where he told them the story of how he received his power. Then, the next hurdle would be the genealogy.

On Brandon's twelfth birthday, he woke up that Saturday to a note from his mother listing a few chores she wanted him to finish, but then he could do what he wanted to do. Clipped to the note was twenty dollars. As like most weekends, Max was traveling abroad, but he would probably make his birthday call somewhere between three and four when he would be between meetings. This was commonplace for Brandon. Most children Brandon's age would have ignored the chore list until later, but he figured out quite young that finishing the list first left him more time for himself. Evelyn didn't have a temper if the chores didn't get finished; she would just raise her eyebrows, push out her lower lip, and walk away—the guilt would eat away at him. After he did his laundry, folded it, and put it away, he cleaned his room, emptied the dishwasher, cleaned the fish tank in his room, and then he snatched the twenty dollar bill and headed for Newton Centre to take the T to the Franklin Park Zoo, his favorite place in the city. Visiting the zoo by himself wasn't uncommon for him; he would spend most Saturdays there when his parents weren't around, and this visit was even more special: a new exhibit was opening, the Circle of Animals.

Brandon noticed his parents' silence as they walked through the park; he expected as much since they needed to adjust to his physical form, but they also needed to deal with their guilt of not being there for him as much as they should have.

The twelve-year-old got his ticket, showed his ID, and had his retina scanned as he entered the circular building, its red neon sign above humming ever so slightly. The zoo had broken down each section of the exhibit by the four elements, and his first room was painted with fiery reds, oranges, and yellows. Each habitat measured ten by ten, complete with whatever each inhabitant needed to survive. A wild ram came first, and then a lion, followed by an intriguing breed of horse whose name was listed as 'Arrow'. How odd, he thought, to put animals that didn't even live in the same habitats in the same room, but he didn't blink even once as they took in all the visuals.

Colors turned from those of fire to earthy browns, beige, and amber. A large black bull stood in the first habitat, and Brandon lingered a little on the last one. A goat was lying in a low pool, but then Brandon could have sworn he saw a fish's tail on the bank. For a moment, he thought they were connected, but that would be impossible.

White, gray, and pastel blue swirled along the walls of the next room. Two zoo workers cleaned the first habitat; Brandon could have sworn they looked alike, too. Next to that stood a large scale with a placard that explained the weight of each animal in the exhibit as well as everything in the natural world required balance. Finally, the last glass chamber showed pinwheels and how the movement of air helped nature to prosper, from moving seeds to eroding mountains. He remembered that from science class. All along the ceiling were polychromatic kites, their tales swaying around in the artificial breeze made by fans.

Finally, in the last exhibit, each wall was a glass enclosure with water symbols everywhere. Habitat one showed a variety of crabs in an artificial tide pool; the array of claws sent chills through Brandon. Next, he saw scorpions, one of which was at least a foot long—he was quite thankful that thick glass stood between him and that stinger. Just before he left the building, he wandered through a maze of aquariums, each stocked with a diverse panoply of fish. It wasn't until he left the building and entered the light of day that he realized his heart was racing. Water just seemed magical to him.

Hours merged together as he took in every other exhibit, even though he knew all the placards by heart, and he even felt like some of the animals knew him. As usual, he indulged in a hot dog and cotton candy before leaving around three p.m., but not before he stopped at the gumball vending machine. Each plastic or wooden container contained a toy or a souvenir from the zoo; he was getting to the age where he didn't really need any of them, but he had a quarter and felt like taking a chance. In went his money, and out popped a small wooden box with a gilded edge. A ring of weird symbols marked the top of the box, but he had no idea what they were. Inside the box was an opaque, pale blue marble about an inch in diameter, polished to a gloss, and flattened slightly. He shoved it in his pocket and headed for the T station.

By the time he arrived home, his mother was there arranging some flowers in a crystal vase, and he fumbled through his pocket to find the wooden box to show her. Evelyn didn't look at the object or her son, and didn't see his wide-eyed expression, but she did make sure to tell him to wash the marble first if he was going to play with it. You never know where things came from, she'd always tell him. When he walked into his room, he opened the box and rolled the glass piece in his hand. He couldn't see through it when he held it up to the window, but it did shine in the sunlight. Rather than wash it, he thought it might look 'really cool' among the rocks in his aquarium, so he placed it next to a tiny statue of Poseidon holding his trident. Brandon just stared at it until his mother called him down to dinner, but he stopped at his doorway and ran back in for one more peek. Dinner was the longest hour of his life. He didn't even realize that Max hadn't called until just before he went to bed.

Brandon's bedroom window faced east, and the arrogant sunlight pushed its way through the slits in his blinds, poking at him while he slept. At seven, he untangled himself from his sheet and jumped out of bed, pulling the blinds all the way up. He loved sunlight. On his way to the bathroom, his eyes caught the shimmer of the aquarium, but he stopped at the door. As if in slow motion, he turned around and crouched down in front of the tank. His eyes came alive, darting all over what he saw. In place of the small pale blue flattened marble sat a silvery disk leaning up against the glass. Five inches in diameter and half inch thick, it had twelve different faceted gemstones embedded in a circle around the edge surrounding a ring of symbols, the same ones on the cover of the box. In the center was a blue gemstone, one inch in diameter, faceted like the others, but this blue was like nothing he had ever seen: a combination of the dark blue of the night and the pale blue of the morning, and every blue in between. Swimming around the disk were two of his fish, intrigued by the sparkling from the young day. As he pulled it from the water, he then noticed the chain attached to it. Like at the zoo, he hadn't blinked yet.

Brandon dried it off and put it around his neck, admiring it in the mirror, his fists on his waist and a sporting a wide grin. This was the best birthday present ever.

A few weeks later, he made a second discovery, one that would make this one even better. He had been cleaning his closet, yet another task he found on a list from his mother, and slipped on a book, falling back against the closet wall. When he got up, he thought he felt the wall break, but when he moved his hanging clothes out of the way, he saw that the wall had just opened along a vertical seam, leaving a quarter inch gap. He pulled it open, and the quarter inch gap became a two-foot opening into a room behind his closet. Blades of light cut into the room from somewhere inside; he grabbed his flashlight. The dormer on the left had some boards over it; that's where the slivers of light originated. Not being one to think things through, he grabbed one of the boards nailed to the dormer and let his body weight do the rest. A window! With the removal of the other boards, light poured into the room, an eight-by-eight foot room lined with wooden shelves, some of which had old, dust-laden books. As the dust settled, he peered out the round one-foot-wide window, and he could see the acreage behind his house. He thought his heart had raced that day in the zoo; today, he soared.

It only took him a day or so to clean up the room, dust the shelves, and wash the window. No list prompted him this time. He dragged some pillows into this secret chamber and would lie awake after he was supposed to be asleep, holding the disk up so that he could make it fill the window. During the day, the sunlight coaxed the gems to life; at night, the moonlight did the same. When he held the central blue gem to his eye and looked into the sky, colors moved like living beings. He'd sleep in the secret room and awaken refreshed, inspired.

A year later, he learned by accident that the gemstones drew power from the symbols on the disk, symbols he figured out where the Zodiac signs. He had come to a tree trunk blocking the bike path near his school one afternoon, and thought he could push it out of the way. It didn't budge, but he kept trying. The harder he pushed, the faster his heart beat, but he had no success. Adrenaline, more than usual, pumped through his body, and he kicked the trunk, hearing a crack. On his chest, his amulet—which he had taken to wearing every day—felt hot against his skin. The emerald, the gemstone for Taurus, glowed. He put his hands back on the tree and closed his eyes, focusing on the bull and the emerald. He felt a surge of power in his muscles and pushed, nudging the log a few feet. Two more tries moved it off the path. Over time, other skills surfaced, each he attributed to other signs. He never did figure out what Virgo did, though. It wasn't until he was twenty that he experienced Sagittarius.

Brandon, who wore the amulet all the time, had been running along a beach one sunrise in Ecuador, during his semester abroad where he took courses for his bachelors in zoology. A gray mare had wandered onto the beach and ran beside him, but then passed him. Brandon took that as a challenge and tried to catch up. When he did, he then noticed his transformation, as well as the quiver of arrows on his back and the bow that just materialized in his hand. The two equines played on the beach a bit before Brandon needed to go. That was the last Zodiac sign he had mastered; Virgo remained a mystery.

This was the first time Max and Evelyn had heard of the secret room. They had just been too busy to notice. Some time during the story, Brandon had resumed his human form, and his mother realized this when she went to embrace him. Heading back to the car, Max, who struggled with his, awkwardly embraced Brandon. He said he would need more time. Brandon felt that, even with this new information, Max would be even more distant from him. Evelyn commented that she had seen a few news reports over the years about monsters or creatures, the ones Quinn had been unable to suppress, and that just made this easier to take in. Standing next to the Mercedes was a couple, two people that Brandon immediately recognized. Today would be the day for all of the past to become known, so Brandon introduced Paul and Alkinoë Fairmont as his birth parents. Just when Evelyn thought this might be easier to deal with, since she had known for years that Brandon might inquire about them, she had no idea how she would react once they started talking. Not one for subtly either, Paul said he had a story to tell them, nodded at Brandon, and transported his wife and the Jeffrieses to Delphi. Brandon could only imagine how Max and Evelyn would take everything, but he had learned long ago that he wasn't responsible for how people reacted to the truth; he was responsible, however, for always telling the truth—it was something he had learned from both fathers. He sent a text to Dan to let him know what was happening and headed back to the apartment. He knew the Jeffrieses would need some time, so he didn't expect his phone to ring when they returned.

An unknown future lay before Dan, Sarah, Aleta, and Brandon, but each finding closure in his or her own way would facilitate concentrating on the coming battle, one that they weren't even sure they could win.

29—AWAKENING

Sarah stared up at Mount Olympos from the Vale of Tempe, the valley between the southern Olympos and the northern Mount Ossa. Apollo had told her that an ancient cult used to convene there, and he felt it was an appropriate place to start her journey. The midday sun painted the rocks a greyish orange, and she could see where the mountain disappeared into wispy clouds, the *Nephelae*, even though no other clouds dotted the skies. Apollo told the team that none of the gods could access the mountain, but as Sarah was mortal, she wanted to try. She tried to convey her intentions to Olympeia in her mind, since she had connections to Gaea, but the *ourea*, or mountain spirit, ignored her. The closer she got to the mountain, the rockier and less accessible the terrain became, but she had summoned a wind to lift her over the more precarious sections. At almost ten thousand feet tall, the physical mountain projected a stubbornness that she had never really experienced before. This wasn't the gods' home, she knew, but it provided the foundation upon which the gods built their more ethereal citadel. When she was within a half-mile of the base, the *Protogenos* deigned to tell Sarah that she had the stench of the gods on her and would never be permitted on the mountain. Since one fourth of Sarah's power came from an Olympeian goddess, that would be enough to preclude her advance. Of course, Olympeia could also have meant Apollo, since Sarah had been in contact with him. It didn't matter; Sarah could feel her ability to walk toward the mountain getting progressively more difficult, as if her own legs resisted moving forward. She had prepared for this particular mission, with Quinn's assistance on research, even down to what she wore; the United Nations preferred discretion and issued each team a uniform, but Task Force: Gaea chose to avoid that regulation. With the power they wielded, no one really challenged them. Sarah had chosen her black catsuit, the closest thing to a uniform she would concede to wear. The skintight black leather ensemble made her feel like a superhero of a sort, although she would never say that aloud. Nonetheless, Olympeia wasn't being cooperative, so Sarah would try a more direct approach.

Summoning the winds, she ascended, but as soon as she was approaching the *Nephelae*, the cloud spirits solidified, barring her advance to the immortal realm; they followed the mountain spirits edict. Sarah's ability to manipulate the air had no effect on these clouds. She could be persistent as well, no matter how an ancient *Protogenos* felt. Every time Sarah tried to move up the mountain, rocks would block her path. She simply moved the obstacles, but as she tried to go further, an impenetrable force pushed back, like a magnet repelling another magnet. Sarah tried repeatedly, managing to get a little higher, but this time the ground shot up before her, almost decapitating her. With one swipe of her hand, the earthen wall crumbled, but then a wall of dirt shot up once more a little taller. The third time Sarah tried, the wall fell forward pinning her to the mountain itself, conforming to her body like a second skin and trapping her against the ground. None of her power worked on it. In fact, the dirt spread closer to her face and covered her mouth and nose. Olympeia would not be challenged.

Once the dirt had eveloped Sarah, she pushed muffled screams through, but soon even those stopped. Then, as if nothing had happened, silence and wispy breezes blew around the base of the mountain, carrying with them the scent of nearby flowers. Minutes passed in silence, and a butterfly flitted by. The ground began to rumble, and soon the casing of earth cracked, traces of human blood seeping through a little; from within the shell, a cry emerged, and seconds later, stony shrapnel flew. Sarah rose into the air, her bloody arms extended out from her sides, fists clenched. Her eyes, once a verdant hazel, now glowed like fire, as drops of blood trickled down her cheek.

Sarah's voice grew deeper, grittier: "Spirit of Air — *Khaos* — bring down your winds!"

Gale force winds grew around the base of the mountain where she hovered, ripping plants and wearing away and battering part of the physical mountain. Sarah could hear Olympeia in her mind, and the *Protogenos* felt... discomfort. *Good*, Sarah thought.

"Spirit of Fire — *Hesteia* — bring your flames forth!"

Normally, with her ring, Sarah could manipulate nearby fire and make it grow. When she called upon the elemental deity itself, her power could reach much further to find that fire. She had prepared for this obstacle,. Before she arrived at the mountain, she had lit a fire in an iron bowl nearby. Having invoked the goddess' power still present in the world, Sarah called the flames to her, and the growing conflagration grew as it rushed the valley, bashing into the foot of Olympos, fed by the hastening winds. Olympeia's barrier keeping the gods out held fast, however. Assaulted by two mystical elements simultaneously would bring agony the *ourea* had never felt before, and being touched by the elder god, *Æther*, through the ring amplified the effects; Sarah wasn't finished, however.

"Spirit of Water, Thalassa, bring up your waves!" Waters from the Mediterranean Sea followed her command, and a tidal wave bypassed Litokhoro and crashed through the valley and into the mountain's base. Sarah's control over three elements pushed her toward a madness she had never known, and the waves of energy amplified through her. She knew that if she kept this up too long, the power would destroy her. Normally, such elements would have no effect on such a mighty mountain, but heightened by primeval magic, these elements brought quite a blow; Olympeia had no frame of reference, and no defense, so she did what she had always done—cried out to her sister, Gaea, but the earth didn't respond.

That had never happened before.

Sarah gestured, and the waters receded, the winds died down, and the fire ceased. She slowly touched down, and her eyes returned to her normal hazel.

"You summoned her, didn't you? I can tell. I'm connected to her, too." Sarah smirked. "She empowers me."

A disembodied voice echoed throughout the valley surrounding Olympos.

"Daughter, hold. My sister has but one purpose and does not comprehend what you do. Millennia have not brought her wisdom. She will not relent."

"Then, what can we do, Gaea? We need to get to the *Ptinotrofeio*."

In the silence that followed, the Mother of All then showed her sister Lismonia's atrocities, the lives she had destroyed, the sheer abomination that Nyx's daughter was and the toll she had taken on humanity, but Olympeia only knew the Pact was invalid, and the gods wouldn't enter.

"I'd hoped to get to the Hall of Tribunals, but Olympeia says I have the smell of the gods on me. I can't break through the enchantment." Sarah fell to her knees.

"With my aid, you would have broken through—"

"That won't be necessary." Dan materialized through a portal near Sarah. "Gaea, I couldn't ask you to go up against your sister. I have too much respect for her for that. I believe I have what we need." He took out the wooden box that Ari had given him. "My father has always told me that some truths are universal and transcend all, even that of the elder gods. No matter how strong

Lismonia may be, she cannot change those ubiquitous ideas. Spirit of Olympos, behold this undeniable truth."

He opened the box and held it out toward the mountain. Olympos shook like it had never before, and rocks loosened from above and cascaded down; Sarah, weakened, managed to deflect them, as did Dan with his shield. A resonant shriek pierced the sound of the trembling mountain, and both Sarah and Dan held their ears because the sound of a primordial screaming could potentially liquefy one's mind. It took a few minutes, but then the tremors stopped.

"What just happened here?"

Dan held out the box. "Take a look for yourself."

Sarah took it, looking at Dan, and then removed the lid. Waves of memory crashed upon her, bringing with them that one truth that the contents of the object carried with it. Unlike Olympeia, whose faculties were not meant for complex ideas, Sarah neither shuddered nor screamed. Her face illuminated by knowledge and wisdom, she smiled faintly. Dan took back the box. She looked at peace.

"I remember now."

"So does Olympeia," Dan replied. "Let's go to the Hall of Tribunals."

Apollo appeared, dressed as he would for an Olympeian. Dan nodded once, and the sun god took his son's and Sarah's hand, all three vanishing in a burst of light.

A white marble floor stretched out beneath Dan, Sarah, and Apollo's feet, with fluted columns rising into the sky bordering it and no ceiling above. Beyond lay the bluest sky, vast and powerful, a canvas for the emotions of the gods. At the center of the floor was a ring of marble, twelve feet across, with only a tiny ember burning. This was the hearth of Hesteia, the one who nurtured the gods. Sarah extended a palm over the fire pit and gently coaxed the flames to life, playing with them like a puppeteer. Realizing where she was, she pulled her hand back, fearing that her effrontery might rouse the goddess' anger.

"Don't worry, Sarah." Apollo looked up. "She's not here, not yet anyway, and she wouldn't mind. You honor her." He smiled, and she lowered her head. Normally, in the mortal world, she thought of him as Paul Fairmont, dressed in casual clothes, but here, he was Phoebos Apollo, god of the sun. Here, she felt different... humble.

"Soon..." Dan whispered. "The year is almost up. I can feel it." He looked all around, as if he wanted to see something specific, but above him was the sky, slight clouds appearing and then disappearing.

Apollo stood at the edge of the floor, looking down into the clouds. A deceptive peace lingered, like a tentative guest. The gods would return after their self-imposed exile, he thought, and they would have many tales to tell, but he wondered if his father would be among them. Lismonia had taken Zeus' memory from the world, and Apollo had no idea where his father's mortal form was, and whether or not he was still alive. He supposed that if Zeus were dead, he would have felt it.

Dan joined his father. "What do you see when you look out there?" he asked.

"Possibilities. Endless ones. And what do you see?"

"The playground for the *Moirae*. Deception. Duplicity. Paranoia."

"Always the optimist," Apollo laughed. "Look beyond that. Danelos, you've never known any other life than this one. Not only have I lived as a mortal man, but I've also been down a different timeline, and I couldn't even begin to tell you what that does to someone. I've known madness and clarity, deep founded hatred and unrelenting love... I learned that the world needs *issoropia*."

"Balance. I know." He paused briefly to pull out a piece of parchment. "This prophecy that I acquired says that only four of us face Lismonia, this elder goddess, nurtured on hatred. Can just Brandon, Sarah, Aleta, and I really stop her? Will our weapons and experience be enough?

I mean, look down there, Dad. Really look. Our world's countries spy on one another, demand we prove who we are day after day, and would rather act than question. We've battled chimerae, drakones, and even Ladon – but they were monsters we could assess and target. How do we target a goddess of darkness who feeds on the souls and memories of others?"

Apollo kept staring out beyond the clouds. "Assemble your team," he said, his voice taking on a regal timbre. "You're about to find out the answers to some of your questions. Lismonia's been through China, and… *Gaea help us*… she's already destroyed Korea, north and south. Look…"

The god cleared the clouds and showed Dan the earth, a black growth like a bacteria having encroached on China and moving east. Apollo closed his eyes for a moment.

"Gaea seems to think she's headed for Japan. I'll meet you there." Apollo vanished.

Dan could get him and Sarah there instantly, but even at top speed flying, Aleta couldn't make it there fast enough. He opened a portal to his apartment where Brandon and Aleta were waiting.

Once they came through, he pulled Brandon aside. "Listen, I need you here. When the fire in that hearth flares, it'll be time for the gods' return. Your amulet, like my sword, can open the *Ptinotrofeio* and release the gods. Their avian forms will seek out their mortal selves. Then, I need you in Japan. Just call on your communicator when you're there."

Even with all the power at his command, he knew his brother was right. "Understood. What do I do in the meantime?"

"Pray." He embraced his brother. "Let's go, Aleta."

Alone on Mount Olympos, Brandon paced in the great hall, fiddling with the amulet. He wandered to Apollo's seat in the hall, wondering just what they would find when they arrived in Japan.

Apollo appeared in Kyoto at the center of the main island to try to head off Lismonia, but his knees buckled with what he saw. He was too late. Black scorches marked where roads and buildings once were, and the carnage had left half-dissolved skeletons and partially burned bodies. He crouched and picked up some of the dirt, and it blew from his hands in a soft breeze, a breeze that carried the smell of burning flesh and bone. In a way, he felt like Lismonia was giving her own burnt offering to the gods, but human sacrifice was forbidden. Lismonia didn't care. She had rendered the earth here inert, unable to bring forth any life. Apollo even wondered if Gaea could restore this much destruction. It didn't matter. The next major city was Tokyo, a city of over 50 million people, so he disappeared once more, his soul burning with rage. Such senseless chaos...

Six p.m. in Shibuya Crossing in downtown Tokyo redefined lunacy. Hundreds of thousands of people rushing across major intersections, taking advantage of the largest shopping district in Tokyo, resembled an army of ants on the move. Tourists tended to flock here because it reminded them of Times Square in New York City, but Shibuya's lights and billboards surpassed even that American city. A myriad of lights and sounds, billboards and electronics — not including the ubiquitous cameras — gave Shibuya the feeling of a video game. North of the city was Yoyogi Park, once a rundown landfill, the site of Olympeian Resurrectionist activities, but now a thriving gardens enjoyed by the citizens and tourists. Apollo appeared in the park, near the Meiji Shrine, and looked up at the *torii*, the Shinto gate. It reminded him of the Portara on Naxos.

He wanted to be the one to meet Lismonia, to weaken her before his son and the others would encounter her. He owed them that much. The daughter of Nyx had gone up against Zeus, but he was mortal then, so he couldn't have stopped her. But, Apollo was different. Being the first and only god to devote himself to a *Protogenos* so fully, he could surely withstand Lismonia's power. That, plus he knew he had an advantage. Blustering winds from the underworld swept through Yoyogi Park, killing everything in its path. Even Apollo could feel its power approach, but he had felt it before and knew how to protect himself. Icy winds tinged with rage, laden with souls, blew through the gate, splintering the cypress wood, and Apollo held his ground. Darkness spread across the skies, the bubbling, gelatinous form of Lismonia charging toward the city center and the lone god.

Rising above the singed trees that remained in the park stretched the elongated neck of Lismonia, her red eyes flaring, and like serpents, black tendrils of her body moved across the earth until they found their target of the sun god. Her exuberance showed in how quickly she tightened her grip on him, pushing her eyes toward his. Apollo didn't resist. He knew what was coming and wouldn't lose his mental control like Esteban did, succumbing to the madness. He felt her force her way into his mind, but he took down all the barriers, giving her complete access. That simply excited her. Under the blackness that covered his mouth, he smirked, but he also began to feel that fear that her victims can't help but feel in her embrace. Lismonia pushed in and found that inner core of memories he had kept deeply nestled, the ones he agonized over, the ones he had told Zeus about. Then, Apollo felt Lismonia jerk back a little, and he knew he had her.

Two disparate timelines appeared simultaneously, showing the same moments, but different events: an impudent god's mortal sentence to Gaea was coupled with the same god's decision to relinquish his mortality willingly and find his path. One coronation in Arkadeia took place on a bright day, dripping with sunshine; yet, another happened on a day rife with thunderstorms. Which one was true? Which should she rip from the hearts and minds of those who knew him? Wait—here was the birth of a child, one whose immortal soul was ripped in two, while the same child was born into mortality, in the modern world. And then she hit upon a memory that she couldn't reconcile: in one timeline, Zeus and her mother embraced in the shadows of the Scales, and she emerged in Megara.

In the other timeline, she was never born. How was that possible?

Confusion and doubt filled Apollo's mind, but it wasn't his... it was hers. She couldn't latch onto anything in his mind, and that filled her with one more emotion she hadn't expected: fear. Withdrawing from him, she recoiled into a churning mass before the god, who crumbled to the ground, enervated but alive. A voice rose above the tumult, and another figure ran up toward the entrance to the now-destroyed Meiji Shrine.

"No! You will not take him!" Dan dragged his unsteady father away as much as possible. He then stood before her in defiance, his fists clenched at his sides. He didn't know that Lismonia had already touched Apollo. Aleta flew above doing crowd control.

Seeing this other man before her, one she recalled from back in the quarry, Lismonia gathered herself and, like a whip, enmeshed herself around him, knowing that she could punish Apollo by extricating the memories of his son from him. Like his father, Dan felt no fear. He had been raised the son of Apollo and Alkinoë. He was an Arkadeian prince, and he would not waver, *Moirae* be damned. Apollo recovered enough to see Nyx's daughter embracing his son.

"No!" his word echoed, a wave of power emanating from him in all directions. Lismonia rippled, but she didn't let go. The son of Zeus and Leto reached out to his child. He knew that it was too late and would only be a manner of moments before the world would forget Danelos Fairmont. He might remember, like he remembered his father, but that wouldn't be so for anyone else, and Alkinoë would lose a son again. He blasted her with bolts of light, but they merely fizzled on her. If he didn't know any better, he thought he felt her smile.

Dan felt her invading him, pushing herself into his mind, and he felt nauseated, but he tightened his gut and withstood what she was doing. If he were to die, he would do it as the son of a god. When he sensed she was at the core of his memories, he let her do what she came to do. But, then, she flinched. *It wasn't possible.* Before she could press on, she felt it was time for their return. The gods would be in this world soon, and then she would shred them out of existence. She relinquished her hold on Dan, who fell into his father's arms, but before she disappeared, Dan took a small box form his pocket. Reaching up toward her, he flipped the lip open, his arm shaking, and her psychic scream just about overwhelmed his senses, but the truth had now been revealed.

One of the universal truths in the world was the Omphalos, a sacred rock seated at Delphi. Ages before the *Titanomachia*, the *Moirae* had prophesied that the offspring of Kronos would rise up and defeat him, so when his sister-wife Rhea gave birth, he ate his offspring whole. Competing against this prophecy was his desire to assert his masculinity, so he continued to impregnate his wife, and each time she gave birth, he ate the child. Finally, fed up with this, and pregnant again, Rhea approached her mother, Gaea, who advised her to give her husband a rock in swaddling clothes when the baby was born. He wouldn't even know. The sixth child was taken to the island of Crete where the goat-goddess Amaltheia wet-nursed the infant while the Korybantes banged on their drums to drown out the child's cries. When the child reached the age of ascension, he was advised by his grandmother to offer a drink to the glory of the Titans to Kronos. Swept up in his own ego, the Titan king didn't recognize this young man as his own son, and he gladly drank a chalice of nectar, poisoned by his grandmother. Nauseated, he vomited up the contents of his stomach, including five offspring and the stone. The sixth child, Zeus, joined with his brethren to challenge the Titans for Olympos. The stone landed by Delphi, and the high priests of Gaea oiled it and kept it from harm. Some said it possessed great power; others thought it was more symbolic. Nonetheless, priests would etch prayers and statements into the stone like 'Long live the glory and power of Zeus'.

The box contained a piece of the Omphalos with Zeus' name etched into it, and since the stone is older than the gods, it remained a universal truth espousing Zeus' existence to the world. Confronted by this truth, Lismonia's power was undone, and she headed for Greece.

"Olympos..." Dan uttered, sitting up.

"Yes, we're going." A burst of light took them there.

Matsuyama, Ehime Prefecture, Japan

In the Sonkei Elder Care Facility, a nurse had just walked into check on her patient in room 205, an elderly man who was brought in a few months prior in a catatonic state. No one knew where he was from, if he had any relatives, and he had no identification on him when emergency responders found him on Nikkuna Street. He had been kept on a respirator since his admittance, and the nurses would simply change his diaper and transfer him from one bed to another so they could clean his bedding once a week, more if he had an accident. A needle in his arm fed him a nutrient solution that would keep his organs from shutting down, but it did little more than that. The Japanese government, in conjunction with local businesses, ran Sonkei, so whatever the minimum standard was, they tried to meet it. Just before the nurse left, she double-checked the chart to make sure the patient had received the care he was supposed to. Leaving to resume her rounds, the door had just clicked behind her when the slow blips of the heart monitor increased gradually, and the patient's chest began to rise and fall on its own. As his eyes opened, he put both hands on the breathing tube and gently removed it himself, coughing after he dropped it on the side of the bed. He took out the IV from his arm, sat up, and realized where he was. *It is nearby*, he thought. *I feel it.* An alarm sounded once the IV had been tampered with, but when the nurse and an orderly saw the patient sitting up, they stopped.

"Katsuo, tell Dr. Saito that his patient is not only awake, but sitting up in bed." The orderly, amazed to see the man awake, did as she asked.

She took small steps toward the man, not wanting to frighten him. "Everything is okay. You're in the Sonkei Elder Care Facility. Can you tell me your name?"

His mind was clearing from the fog that he had been living in for months. He didn't want her to think he had dementia, so he gave her the name he had been using since he arrived.

"Rakurai Saro." His voice was raspy from disuse. He looked around. "Is my wife here? Kujaku?"

"I'm sorry, Saro-san. We didn't have any information for you. You came in with no identification."

He went to step down, but the nurse tried to stop him.

"You have been in a coma for months. Please, stay in bed. I will have to sedate you if you do not."

She had no idea to whom she was speaking. He put his hand over hers. "You are more than welcome to try." He jumped down, his feet not used to being used for quite some time. This mortal form had so many limitations.

"I'll be right back, Saro-san. Please stay right here." He nodded.

Parting the curtains, he looked out at Matsuyama, but he was trying to look beyond. In this form, his vision was limited to that of an eighty-year-old man. His ancient eyes, however, scanned the city that he could see, wondering where the source of the power was. He had not seen it or been near it in... millennia. How could it be here, in Japan, he thought. But, it was. That energy was undeniable — a piece of the Omphalos was not far away. That had been

303

what brought him back. A calendar on the wall told him what he needed to know—the time for their return was imminent. How fortuitous for it to happen on a Thursday. Now, all he had to do was keep his eyes to the sky. He hoped that his wife wasn't too far away, but when the *Ptinotrofeio* opened, they would be reunited once more.

Mount Olympos. The Hall of Mortals.

Long ago, when the gods were young and had just taken Olympos, the pungent smell of the battlefield from the *Titanomachia* lingering in the air, Zeus and his five brethren met often in this hall, the only one with actual walls of marble and no visibility to the skies surrounding Olympos. Torchlight illumined the chamber, and the new king met with a Titan lord, Prometheos, to discuss how to bring about a stronger mortal race, one whose worship would strengthen the gods. It was from these meetings that Mankind emerged, and it would later be that Prometheos would steal one of these very torches to bring to humans so that they might know fire—warmth, nurturance, and protection. As more gods populated Olympos, mostly thanks to Zeus, marble stools appeared around the central table. Upon each lay either a chiton or perhaps even a himation, each belonging to one of the deities who frequented the room when austerity was required. Along the walls hung tapestries woven by Athene depicting some of the proudest moments in the history of mortals as well as emblems of each of the Ages of Mankind: Gold, Silver, Bronze, Heroic, and Iron. Historians and bards knew nothing of this chamber, so neither Hesiod nor Ovid could write of it in his exploits of the ancient world.

As large as the Hall of Tribunals, this place had no hearth; the torches stood for Hesteia's presence. Unlike the other gathering places on this mystical mountain, this chamber was the only one that could be sealed by enchantment. Within these massive walls now sat Apollo, preparing for the coming onslaught. Gaea had told him that Lismonia ventured to Tartaros once more, and he feared to know what havoc she would bring. Would she convince the five *Potamoi* to leave their watery thrones and besiege Olympos? Could she entice Cerberos to climb the mountain? Too many gods and creatures moved beneath the world of Mankind for him to count, and he prayed that the *Moirae* hadn't woven the outcome of this day's events too soon. In his peripheral vision, he saw something seep beneath the door — he hadn't sealed the chamber! Lismonia hadn't returned just yet, but this entity wanted to even the playing field a bit. Liquid blackness rose around the chamber, filling it inch by inch. Apollo felt the cold on his feet and then his ankles: Erebos. He thought to trap the sun god here until Lismonia could defeat the gods. She had promised Darkness Incarnate a place in her dominion, and like most simple entities, he was caught up in her power. The last time he and Apollo met at Delphi, the god had bested him, but now Erebos felt he would be victorious. Unbeknownst to him, the ancient power that Olympeia infused into the mountain was only accessible by those she deemed worthy to receive it.

Spilling forth into the tombs of the Titans, Lismonia's fury pooled around the encasements, but it was only one she lingered by. Oozing from her blackness came caustic bile and pus, byproducts of her emotions, and flashes of memory came to her from her mother: power is an extension of will. Hundreds of black fingers manipulated the rocks, injecting the most minute cracks with her acidic secretions. Within the obdurate sarcophagus of stone, supplemented by the energies of Zeus, Poseidon, and Hades, the Titaness of Memory, Mnemosyne, lay, not yet expired, but hardly alive by even any immortal standard. Even though she had been an unwilling coconspirator in the

Great War that brought about their downfall, she was punished along with her brethren. Lismonia's amorphous tendrils worked their way into the tomb and ripped it open, exposing the desiccated form of an elder goddess, her eyes hollow and longing. Faint pulses of life glimmered on the body, and Nyx's daughter wasted no time: she sought specific knowledge. Unable to resist the corrosive discharges eating away at her divine flesh, Mnemosyne surrendered what Lismonia needed to know. Tentacles of darkness dropped the near-corpse of the Titan, not even bothering to replace her within the tomb, and slithered her way toward the mountain.

Gaea returned the body to its resting place and sealed the tomb. The *Moirae* had woven into their intricate tapestry that she wouldn't be able to stop that foul creature. Mother Earth grieved once more the loss of her daughter, but she knew that Lismonia's reckoning was coming. That would bring her great comfort.

30—MEMORY'S CURSE

Gathered in the Hall of Tribunals, the members of Task Force: Gaea and Apollo prepared for the return of the gods, and Nyx's daughter. Hesteia's flames flared in her hearth, the signal to open the *Ptinotrofeio*, the sacred vault of Ouranos that had functioned as the aviary of the gods for a year. At the ready, Aegis had reviewed tactics and possibilities with his teammates and had prepared for the inevitable attack of Lismonia's, the one that he feared would not only overpower them but also the gods. She who had been called *The Nebulous One* had learned quite a bit since her arrival in the mortal realm, using finely honed senses and strategies that went beyond the one-dimensional attributes of other elder gods. Although she wasn't a *Protogenos*, like her mother, she possessed the aspects of an amorphous immortal that acted beyond the boundaries of human law and custom. The taking of lives, in the most heinous ways conceivable, was merely the surface layer of her transgressions. Balance must be sought, though, and everything had its counterweight.

Apollo stood next to the hearth, glancing down at the flames. Atop the stones that encircled the hearth, a two-inch-wide channel sat filled with water. The son of Zeus looked over at Aether and remembered how she was such an ingénue when they first met a few years back, but now she had grown into a powerful elemental and Wiccan priestess in her own right. Zodiak had come far in the past year, learning so much about his past. Perhaps it was his Arkadeian genealogy or perhaps it was how the Jeffries reared him, but Brandon had accepted the changes with great aplomb. He had also learned about Virgo, the elusive sign that gave him access to a spiritual element. Not something to use on the offensive, the sign would anchor him to the others, much like *Æther* does for Sarah. One of the strongest women he had ever met was Talon. To look at her, one might not see she had Amazonian ancestry, but to see her in action would immediately bring that out. Charged with her javelin, she was the last protector of her lineage, the *Eklektos*—the Chosen One. He cast his eyes on Aegis, the protector, and wished he had grown up with his brother. Apollo hated himself for having to deprive his family of its completeness, but he did what he thought was best.

This foursome could handle whatever the *Moirae* put before them, he thought. Anything.

Sarah scoured the hall for anything that would signal Lismonia's return. Unfortunately, the gods kept an austere meeting place, so nothing could really look out of sorts. She heard a whisper, though, behind one of the marble seats, and thought for a moment that she had seen something move. Dismissing it, she continued her surveillance. A minute or two passed—she really couldn't tell on Olympos—but then, she heard it again, this time more clearly. Taking a defensive posture without rousing suspicion, she narrowed her eyes and focused her hearing. Out of the corner of her eye, something moved, but as soon as she looked, she saw nothing. Just a delusion, she thought. She let her eyes rove in a pattern: left, up, and right. The whispering became a louder; it was still indistinct, but a chill crawled over her. Her mind had figured out what it was, but she couldn't rationalize it. As soon as she looked left, something leaped out of the shadows and pushed her to the floor, and she put up her hands defensively. Hot breath pulsed on her arms, and she remembered that smell, the smell of rotting flesh and coagulated blood.

"Oathbreaker!" the gravelly voice uttered. Horkos pressed down on her body, and his teeth snapped near her face. "Oathbreaker!"

Sarah pushed back, freeing herself for a moment, but then Horkos grabbed hold of her left foot. She pushed winds at him, but he kept his hold on her. Then, her right foot was immobilized. Horkos moved over her once more, his long teeth dripping that acid on her legs and abdomen, burning through the leather into her skin. She felt numb from the waist down. With both hands, she pushed the air against him, but he had latched himself into the marble floor, and her with him. She tried to concentrate on the water in the hearth, but the searing pain in her legs kept her distracted. When she opened her mouth to scream for help, nothing came out. She could still breathe, but she couldn't utter one sound.

"Oathbreaker... punished you will be," Horkos said, his raspy voice striking upon the fear she had been suppressing. He moved closer to her face, hissing and breathing his fetid air over her.

Moving the javelin from one hand to another, Aleta watched the other side of the hall, the side where Zeus and Hera's thrones rose above the others. Patience wasn't her strength, though, and her wings twitched at every little sound. The air around her felt electric, but not because of her power. Her instincts told her something was amiss, but she couldn't place it yet. The irony wasn't lost on her, either. Here she was, possessor of Zeus' greatest power, but she couldn't do anything to stop Lismonia. Perhaps this wasn't his greatest power after all. Needing to ignore the upside down feeling in her stomach, she jumped into the air to get a better vantage point and focus on something else. From behind Zeus' white marble seat of power, a shadow lurched by, but Aleta assumed her wings had made it. An echoing snarl broke the silence, and a dark shape jumped up at her knocking her to the floor. A duet of growls pounded against her ears, and she couldn't find her bearings. With her javelin held out in front of her, she managed to hold back the snapping canine jaws of Orthros, the beast who fragmented her life by killing her mother. She used her wings to give herself some leverage, but he kept pushing forward against the silver bar. *Nephoskizetes* could withstand much, she thought, but could it take on the full force of Orthros? Barking that resonated throughout the hall replaced the growls, and Talon pushed every iota of strength into keeping the jaws at bay. Her positioning made it harder to push up, pinning her wings behind her. Tightening her gut, she gripped the javelin and concentrated. Arcing electricity jumped from one end to the other, jolting the dog long enough for her to reposition herself and stand up. A sweeping motion of a tail sent her back to the floor, her head colliding with marble. Blood trickled from a wound on her forehead, but she pushed against the pain. Focus, she thought, just focus, but the throbbing in her skull kept her from getting a firmer grip on her awareness. The next thing she felt was the sheer agony of powerful teeth piercing her leg as one of Orthros' heads latched on.

Pacing near the hearth, its flames burning brightly now, Brandon mentally lingered on the last visit he had with his adoptive parents and how they were actually trying to accept what had happened to him. Apollo told him that Max looked as if he wanted to throttle him after hearing about the kidnapping and, even though he understood the rationale, Max couldn't accept that a man would do such a thing to his son and his wife. That was the first time Apollo actually seemed contrite, when he realized that his actions affected more than just his immediate family. Perhaps they would all have time together to talk further when this was over, but the future lay enshrouded in uncertainty, as usual. Brandon played with his amulet, not really paying attention, and saw a reflection in the silver Earthsteel. When he looked around, nothing was out of the ordinary. He continued to walk back and forth, his boots making no sound on the polished marble floor. Intuition made him look up. A scaly tail dropped and encircled his throat, lifting him off the ground, its constriction cutting off his air supply. Brandon pounded against the tail with his fist as the serpentine appendage suspended him off the ground, but the grip simply grew tighter and tighter. He had no weapon, but he also had no air left, so he swung his legs back and forth until he had enough momentum to wrap his legs around something above him. This gave him the ability to loosen the tail around his throat enough to pry it away; channeling Taurus and Cancer gave him the strength and grip respectively to do it. Smooth claws latched onto him, swinging him around until he landed on the floor, the creature landing on top. He felt thick pus dripping down his arms and face, and it was at that moment he knew his opponent: Lyssa.

Dan's fingers laced together, he cracked his knuckles before then removing his sword. *Thyroros* shimmered in the firelight, shadows playing on the smooth blade's surface, highlighting the text in an ancient tongue known only to *Protogenoi* and those chosen to know. This vigil that he and his teammates were performing just made the anxiety level grow, never knowing when Lismonia would strike, but with the gods about to return, Nyx's daughter had no choice but to do something. This hall had always held Dan's curiosity, especially when his father first brought him shortly after he accepted the manacle and sword. Apollo felt it would be best to meet those to whose service he was bound. Not all the gods met Dan that day, but enough of them present gave the young boy a sense of grandeur and power. Hera's peacock took a great liking to him, too, which was odd since, according to Zeus, that bird only liked Hera. Ever since she put Argos' eyes on the feathers, Zeus always felt like he was being watched. He probably was.

As the son of an Arkadeian warrior, Dan had been given the benefit of Athene's training when the goddess could visit, but mostly he learned from his mother. She kept a sword in the closet for those impromptu training sessions, the times when she told Apollo she was taking her son to the zoo. An abandoned dance studio a few blocks away served quite well as a sparring station. Alkinoë assumed her husband knew what she was doing and didn't say anything, but he never once let on that he knew, if he did. Focusing on one of the columns and the fire's dancing shadows on it, Aegis moved the sword around, slowly at first, but then he got into a rhythm. He'd thrust into an imaginary foe, swing the blade around low as if he were going to disable someone, bring it behind his head, and then twirl around, both hands on the hilt. Athene had told him that combat and dancing had similar moves, and she felt dancing could be more dangerous. This shadow sparring kept him focused, although it tended to disturb those around him. Coming up from a kneeling position, he stepped back to swing around, and his blade struck something hard. He didn't think he was that close to the column. A voice brought him back into the moment, and then he saw his adversary, sword extended.

"Ares... You can't be here."

"I am." The war god pulled his blade back. Hesteia's fire brought his dark bronze armor to life.

Dan knew the moves of battle as well, but this was a war dance, one where a victor always emerged. No stalemates — ever. For as well-trained as Dan was, Ares was more so. His entire existence revolved around combat and conflict. The war god never removed his helmet while fighting, either; he didn't care about looking into his opponent's eyes. He wanted to spill blood.

Bloodstained *Ochieleos*, Ares' sword appropriately named 'No mercy', crashed down toward Dan who leaped out of the way just in time, somersaulting over the hearth to the other side. Ares jumped onto the hearth, never taking his eyes off Dan through the fire. His eyes glowed red for a moment before he, too, took to the air, landing hard. In a flurry of movement, he swung his blade, and *Thyroros* met every thrust or stroke, a duel of Earthsteel blades. Ares turned, bringing his own sword down, but Dan's wrist flew up and his impact shield caught the blow that could easily have killed him. A swift swing of his foot brought Dan to the floor, his sword landing a few feet away. Apollo's son crawled to retrieve his weapon, but Ares picked him up by the feet, spun him around, and threw him into a column about twenty feet away. That maneuver wasn't meant to kill Dan; Ares was like a shark playing with his food before the kill. Having had the wind knocked out of him, Dan couldn't get his feet to work, and the war god strode over in just a few steps, kicking Dan further across the floor. That cracking noise Dan heard was his own ribs cracking from the impact, and slumped over, blood trickled from his mouth.

The sensation of Horkos' fangs along Sarah's body, their polished sharpness dripping acid on her, ate away at her resolve. She couldn't think of a way to defeat him. Pain interrupted her thoughts as his fangs sank into one arm, then the other. He hadn't taken any flesh away when he removed his mouth; perhaps he was playing with his food. Her eyes grew foggy, but she remained conscious. Horkos walked around her, snapping his jaws near her face as he passed by, and she couldn't figure out what he was doing. If he was going to devour her, as he had her mother, he should just do it and finish the job. Then, perhaps, she could see her mother in the underworld. Paralyzed from her neck down, Sarah's will power seeped out of her like the blood from her arms. Shock had started to set in, but she didn't want to give up. She wasn't ready. Where had Horkos gone? He seemed so eager to destroy her, but then she couldn't feel him near her anymore. Had he just come to do this and let her die on Olympos?

The day her mother died came to her in spurts, and she could see that moment play over and over again. Horkos had taken great pleasure in consuming Annabeth Jacobs because he claimed she had broken an oath. What kind of oath had *she* broken, Sarah thought, fighting through the pain. The silence haunted her now, and she thought Horkos would be back any moment to finish what he started. She asked herself again, what oath? As the past kept bombarding her, she pushed her own thoughts into them, going back in her mind to see what she could have done to draw Horkos here of all places. Her agony had reached that point where she could easily pass out, which would surely mean her death. Remaining conscious would be her only hope. Sarah felt Horkos with her again, even though she didn't see him. Something about the air changed when he was nearby. Death would be better than this. Perhaps she should just beg him to kill her.

As Orthros shook her like a doll, Aleta felt pieces of her leg rip away from the razor-sharp jaws. She flapped her wings to get him off her, but then she felt mind-numbing pain as one of her wings was ripped from her back, but she couldn't scream. One of the canine's heads shook it like a toy then tossed it away. Blood oozed from the stump on her back, trickled down her shoulder blade, and pooled on the marble. Silence followed. The only sound was the thumping of her own heartbeat in her head.

Strange scenes rushed around in her mind, scenes of women dressed in ancient leather armor running across a bloodstained valley, each bearing a wooden spear. Another flash brought her to a wooded area, a sacred ceremony where a woman in white lowered a feathered headpiece on the head of another woman kneeling before her.

Aleta reached out to pull herself forward, thinking that if she could get further away, somehow this would all end. Every time she pulled herself along the cold marble, percussive pain spiked through her shoulder. She noticed she couldn't smell anything, either, as if Olympos had no scent. This would surely be the end, she thought. Double growls made her heart pulse for a moment, and she prayed to any god listening that Orthros not do anything more to her. She would bleed out soon and then they could have her corpse.

Brandon didn't remember Lyssa being this heavy or strong, but Dan had been the one to contend with her in the Ganges, not him. She dragged her claws down his arms, and ribbons of blood flowed onto marble. He cringed as the pain shot through his body like a lightning strike, meandering along his nerves. Gathering up his strength from various signs, he bucked, getting Lyssa off him. When he tried to prop himself up with his arms, his elbows slipped in his blood, and he fell back down. He felt his boots take hold on the floor and pushed himself away a bit, giving himself a chance to get up. The wounds she had inflicted weren't deep, but they were painful. A swish of her tail came by, but he jumped up just in time to avoid it. Every sign he could muster flooded him, and the next time Lyssa's tail flew toward him, he grabbed it, swung her around, sending her to smash into a column. Rage goddesses didn't need much recovery time, apparently, after crashing into Olympeian marble, so as long as he could remain standing, he had a chance to defeat her.

What felt like a migraine, sending waves of nausea through his gut, compromised his ability to strategize. Adrenaline took over and forced his heart to beat faster. Lyssa pushed him psychically toward the precipice of rage; once crossing that line, the mind had little ability to rationalize and acted purely on emotion. Ironically, should he succumb to her power fully, she could control him. He felt his hands squeezing his head, fighting against her. Dropping to his knees, he screamed, and he felt the columns reverberate his voice, nudging him closer to the edge.

Despite his injuries, Dan engaged Ares once again, rebuffing each attack with either his sword or his shield. He hadn't been able to get one offensive shot in, but that didn't surprise him: Ares was the expert. As long as he could keep the melee going, he could try to control it. Broken ribs or not, he wouldn't allow the god of war to best him. Athene had told him that to control one's pain was to channel a form of energy. If he didn't think of the sensation as debilitating, he wouldn't be weakened. It was a challenge, though. Every sword strike vibrated through him, but *Thyroros* held true. Dan was indeed the key to boundless vision, and if he could just find a way to activate the sword's magic, he could send Ares away. How did he get out of the *Ptinotrofeio*, though? He would try to put that question out of his mind, but like a boomerang, it would return. His distraction cost him as Ares landed a spinning hook kick on his head, sending him down.

Ares' bronze greaves had removed some skin from Dan's cheek—yet even more blood. The son of Apollo was giving his uncle exactly what he wanted apparently, so he just stayed hunched over while he regained his focus. Athene had taught him everything he needed to know, especially how to take down Ares; why was he not able to channel anything into this battle?

While awaiting death to take her, her mind fading in and out of consciousness, Sarah started muttering something. At first, she didn't realize what it was, but the more she said it, the clearer the words became. With the beginning of some lucidity, she focused on the syllables that she realized she was saying, and her voice slowly lost its quaver: she was invoking her spiritual anchors. Through tears, she directed all her spiritual energy on her voice while she lay on the cold marble.

"*Khaos. Thalassa. Hesteia. Gaea.*" Her voice was barely above a whisper, but she repeated the names.

That dreaded feeling of Horkos' presence returned. Sarah wouldn't stop, though.

He kept growling, "Oathbreaker!" Her strength was slowly returning.

With some of her spiritual center regained, she focused her energy on calling quarters. That would certainly provide her with support.

"Those of *Aer*, of the living Air, *Aetoi* who guard the Eastern gates, I call on your strength."

Horkos jumped on her. He opened his mouth to rip out her spinal cord, but the winds came, pushing him away.

"Those of *Pyr*, of the living Fire, *Drakones* who guard the Southern gates, I call on your energy."

Every time he tried to move closer, flares from the hearth lashed out at him like a whip.

"Those of *Hydor*, of the living Water, *Naiads* who guard the Western gates, I call on your presence."

From the ring of water on the hearth rose liquid daggers, each one flying at Horkos, piercing his skin.

"Those of *Gaea*, of the living Earth, *Leimakides* who guard the Northern gates, I call on your nurturance."

Electricity sparked beneath her, the essence of the earth's healing power pushing its way through the floor.

Wounds closed, sensations returned, and then she stood up, using the hearth to lean on. It would take a few moments to gain her footing, but she was ready now to face this demonic spirit.

Fire, air, and water formed concentric layers around Horkos, who pushed against the elemental boundaries with all his strength. It was then she realized that she didn't see her friends, but she could feel their energy. They were indeed there with her.

Sarah held out her hand toward Horkos and made a fist. Each of the elements converged on him, ripping through him, until all that remained were pieces of his monstrous body. With her nemesis destroyed, reality came into focus, and she could see Dan, Aleta, and Brandon trapped in their own personal anguish. Despite her efforts to intervene, she found out quickly that she couldn't directly help them, but she could try to strengthen their energy through her connection to *Æther*. She stepped into the hearth and allowed Hesteia's fire to consume her. Then, she invoked the other three *Protogenoi* whose elemental presence was under her command. When she had created a spiritual rhythm, she invoked the last power:

"*Æther*, son of *Erebos* and *Nyx*, I invoke thee. Father of the *Nephelae*, I invoke thee. He who guards the upper air, the essence of light—I invoke thee!"

Aleta could feel her thready heart beating in her chest, but she also could feel the disappointment. Her grandmother knew just how much being a part of something bigger meant to her, but Talon was about to die and have nothing to show for it. It was in that moment that she remembered the day her grandmother spoke to her about her heritage.

"We and the earth were one. We and the sea were one."

Grandmother was right. She *was* a part of something

bigger. Her ancient tribal origins spoke of the *Eklektos*, a chosen one who would bear the tool bequeathed to them by the sky god, who she had come to know was Zeus. This tool, *Nephoskizetes*, was hers to command, and she drew strength from it. She turned her head toward the silver javelin and reached out to it, fighting through the pain and fog of consciousness. Clenching her fist, Aleta felt the lightning bolt first strike the javelin and then her hand. Divine voltage surged through her body, the living light replenishing her. She managed to get to her knees and relinquished the javelin back to the skies. Her solitary wing disappeared, as did the bloody stump. Hanging her head, she closed her eyes tightly and pushed out her lower lip.

"For you, Grandma, I do this," she whispered. Orthros growled in the background.

She reached her hand toward the skies, and the clouds attended her command, bringing with them a lone filament. Gripping the javelin once more, she stood up, extending two white wings. The two-headed dog leaped at her, but whimpered as the tip of the javelin protruded through its back. Aleta clenched her jaw and a tendril of energy descended, making contact with the silver. Fur and fang exploded all over the floor, wisps of smoke taken up by the wind. It was then that she saw Sarah in the hearth.

Guttural sounds, like those of a chimera or Minotaur, flew from Brandon's mouth, as the rage radiated through him. Part of his mind could tell what was happening, but that part was diminishing. Fueled by so much vitriol, he ran into columns, but he felt his own bones crack with each collision. Pain simply added to the heightened emotions, as if he were throwing kerosene on an open flame. Every pulse diverged through him, the cells in his body overloaded. He couldn't understand why he couldn't regain control; he had never been so susceptible to Lyssa, even when he was near her before. Had Lismonia strengthened her somehow? Thoughts vacillated, not allowing him to anchor himself on anything. He remembered the Ganges. Aegis. Aquarius. Apollo. Like flashbulbs, these images appeared and then disappeared. Brandon's stomach churned, and he leaned over to vomit. Hunched over on all fours, he felt the amulet swinging from his neck and forced himself to concentrate on any of the signs just to give him an anchor. Another flash burst in his head. Erinyes. He remembered his encounter with them, how Megaera licked his cheek.

The silver disk fell against his chest as he rose on his knees, and he clutched it with both hands. Other images rushed by, but these seemed different. Sarah. Dan. Aleta. Brandon found his center, the sign of Virgo, and allowed it to embrace him like he had when he fought the Erinyes. The gemstone attached to Virgo, the onyx, pulsed with light, but it wasn't just light. It was his psyche. He concentrated on those others from whom he had learned much and taken comfort; the rage faded, despite Lyssa impelling more toward him. Brandon realized that the rage wasn't just from her. He owned some of that, and that rage sought out his guilt and fed on it for almost allowing his brother to get hurt in India. Virgo's purity couldn't be challenged, since it came from a deeper place than Lyssa's power. Once his mind became his own once more, he channeled his favorite sign, Sagittarius, and shot twelve arrows into the daughter of Nyx. He walked over to her twitching body, having regained complete control, and just felt pity for her. Brandon looked over his should and saw the fiery form of Sarah in the hearth.

Dan could have just stopped fighting and dropped his sword, going with the mistaken premise that Ares wouldn't engage an unarmed man, but the god of war didn't care for honor. He hungered for—no... lusted after—anger and strife. Bloodshed and the urge to kill were foreplay to him, with piercing the flesh of the weak as the consummation of the act. Watching warm blood flow from a wound aroused Ares, and he yearned to make each adversary a gory fountain. This orgiastic melee invigorated his desire. Dan had no interest helping Ares satisfy those desires. He would no longer take the offensive, trying to disarm the god. Goading him with insults meant to inspire impulsive attacks, Ares threw words dripping with venom at his adversary. *Ochieleos* fell hard on Dan, but he just trusted in Athene's training. Gaea had forged his impact shield, and he trusted Gaea. Ares' words he could deflect easily enough, but the sword shook him with each blow. If Ares spun around to swing a decapitating blow, Dan lifted *Thyroros* to parry it. When the god reached out to plunge his armored gauntlet through Dan's chest, the son of Apollo used the momentum to flip Ares over onto his back. His heartbeat remained normal; he would give no satisfaction to Ares for even the slightest moment.

Being on Olympos heightened Dan's awareness, although not as much as his opponent's, but he had realized something while he avoided fighting Ares: as he was indeed Apollo's son, he could tap into the same power as his father, although he had never tried. Ares was on his feet again, but Dan was ready this time. He opened his left hand and let the ancient power loose, conjuring one lone orb of light, no larger than a marble. That was all it would take. Illuminating the sword's gem, *Thyroros* shimmered, and Dan had never felt such raw power in his sword before. Of course, he had never used it on Olympos before. Or had he? Striding over to his nephew, Ares lunged for him, but the portal enveloped the god and sealed. Dan smiled. The figure of Sarah in the hearth appeared.

31—REVELATIONS

Sarah landed on the floor, and Hesteia's hearth continued to burn strongly. The others had questions, and
she knew what to tell them. Lismonia had used the
powers of Mnemosyne to tap into their darkest memories,
bringing them to life. The Titan's power was such that, if
they had perished while engaging that memory, they
would have perished in reality. Aether couldn't say more,
mostly because she didn't know more, but her instincts
told her that Lismonia wasn't done. As soon as she realized the four of them were still alive, she would attack directly, and they didn't have much time at all to prepare.

"Who did you have to face?" Aleta was looking at Sarah, and she knew the answer.

"Horkos. He almost had me, too. I thought I had gotten rid of my guilt over my mother's death, but apparently
not. You?" She, too, knew the answer.

"That damned two-headed mutt, Orthros. He ripped
one of my wings off." She flapped them both to prove she
was back to normal. "Brandon?"

"I think I know." Dan stepped in. "Lyssa. Since you
mentioned guilt, Sarah, I just figured. Right?"

Brandon nodded without speaking. Dan pulled his

brother to him in a firm embrace.

"Stop obsessing over that, okay? You didn't hurt me."

"And you, Dan?"

"Ares."

Footsteps from the shadows revealed someone who had just arrived on Olympos from tending to other matters.

"How intriguing." Apollo didn't expect that response. "But, you've never faced Ares. In fact, you've never met him. When I brought you to Olympos as a boy, he was on the Areopagus."

Dan looked at his father in a way he had never before. "I have indeed faced him before. In fact, you know when. In that other timeline, I was known as Demetrios first, and I was born in Arkadeia. Zeus had sent me on a mission to free Ares from Gaea's *adyton* deep within Tartaros. It was there I faced Ares and brought him back to Olympos to restore the balance. Lismonia used Mnemosyne's power to reach into my mind and pull a memory of a conflict where I had felt great guilt. She just chose the wrong timeline."

Apollo had no words. Brandon walked up to Dan.

"So, you remember that timeline, like Apollo? You never said anything to me. To us."

"He couldn't," Apollo uttered. "If he had, Lismonia would have targeted him early on, but he probably suppressed that knowledge so deeply that only if she were looking for him would she find him." He felt numb. "That was why you lured Lismonia to you in Tokyo. You knew that if she took your memory from those in that other timeline, the one that never existed, no one here would be affected, but she wouldn't know that." He was too stunned to say so, but he was actually proud of Danelos for thinking of that.

Dan turned to his brother. "I know you feel betrayed, but remember, I couldn't tell anyone. No even Ari knows. When Lismonia took Zeus' memory from the world, I felt something change, but I remembered him when everyone else shouldn't. I would have made you all targets, more so than you already are."

"I understand. And I agree with your choice. This had to have been hard for you, not telling us. Not telling your father." Sarah looked over at Apollo.

The sun god had conflicting feelings. On the one hand, he now had someone to talk to about that other time, but on the other hand, he did feel a twinge of betrayal. Gaea then told him that she had helped to shield Dan from Lismonia so that he could use this knowledge at the appropriate time. Knowing that she had intervened made him less bothered, but he had lived as a mortal for so long that emotions like that just crept out of the darkness.

Dan stepped over to Brandon. "I want you to know that, even though you weren't my brother in that other time, I always felt you *were* one. So, I guess that was always meant to be."

Apollo asked Gaea if she knew where Lismonia was, but she didn't, and to hide from a *Protogenos* meant she could be anywhere. Apollo reminded them that prophecy dictated that the four of them had to finish these tasks, but he would see if he could track down Lismonia. As he left the Hall of Tribunals, he concluded they were more than ready to face Nyx's daughter. They would just need the right plan. The gods could wait a little longer.

32—ASCENSION

Dan sat in the Hall of Mortals, one lone torch burning. Like his father, he found peace in the darkness, and after what had just happened, he wanted a few moments to himself. *Thyroros* sat on the stone table, and he stared at the inscription: 'He who bears Thyroros holds the key to Boundless Vision.' Was that some sort of cosmic joke? Was his boundless vision the ability to see into a timeline that only he and his father had experienced? Would he be the visionary who could lead this team to victory over Lismonia, or anyone, for that matter? These smaller battles over the past year had taxed not only their bodies, but also their minds and hearts. This gelatinous cloud of darkness had vast power, and she could most certainly destroy them today. He didn't even think his father could stand up to her.

"Gaea and Olympeia, I need your strength now more than ever." He brushed his fingers over the inscription. "If you have chosen well, then we shall win. I have to have faith."

He extinguished the torch and sat in utter blackness.

Sarah watched from the Hall of Tribunals as Aleta soared in the skies around Olympos. It might be the only chance she would get to spread her wings in such a place. As she set down, she saw Brandon by the hearth. All three watched the flames, a different type of fire than they had ever seen—this was tied to the First Fires.

"Are you still mad at him?"

"I'm not mad, Aleta. It's just a lot to take in."

She put her chin on his shoulder. "I know. But, he's your brother, and he loves you. He would have said something if he could."

He nodded.

Sarah saw Dan step out from behind the thrones. "He's back."

The shadows that plagued him were gone; he left them in the Hall of Mortals. He had to.

"We're a team, and we need to remember that no one person here is any more than anyone else. You have all allowed me to be team leader, your *aegis*, and I'm grateful, but today... we're one. Here's my idea, but I want your input."

Minutes, hours, days... some span of time passed, and Olympeia spoke to Dan in his mind. "Holy shit. We're in trouble. This isn't what we were expecting."

Mount Olympos quaked—the marble columns lining the outside of the Hall of Tribunals crumbled, and striated cracks surged through the floor. A roar that sounded like no creature in existence echoed in the heavens, and then the tips of wings became visible, the flapping of such monstrosities raising hurricane-level winds. With a wingspan a mile wide, these bronze feathered appendages rattled as they moved. Coming into view was a dragon's head, a quarter of a mile across, on top of a long serpentine neck and bronze scales covering its skin. Eyes like Erebos himself looked down into the Olympeian hall as its arms reached up and grabbed hold of shattered columns, each arm ending in fifty writhing serpents. The thunderous howl again vibrated through the air, and each mass of serpents crashed down on the already-splintered floor. Although Dan and the others couldn't see from where they were, the creature's torso split into two vipers for legs, each constricting the mountain at the base. This creature's head could scrape the starry heavens while its legs latched onto the earth.

"Typhon," Dan told Brandon, who stood behind him holding on to a broken column. His voice barely made it above the ruckus. "I don't know how Lismonia managed to free him from under Mount Aetna, but we need a different plan. Get Sarah and Aleta now!"

Hesteia's hearth was mostly unaffected by the battering, for the moment—perhaps a stronger magic protected it—so the four gathered on its far side, as far from Typhon as possible. Dan was looking for any suggestions, but he felt their original plan might work if they could get rid of Typhon, but that would be near impossible. History told of only one way to vanquish Typhon.

"Here's the deal: Typhon's the daddy to almost all of the monsters we've fought. He and Ekhidna populated the world with chimerae, hydras, etc."

"Who defeated him last time he came around? I should know this, shouldn't I?" Sarah wished she'd paid more attention to Dan's stories.

Aleta knew. "Zeus."

"Yep. Like I said, Lismonia had to get some help to free him. I'm guessing Nyx found a way. We're out of time, guys. Ready?"

Before they could put their plan into action, creeping over the edge of the floor from outside came the black mass they had seen many times before, and Lismonia situated herself between the hearth and Zeus' throne. Typhon reached out toward the hearth, but *Thyroros* sliced through some of the serpent fingers, and then Dan rolled out of the way. Angering this elder god wasn't part of the plan, but it was an unavoidable consequence. It didn't matter since the serpents grew back, wriggling more than ever. The other arm snapped like a whip, entwining Dan in the mass of fifty snakes, and the sword fell into the hearth. Typhon's other limb snatched Sarah, the serpents constricted around her. Aleta turned toward Lismonia and discharged a bolt of lightning that encircled her, pouring every ounce of will power into the attack. Nyx's daughter pushed against the web of light, but she couldn't escape it. Aleta's wings flapped to help her keep her balanced, but she couldn't do anything to help the others.

"Now, Brandon! Do it now!" She was playing tug of war with the electric filament.

Brandon saw Dan and Sarah trapped in Typhon's grip and wanted to help them, but he eventually grunted and ran behind the thrones. As Typhon's snakes squeezed the life out of both his victims, he hadn't noticed Brandon's departure. Like most primordial gods wielding massive power, he also had a singular purpose and didn't think beyond that. He swung his arms into the other columns and roared his revulsion for the mortals in his grasp. Dan struggled against the tightening of dozens of snakes, but Sarah wasn't moving. The longer Typhon flailed, the less likely Sarah could survive; she didn't have the genealogy Dan had.

Having a nebulous form should have given Lismonia an advantage, but she couldn't break free from the lightning containing her. Aleta knew that, should she falter at all, the gods would remain trapped in the *Ptinotrofeio* forever. Even if Lismonia had Brandon's amulet, she wouldn't be able to use it anyway. At first, she might revel in the gods' caging, but her ego wouldn't rest until she was the means of their oblivion, and that frustration would bring madness. When Aleta glowered at her ensnared foe, she was reminded of Orthros and how he killed her mother. That alone kept her arms from faltering.

From behind the two thrones ran Brandon carrying a torch, followed by the pounding of heavy feet and the sound of metal on marble. An arm the length of a school

bus and just as thick swept away the seats of Zeus and Hera to make way for three figures from deep beneath Olympos. Just as Lismonia had planned for Typhon to aid her, Task Force: Gaea had a contingency as well. Three one-eyed giants climbed onto the floor, dragging an iron anvil behind them with chains, sending up sparks that fizzled out in the cyclonic winds of Typhon's wings. Each Cyclope carried an iron hammer over his shoulder, too, that bore the indentations of millennia of blacksmithing.

Caught within the lightning web with Lismonia was Hesteia's hearth, its flames dancing proudly — something Aleta had intended — and Nyx's daughter tried to smash the stone ring with dark tentacles, but this fire wasn't mortal fire, but rather flames that predated her own mother's existence. Battering the stony ring brought no success.

"That must be frustrating," Aleta smiled. "You can't put out a little fire. I hope you like mine. Brothers Brontês, Steropês, and Argês, help me contain Nyx's daughter."

The three Cyclopes pounded the anvil, each impact sending lightning bolts into the surrounding air, strengthening Aleta's bolt.

As would any cornered animal, Lismonia lashed out with multiple black tentacles, wriggling around the necks of the Cyclopes, but her body couldn't pass the ring of light girdling her. With each successive hammer strike, electricity snaked around the tentacles, repelling them. They had forged the thunderbolt for Zeus long ago from their anvil tempered in the First Fires. Aleta's javelin had been forged on this very anvil as well. Striking out in all directions, the black shapelessness shifted, but no form she took could escape the power of the Cyclopes. She was trapped encircling the hearth — light on both sides of her.

Brandon fought back every urge to help his brother and Sarah, but if he didn't act now, it wouldn't matter if he could free them. He held his amulet in front of the torch, one he had taken from the Hall of Mortals, and the constellation gemstones irradiated the sky above with patterns of color. Being the only one who could use the Eye of

Ouranos, he didn't need an incantation or enchantment; a rift opened above them, and a large white eagle flew into the hall, circling around the chamber, screeching its gratitude. Aleta saw the avian form of Zeus and his eyes showed both gratitude and the pride that one shows a daughter. His wings took him over to the Cyclopes, and all three slammed their hammers down simultaneously. The bolt they generated fed Zeus, revitalizing him after a year in captivity, self-imposed as it was, and he grew to where his wingspan was as wide as Typhon's head. The son of Tartaros and Gaea saw his former jailer and roared, flapping his own bronze wings harder to destabilize him — perhaps an ordinary eagle might be affected, but not the son of Kronos and Rhea. Authoritative wings moved him closer to the dragonhead, and Zeus discharged surges of power from his eyes and talons. Chills traveled through Aleta to see such an awesome display of power; Brontês and his brethren continued to pummel their anvil, charging the air itself. A second rush of energy loosened Typhon's grip on Dan, who wriggled free and fell to the floor. Despite his own Olympeian heritage, his wounds needed a little time to heal. Sarah, on the other hand, remained caught in the serpentine web.

A volley of arrows from a centaur's bow struck half a dozen snaky fingers. Another barrage followed. With the third, Typhon's grip slackened to where Sarah slid out of his grasp, and swift horse legs carried Brandon to catch her before she slammed into the marble. Unconscious, Sarah looked misshapen after having been constricted for so long, and Brandon held her close. He brushed hair from her face to see bruises on her cheeks, and felt the broken bones in her arms and legs. His eyes clenched shut to keep tears in, he gently held her against him, rocking back and forth. When he looked at her face, he thought he saw her lips quiver. As he leaned in, he couldn't hear anything, but he felt slight movement.

Aleta glanced back to see Brandon cradling Sarah and fed more will power into her onslaught of Lismonia. She felt a strange warmth on her back and a different kind of light emanating from them. Brandon has his eyes closed, rocking back and forth. The essence of Virgo, the Nurturer, took over where his desire to help her couldn't. If she could just take some of his own power to kick start hers, she might be able to find her healing center.

Zeus had managed to get Typhon further down Olympos so the other gods could fly to the mortal parts of the world where their human selves resided. Once they were whole, they would return to reclaim their home.

Sarah's eyes fluttered a little, but she didn't otherwise move. Brandon couldn't be sure how much time had elapsed, but he felt her body move on her own. Her limbs no longer felt broken, either. Once her eyes opened fully, she inhaled deeply. He helped her to sit up, and she started calling quarters to find her center; Brandon repeated each line. With her mental focus restored, so did her connection to the divine power of *Æther*, and her healing accelerated to where she could move her arms.

Having to crawl over to them, Dan sat next to Sarah as she gradually healed. He, too, felt the strength in his legs returning. Holding on to each other, they moved along the floor, and then Sarah slowly slid toward Lismonia, taking her place in the circle. Hobbling a little, Dan found his place as well, as did Brandon. With all four of them surrounding Lismonia, the Cyclopes ceased their hammering, but the ring of lightning remained.

Even though their hands couldn't touch, they extended their arms around the hearth, forming yet another circle of influence. Dan began the final ritual.

"I look to the north and call upon thee, *Gaea*, Mother Earth, Mother of All, I invite your presence."

Aleta, Sarah, and Brandon repeated his words. Vines of earth, Gaea's strength, rose through the marble floor around Dan's legs, his eyes like two bright suns, and *Thyroros* rose above his head from the hearth, pointing to the sky, spinning in place. This created the first pillar of binding.

Fearing what might come, Lismonia whipped out at him, but their collective will had secured her imprisonment. Churning in on herself, she pushed and slashed, but she couldn't move beyond.

Sarah delivered her part, her voice strained, but determined. "I look to the east and call upon thee, *Æther*, Bright Upper Air, Light Above All, I invite your presence."

Again, the others repeated her words, and Sarah's whole body radiated white light. Her ring left her finger and hovered over her head, twinkling, establishing the second pillar.

Lismonia continued to try to free herself.

"I look to the west and call upon thee, *Olympeia*, Spirit who flows through the Sacred Mountain, I invite your presence.".

Nephoskizetes rose above Aleta's head, arcs of light passing up and down the silver javelin.

Now, Lismonia felt the third pillar.

Brandon completed the rite. "I look to the south and call upon thee, *Ouranos*, Father of the sky, All-Seeing One, I invite your presence." Even though the god Ouranos was no more, the power of the sky itself overtook Brandon, his eyes glowed blue, and his amulet rose above his head.

With the fourth pillar established, Lismonia's fate was sealed.

The *Ptinotrofeio* had remained open from the gods' departure, and in a singular voice they spoke, and the heavens rumbled with stentorian thunder.

"For your evil, we bind your power and banish you.

By the power of Earth, Sky, Air, and Mountain, we bind your power and banish you.

By the sword, the javelin, the amulet, and the ring, we bind your power and banish you.

Three times, we bind you, three times, we banish you.

We bind you from the North.

We bind you from the South.

You shall do evil no more.
We bind you from the East.
We bind you form the West.
You shall hurt others no more."

All four lifted their arms, and Lismonia rose up until her form was contained within the *Ptinotrofeio*, at which point the lightning extinguished and the rift closed. Twelve orbs of light entered the hall, hovered for a moment, and left in the direction of Zeus. One appeared seconds later, lingered by Dan and Brandon, but ultimately departed as well. The young men then realized their father had joined with the gods to battle Typhon.

This day, the *Moirae* would weave a tapestry with threads of iron and steel, with lightning and earth of four mortals battling Oblivion and emerging victorious. A heavy silence filled the gap left by the tumult, and they had no words to express, collapsing against the hearth, the flames now a gentle but steady flicker. Morpheos brought his gift of healing slumber to their eyes, and both Gaea and Olympeia would fulfill their destiny, too, and heal their body and spirit. They deserved that… and more.

33—ROADS LESS TRAVELED

Brandon surfaced from his deep slumber as if he had been swimming up through dense fog, finding he had slept better than he had in years. He wasn't sure how much time had elapsed, but it couldn't have been longer than a few hours. Or, was it longer, he thought. Propping himself up on his elbows, he scanned the room: marble columns, white with gray, and no walls, like the Hall of Tribunals. A gentle zephyr carried the scent of lilac and rosemary, and iron braziers burned anise incense, a favorite of Apollo. He looked over to see Sarah and Aleta still asleep, but Dan was sitting up on a bed, like his, draped in white silk.

Dan stretched and twisted his torso around. "Where are we?"

"The Hall of Healing," a voice replied. Dan recognized it as his father's. "Welcome back. You've been asleep a week, by the mortal standard, anyway. How do you feel?"

"Considering I had my ass handed to me by Typhon, I feel pretty good."

Attendants to Apollo checked on the women, but they remained sound asleep. Brandon, not entirely coherent, gave a thumbs up to his father.

"The Cyclopes moved you here while we took care of Typhon. I'm glad my father freed them from Tartaros way back. They're good to have around." Apollo walked over to Sarah, whose eyes had fluttered open. "Nice to have you back." His smile was as warm as a sunbeam.

"Thanks," she managed. "Wow, did I sleep hard or what. Everyone okay?"

"Yeah. How are *you* doing? You had a rough time there for a bit?" Dan walked around.

Sarah turned on her side. "I have friends in high places that were willing to help me out." Apollo knew he was included in that, but she also meant the elemental gods. "So, whatever happened to Typhon?" Despite her grogginess, she was eager to know the outcome.

Apollo sat on a nearby marble plinth. "It took some work, but we managed to get him under Aetna again. Last time, Zeus handled it himself, but with the rest of us, it happened quickly. We had to trick him to Sicily. Once he saw the island again, he lashed out at us, but my father knows how to throw a thunderbolt. Gaea was more willing to help this time, too, so I don't believe we'll see Typhon again. The downside is that Aetna's an active volcano once more, but no one lives nearby."

The last member of the team made her way to consciousness. "Holy hell," she yawned, pushing Morpheos' gift out of her mind. "I feel like I was hit by a bus. Repeatedly."

"I have to hand it to you all, Ares has been here more times than I can count, and he hasn't recovered as quickly as you have. Plus, he tends to whine when he's injured. My attendants would just ignore him." Apollo smirked.

Olympeians have a keen sense when things change around them, so it seemed convenient that the moment all four of them felt better that Hermes flitted in. He looked a little like Apollo, but younger, and—aside from his winged helmet and sandals—dressed only in what looked like a skirt. He always carried his caduceus, a winged staff with two snakes entwined around it, the vessel for his power.

"Brother, Zeus wishes to see them now."

The sun god simply gestured. Moving faster than mortal eyes could follow, Hermes transported them all back to the Hall of Tribunals. Apollo would join them shortly.

⤜⤛

They had to pass by the thrones of Zeus and Hera to enter, and they saw that all the damage wrought by Typhon and Lismonia had been restored. Now they saw the true majesty of the Hall of Tribunals as it was meant to be, with each god seated at a throne, and Hesteia tending the hearth. Only Hades was absent. Hermes guided them before the king of the gods, whose presence radiated newly kindled power, a consequence of mortal clarity. He stepped down the dais, and the four heroes bowed their heads. Like a general inspecting his troops, he walked by them, his arms behind his back. Dan was his first stop.

"All of Olympos owes each of you a debt of gratitude for your recent actions, but also for your devotion to the gods. Danelos, you took on the sacred pledge when you bore that manacle, and it has bound you into our service. Having lived a mortal life as well as a divine one, I would be willing to free you from that bond so that you may pursue your own direction."

His grandfather's eyes shimmered with power, and he felt Zeus' pride wash over him. After all that had happened to him since that day on Mt. Graylock, he had his answer. He touched the manacle and looked up at Zeus.

"I freely chose this life, and I will continue to do so. This manacle doesn't bind me into enslavement. It shows me that there are always higher ideals to strive for, and I'm not yet done learning."

A gentle squeeze on Dan's shoulder from his grandfather's hand showed approval. Next, Zeus moved to Sarah who was wringing her hands. This was her first audience with the gods on Olympos.

"Not since my daughters Artemis and Athene came into their own have I witnessed such strength of character and dedication to a larger cause. You, young lady, have proven yourself many times over and honor the elemental gods." He leaned and kissed her cheek.

Hesteia left the hearth, something she didn't often do, and approached Sarah. Flames in the hearth diminished slightly, but maintained their energetic flickering. The goddess' amber eyes sparkled like embers framed by the himation over her head. Tears in small trickles fell down Sarah's face as Hesteia took her hands.

"You honor me each time you touch fire, daughter. Even when I was in the *Ptinotrofeio*, and you reached into my hearth, I felt it." She leaned in. "I, too, shed tears knowing someone had reached out to me. May you always have wisdom and grace." She returned to the hearth with a faint smile.

Zeus stood by Brandon next.

"A worthy son you are to Apollo, and an even worthier brother. As far away as our aviary was, I sensed your guilt in India. All things have come to pass, as they have needed to, and know that you have made all of Olympos proud. Were Ouranos here, I do believe he would echo my sentiments. You honor him."

Brandon smiled, but then he replied to Zeus. "I feel so unworthy."

"For what reason? The *Moirae* wove your past, as they have us all, and we all have choices on threads interspersed within our life. As you made certain decisions, those threads remained while unused ones withered and fell away. Of the infinite possibilities set out to us, the choices you have made brought you to this place, in this moment." Zeus hadn't felt this impassioned for quite some time, but he sensed something within Brandon that could impede his life.

"I'm not sure you understand," Brandon replied. "I look at my brother and see a man who has lived not one, but two, lifetimes, each as the prince of Arkadeia. He grew up with the love of Apollo and Alkinoë, knew of his ancient history, and had the support of Gaea and Olympeia. Sarah's knowledge of her genealogy and strong beliefs ground her. Aleta's grandmother told her about her Amazonian background, how her ancestors broke away from their patriarchal limitations and wielded transformative abilities to become something more. *My* upbringing, while I do love my adoptive family, has given me no family history to cling to. Both Max and Evelyn Jeffries have limited ties to their own families, so I grew up with knowing a few aunts or a cousin or two. I feel unworthy because, for as much as I have embraced my power, I don't feel I deserve it."

Hera glided down the stairs of the dais and put her hands on Brandon's cheeks.

"And that is precisely why you *do* deserve it. Knowing you can trace your lineage a few thousand years may seem impressive, but the bonds you create on your own help define you. Your father, by inspiring us to live a human life, showed us that was truer than we ever cared to imagine. Look around you. Your three friends here *are* your family. But, I feel your disconnect. Perhaps, your father could share his memories of Arkadeia with you."

Brandon looked at the floor.

"I've been there... once." He smiled at his brother. "Perhaps you're right. I do need to learn more about my homeland."

"And, you." Zeus addressed Aleta. "With prowess and aplomb you brandish my lightning. Forging an alliance with the Cyclopes was a keen maneuver. I did it as well. The bolt can do more than you think, so keep working with it."

With a glance, the king of gods signaled the other gods to rise. Bowing his head, the other gods did the same; this was the first time the gods had honored mortals as

338

such. A crow squawked, soaring in through clouds, circled over the gods, and materialized as Apollo in front of the others. He, too, genuflected toward the four heroes before addressing his father.

"Father, may Gaea's glory surround you. I wish to speak with you… alone." Both gods vanished.

Black mist rose from the floor by one of the two empty thrones and coalesced into Hades, silencing the other gods. The god of the underworld rarely ever visited Olympos, and when he did, he had good reason. Taking his throne, more symbolic than actual, his ascetic tone took none of his brethren by surprise.

"I have restored my governance in the underworld. The *Potamoi* had the choice of returning to their riverbeds or simply ceasing to exist. They chose the former." With a gelid countenance, he looked at Dan. "In one cycle of the moon, I shall send Hermes for your beloved."

Zeus' thunder crashed, the sky god's eyes glowering at his brother from the heavens.

"He needed to know." Hades blew away on a breeze, returning to his wife.

Aleta and Sarah rushed over to Dan. Brandon stood there thunderstruck.

"Has something happened to Ari?" Aleta shrieked.

"What happened?" Sarah asked, her voice cracking.

After taking a deep breath, Dan told them about the deal Ari had made with Persephone to get the Omphalos. After the gods' return, he would take Charon's place until the gods could resurrect the ferryman. Brandon asked how long that would take.

Dan's eyes moved from one friend to another, and then he looked down. "A year."

Brandon looked at Zeus and Apollo, who had just returned. "One or both of you needs to do something!"

Again, thunder crashed around them, and flashes of light filled the hall. Apollo put a hand on his father's shoulder. Zeus would overlook the effrontery of his grandson under the circumstances.

"I can do nothing. He entered into that arrangement freely."

"Look, guys," Dan began, "it'll be fine. Ari and I have discussed this at length. It's only one year." He turned to Zeus. "One year, Zeus. One minute more and Olympos will feel..." He clamped his mouth shut before his words caused more harm.

Apollo spoke more with Zeus while the others stood with Dan. By the time the two Olympeians had finished their conversation so had the four. Apollo nodded at Brandon who then knew it was time.

"Guys, I've made a decision that will affect our team. Hera was right. I need to know more about where I'm from and what it means to be an heir of Arkadeia. So, effective immediately, I'm taking a leave of absence from Task Force: Gaea."

"What will you do?" asked Sarah. "I mean... will you and Apollo be spending some time together?"

Brandon again locked eyes with his father. "Not exactly. Zeus has given Apollo permission to send me back to Arkadeia, to the time just after we left when I was a child. As it's a long-term enchantment, Apollo would rather not use *Thyroros*. While there, I will learn from the people about what it means to be Arkadeian, and also what it means to be royalty. Apollo will speak with his priests, with Morpheos' help, through dreams and auguries to prepare for my arrival. Kleisthenes will remain the captain of the Royal Guard and will advise me while I'm there."

"How long?" asked Dan. His tone sounded more like that of a soldier understanding a military strategy than a brother and friend. Detachment helped him from unraveling.

"Not sure. But, remember, time passes differently there. I might be gone a few months to you, but it might be a few years to me. This is the best way for me to do what I need to do."

"How will you not affect the past? Won't your actions change our present?" Aleta, too, approached the situation disengaged a bit from the reality.

Brandon nodded. "The Eye of Ouranos in my amulet will alert me to things before I do them that would affect the future, or your present. If I cannot do them, Kleisthenes will. It does mean making some difficult choices. If I absolutely have to leave, I will convey a message to Apollo through his high priest to bring me back."

Sarah wrapped her arms around him, sobbing into his chest. "What if you don't want to come home?"

"Worse yet," Aleta asked, "what if you die there?"

Apollo replied, "Those are certainly possibilities, but neither of which is likely, especially the latter. Brandon will leave in a month. That will give him time to set his affairs in order, as well as have time with each of you."

Dan gestured for the other three to join him. "We need a moment." That was Dan's way of saying he didn't want his father or grandfather to eavesdrop.

Approximately fifteen minutes of mortal time elapsed before they returned.

"We have decided to take a break from the hero business for the next month. I want to spend time with Ari and Brandon, and we all have personal lives to return to now that the imminent threat is gone. I trust that you, Dad, can keep an eye on the mortal world during that time?"

"Yes, Dan, I can. I promise," Apollo answered. He knew better than to argue with them at this moment. "Here," he said, giving him a small ball of light. "You should all return home and enjoy each other. We have things to talk about here."

After *Thyroros* opened the portal back to Dan and Brandon's apartment, three people left Olympos. Dan turned around, and his eyes told Apollo things words could never convey. Soon, the portal closed.

Zeus asked, "What was that look on Danelos' face?"

Apollo continued to look where the portal had been. "Soon, he will lose both his brother and the one he loves. That is too much."

"A heavy heart weighs more than the heavens themselves, my son, but I have faith that Danelos will show himself to be stronger than Atlas. Come, we have much to discuss about mortality. The gods await us."

"Here in the Hall of Tribunals?"

"Nay, in the Hall of Mortals... a more appropriate venue, I believe."

In the mortal world a few days had passed, although weeks had gone by in the immortal realm. The gods had stories to tell that reinvigorated Apollo's faith in his own kind. Some had experienced epiphanies, others felt nothing, but at least they had been something they had never been before and learned from the experience. When he first told Zeus about his experiences, he didn't think his father understood at all. Now, he was sure he did. Olympos would evolve into something it had never been before, and Apollo couldn't wait to see what, but now he had other matters of his own to attend to back in Boston.

He had climbed the two sets of granite stairs and stood outside the door at 1236 Commonwealth Avenue, looking like his Paul Fairmont persona. He had never felt so helpless before, and he couldn't bring himself to go inside. He and Alkinoë had never truly come to any accord about what happened, although she had gotten closer to understanding what he had done to protect their son. In his mind, he rehearsed what he would say so that he wouldn't sound like a fool, but each time the words came, he couldn't put them into any reasonable sense. Who knew a varnished wooden door could prove to be such an insurmountable obstacle for an Olympeian god? Each time he reached for his keys, his hand wouldn't respond. Back when the gods ruled supremely, all he would have had to do was raise his hand, and a city would fall or a field would prosper—simply because he willed it to be. Now, he was impotent.

Finally, he tapped his knuckles on the door, and his heart echoed the impact. Each passing second lasted an eternity before the door opened and Alkinoë stood face to face with him. Again, time just stopped, but then she gestured for him to enter. It had been a while since he had been home, and he didn't want her to feel uncomfortable. He had been the one to err, so she was entitled to feel however she wished. Her cup of Earl Grey, still piping hot, sat on the coffee table next to her most recent novel. He sat stiffly on the chair across from the couch.

"How have you been?" He found it a challenge to know how to sit around her.

She brought the teacup to her lips. "Fine." She sipped. "You?"

Alkinoë laughed to herself.

"Why are you laughing?" He wasn't sure if he should smile or not.

"I may be mortal now, but I know where you've been. Dan and Brandon stopped by earlier and filled me in. I was just wondering how long you would have sat there unsure and nervous."

Slightly relieved, he didn't quite know how to take her demeanor. For the moment, he decided to play along. He sat back and crossed his leg.

"Let's cut to the chase, shall we? Are you still upset with me? I don't blame you if you are."

She sipped her tea again. "I remember a lesson that Chiron taught me, oh, millennia ago, when I was still a cadet in the Royal Guard. This was before we met. He said to me, 'Alkinoë, sometimes you will have to slaughter the whole flock to save one sheep.' I didn't understand it then, but when I was crowned queen, I learned the hard way that tough choices had to be made, and consequences always followed. The next lesson I learned was that I had no control over those consequences.

"Apollo, I've known deep down that your decision to kidnap Kidemonas was in his best interest. Am I happy that he's safe? Of course. Am I happy that another woman got to raise him as her own? Well, I think you know the answer to that question. I think I've moved beyond it. I've seen what kind of man Kide... Brandon has grown into. His adoptive parents love him and raised him well. He's certainly a good man. I'm just glad that he's back in our lives again. Both my sons are."

Those words changed Apollo's expression just a little, but since she had been a negotiator between warring nations, she could read faces well.

"What is it? Don't keep it from me. For Gaea's sake, Apollo..."

"Brandon wants to learn more about his heritage, and I said I would help him."

"Okay, but why do I see apprehension in your eyes?"

Apollo sat for a few seconds, taking a deep breath. "I am sending him to Arkadeia for an indeterminate period of time. Zeus has allowed this."

More silence. *By holy Olympos*, Apollo thought, *I have had enough of silence!* He stood up.

"Alkinoë, if you have a problem with this..."

She held up her hand. "Apollo, that is his choice to make. I know you will have set up a contingency so he can return, so I'm fine. Sit."

This time, he sat next to her, on the edge of the couch. "Did Dan tell you about Ari?"

"Yes, but he's taking it better than I would have expected."

"Denial."

She shrugged. "True, but we'll keep an eye on him, as will Sarah and Aleta."

"Did he tell you about his memories?"

"No," she replied, "what memories?"

He explained how their son remembered his life in that other time, like his father, and that was part of the reason why Brandon wanted to go back to Arkadeia.

Apollo couldn't explain why their son remembered something that only one other god did, but it didn't seem to have an ill effect on Danelos. Not knowing this information, and reflecting on Dan's earlier years, neither one of them could ever say that Dan didn't seem well adjusted. If he felt odd or even the slightest bit unstable, they had never seen it. Alkinoë simply told him that if a reason existed why he and his son shared those memories, Apollo would indeed figure it out.

"So, tell me. Do you have any other secrets?"

With no other recourse but to live by the standard he espoused as a god, he simply said, "Yes."

As one of the gods of Mount Olympos, he had many secrets: some he was bound never to repeat at Zeus' behest; some Gaea or Olympeia had sworn him into secrecy over. But, he continued, no secrets he held had anything to do with her or their marriage. Keeping the order of the cosmos was a priority, so kidnapping his son had been part of that.

"Would you ever harm one of your sons or me if it meant keeping the order of the cosmos?"

"No," he said, without even having to think. "I would sooner end my own life. After what I have experienced, I don't have it within me to carry out such heinous actions, no matter the cost to the universe. Creation be damned. I would rather die with you, and our children, than ever allow anything to befall you."

She hadn't expected that. "Apollo…"

"No, Alkinoë."

No matter his protestations, she knew he would do what he needed to do for the greater good. Too much was at stake for him not to do it. But, they didn't need to discuss this at the moment. She pulled him close to her, resting her chin on his shoulder, and was glad to have her husband back. She silently asked the *Moirae* not to reveal anything about the future that would prompt Apollo to act, at least not right away. The void between them had felt like Tartaros, and she never wanted to feel that way again.

∽

One month later, outside The Beanery at 10:00 a.m., Boston traffic provided a cacophonous backdrop of horns and voices. Dan sat next to Ari, both enjoying a Guatemalan blend, while Aleta knocked back espresso shots. A little too early to drink coffee, Sarah had a tea blend with her croissant. A sharply roasted African blend with a shot of half and half gave Brandon his morning dose of caffeine. Dan had been staying at Ari's apartment so Brandon could have some time to himself. He would be off the grid, as it were, for a while, and had to make arrangements. Aleta and Sarah had sent text messages over the prior month, but they hadn't seen each other since that day on Mount Olympos.

"As I was saying earlier," Sarah said, "my latest pottery showing will be in a few weeks. I'm about ready to send out invites. This could really be the break I need. I'm going with a whole serpent motif."

Ari laughed. "I am happy for you. I hope to see your work when I return."

"I'll make sure of it," Dan squeezed Ari's hand. "Let me know when, Sarah. I'll bring people from the university."

"As soon as I have dates, I'll email everyone. Aleta, maybe you'll bring someone?" She smirked, popping the last piece of croissant into her mouth.

"I'm not telling you anything anymore," Aleta laughed. "You're telling everyone all my business."

Aleta had jumped right back into work, and her colleague, Dr. Forrester, had wanted to explore some other genetic avenues that he felt Aleta would be perfect for. Collaboration had kindled a budding romance, so it was possible that she might have a date for Sarah's show. Normalcy was hard to establish, but once roots had been placed, it seemed to grow quickly. With no real threats to focus on, and with Apollo keeping an eye on things for a bit, Aleta could focus much more on herself. Brandon commented that he struggled with telling Max and Evelyn about his upcoming travel plans, so he framed his trip as family research since time travel would be too challenging. Dan had done his best to reconcile both his brother and his boyfriend going away; it would be after they left that would be the true test. If anything, he had to understand his dual memories, something Apollo had already learned how to do. Sarah wanted to know more about that.

"As a boy, I had dreams about a magical palace, but I always assumed they were just dreams, so I dismissed them. They grew more and more vivid over the years, and I came to realize they had to be memories since what I knew was so detailed. I think I finally felt like I knew something was different when my father took me to Mt. Graylock as a kid. He wanted me to understand what it meant to fight for something I truly believed in, so he created a doppelgänger of himself to try and fool me. Once I figured out the sword, I sent this shadow to another place — Arkadeia — the Arkadeia of that other timeline, actually, the only one I remembered. The sword could only open a portal to a place that actually existed, though, so that doorway led to your birthplace, Brandon. Fortunately, my father's enchantment would have faded so that shadow would cease to exist.

"I was glad you had had the chance to see part of the city before we had to go back, but now you'll be there for a longer period. I can go back whenever I want, but I won't. You need to experience it yourself."

Staring off, Brandon looked over at his brother. "If you need me, really need me, you know how to find me."

"Brandon, I never ventured much into the city, but I can recommend a few places just outside the city in the surrounding countryside I think you would enjoy," Ari added.

Sarah jumped up and sat in his lap, wrapping her arms around him. "I'm going to miss you so much. Don't forget us."

"Never." He squeezing her in return.

On her fourth shot of espresso, Aleta fidgeted in her seat. She didn't do as well with emotional scenes, and goodbyes, no matter how temporary, made her detach. "So, what are you most looking forward to when you get back there?"

Brandon smiled, then chuckled a little. "There was this orange kitten that latched onto me when I was there with Dan. I'm curious to find it again."

Laughter rose above the din of the city, sheltering each of them from the darkness lurking beneath.

By the time noon arrived, Dan announced that he and Ari needed to go. Ari would be leaving soon.

Brandon pulled Ari into a tight hug. "Take care of my brother," he whispered. "And, take good care of yourself."

"I promise," Ari replied. "You as well. Say hello to Arkadeia for me."

Just before they all walked away, Dan pulled Brandon aside.

"Do what you need to do, however long it takes, and then come back. Okay?"

Brandon tightened his mouth and nodded.

Dan pulled his brother to him wasn't prepared to let him go. "I lose you and Ari both today."

"*S'agapo*," Brandon choked out, having a hard time holding back his tears.

Dan couldn't just go into the next room anymore and wake his brother up when he couldn't sleep. They couldn't have their sushi every Wednesday. No more sparring sessions at the university gym.

"*Kai ego s'agapo.*" And, I love you.

Ari had been talking with the others and called Dan's name. The brothers parted, and Brandon headed back toward Apollo and Alkinoë's townhouse. He couldn't turn his head to look back or he would never go. They were his family, and in a way, he was abandoning them. Once he turned the corner, he stood taller, pushed back his emotions, and walked on.

Later that afternoon, Dan and Ari sat against a tree in the Charles River Reservation having a makeshift picnic of falafel and diet soda, two things Ari had come to love. Sailboats cruised down river, and a few shells from local universities practiced for crew. The John Hancock tower sat behind them, as did Prudential Tower, with the Massachusetts Institute of Technology and Genetics across the river. Playful zephyrs brushed by, and not far from where they say children flew kites and played Frisbee. If it weren't for the ubiquitous surveillance cameras, it might almost seem idyllic. Speckled throughout the park were plainclothes police, more obvious than clandestine, as was typically the case. Nonetheless, they were doing their best to enjoy what time they had left.

Dan shoved falafel into his mouth and then reached around to feed Ari, who was lying back against him. The irony of the situation wasn't lost to either one of them: Ari would spend the next year taking Charon's place, guiding souls across a river in the underworld, and they were watching the living traverse and enjoy the Charles. Those thoughts went unspoken. Each had already said his goodbye earlier, and they didn't want to cast a shadow on these last moments with heavy emotion. Dan had asked Apollo to keep an eye on Ari, if possible, although spying on the underworld wasn't an easy task.

Ari wanted to compare Boston to Arkadeia, since much of the river area reminded him of his home, but in incalculable ways, these places looked nothing like one another. Pure and untainted by technology, byproducts of that technology, and just human consumption, the land of Arkadeia lay as picturesque and mystical. One truly felt Gaea's presence there.

"You do not have to worry about me. I understand more about the underworld than you might imagine. Plus, I believe I have an ally there now."

"Persephone will act on your behalf? That would make me happy, but I wouldn't hold my breath."

Idioms sometimes escaped Ari. "Eh?"

"I wouldn't put confidence in that idea. You're the one who spoke with her, but she follows Hades' lead. His unsympathetic means of communicating leaves much to be desired, too."

"If he remembers me, I should be able to get an audience with him. He had great respect for my father. Plus, I am returning the Omphalos. That should get me bonus points, right?"

It always made Dan laugh when Ari tried to use slang. "Yeah, bonus points." He squeezed Ari around the shoulders.

The breeze picked up a bit, and the perfume of asphodel touched the air.

"Hermes is coming." Ari knew that smell all too well.

Darting through the skies, the figure of a man landed before them. He appeared to them as human, wearing a baseball cap embroidered with silver wings, a "Chaos Theory" T-shirt, and black Jimmy Choos also embroidered with the same wing insignia. On the inside of his right arm, a caduceus tattoo ran from his elbow to his palm. Ari stood up next to Hermes, but Dan wanted one more moment. He held out his right hand, Ari placing his palm down on top, and he wound a red ribbon around both hands.

"Aristeides, I love you. With this ribbon, I want us to be bound together. Your soul complements mine, and I am yours for all time. I *will* wait for you."

Hermes flitted back a bit to give them this moment, smiling to himself. Ari's grin placated Dan, and he responded.

"Danelos, you are my love and my prince. For all time."

With one last kiss, Ari went with Hermes to the water's edge where they both vanished in a cloud of hummingbirds. Dan sat back down by the tree and watched the ships pass, praying to the gods.

34—FULL CIRCLE

Three months later. Naxos, near Stelid.

"Aether, I need you over here!" Aegis shouted over his communicator. His sword flashed in the midday sun, severing wings and limbs, scaly debris lying all over the beach. As had been the case in the years past, before major metaphysical threats tormented parts of the world, hidden caves and faulty magical portals allowed Hadean monsters to roam into the world of mortals. Quinn didn't get the message in time for them to stop the full-scale assault on the island, but she had the wherewithal to get her team on location as quickly as she could. Human casualties equaled in the dozens; not desirable, but acceptable loss in a military perspective.

"We have to move the civilians!" Aether told Talon soaring above her. "Aegis, I'll be right there."

A whirlwind carried Aether to the beach where Aegis kept knocking back sea serpents, but they kept slithering from the ocean. She raised a dirt wall between the surf and the civilians still trying to flee, but the Ethiopian Cetoi kept ramming into the wall. These were the same sea serpents that had tormented Andromeda when Perseus rescued her. At their full size, they could be as long as eight to ten football fields, and these snakelets were newborns, only about the size of one field, just about three hundred feet long.

"How many are there?" asked Aether, pushing all her energy into maintaining that wall.

"Not sure, six? twelve?" Aegis answered, leaping on the head of one who had slipped over the wall. One quick stab with *Thyroros* through the skull did the job. He grabbed the tail, swinging the corpse back into the sea.

Salty surf crashed into the wall, sending random waves over it onto Aether. "Funny guy," she mumbled. With one push, she sent the wall a quarter of a mile into the water. That wouldn't stop the Cetoi, but it might slow them down. Drawing in the sea, she focused on Thalassa, the primordial ocean goddess.

"Goddess, give me strength!" She concentrated on making a waterspout big enough to distract the Cetoi and moved it down the beach, away from civilians. A column of spinning wind and water moved at Aether's whim, getting in the way of the young serpents. Aegis took a leap into the shallows to stop another one trying to swim its way to shore. Earthsteel severed scales, letting ochre blood pour out into the sea. Neither Aegis nor Aether could help the other, and doing damage control or creating stopgap measures to protect the people wasn't effective.

Screeching her arrival, Talon swooped down, sending lightning into the throng of writhing sea serpents; that just made them angry. Aegis radioed to both of them an idea, but the salt water had corroded some circuitry, making his message garbled. He hoped they understood. Aether changed her tactic and moved the waterspout northeast toward the shrine of Apollo that jutted out into the bay. She *had* gotten the message. Talon used lightning strikes to force the serpents to stay in one group. Aegis ran toward the shrine along the beach. He wasn't Hermes, but he could move when he needed to do it. Pushing his way through tourists and citizens, he shouted that they leave the area immediately. Their confusion vanished as soon as they saw a bevy of sea serpents coming in their direction. With a flying somersault, Aegis landed on top of the Portara, the doorway that should have been attached to the temple of Apollo. He had maybe two minutes before they arrived, but he knew exactly what to do. The last time he had been here, he and the others helped dispatch a hydra that had gotten too close to a weakened portal in the Portara itself. He wondered whether that doorway still existed.

Timing was the key. If he did his job too soon, the serpents might catch on; if he did it too late, he wouldn't have any other options. As a group, even diminished by one, they had formidable power through Olympeian magic, but they didn't have time for that. One minute more. Thirty seconds. Fifteen seconds.

Now.

He leaped straight up as high as he could and, as he fell, he used the sword's power to slice a colossal portal into the underworld. Unfortunately, he had to slice right through the Portara to do it. Aegis rolled out of the way of the stone arch seconds before the waterspout and wind pushed the six remaining Cetoi, and the surrounding water, through the gateway. Hades might get a little wet, but that would be a small price to pay. As the last waves crashed around the rubble of the Portara, the tide returned to the sea. Talon circled once and landed next to Aegis. Right after, Aether set down after a wind transported her to their location. The crisis had been averted.

Aegis commented to his teammates how much he really hated serpents.

Once they saw no one had been hurt on the island, Talon radioed Quinn to send a TF-18. At various moments in the melee, each had thought about Brandon, but they concluded he was where he needed to be for now. And, they were, too. Even though their team consisted of only three members, they were still Task Force: Gaea.